THE THIRD TSUNAMI

MICHAEL J. SUTTON

This is a work of fiction. Names, characters, businesses, shrines, temples, temple leadership structures, tsunami response activities, and supernatural beings, are the products of the author's imagination. Any resemblance to actual persons, living or dead, or actual events is purely coincidental. The author has sought to accurately describe the events of March 11, 2011, in and around Matsushima. If the Tengu, Nue, Tanuki, Kitsune, and other yokai do exist, a more detailed understanding of their origins, habits, and hobbies would be appreciated by the author to convey a more accurate picture.

Published by Hidden Road Publishing

Volume 1 of **THE LAST DAYS OF OLD JAPAN**

ISBN: 978-0-6455671-4-4

DEDICATION

To all who seek Truth, who walk on the hidden road.

ACKNOWLEDGMENTS

I would like to acknowledge many people who influenced the hidden road I took in writing this novel. I would like to thank the people who created, and care for the botanical garden on the island reached only by the red bridge at Matsushima. It is one of my favorite places in all of Japan. The town of Matsushima, despite the tourism and souvenirs, has an enduring beauty and presence, the stone statues of Zuiganji stand tall and speak of centuries of devotion.

I would like to express my thanks to the priests in the massive complex of Myoshinji in Kyoto who allow people to walk the cobbled path at dusk and let us sit under the dragon whose watchful eyes look at us in wonder and amazement as we stare into the heavens through him. I thank the priests of Kurama who have kept alive the tradition of the Tengu and his role in shaping ancient Japan. I thank the shrines and temples whose precincts house the many stories of some of the characters I have sought to write about in this book. I thank the writers, poets, priests, and people who have curated and spoken the ancient stories of the yokai, the non-humans, who speak to us today as we struggle with our own identity, and with the elusive goal of mutual acceptance.

I would like to thank the many people who shared with me their experiences of that fateful day on March 11 in Matsushima. I have tried to give an accurate account of the tsunami that wreaked death and destruction on that terrible day. I published this edition of my book on March 11, 2023, and will publish each novel in this series on the anniversary of this infamous day. This edition is in English, but my intention is to translate the books into Japanese. The Last Days of Old Japan series will tell the story of five people whose lives are forever intertwined by the tsunami as a way of talking about the challenges and experiences of the people of Japan, China, and America in the twenty-first century.

I would like to acknowledge the people of Japan, China, Korea, and India, whose legends, characters, stories, and memories resonate, rejuvenate, and reveal the human heart. I would like to acknowledge the richness of their cultural tapestries and a future where what unites us is greater than what divides us. We eagerly await peace in our hearts and in the world around us.

1

Masayoshi Kato said nothing when he shot his best friend dead. His only thought was to leave the island as soon as possible without being seen. As he walked quickly through the forested garden, toward the red bridge that would take him to the little town of Matsushima, he kept contemplating the awful possibility that he was being followed. In his mind, he kept going over the events of the past ten minutes. Only one question mattered: did he get away with it?

Ten minutes earlier, he stood waiting for his best friend like a stone statue in a graveyard. He wore a black coat, a black suit, a faint blue shirt, an obscenely red tie, and neatly polished black shoes. Black gloves covered his cold hands. He was tall for a Japanese man, relatively thin, with thick and grey-tinged eyebrows, an angular face, an unusually long nose, and a mouth that frowned downwards. His hair was dark, but grey around the edges. He had recently bathed, after which he doused himself in a pungent aftershave and hair tonic.

He stood silently on a raised, weathered, wooden platform lookout, on the far edge of a small island that overlooked the still waters of Matsushima Bay, an archipelago of little islands that stretched out to sea, on the northeast coast of Japan. No one could see him standing on the lookout unless they were in one of the fishing boats in the distance, tending to the hundreds of tall wooden poles standing together that collected seaweed, driven by the ebb and flow of the tide. The lookout was concealed by a forest of tortured, prostrating pine trees that had been twisted by years of exposure to unrelenting gales.

The lookout could only be reached by a narrow path smothered by pampas grass that rustled in the wind, like nails scratching tin.

Behind him was the island, usually deserted this time of day, a curated botanical garden, a place of forgotten trees, a desolate and lonely place. The island housed a small café. It was boarded shut. Leaves gathered at the door. Few sat on the wooden seats littered near the most scenic views of the bay. The paths on the island had not been swept for some time, and pinecones were scattered on the ground, tossed by the wind. Few people came here, especially on a day like this.

The island was connected to the town of Matsushima, in the city of Sendai, on the east coast of northern Japan, by a thin, but weary concrete bridge. The railing of the bridge had once been painted red, but the rust glimmered in the sun as it fought to come out from behind the clouds. In trees and rocks, little round wooden painted dolls sat, as if sheltering from the wind, their eyes ever watchful. People would place them there for good luck. For Kato's best friend, his luck had run out.

Kato Masayoshi held tightly onto the wooden railings of the hidden lookout, looking out to sea, as the waves splashed onto the jagged rocks below, covered with empty oyster shells. It was bitterly cold. He had traveled up to the city of Sendai from Kyoto in the south the day before, with his wife Akiko and daughter Ai. He did not want them to join him, but they had insisted. After all, he said he was just on a business trip. They wanted to do some shopping. Akiko wanted to see her old school friend who lived on the coast. She wanted to talk about old times and their daughter Ai just wanted to get away for a few days. They did not know the real reason. Kato had come to kill his friend in cold blood.

He had been on the lookout platform for only a few minutes when he thought he could hear the footsteps of a man coming up the path behind him. Maybe it was just the wind rustling through the pampas grass, he thought. He wasn't sure, so he turned around and sure enough, it was the man he had come over 500 miles to meet.

It was Kenji.

His face was dripping in sweat, his coat was open, and a scarf was hanging loosely around his neck. He looked like he had been running.

'I am being followed!' he blurted out, panting heavily, and wheezing deeply, gasping for air. He staggered over to the right of where Kato was standing and grabbed onto the wooden railing. Kato did not look to see if anyone was behind him but instead looked at his friend, genuinely concerned.

'What makes you think you are being followed?' he asked calmly.

'There was a priest,' panted Kenji, 'He was walking behind me.'

'A Buddhist priest?' scoffed Kato dismissively. 'There are always priests around here. He was probably from Zuiganji, the temple in the town.'

'He was following me,' insisted Kenji. 'I am sure of it. From Matsushima, across the red bridge. Whenever I looked behind, there he was.'

Kato paused and raised his eyebrows. 'Where is he now?' he asked cautiously, now sufficiently concerned to turn around, looking into the path obscured by pampas grass. He couldn't see anything unusual and heard nothing out of the ordinary.

'I lost him after I crossed the bridge on the other side of the island,' replied Kenji, still wheezing deeply. 'I could feel him getting closer to me. I know he was after me, but then he was interrupted by another priest who was already on the island. The other priest was having a smoke and drinking a can of coffee. The other priest called out to the one following me.'

'Did you hear his name?'

'It was a little odd. It was more of a kid's name. I think I heard 'Ka-chan.' It was something like that.'

'How old was the priest?'

'Maybe in his mid-twenties.'

'Well, Akiko calls you 'Ken-chan,'' remarked Kato. 'But I admit it is an odd name for a priest. Maybe the two men went to school together and it is just a nickname. Who knows?'

'I am sure he was following me,' Kenji insisted.

Kato sighed and dismissed his friend's paranoia. He looked at Kenji. He was visibly unwell. He looked like death itself. He was gaunt and skeletal, like the barren branches of a tree in the middle of winter. He could tell that his old school friend was in a lot of pain.

'How are you today?' he asked sympathetically.

Kenji coughed violently, his whole body shaking. It was a deep cough that went on for some time. When he had finally, stopped, he cleared his throat and tried to breathe. 'I will be dead soon Masa,' he said, with his eyes shut in pain.

Hearing his friend utter those awful words out loud, made Kato look away and out to sea. He gripped the railing. It was awful for him to see Kenji in so much physical pain. Kato had heard those words before, but on this day, it felt like a final confession.

'I have withdrawn all my money,' he heard Kenji say.

'Why did you do that?' asked Kato, still staring at a tree that stood on top of an island in the distance. He felt Kenji tugging on his coat.

'Here,' Kenji said, 'Take it!'

Kato looked and saw Kenji holding a large envelope. He pleaded with Kato to take the money, but he refused to accept it. He was offended by the very idea of it.

'I don't need any money,' he protested. 'I am not here for money!'

Kenji grabbed Kato's right hand and forced the envelope into his palm and closed the fingers around it. 'I will not need it,' he said emphatically.

'Buy Akiko something, or Ai-chan!' insisted Kenji frantically. 'It can pay for the bullet train and the hotel accommodation, anything.' His eyes were bloodshot and desperate.

Kato realized it was pointless to argue and so he bowed politely and reluctantly put the envelope in his coat pocket. He sighed deeply, biting his lower lip.

'There is one more thing Masa,' said Kenji. He coughed again, this time even more violently. When this bout of coughing was over, he found it hard to stand up again, but he eventually did and lent on the railing wearily. He turned to face his old friend.

'I told you before I didn't know who kidnapped me.'

Kato nodded but kept his eyes on the ocean.

'As I told you three days ago, they kidnapped me in the park at Arashiyama, up from the river there, near the bamboo grove. It was late in the afternoon. They took me to a room near the tram station. I was bound and gagged. I could hear the sound of trams coming and going. I don't know when they administered the poison. It could have been in the tea, during the first meal. I was moved to a quiet street in downtown Kyoto. It just felt familiar. They interrogated me there. They kept asking about a scroll, an old document they wanted. They assumed I knew where it was. I had never heard of it.'

Kato wondered why Kenji was telling him all this. He already knew this. They had planned this day meticulously, but Kenji kept talking and Kato did not have the heart to stop him.

'When I escaped, I found out the truth. There was no antidote to the poison. But, in my heart, I knew that already. You know when you are dying. You can feel it in your bones, a light goes out in your heart, and you know it is only a matter of time before the darkness overwhelms you. I thought I was kidnapped by Miura's men. That is why I came to you. I remembered that you know him. Imagine my surprise when I found out that my old friend Kato was a drinking buddy of the leader of one of the largest yakuza syndicates in Kyoto. Also, you know about guns due to your time in the army. You are also the only one I trust. I assumed it was Miura.'

Kenji paused and sighed. He had something to say but he knew it would be something that Kato would not like to hear. 'But Masa, I found out, it was not him. I spoke to a friend. I will not give his name. It is better if you don't know. I'm sorry, but the man who wants me dead is some other man I have never heard of before. He wants the scroll. His name is Kawabata Koichiro. He is a gun for hire. I do not know who hired him.'

Kenji looked at Kato with tears in his eyes. 'I am sorry I got you mixed up in all this.'

Kato knew exactly who Kawabata Koichiro was, but he did not tell Kenji. As soon as he heard that name fall from his friend's lips, his heart fell, though he tried not to show it. He knew immediately his life was in great danger. He smiled at his old friend and changed the subject. It did not matter if Kenji was being followed or not. What mattered was that Kato needed to return to Kyoto immediately. In Matsushima, he was alone without any backup, and completely vulnerable. What Kenji had just told him, changed everything.

Kato pointed out to the ocean. There was an island in the distance, only small, jutting out of the sea. On the summit was a solitary tree, bending in the breeze. Kato had noticed it the moment he stood on the lookout. It would bend with the strong wind, but it would not break. It just kept growing, despite being exposed to the elements.

'Look at the tree Kenji,' he said gently.

Kenji turned away from Kato, looked out to the ocean, and smiled. 'It is beautiful Masa, simply beautiful. I am glad I came here. I used to come here as a boy. This is the most beautiful place in all of Japan.'

Kato said nothing. He reached into his coat with his right hand and pulled out a small pistol with a long silencer on the end. In the pistol were two bullets. Without a word, he pointed the gun at Kenji's left temple and pulled the trigger. Kenji died instantly and fell sideways onto the wooden platform. He grabbed Kenji's left hand, wrapping his fingers around the pistol, and carefully forced Kenji to fire another shot that went aimlessly into the air. He wrapped Kenji's fingers tightly around the gun, and took off the silencer, putting it back into his coat.

He said nothing. He left the wooden platform, not even looking back at the corpse of his oldest and dearest friend. Silence followed more swiftly than any regret. He walked quickly through the pampas grass and up the small hill to the main path that led around the island, back to the red bridge that would take him to the small town of Matsushima. He needed to get there as soon as possible.

Even though he had been on the lookout platform for a short time, he felt he had lingered too long. He hoped he had not been seen. He wanted to be as far away from the scene as he could before he met another person. If he reached the bridge, it would be far enough distance away. His pace quickened, and he buttoned up his coat as he walked, the cold wind forcing him to breathe only through his nose.

What worried him was what Kenji had said. The very mention of the name 'Kawabata,' spooked him. Deep in his stomach, he felt an anxiety stirring and he began to furtively gaze to his left and right scouring the botanical garden to see if anyone had noticed him. His heart was unsettled by every rustle of the pampas grass, every bird call, and every creak in the trees. He felt as if the island knew exactly what he had done and it was looking at him disapprovingly.

Not that he felt guilt. He felt no guilt or shame. He had just killed his best friend. But in his mind, it was not murder; it was mercy. He had done was he had been asked to do, nothing more. It was a clean, uncomplicated death and Kenji died instantly. He had taken a risk killing in the open, but he was willing to take the risk. Kenji had decided on the place of execution. It was not up to Kato. It was where his old friend wanted to be. As he said, it was a special place from his childhood. It was risky but it was not the first time Kato took such a risk and it would not be the last.

None of this worried him. Both men suspected that they had been followed since their first meeting in Kyoto three days before. They did not know by whom, but their plan was based on the key assumption that the people who kidnapped Kenji were men associated with one of the yakuza, Japan's organized crime syndicates. It was a reasonable assumption. The yakuza ran prostitution, gambling, and extortion, held to a strict code of behavior, and were easily recognizable by their tattooed bodies. Kenji had already mentioned the name of Miura during the first conversation, and that was enough information for Kato to overcome any uncertainty over whether to help his old friend.

Miura Hajime ran the city of Kyoto, or parts of it. Kato knew him. He knew his daughter. She was the same age as his daughter, Ai. She was a nice kid, very bright. They were attending the same high school. He had his kimono textile company make Miura Hajime a beautiful kimono for his late wife, long before she was diagnosed with cancer. Miura had a solid reputation as a gangster boss, but he was also affable, cultivating friendships outside the yakuza. He even moved openly in more polite Kyoto society. His wife eventually died from crippling bone disease. Kato paid his respects at her funeral.

The last time he saw Miura, the gangster was head over heels for a Chinese woman who had moved to Kyoto, her son studying at a university called Ritsumeikan. In January that year, Kato bumped into one of Miura's lieutenants, a small pudgy man by the name of Terada Yujiro, who told him that his boss had raised many eyebrows by his public association with this new woman. She had a strong personality that irritated some of the men who guarded Miura. The old guard in the gang did not like it. It made them uneasy. It made him a target. Terada thought Miura was getting soft and there were murmurs of a possible leadership challenge in the ranks. Kato told Terada that the last thing Kyoto needed was a change at the top and that if Miura's head had been turned, it would only be for a moment. He reminded Terada that loyalty to his boss was the most important principle to follow.

Two days later, the murmurs stopped when the dissenters were found dead in some disused warehouse on the edge of the city. Even though Terada knew Kato was not in the yakuza, he was respected. Everyone knew him as a man of loyalty and honor. Kato was a man who kept his word. Kato knew Miura like he knew an old pair of shoes. He and Kenji had assumed the one following them was related to Miura's gang. Miura would not have been a problem. But Miura's man was not following them.

It was Kawabata.

He cursed to himself several times. He did not usually curse.

Kawabata!

He had never met the man. He knew him only by name and reputation. Kawabata was a mystery. Kawabata Koichiro was the head of a distinguished and expensive tea ceremony school in Kyoto. The family boasted a lineage back to the 1600s. Most of his students were daughters of prominent families in the city. He was notoriously secretive and aloof. He was rarely seen in public. His tea house was more like a fortress in the town of Arashiyama on the western side of the city of Kyoto. The locals called it 'the castle,' and it was only open to his students. His school was patronized by several devoted and traditional Kyoto families who supported him and his philosophy of life. He had taught many of them over the years.

It was his drinking buddy Miura who let slip something that was known only to a few who were still alive. It was the kind of information that got people killed. A few years before, around the time Miura's wife died, Kato and Miura had been drinking a bottle of expensive sake from Miura's hometown of Sado island off the northwest coast of Japan. Miura never showed emotion in front of his men, only with his close friends, of whom Kato was one. That night he was in deep mourning. Miura was very drunk and he told Kato that Kawabata Koichiro was much more than a Tea Master. He was the go-to man for discreet political assassinations, the kind of work the yakuza kept well clear of. He had powerful political connections going all the way to Tokyo. Kawabata would either fulfill the commission himself personally or contract out the work.

According to Miura, Kawabata Koichiro had been killing people since the 1970s but had recently retired. His retirement was of great concern to many, and a great relief to others. Kawabata had passed his 'hobby' as Miura called it, onto one of his grandchildren. Miura said that Kawabata was perhaps the most dangerous man in Kyoto if not all of Japan.

Kato was angry that Kenji had gotten mixed up with Kawabata. He was only doing a last favor for his old friend. He had never crossed paths with Kawabata. He had not, to his knowledge, met the grandchildren either. He had no idea what any of them looked like. He assumed that Kawabata was most likely in his seventies or eighties. He was probably around the same age his father might have been if he had not been fatally stabbed in the back in 1995.

But Kato did not fear Kawabata, nor was he unwilling to kill him. He was able to do that. If he could get away with it, he could easily kill anyone, but only from the shadows. Kenji was not the first person he had killed. Kato had not made a formal tally, but it was close to twenty. He rethought a few dates and times as he walked quickly along toward the bridge. No, it was closer to thirty. What he feared was discovery and the shame it would bring on his family, his wife Akiko, and daughter Ai. If they discovered half the things he had done in his adult life, they would leave him, and he would be alone. He did not want to be alone. The idea of being alone in his house would drive him to despair.

Despite the rising anxiety in the pit of his stomach, Kato was relieved that his best friend, Kenji, was dead. He would now be at peace. Far better to be laid to rest by an old friend at a time and place of his choosing than being shot in the back by a stranger along one of the backstreets of some town. Kenji was dying anyway. He barely recognized his old friend, even though the two had met three days before in Kyoto. In those three days, the poison in his blood and organs was rapidly consuming him, and he would have died an excruciatingly painful death. Kenji would not have to worry about the pain of his impending death, nor would he need to fear the assassin's bullet haunting his every step. Kato was amazed Kenji was even able to walk out to the island by himself. It must have taken the last of his energy. He had done something very risky and perhaps outrageously foolish, but Kenji was a friend, a good friend. He did not have many, but Kato would do anything for his friends.

Kato had finally reached the top of the steps leading to the red bridge that took him back to the town of Matsushima. It seemed to take forever, but he was still alive, and he had not met anyone or seen anyone. He was probably in the clear, so long as he did not meet Kawabata before he could return to the safety of Kyoto. This new information about the assassin bothered him and forced him to change his plans for the rest of the day. Assuming the men searching for Kenji were sent by the bumbling Miura, Kato's plan was originally to go to a local shop and buy a handmade wooden doll, a kokeshi, for his daughter Ai, whose birthday fell in two days and then return to Sendai. A few months before, Ai had seen a bunch of kokeshi dolls huddling forlornly together in a cramped wooden box at a second-hand market in Kyoto. She felt sorry for them, wanting to rescue at least one from oblivion. But her mother Akiko refused to buy one for her, saying that it was bad luck to buy a used doll.

When her father proposed a sudden business trip to Matsushima, Ai was insistent that she have a new wooden doll to put in her room. The way she looked up at him, with those eyes and that smile she could pull, how could he say no? After buying the doll, his original plan was to meet up with Akiko and Ai at Sendai station late that afternoon, go to their hotel, stay the night, and return to Tokyo the following afternoon on March 12.

But Miura's man was not following him. It was someone associated with the secretive and dangerous Kawabata. It was either Kawabata Koichiro himself or one of his family members. Kato needed to return to Kyoto that afternoon. As he stepped onto the bridge, he took his mobile phone from his coat pocket and called his wife. He looked back to the island and then forward to the town of Matsushima. She answered.

'It's me,' he said.

'How is Matsushima?'

'It's fine. How is your friend?'

'She is very well.'

Kato could hear voices in the background. They all seemed happy.

'Sayako says hello to you Masa,' said Akiko.

'I hope she is well,' replied Kato reluctantly and politely. He loathed the woman, whom Kato saw as an odious busybody and gossip. She never liked him as Akiko's husband and often criticized him behind his back. Sayako wanted Akiko to marry Kenji, as he was more handsome and came from a wealthy family. She always told Akiko that she married the wrong person, but his wife just smiled and laughed. Given her obnoxious personality, Kato always wondered why his wife would keep her friendship with such a person.

'Really Masa, you are so kind,' said Akiko. 'I will tell her.'

'Tamura called me just now,' he lied, realizing he needed to have a convincing ruse to get them to cut their holiday short so they could return to Kyoto as soon as possible. 'We must go back to Kyoto after lunch. I'm sorry, I know you wanted to do some more sightseeing.'

There was silence on the other end of the phone. Kato knew his wife was upset.

'I am sure Tamura can deal with it,' she protested.

'Tamura is only my manager. The final decisions rest with me. I need to be there. There are deadlines and orders to meet.'

There was silence from the other side of the phone. Kato could hear some muffled voices. Akiko must have put her hand over the phone and was talking with her friend.

'Ok,' she said finally. 'I understand.'

'Listen,' said Kato. 'I can meet you at the hotel after you have lunch with Sayako, and we can get the Shinkansen. Is Ai with you?'

His wife said that she was. 'Did you get the kokeshi?' he could hear Ai ask in the background.

'Not yet,' said Kato. 'I will buy one now. We can get a bento for us to have on the train.'

'We don't need one. We have just eaten lunch. Sayako made us a banquet.'

Kato could sense from the tone of her voice that she was upset.

'Masa,' she asked. 'Is everything ok?'

'Of course, Akiko, everything is fine,' he lied.

There was another, longer pause in the conversation. Kato thought for a moment that his wife had hung up on him.

'Your voice sounds different,' she insisted. 'Has anything happened?'

'No, everything is fine, nothing is the matter, I will see you at the hotel, the earlier the better.'

He hung up and put the phone in his pocket. If he knew that he would never hear her voice again, he would have said something else, maybe even some words of affection or gratitude for their many years together. During the conversation, he mentioned her name and it surprised her, making her feel anxious. He could sense that in her voice. It was a mistake on his part. He regretted it. He let slip that something was wrong. That is why she asked. He rarely mentioned her name to her face, except when they argued, when he needed her to listen to him. Those times usually revolved around appointments that conflicted with her social schedule. He rarely interfered with her life.

Normally, his conversations with her would be short and to the point, not that they really talked. Even when they met at university, they rarely spoke. Kenji had introduced them after a tennis match, and they found in each other a companionship that was both inexplicable and irresistible. Their marriage was a surprise to everyone, including Kenji who had long been interested in Akiko since junior high school but never made a move. Kato had been absolutely devoted to her and faithful as a husband.

Kato worked himself to death trying to make Akiko's life as comfortable as he could. He had to overcome the constant taunts from Kenji and people like Sayako that Akiko married beneath herself. Her father had been a minor statesman in the government. Her family had a long association with the Japanese Self-Defence Force. Her uncle had been a general. He knew that Akiko understood that his love for her was expressed through his work. He had never told her verbally that he loved her. But she knew. She did not need to hear it.

But Kenji made a fuss about this lack of communication when Ai was born. He called Kato to task over his customary but curt demands and lack of communication. Kato never saw it like that. He kept his family safe and provided for them. Akiko had lots of friends and spent most of her time with them, while Kato worked almost seven days a week.

He hoped to keep his family out of this trip to Matsushima, but Akiko had insisted upon it when he mentioned it three days before. She wanted to get the kokeshi for her daughter and she saw it as an opportunity to see her old school friend again. At the time it seemed quite harmless, especially if there was no real danger. But now that an assassin associated with Kawabata might be closing in, he knew bringing his family was a mistake. He put them accidentally in harm's way. He reprimanded himself for being so foolish and told himself that like Miura, he was getting too soft and weak. He had spent too long letting things slide and now he had made a mistake. He was still reprimanding himself when he started walking quickly across the bridge.

2

The bridge was deserted. The weather was still cold. Kato kept his coat buttoned. He still wore his gloves. While he clenched his fists to warm them, he realized that the island he left would be forever scarred as the scene of a murder. He had not thought about that before. He dismissed the thought and continued walking along the bridge. Each step closer to Matsushima was one step away from the past and that felt good. Indeed, killing Kenji on the viewing platform on the far side of the island was better because the island was separate from the mainland and by crossing the bridge he was in some psychological way, distancing himself from the crime. Maybe, he thought, when he reached the end of the bridge, the fears of uncertainty over the Kawabata family might cause him less anxiety.

He was thinking about this when he reached the middle of the red bridge. He had been deep in thought and kept his eyes down. When he lifted his eyes he realized, much to his surprise, that an elderly man was walking towards him, from the Matsushima side of the bridge. From what he could discern, the man was possibly in his eighties and walking with a distinct limp. His painful step was aided by a walking stick, and he wore a thick grey coat that seemed to cover him entirely. His legs seemed unusually long, and his clothes did not seem to fit him very well. It was as if he had dressed in a hurry.

Kato did not alter his pace but kept walking along the bridge, toward the old man. Surely, he thought, this man must be out for a stroll or something like that. He was probably from Matsushima, maybe a fisherman or a laborer. That might have explained the slightly disheveled appearance, or maybe he just didn't care much as he was obviously retired and just needed something to wear for his stroll, a brisk walk across to the island and back to his home in the town.

But as each step brought the two men closer, he began to suspect something completely different. He could not dislodge the suspicion forming in the back of his mind. It was a possibility, not entirely out of the realm of possibilities, that this old man was the man he had hoped he would not see that day in Matsushima. Could it be that this elderly gentleman was Kawabata the Tea Master and assassin? He had never met him before, so there was no way of knowing if he was Kawabata or not. If this man was Kawabata, then this meeting on the bridge was not a coincidence. If his reputation was anything to go by, then this might be the last day of Masayoshi Kato.

As the two men approached each other, he could see that the elderly gentleman was watching the sea, and quite innocently seemed to gaze in his direction. His eyes passed Kato's briefly but when they did, they widened as if he recognized something. The old man stared at him again and looked at him intently, but then just as quickly, his eyes returned to the ocean.

The man's facial expressions gave it away. He knew immediately he had been recognized. The eyes of the old man said it all. Though it was the briefest of glances, it was all that was needed. Kato stopped walking and stood waiting for the old man to make his move against him. He had no weapon, no gun, no knife, only the cylinder of the silencer in his coat pocket. The gun he used on the island to kill Kenji was not his own. Kenji had produced it and the silencer a few days before when they met in Kyoto. Kato agreed to use it and then put it in Kenji's hand to give the impression that he had committed suicide. It did not occur to him to bring another gun. He was not expecting to have need of one. Kato calmed himself down and waited for the old man to strike.

To his amazement, nothing happened. The elderly man walked straight past him. Kato sighed deeply, greatly relieved. He had made a mistake. The anxiety of the tension of the day had given him an excessive sense of paranoia. He heard the distinct sound of the old man limp past him, the thud of his left leg on the ground suggesting a natural fracture. The old man was obviously just out for an afternoon stroll and nothing more. Kato wiped his forehead, leaving beads of sweat on his glove. He turned to the railing of the bridge and placed his hands on it, looking out to sea.

But Kato was not yet in the clear, because the man also stopped walking. His footsteps had fallen silent, and the old man stood still a few steps from him, closer to the island, staring at it in front of him. Kato could hear him breathing behind him. He turned his head slightly and as he did, so did the old man until they were looking at each other. The face of the old man however, was not angry or devious but inquisitive and curious. It was the look of astonishment as if in him, he saw someone he did not expect to see. But it was more than that. It was the look of disbelief, that his eyes betrayed something that he could not possibly be seeing. The man looked at him, his eyes wide as if he had seen an old friend from long ago.

'Ichinosuke?' asked the old man.

Kato said nothing in reply. He didn't know what to say. His name was not Ichinosuke.

'Ichinosuke?' asked the man again.

The old man had obviously made a mistake. He mistook him for someone else. It was easy to do because Kato's face was so ordinary that he was often mistaken for other people. He had no remarkable features, except for his long nose, a few wrinkles around his eyes, a narrow mouth, and chiseled cheeks which were almost gaunt due to his strict diet. His hair was completely black except for the grey edges, and it sat neatly on his head almost as if it had fallen out of the sky and plopped down on his scalp.

The old man turned round and using his walking cane, he moved and stood within speaking distance from Kato. He did not move forward, but his eyes looked at Kato's face as if trying to recognize something. Kato also turned to face the old man. He let slip a thin smile through his frowning mouth as a sign of respect and bowed, as his impulse for politeness overruled any urge to move on.

'Do I know you?' he asked the old man politely.

The man looked at Kato from top to bottom and then stared up at him, his right hand pressing on his walking stick. He breathed in heavily and his face winced as if in pain, forcing him to close his eyes. He sighed and when he opened his eyes they were tinged with redness.

'No,' replied the man, disappointed.

'I have a typical face,' protested Kato politely. 'I am often mistaken for someone else.'

'Then that can be very inconvenient,' said the old man loudly, in a deep voice. leaning on his walking stick precariously as if he were about to topple over.

'They think you are their brother, but you are not, or they think you are their husband, but you are not, or perhaps they think of you as their friend, but you are not, are you? Just another face in the crowd, just another set of eyes and ears and mouth, but you are not, are you? To your wife you are someone quite particular, to your family you are quite remarkable and to your friends you are quite memorable.'

'I am not remarkable, or memorable or particular,' protested Kato.

The old man came closer to Kato, so they were within only a few steps of each other. The man seemed taller and stronger than before, and his eyes seemed to look right into his heart. He felt as if this disheveled, limping man was inside his head, poking around.

'So, who am I then?' asked the old man abruptly. 'An old man out for a walk across the bridge and so old that he cannot remember a face from long ago? Is that what you are thinking?'

Kato said nothing. The man looked at him more closely, but like a wild animal might size up its prey before pouncing.

'I'm sorry to keep you,' the old man said abruptly. 'You seem to be in such a hurry to leave the island and return to Matsushima, I will not delay you any further.' He turned to leave, but this time it was Kato's turn to protest.

'I am not in any rush,' he replied emphatically.

The old man scoffed. 'If you say so,' he slurred with a surprised look. 'You don't have to kick up a fuss about it. From your demeanor, I simply assumed that you wanted to be as far away from the island as possible.'

At this Kato began to become suspicious. It was such a strange thing to say. Perhaps his carefully laid plan was about to crumble like a paper lantern in the rain. Did he know about Kenji? Maybe he was Kawabata after all. 'Why would I be in a hurry?' he asked.

'To escape what you left behind I suspect,' replied the man quietly but firmly. 'To put distance between what you left behind and yourself, to slip back to the world of people with your humanity intact.'

He spoke the last few words slowly and they lingered in the air. These words convinced Kato that the man must be Kawabata. How else would he know about Kato's movements in the last hour? Kato stared at the man. 'Who are you?' he demanded.

A faint smile emerged at the corners of the man's lips. 'Who am I?' he asked.

Kato repeated the question. The old man seemed so fragile with his walking stick. Even a gust of wind might knock him over. He hobbled forward but slipped and Kato went to grab him to stop him from falling but the old man instead held onto Kato's shoulders, his hands gripping him tightly. Kato was wearing a coat and a suit and a shirt, but the fingers of the old man seemed to go through all three layers and burn into his flesh. He could feel warm fingers through three layers of clothing. How was it possible? The old man's head was fallen, but he lifted it up slowly so that his face was in front of Kato's. Kato could see every wrinkle on his face, every pockmark, every scar. His teeth seemed old but impeccable, and his lips were large and bulbous. He smelt of the sea as if he had just come out of the water.

The old man looked at Kato and he began to smile. His smile grew and then, he could feel a rumbling in the old man that reverberated right up to the two strong hands gripping his shoulders. The man began to laugh. He stopped and then began to laugh again until his entire body shook. He then released his grip on Kato's shoulders and ran his fingers down his chest and then pushed himself away standing tall on his two feet by himself, unaided by his walking stick which he had dropped on the bridge. The man looked at him.

'You want to know my name? What if I said my name was Kawabata? What does that name mean to you?'

Kato's hand instinctively reached into his pocket for the long cylinder of the silencer. It was his only weapon; it was better than nothing, but to his surprise, it was no longer there. His hand rummaged around every corner until it dawned on him that the piece of metal was gone. He looked back at the old man, his face both alarmed and angry, but what he saw astonished him.

'Are you looking for this?' asked the old man, holding up the silencer in his right hand. The old man dangled it in the air between his fingers.

'That is impossible!' exclaimed Kato, deeply shocked. The old man must have taken it from him when he fell. He realized that the stumbling of the stranger was just a ruse to take any weapon from him, to disarm him completely.

'Ah!' replied the old man with a smile. 'The silly old man out for a walk who mistook you for someone else, now has this little toy. Today is the day for surprises!'

He held the cylinder up to his face and sniffed it like one would a flower. His nostrils flared and he moved the weapon away from his face as if repulsed by its very presence. The man turned his face to Kato and shook his head. 'Recently used it seems, on the island over there am I right?'

His eyes examined the silencer closely, not as an expert, but more like a child might examine a newly discovered pebble or a fallen leaf, his nose almost touching it. 'Ah!' he exclaimed as if he had found something fascinating. 'This is a new model. It is well made. Is it Japanese? I am fond of knives and swords myself. The gun leaves less to chance. The sword is much more exciting. It gets the blood pumping. This little cylinder muffles the sound. How splendid. You know I have not held one in this make and model in my hand before. It is the weapon for a coward, which you must be, sneaking around, hoping no one notices, able to creep up behind someone and shoot them without them ever knowing you were there. This is the tool of an assassin,' he said, his eyes bulging, his face still expressing excitement.

He turned his head away from the head which he kept in the air and towards Kato. His nostrils flared and a smile began to protrude from both sides of his round face.

'I am not an assassin,' protested Kato.

'I didn't accuse you of being one,' retorted the old man quickly, his nose returning to sniff the silencer. He looked about him as if he saw something in the wind, a scent, a whiff, a breeze, and he breathed deeply. He held the cylinder with his hand away from his face, in the air, as if it had a repugnant smell. The man spoke again.

'But it was not, as I thought, an act of cowardice, but one of friendship, am I right? No, this was an unusual death,' speculated the man, staring at Kato once more. His eyes seem to be scanning Kato for further information.

'I surmise that you killed an associate, no, a friend, a close friend.'

The man stared into Kato's eyes.

'Even if he were a close friend, don't you think, Masayoshi Kato, that you should have found a less painful way for him to die?'

With that remarkable statement, the old man casually threw the silencer over his shoulder into the water. It disappeared beneath the waves and Kato never saw it again. Kato was speechless. His mind was full of questions, his heart full of fear, and his fists clenched. He did not know whether to strike or run away. How did this old man know his name? He must be Kawabata. Why doesn't he do what he came to do and why did he throw the silencer over the bridge into the water? Did he have his own pistol in his pocket ready to use at a moment's notice? Were there others waiting for him at the end of the bridge to take him to his death? He looked quickly at both ends of the bridge. There appeared to be no one. Again, the only one he could see was the old man.

Kato felt like he was being pushed into a corner by this enigmatic, strange person who seemed to speak in riddles and questions. Is this why he was the most feared assassin in all of Japan? How bold, how outrageous, thought Kato, that this assassin would toy with him as a cat plays with a mouse. He had nowhere to run. He thought of jumping off the bridge into the water. That might give him a few seconds before the old man pulled out his own pistol, but it might have given him all the time he needed to get away. Maybe this Kawabata was expecting it and he would relish the thought of gunning down Kato as he leaped into the ocean. Every fiber of his being was screaming for him to move or at least do something, but he retained his composure and forced the anger back down into his heart and stomach. It was the control of his emotions that kept him alive all these years, encased in a mold of stubborn politeness the result of many hours of dedicated meditation.

Kato was capable of rage and deep anger, but the door to this was normally locked, bolted in chains and ropes, deep inside his inner being. When roused or provoked, Kato had the capacity for an outpouring of anger. He did not know where this came from, but he knew the triggers that could unleash it, a time of uncontrollable rage. He could easily kill without this door to rage being open. He killed Kenji without a moment's hesitation. He was not angry about it. He felt sadness for his friend. But this was different, here on the bridge, with this man. It was as if the old man knew about the locked room in Kato's mind and was trying every door in his head to find it. He could hear the man walking through the corridors and staircases in his brain searching for that room. But even if he found the door, the ropes, and chains would keep him busy for a while. If successful, if the man breached those doors, then he would be forced to relive the most painful moments of his life. If that happened, then he would be unable to stop the rage. He knew the door would be in danger of being breached if he could smell smoke in his nostrils or feel fire licking at the back of his eyes.

He knew why the triggers were fire, and he knew why smoke would trigger his rage, for the most painful moment of his life was finding his father, his poor, innocent father, lying still a few feet from a burning house. It was a lifetime ago. It was the night he went into the burning house, saved a little boy, and then found his father lying outside on the ground. He had been stabbed in the back by a coward, obviously a good friend, obviously someone he trusted. As he cradled his father's head in his lap and heard the last words that fell from his lips, Kato was reborn, and the anger he had always felt dancing around the edges of his heart, took control and transformed into rage. Within a few hours, he did something unspeakable, and he could not describe how it felt afterward.

It took several days and hours of dedicated meditation to calm down. In his mind, he locked the rage, the memories, the pain, the regrets, and the anger into a special room in his mind, and bolted it with ropes and chains, mental disciplines designed to prevent him from opening the door. If the door opened, then he would cease to be a polite, respectable seller of silk kimono and become a cold-blooded killer. Then, anything was possible, and he would start killing with earnestness, the rage would take over and he would be unstoppable. As Kato regained his composure and relaxed his facial muscles, he felt that the old man could see through his politeness and in some way, read his mind.

The old man had picked up his walking stick and was leaning on it again.

'At some point, you should tell me who this Kawabata is,' said the man. 'I can read your thoughts. They are spilling out onto this bridge everywhere. It reminds me of the steam spurting from a pot of boiling buckwheat noodles. They have leapt so far that I have to stand back in order not to be splashed in the face.'

Kato did not know what to say.

The old man continued. 'You fear a man by the name of 'Kawabata,' an assassin in Kyoto. You think he is tracking your every move. You believe that he wants to know what you know about your dead friend Kenji Nomura, and why he was poisoned.'

This confused Kato greatly. How did this man know all this information? How could this man read his thoughts if that were indeed possible? How could he have known about the death of Kenji which took place only a few moments before? Maybe his crime was seen by one of this old man's associates and this information was conveyed to him by phone. That must be the only rational explanation. He was convinced this old man was Kawabata Koichiro and that he had placed men on either side of the bridge who would prevent him from escaping. Kawabata was simply toying with him, playing with him, delaying the inevitable.

The old man laughed out loud. 'You look like him, but you are certainly not Ichinosuke!'

Kato had forgotten about this 'Ichinosuke.' The ruse had not worked. He did not care who this 'Ichinosuke' might have been. He wanted this charade to end and for this man, who was obviously Kawabata, to reveal himself and make his move. 'I don't care who Ichinosuke was!' spat out Kato furiously. 'I am not he. I am Kato Masayoshi, but you know that, so why don't we stop this charade now.'

'Charade?' exclaimed the man, 'you think I am Kawabata?'

Kato nodded.

'If I wanted you dead,' said the man. 'Then I would have killed you before you had time to take another breath. I would not bother with a conversation.'

It was Kato's turn to scoff out loud. He laughed. 'Will you kill me with boredom?' he asked angrily. 'Make your move or move on!' he ordered.

The man ignored his insults and stared at Kato again surveying him like one was performing an inspection. 'It is truly remarkable,' he said. 'I am amazed. You look exactly like him, the same face, the same eyebrows, the same expression. It is not an accident for us to meet, no it is certainly not an accident. But Kato, you are right, you are not Ichinosuke. You are a man of deceit and deception, who hides even from his wife and child. If they knew what you did to Kenji, you would lose them forever, you know how people are with these moral sentiments, but you do not live by them at all, you have your own personal code and you bow to no one except yourself. You are certainly not Ichinosuke.'

This was the first thing that made sense to Kato. The old man was right. He would lose them. They would run so fast to get away from him the moment they knew what he had done. His daughter would never look him in the face again and his wife would turn her back on him, leaving him completely alone. Yes, the old man was right. He was a man of consummate deception, an excellent liar, and a peddler of deceit.

'But, despite your failings,' said the old man. 'You remind me such much of Ichinosuke, especially the eyes. You have the same face. Maybe you took it or maybe it was given to you by someone when they no longer needed it. Do you take faces? Is that your profession? Maybe there is someone else under that skin of yours. Do you know anyone who takes faces?'

'I have no idea what you are talking about,' said Kato frustratingly.

'For someone who has lived in Kyoto all his life, you know little about old Japan. Someone who steals faces is one of the most dangerous creatures in our beautiful world today. There are not many left these days, but they are still around, and you will never see them until it is too late. I hope you never meet one Kato-san.'

Kato was anxious to get away, but he felt drawn to the old man and this bizarre conversation. Kato realized that the old man seemed to speak only in riddles and puzzles and the only way to find out answers was to humor him and find out the truth concerning this 'Ichinosuke.' Maybe, then, once the ruse had run its course, would Kawabata reveal his identity.

'Who was 'Ichinosuke?' asked Kato politely but wearily.

The old man smiled. 'Finally, you ask a good question. What do you know of your ancestors?'

The question came out of nowhere and was not what Kato was expecting. The old man was smiling. He looked excited as if he were about to tell him something fascinating.

Kato was surprised by the question but decided to answer it anyway. He sighed. 'My family has been in the kimono business since the 1880s. Before that, I do not know. Our family records were lost in a fire. I always assumed that they might have come from the samurai warrior class and moved into business after the government made them destitute.'

'I can answer that question with some certainty,' said the man smiling broadly, still visibly excited. 'I don't know much about this century or last century, but I know a lot about the one before.'

Kato said nothing. What was saying made no sense to him.

'Your family did enter the merchant class around that time, it is quite possible. I lost track with them then. I was not interested in them, but I knew Ichinosuke. I could not forget him. Your ancestor Ichinosuke could open the kimono shop because I was unable to kill him in 1868.'

'Surely you are just joking with me old man,' said Kato. 'That is not possible.'

'Anything is possible in this world Kato, anything at all,' replied the man. 'Just looking at you, I realize this day is important as if the goddess herself has conspired to bring us together once more. When I look at you, your face is blank, but your heart is as violent as the ocean depths. You do not know how deeply this all goes. Our lives are intertwined. Your ancestors knew me. Some of them even fought alongside me. Our past is tied together as is our future.'

The old man hobbled over to the left side of the bridge and placed his hands on the railing, looking out over to the town of Matsushima in the distance. He sighed.

'The emperor visited Tokyo for the first time in late 1868, by road from Kyoto. He had betrayed us. Most of us were dead or in hiding. But those who survived hatched a plot to kill him as he traveled from the ancient capital. I almost succeeded. Only one man stood in my way. It was Ichinosuke. He stood resolute and refused my demands to pass. He had never seen so much blood. I skewered his friends like barbequed chicken on a stick. He shook like a leaf in the wind, but he did not move. I remember his name because someone called it out, I do not remember who, it might have been the emperor or one of his advisors, but it stuck in my mind. I have forgotten all their faces, but I remember him, like it was yesterday and yours is the same face staring at me now.'

'There must be a rational explanation for all of this,' countered Kato. 'I don't believe a word of what you are saying. You obviously know about me and for whatever reason, you are toying with me drawing me into your deluded world of fantasies.'

The old man interrupted him.

'You are absolutely right,' he said. 'Perhaps after killing your best friend, your mind has collapsed, and I am a figment of your imagination, and you are standing on the bridge here at Matsushima staring out to space your mind wrestling with the reality that you murdered your best friend. Perhaps I followed you to the island early this morning, crept up behind you and saw what you did there to poor old Kenji, and heard you muttering his name to yourself. Perhaps I read about you in the newspaper or visited your shop in Kyoto and decided to follow you all the way to Matsushima to frustrate you with this bizarre story, but then it would be an incredibly complicated and irrevocably pointless exercise. To what end would I engage in this adventure? What would I possibly gain from it? I was out for my daily stroll to the island when I saw your face and immediately, I remembered Ichinosuke. You look just like him.'

The old man seemed genuinely disappointed that Kato failed to believe him. But as these last words fell off his lips, the voices of two men could be heard coming from the island side of the bridge. The two men wore the garb of Buddhist priests. Kato assumed quite naturally that they served at the temple that was famous in the Matsushima area, Zuiganji. The temple was at the end of a forested path on the edge of the town, near the station. These were also the two men Kenji must have seen earlier in the day. They looked harmless enough. Poor Kenji was probably just paranoid.

'Ah, two priests from Zuiganji,' said the old man, changing the subject, and pointing to them. 'One of them I know quite well, the one on the left. The other is unfamiliar to me.'

The two men were deep in conversation. The one on the left was overweight and short while the other one was tall and slender. As soon as they looked up, one of them, the shorter man, recognized the elderly gentleman.

'Good afternoon!' exclaimed the plump priest on the left, bowing deeply. The old man and Kato bowed. The priests walked over to them. 'Out for your stroll around the island Yamaguchi-san,' asked the priest. The old man bowed to him and smiled.

'Yes, I was on my way, but I met this gentleman on the bridge.'

The priest looked sympathetically at Kato as if he had also been stuck in a conversation with Yamaguchi-san at some point in the past. Kato, for his part, saw this as his chance to escape and return to Sendai.

'Actually, I was on my way to find a kokeshi doll for my daughter,' said Kato to the priests. The eyes of the plump priest lit up.

'My father-in-law has a workshop in town and his shop is open today. He is an accredited craftsman with the government. They are all genuine dolls. They are quite beautiful. His workshop is on the way to the station. I can take you there if you like?'

Kato bowed in appreciation, and turning to the old man, Yamaguchi-san, he bowed and smiled. He had found his chance to escape, and he took the opportunity. He had lingered on the bridge for too long. He did not know why the old man knew so much about him, but there must have been some reasonable explanation. Yamaguchi's story about Kato's ancestor was complete nonsense. He liked a funny story as much as the next man, but the rambling rubbish about samurai and stealing faces and emperors and all that was a sign of an unhinged mind.

The two priests bowed to Yamaguchi and moved on. Kato followed then and the three of them began to walk across the bridge together. Kato was in the middle of them, and he was glad that these two men had brought an end to a strange conversation. Yamaguchi was obviously not Kawabata but some weirdo who lived locally and accosted people at random to confuse them with his crazy theories on life. He was very strange, and his mind games were manipulative and alluring. Even Kato with all his innate rationalism was getting pulled in. The image that came to mind was that of giant spiders from one of the old Japanese legends who cast their web-like nets onto pilgrims who got too close to their lair.

The priests had arrived just at the right time. He was eager to get back to Sendai, grab his family, and quickly return to Kyoto and safety. It was all perfectly simple and straightforward. He would contact his old friend Miura and together, they would deal with Kawabata. Once Kato killed Kawabata Koichiro, Miura would gain a stronger reputation among the yakuza and his position would be elevated. He would end up owing Kato another debt, while Kato would be safe. That was Kato's new plan. He was improvising.

In a few moments, Kato would have reached the end of the bridge and he would have caught the next train to Sendai, and he would never have met the people he would meet this fateful day, nor would their lives be forever intertwined with his, nor would he undergo such a deeply personal change that he would reshape the future of Japan itself.

Often life hangs like a thread in the wind, and this was one of these moments. Even if he made it to Sendai, he would not have met his wife and daughter. At that moment, they were enjoying food, friendship, and laughter with Akiko's old school friend Sayako and her husband was washing up in the kitchen. They would soon leave the house and Sayako's husband would drive them to the station. They would never reach it, but they would all die in the car. A huge and violent wave would soon knock the car off the highway. Ai, Kato's daughter would be knocked unconscious, and Sayako's husband would break his way out of the car, only to fall into the water and drown. Akiko would also drown, but she would do so holding her daughter and calling out for help. It never came. Every house on Sayako's street would be obliterated and every person in every house would die. On this day, the day Kato went to Matsushima, the day Akiko and Ai went to Sayako's house, more than eighteen thousand people would die in a tsunami. They never saw it coming.

This was all the future for Masayoshi Kato, the grief and anguish that would destroy his world, but as he walked along the bridge that day, he thought that he had planned for every contingency, and he was in complete control of the world around him. The reality was quite different. He could not even control the weather.

As he walked with the two priests, he felt the urge to look back. It was subtle, a kind of involuntary reflex, most people have them, the glances people often make for no reason at all. Had he not looked back, his life might have been different, and the conversation with Yamaguchi might have simply gone the way of all previous conversations, lost in distant memory in the deepest recesses of his mind. His life would have been tragic and indeed it was, especially on that day. The man who left the bridge was not the man who returned to Kyoto a few days later. He was about to lose everything he ever cared about, but it was nothing compared to the sufferings and trials that lay ahead in the years that followed. It was all because he looked back on that day on the red bridge at Matsushima. The path that Kato would cut through life would lead to the deaths of so many people, so much blood, that would make Yamaguchi's tale of Ichinosuke pale into insignificance.

Kato felt a chill at the back of his neck and a stirring of queasiness in his stomach. It seemed colder than before. The sky was grey, but Kato could sense a foreboding behind him, a creeping darkness spreading across the world, and he looked back, just for a moment. What he saw that day he could not describe to anyone, and his mind could not explain to him what he saw. This image would torment him for many years and often when he slept, this moment would be replayed again and again in his subconscious.

Yamaguchi, or whatever he was, had changed. He was no longer in human form. The shape was indefinite. He could see claws, terrible claws, wrapped around the railing of the bridge, sharp and long. He could discern a fur-like skin wrapped around the shape, like that of a bear or a large cat. Yamaguchi's face was still there in that he was recognizable, but his eyes had turned jet black, and he exuded fear, dread, and decay. Simply by looking at him, even for a moment, Kato was drawn into a whirlwind of rotting flesh, bones, and carcasses. He could smell the odor of death. At Yamaguchi's feet were the dismembered remains of hundreds of human bodies, skulls, bones, and pieces of flesh torn, and as far as he could see, there was a cemetery of unburied corpses. Kato could see samurai swords and helmets and banners strewn across the ground. He recognized a torn banner of the hollyhock emblem, the symbol of the old government ruled by the last of the Shoguns, the Tokugawa family, swirling in the wind, held by a fallen soldier. Next to it, he could see the crushed emblem of the Japanese Imperial Household, the banner of the Emperor of Japan. It was torn. At the feet of Yamaguchi, on his back, as if turning to run away, frozen in time was a soldier in white and brown clothes, and his face was staring at Kato. Kato looked at the man and realized he was looking into a mirror. He was looking at himself. Kato turned quickly away, pushed past the priest on the left, went to the railing, and was violently ill into the ocean.

3

The two priests rushed over. The one who was not from Zuiganji quickly gave Kato a cloth and a flask of water. Kato bowed appreciatively, drank some, and spat it out, wiping his mouth with the cloth.

'I will get this washed and return it to you,' said Kato apologetically.

'It is only cloth,' said the priest kindly. 'How are you feeling?'

'I hope it wasn't Yamaguchi-san's conversation?' asked the other priest. 'He is known to ramble. I am glad we were able to rescue you from him. He often stops people in the street and confuses them no end, pretending to know who they are and their history and so on. We noticed you chatting here for a while. We were up on the hill on the island having a cigarette. Yamaguchi-san loves history, especially other people's history. He is a bit of a trickster.'

'I don't know,' replied Kato honestly, drinking some more water from the flask. 'It might have been something I ate this morning.'

He was very rarely sick, and his body's response was so strong that it surprised him as he was normally able to control himself. He usually ate vegetables and some fish. He ate meat occasionally. He often drank a lot, probably too much for his age, but he rarely vomited. This sudden regurgitation of his stomach was as if his body had a mind of its own and needed cleansing. He looked in the direction of

Yamaguchi, but to his surprise, the bridge was empty, and the old man was gone.

Kato and the two priests had reached the end of the red bridge at Matsushima, but he still felt quite nauseous. He vomited one more time over the edge of the bridge into the water below before he reached the ticket gate. Both priests showed genuine concern for him. The small, plump priest with an unusually round face and a bald head, introduced himself as Abe. He recommended that Kato sit down and rest somewhere for at least a few minutes before they went to buy the doll for his daughter. Kato, despite wanting to get back to Sendai as soon as possible, agreed. His legs felt like jelly and every time he thought of Yamaguchi, he felt more of his stomach rising to his throat. It was as if he was physically and involuntarily rejecting the presence of the old man as if his entire body revulsed and needed to expel a wretched poison seeping through his veins. It was as if his body and spirit had been preconditioned to respond in a certain way and that deep in his subconscious, he felt an inner voice deep in his flesh telling him to keep a distance from the old man or whatever he was.

Leaning over the red railing of the bridge, feeling drained and nauseous made him think of the last time he felt this way. It was when he had been held captive by terrorists in southern Iraq in early 2006. He had been reckless and stupid that day, wandering through the marketplace by himself, surrounded by the aroma of spices and vegetables, and meat. He felt he was not doing enough to help the local people and wanted to meet some of them and so on his day off, he left the area designated for his unit and went into the villages. His walk took him to a beautiful little town.

He did not notice the unit of American marines passing through the village, but he felt the explosion as it tore through the stalls. A bomb. Terrorists detonated it in the marketplace, at noon, when everyone was there, in a place full of voices, laughter, and conversation. The sounds of laughter and the quiet conversation were replaced by smoke and fire, the screams of the wounded and dying. None of his training in Japan could have prepared him for what he saw. They were innocent people, just going about their day, brutally slaughtered just because some local disgruntled Iraqi terrorists saw an opportunity to kill Americans. Kato held the remains of a young boy in his arms, his body broken by the deafening blast, and he wept uncontrollably. When the terrorists arrived, they tossed the dead boy away like a discarded doll and dragged Kato and the surviving Americans to a place of execution.

There they interrogated and executed the two senior officers and turned their attention to the stray Japanese man whom they assumed was with the American army. They poisoned Kato with a strange concoction of chemicals. He was violently ill until he was completely drained and exhausted. They didn't ask him any questions and seemed to delight in torturing him. There, in that dark, empty room, lying on the floor, next to the beaten but alive four remaining Americans, Kato could smell a burning fire deep in his nostrils and felt as if he could see flames licking up the walls around him. He had no weapon. He did not need one, nor did he remember much of what happened. The last thing he remembered was cutting himself free from the rope with a piece of glass. The board of inquiry stated later that he became like a man possessed. All Kato remembered was an inferno, as if he were on fire. He was the fire. A tsunami of rage. He could not remember how many he killed that day.

Kato felt his shoulders being shaken and realized that he had been lost in his thoughts. He turned to the priest standing next to him, with an anxious look on his face, and leaned on him, as he was too weak to move by himself. He wanted to thank him but felt unable to frame the words with his mouth. Instead, the man spoke to him, filling the few minutes it took to walk slowly off the bridge and back to the town of Matsushima with some words of introduction. He introduced himself as Ka-chan. That was not his real name, but his adopted name. He said that he was always behaving like a child at the seminary and so one of his Buddhist teachers gave him a name that suited his character as a form of rebuke. The name stuck. He laughed to himself and turned to Abe, the other priest.

'This is Abe Sensei,' he said. 'We trained together in Kyoto, and he has moved up to this beautiful place. I am stuck in Kyoto. It is a real shame. I am very jealous of him.'

The three men had reached the end of the bridge. Kato turned around and took one last look at the island. It seemed so far away. There, on the lookout was Kenji's corpse. He had done his duty. He fulfilled his obligations to his old friend. His debts had been paid. Now he was leaving the world of violence and returning to the world of politeness. He was also leaving Yamaguchi. He could not forget what he saw, even if he did not know what he saw. He did not know what to make of his strange encounter with Yamaguchi. Perhaps Abe was right. The old man was a trickster, well-versed in mind games and manipulation. Whatever Yamaguchi did for a living before he retired to the calm of Matsushima, must have caused havoc in the lives of the people he knew or maybe he was just an expert at reading people and manipulating them. It was not Yamaguchi's mind games that disturbed Kato, but something else.

In the span of a few minutes, he had revisited the two darkest moments of his life, two times he was overwhelmed by giant waves of despair. Speaking with Yamaguchi made him think of that room in his mind locked and bolted by chains and ropes. The room kept memories of that fateful day of the house fire in Kyoto, the day his father died. It was the day he pulled the young boy from the flames. It was the day he could not reach the boy's parents. The second was the nightmare of Iraq, his capture and eventual escape, and what he did to make that happen.

It was the day he met the most unlikely of men who would become his friend, the American marine Joshua Tree. Aside from Kenji, Joshua Tree was Kato's closest friend, the only one who could really understand him, for they both survived those few days of hell in Iraq. But Yamaguchi had made him remember the two waves of rage that had swept over him in days he wished he could forget. The first wave was one of despair, the second one was born from desperation. Meeting Yamaguchi called to his mind two very unpleasant memories, days from his past he wished he could erase and experiences he usually tucked away from sight. Yamaguchi had managed in just a few minutes to unravel his mind and unsettle him completely. The frail old man on his walking stick with his clever word games had moved Kato from a safe world of secret motives to a dark world of hidden evils.

As the three men left the bridge and walked on the esplanade that took them back to town, a small cruise boat was leaving the port. It chugged and heaved across the waves as if it were on a tired and weary journey. The boat had seen better days. Orange and yellow stains of rust were smeared across the hull as it limped from the port out into the bay, surrounded by a flock of eager seabirds. Other vessels sat in the small harbor, some fishing boats, and dinghies, side by side. A few men were working on their boats sorting nets and talking. The water was still. In the distance, seaweed was being cultivated, caught by tall wooden poles as the currents drifted past.

The three men reached a street with neatly packed tourist restaurants, emblems of Japan's post-war past, all remarkably staying in business, despite crumbling facades and fading signboards. Abe said he knew one of the owners of one restaurant quite well and often went there for lunch. He led them to this restaurant.

The jaded signboard outside simply said *'Soba.'* The little plastic models of food in the window display may have once resembled real food, but the models were now smothered in dust. Nothing seemed appealing. The restaurant looked like it was closed for the day. The menu was limited. One could choose various types of hot or cold buckwheat noodles, or the specialty of the region, marinated beef tongue. The plastic food models offered noodle bowls of varying degrees of greyness, dust, and age. Even the small round pieces of onion for the buckwheat noodles had lost their color. There were placid strips of plastic beef tongue hanging preciously on a plate of yellow-tinged rice.

As Kato surveyed the menu through the old glass, he noticed the round wizened face of an old woman behind the wooden screen door. She had a blue apron pulled around her waist and a red bandana wrapped tightly around her head, with tuffs of purple hair sticking out. Her face was tired but welcoming, weary but hospitable. She saw the men standing there, examining the menu. Her eyes lit up after a moment or two and she flung the door open with a loud thud and jumped out.

'Abe Sensei!' she announced loudly, frightening all the men. She bowed deeply and then leaned back into the restaurant, calling to someone lurking in the darkened kitchen.

'It's Abe Sensei!' she yelled.

A male voice called back. 'Tell him to come in out of the cold woman!'

The woman giggled and bowed again. 'I'm sorry Sensei, please come in!' she blurted out apologetically.

Abe bowed deeply in return.

'Don't just stand there!' she said to him as she grabbed Abe and dragged him inside. She then bowed to Kato and Ka-Chan.

'Please,' she said to them politely. 'Come in, it is too cold to be outside.'

'Are you going to drag us in too?' asked Ka-chan nervously.

'I am always pulling the Sensei into the restaurant. He just stands in the doorway. Even when he was a little Abe, he needed a good push. Now, he is a priest, but he still needs a good shove from time to time.' She giggled to herself.

The two men accepted her invitation, ducked beneath the blue curtain which stretched across the entrance, and stepped inside the restaurant. She closed the screen door. The restaurant was empty except for a young woman and man huddled in the corner by a kerosene heater. From their appearance, Kato assumed they were from China. The young woman looked up at the men when they entered, but the boy was too busy slurping the soup. Kato paid no attention to them, but Abe and Ka-chan bowed politely. The woman reciprocated. Abe brought his friend and Kato to a large table next to the wall and they all sat down there. Kato was too weak to take off his coat and he still felt the chill of the air outside.

The restaurant's interior reminded him of his childhood. There were faded paintings and photographs of yesteryear and the smell of better days. He liked the atmosphere, and the smell of kerosene reminded him of home. It was obviously a well-liked and often frequented place. The lady with the purple hair returned with some tea and placed a cup in front of all three men. The men nodded in gratitude. The menu was simple, and the choices were sparse.

Abe looked at Kato sympathetically. He seemed worried. 'I think your face is a little pale,' he said. 'Maybe something warm to cheer you up, what do you think?'

Kato knew that he needed to eat something as he was feeling weak. He did not have the energy to go back to the station and knew he would probably miss the next train. The waitress gave them three hot napkins to wipe their hands. Kato buried his face into the hot towel and let the heat soak in. He then wiped his face and hands and tossed it nonchalantly onto the table.

He glanced momentarily at the menu. 'I'll have the barbequed beef tongue.' The lady took the other orders and disappeared behind the curtain which led to the kitchen.

'I should be at the station by now,' said Kato abruptly. 'I have to meet my family at Sendai.'

'First, have something to eat,' insisted Abe. 'I think you have probably missed the next train.' He looked at Kato. His face showed one of sincere disappointment.

'I was actually going to Sendai this afternoon to pick up some incense for the temple,' continued Abe. 'I have a suggestion. Let us have lunch, get a kokeshi for your daughter at the workshop, and then I can drive you to the city. How does that sound?'

Kato deeply appreciated his thoughtfulness. 'I don't wish to impose on you, I couldn't possibly accept,' he protested.

'Don't be silly,' replied Abe. 'It is no imposition at all. I can drop you in front of Sendai station. We can leave within the hour. It will be faster than the train.'

Kato bowed in appreciation. Abe got up and went over to the lady behind the curtain and told her that they were pressed for time. She said she understood and disappeared.

'They are always accommodating here,' said Abe. He sat back down. 'They will bring out the meal quickly. The food is always good. I come here all the time, but I only eat the vegetables, as I am a priest.' He smiled.

Kato could hear a phone ringing. Ka-chan reached into his pocket, gave a quick apology to Kato and Abe, and left the restaurant. 'He is always busy,' said Abe apologetically.

'Where is his temple?' asked Kato.

'His temple is in Kyoto, in the Myoshinji complex in the northwest middle of the city. It is a real temple.'

'What do you mean?'

'Ka-chan has a real congregation, and lots to do, especially funerals, memorials, and so on. My temple, Zuiganji, is mainly for tourists. We do all the ceremonial events and memorials and so on, but most people come here because of the days of old Japan, in the footsteps of Matsuo Basho.'

'The poet?'

'Yes, his book *Narrow Road to the Deep North* brings lots of people, as does the former feudal Lord of this area, Date Masamune who lived around the 1600s. Matsushima is also close to Sendai and so we are always busy.'

'I came here because of Basho,' said Kato. 'When I was young, I came here because of Basho, and because my wife wanted a honeymoon.'

'You came here?' asked the priest incredulously. He laughed out loud. 'What a good choice you made!'

'I think I even remember this place,' said Kato, looking around. 'I don't think we stopped here though.'

Abe turned to the owner who was preparing the meals on the counter.

'Hey Okuda-san, when did you guys open?'

'This place?'

'Yes, the restaurant?'

'I don't know exactly, maybe June 1956, I think it was.'

His wife appeared from behind the curtain and brought out the lunch tray, with a half-dozen slices of beef tongue on a plate, some condiments, rice, soup, and a small ceramic jar of sake.

'Yes, it was June 1956. Ah, it was so long ago!' she reminisced. 'The best days are behind us though. There was a time when the boats were full and people coming and going. It was so popular.' She turned to Kato, 'When did you come here for your honeymoon?'

'1995.'

'Not so long ago then.'

Kato nodded.

Her husband, Okuda-san came out from behind the curtain with his apron on, wiping his hands with a cloth. 'In the 1960s and 1970s, this place was full,' he recalled. 'There was never a spare seat. Everything was new, they were good days. We even had a few pop stars and local celebrities. We had a few sumo wrestlers too. We had little plaques for their signatures on the wall for decades, but the rain came in a few years ago and they were damaged. We had to take them down.'

The conversation was interrupted by the two young people who had finished their meal and were getting ready to pay and leave. As they walked past Kato's table, Abe spoke up. At this time Kato began to eat. To his surprise, the miso soup was boiling hot with just the right flavor, and the rice tasted differently as if it had been harvested locally. The beef tongue had been well marinated, and the pickles were crunchy and flavorsome. He felt he was himself again after a few mouthfuls and in this comfortable little place, he felt all the twinges of queasiness gone.

'Where are you from?' Abe asked the two Chinese, sipping from his soup of miso.

'Beijing,' said the woman politely.

She was tall and athletic, in her late thirties, with long black hair. She was dressed stylishly, and Kato could see that she had all the right designer clothes for a woman her age. He knew the names of them because they were the kinds of clothes Akiko wore all the time. Most of the profits from Kato's kimono business went to satisfy Akiko's preference for designer labels as well as Ai's education at a prestigious private high school in Kyoto. Kato himself lived quite modestly. He was not really interested in wealth. He was happy just to be alive, especially after escaping from Iraq. Despite owning a very profitable business he eschewed all the trappings of wealth, and nothing really mattered to him except Akiko and Ai.

The boy standing next to the girl was younger, maybe the same age as Kato's daughter or a few years older. He was dressed like a university student, disheveled and messy with stubble on his chin and a certain self-conscious nervous disposition, with round eyes behind glasses that kept falling off his nose. His clothes smelt as he walked by as if he had not washed them for a few days and Kato could smell a distinct odor of sweat.

'What do you think of Matsushima?' asked Abe. 'The islands are beautiful don't you think.'

The girl laughed. 'If you say so,' she replied. 'But in China, we have lots of places like Matsushima and they are much more beautiful.'

'Oh, I see,' said Abe, disappointed. 'But you don't have anyone like Matsuo Basho, do you? He was a famous poet in Japan.'

'Everyone knows him,' scoffed the girl. 'But in China, we have many similar poets. All of them were like Basho, but much better.'

'For example?' asked Abe. His prompt response surprised her. The woman looked at the boy as if expecting him to answer for her. He looked uncomfortable and slightly embarrassed.

'Well,' she said, 'we have the great poet Li Bai from the Song Dynasty and Lu You from the Tang Dynasty, both are much better than Basho,' she said quickly with a smile. 'China is like that,' she said.

'I don't mean to interrupt,' said Kato, putting down his chopsticks still chewing a piece of beef tongue. 'I am not much of a poet, but I know poetry is very subjective. My friend Joshua Tree, a native American, half-Japanese man told me that poetry is like the camelia, some people like the flower while others like the tea, but it is the same camelia.' He looked at Abe.

'I like that analogy,' said the priest.

Kato continued. 'That is poetry. It is very subjective. But there is also history that deals with facts, in Japan anyway. I do not know if that is the same in China or Beijing. Li Bai was in the Tang Dynasty, and Lu You was in the Song Dynasty, but maybe your Chinese history textbooks are better than ours as well.'

Abe, Okuda, and his wife smiled, but not as broadly as did the boy, who burst out laughing and then offered to pay for both their meals, pulling out his wallet and counting out the change. The woman just stared at Kato furiously but said nothing.

At that moment, the entire restaurant shook violently as if someone had pushed it over. The boy fell backwards onto the floor, Abe was lifted off his seat and tossed to the ground, and the woman was thrown forward onto Kato knocking him off his seat. They both fell to the floor in a heap, with her lying face down on him. The plates and bowls stacked in the kitchen were thrown off the shelves. Little pieces of tofu wobbled lifelessly on the table and the stock splattered on the floor. Abe was still holding his chopsticks in his hand, but they snapped when he hit the floor. Kato's tray of warm, seasoned beef tongue flew upwards into the air. In the kitchen, Okuda cried out in pain as water from the boiling pot landed on him. Kato grabbed the arms of the woman firmly and lifted her off him.

'Stay down,' he told her and pushed her under the table. She did exactly what he told her to do.

'Get under the table!' Kato yelled to the boy just climbing to his feet, 'help the priest.'

The boy looked and saw Abe dazed on the floor. The boy crawled quickly over to Abe and helped him take refuge under another table, moments before the glass in the door and windows shattered.

The entire restaurant continued to shake violently as if someone was pressing down on the roof and squeezing the air out of it. Kato staggered into the kitchen. Mrs. Okuda had fallen back under the curtain and was lying on the floor unconscious. She had dropped a tray of glasses that had shattered on the ground. Kato went over to her, crouched down, and checked her pulse.

She was alive but hurt with a nasty gash on the side of her head. Mr. Okuda had indeed been scalded and was holding his arms in pain. Kato looked around and found the freezer to get some ice or cold water. He stumbled over, opened the door, and found some bottles of cold water that were not smashed. He took two and quickly dosed the man's burnt arms with the cold water. He went back for two more bottles when the freezer he had opened, literally was wrenched off the wall due to the earthquake and fell towards him. It seemed to hover in the air in slow motion and he felt completely helpless. Two strong arms grabbed him and pulled him out of harm's way as the freezer smashed.

He turned around and the person who pulled him to safety was the Chinese girl. He thanked her and she bowed to him slightly with a faint smile on her lips. She knelt to help Mrs. Okuda who was now awake, though in a lot of pain. Kato climbed around the smashed freezer to get her husband who thanked him for his help. He went to his wife's side and tried to comfort her, when Abe and the boy also entered the kitchen. By now, the earthquake had largely stopped, though there were occasional tremors, and everyone in that restaurant felt like the world was still shaking for quite some time.

The young Chinese woman looked up at Kato. 'We might have the best poets and islands, but you Japanese have the best earthquakes.'

Kato did not respond but looked at Abe, who was very worried. His normal and smooth polite face was replaced by a sea of wrinkles and a deep frown. 'This is not good,' said the priest.

'It was a big one' agreed Kato. 'It is not normal There could be a tsunami.'

'We have earthquakes all the time,' protested the old man, holding his wife's head in his lap. 'They will let us know anyway; they always do.'

'I don't know,' said Abe. 'It feels different. I am going outside,' he said and left the shop, stepping over the broken sliding door that had been thrown onto the street. He looked up into the sky. It was black. He sighed and closed his eyes.

4

Meanwhile, in Kyoto about half an hour earlier, Joshua Tree's mind had drifted off again. His meditation was not going as expected. He could not concentrate. He reached down for the beautifully molded ceramic tea bowl on the polished wooden floor in front of his knees, his legs tucked beneath him, squashed somewhere under his bottom on the red carpet. His legs felt like an extra cushion, and he was able to sit with his back straight in such a way that he could rest relatively comfortably. The bowl was beautifully made, and the tea was especially bitter, but it was satisfying. He was pleased with this tea bowl. It had its own beauty, and it sat well in his hands better than some others he had held in other temples in recent months. Though it was simple, it had its own character. Joshua wondered how many people had been served tea in this tea bowl over the years and where they were now. Maybe he had passed them in the street, unaware that they too had sat in the same place, drinking from the same bowl, and viewing the same scenery.

He held the bowl in his hands and looked out across the garden which lay in front of the veranda. His eyes fixed upon the large pond a few feet from where he was seated. It was an interesting pond, encircled by anciently placed and weathered boulders, some hidden by a variety of flowers, ferns, and grasses. Joshua could hear the bubbling of a brook which seemed to come from the mountains beyond the temple grounds on the left, past the old tea house on the hill, surrounded by a small forest of bright green bamboo. An exceptionally large and strangely shaped stone pillar lay across the breadth of the pond connecting both sides, covered in moss.

A series of stepping stones disappeared off to the right of the pond, half submerged in grey pebbles, adjacent to the white walls of the temple which continued in the same direction. Joshua could not see the larger pond beyond from his vantage point and its small island, or the exquisite stillness of the garden, but these were to be enjoyed after tea. The veranda was open with no railing, so Joshua could look out across the garden which lay in front of him, sitting on a wide strip of red cloth that was draped across the last row of tatami straw mats alongside the polished wood which extended to the edge of the veranda.

Joshua was trying to free his mind of all distractions so he could focus on the cup he held and the tea he had just drunk. The night before he was restless and could not sleep. The day before, his academic supervisor had taken him to task about his lack of progress in his dissertation. She demanded something concrete from him in the new few days. Joshua tried in vain to make some headway at his desk at the university, but he fell asleep in front of the computer. He was just aimlessly doodling and surfing the net. He soon became bored, gave up, and went into the city of Kyoto to his favorite pub, a so-called 'gaijin-bar.' This was a bar for foreigners and a popular place for casual relationships. In fact, He met up with half a dozen women after he stumbled across the place one night after some heavy drinking a few months before. All the girls he dated liked the fact that he was an American and could speak with a deep, resonating accent. They were in awe of the fact that he was in the U.S. marines and had completed several tours of duty in Iraq. It was his foot in the door, so to speak, despite the language barriers. Most of the girls spoke a little English with an American accent, though none had lived abroad. Joshua had developed a 'system' for picking up girls which had worked perfectly until the night before.

The girl was named Michiko and she had slapped him across the face. He was surprised he remembered her name. He had forgotten all the others. Their names didn't matter to him, and his name didn't matter to them. For the girls, he was just another accessory for them to show off to their friends as they walked down the street, like the latest designer bag or purse or umbrella, or whatever it happened to be. They were holding an American man, and that is all that mattered.

That's what he told himself anyway. But his system had collapsed with Michiko. She saw right through his fake compliments, flirtatious manner, and aggressive charm. Joshua had been moving quickly from his basic introductions to the next stage in his cleverly devised system for catching the next Japanese girl when Michiko almost knocked him down with her right hand. The slap echoed right around the bar, and it was so loud, everyone stopped talking. She was the first person to rebuff his advances and left him stranded and alone. He could still feel the sting of her rebuke. He only got as far as her name. She was thirty-five. Her father taught Tea Ceremony in Kyoto. After the slap, she was gone, out of his life. Maybe it was a dream, he thought, an illusion. Maybe it never happened. Maybe he deserved it. Maybe he was just out of control. Maybe a good slap was exactly what he needed. That is why he returned to the temple to meditate. He needed to think.

He tried to meditate by thinking of his favorite spot in the temple he was in. It was a place that inspired him. He created in his mind a different scenario than the one that transpired the night before. This new and fictitious scenario assumed that he showed Michiko respect. She would not have slapped him. They may have enjoyed a pleasant, platonic conservation that may have ended with the polite exchange of phone numbers. That might have led to another meeting. He might have called her and suggested taking her to this temple to have some tea. After all, her father would have approved since he was a tea master. He would explain to her why this spot in the temple was important to him. She might have thought it to be an odd choice, but for Joshua, it really resonated with him.

There was a room at the end of the temple, overlooking the garden, a mausoleum for some ancient leaders of Japan. It was in a darkened room, with a cold stone floor and no windows. In virtual darkness, wooden images of these leaders sat quietly, finding contentment with the odd flower, or offering placed by visitors. These wooden images were placed facing each other as if expecting conversation. He did not know their names or what they did. But they were remembered and treasured hundreds of years after their deaths. But they are remembered only in silence and in the dark, their presence discerned only by the light of candles. He would use this room to try and explain to Michiko something he found difficult to talk to anyone about. That room reminded him of his experience in Iraq, surrounded by the dead, not knowing who they were, what they had said in life, or why they died.

He knew that he would probably never meet Michiko again, but if he did, he would try to have something he really struggled with, a real conversation. He had not enjoyed one for a very long time. His sojourn at the university was more than a chance for him to improve his Japanese language skills and obtain a postgraduate degree. It was compassionate leave. It was one step before a dishonorable discharge. It was to save his career. Every time he heard a loud noise, smelt smoke or gas, saw certain kinds of lights or heard certain sounds, he was unable to function normally. He had left Iraq physically, but not emotionally. He was still there, in the marketplace, on the day of the explosion. He felt a numbing sense of guilt that he survived, and others did not. He remembered the names of all his men who died that day and those he served under. The wife of his commanding officer asked him the day he met her to offer his condolences: 'Why did you survive, and Ron didn't?' He had no answer. He came to Japan, not for answers, but for peace. The temple helped, as did the meditation and the tea, but it didn't stop the nightmares or the guilt.

Joshua was startled by a little cat roaming the manicured garden, leaping from stepping stone to stepping stone along the path which ran parallel to the temple. It stopped on a rock where it could look at the carp in the pond. The cat was entirely black except for tuffs of white on her paws. Bored with the fish, she yawned and scratched behind her ears. The air was still and there was no sound except for the small creek which bubbled past the veranda into the pond.

Seeing the little cat reminded Joshua of when he first arrived in Japan. Despite being half-Japanese (on his mother's side), he knew virtually nothing about Japanese culture. When he first arrived, he was not able to sit in the traditional manner for more than a few seconds before sharp pains would issue from previously quiet parts of his body to demand movement. The first time he tried, he could not stand for a few minutes and promptly fell back down again much to his embarrassment. His Japanese friends understood. He was not accustomed to sitting in this manner. They politely said nothing and helped him to his feet, but not before they kindly admonished him to persist if he intended to spend a few years in Japan.

He resolved to go where few foreigners dared to tread. He would master the art of sitting. His first attempts in his apartment resulted in failure. He could not sit for more than a few seconds and in those few moments, he felt excruciating pain. How the Japanese could do this he thought was beyond him. He could not imagine sitting this way for business, let alone pleasure. Something he never noticed before became something he saw everywhere. Every time he saw someone sitting in the traditional Japanese manner reminded him of his unfinished task and his failed promise.

He lived in a small apartment near the prestigious Ritsumeikan University that suited his needs. His path to his university took him past a small temple that stood beside the campus hidden by a high wall. He thought it was someone's house and garden because no one ever remarked about it or referred to it. The first day he walked past the temple, he saw a little gate. The door was missing but the hinges remained and through it, Joshua could see the outline of a large bell tower and a neat moss garden behind a gravel car park. The roof of the temple with its black wood and whitewashed walls stood in front of the mountain in the distance with the rooftops of the university becoming part of the landscape. In front of the temple, there was a black taxi. The driver stood outside smoking a cigarette, wearing white gloves.

On that first day he went to the temple, Joshua walked under the gate, up the stone path to the entrance, and removed his shoes. The temple slippers were too small for his feet, but he put them on anyway and ascended the stairs. To the left seemed to be the temple office and he could smell something cooking and the voices of women around the corner. To the right, the polished floor shone leading to several verandas. He started to walk down the corridor when a voice stopped him.

'Aren't you going to pay?' said the voice gruffly.

Joshua looked for the source of the voice. He could see no one. He walked back to the entrance booth and hidden behind the booth, was the bald head of a priest, wearing pale yellow garments. Thick glasses sat on his unusually large nose and his bulging eyes seemed to be shut, and for some reason, he did not look up, but held out his hand expectantly. 'Five hundred yen,' he barked, which Joshua quickly drew from his pocket and in return was given a small pamphlet about the temple. Joshua saw the name of the temple on the front of the pamphlet.

'This is Toji-in Temple,' he said to himself.

The man had disappeared even further behind the booth so that now, only the very top of his bald head was visible. While he was standing there, he felt a soft nudging against his legs and looked down, finding a black cat purring. He lent down to pat the cat softly on the back, but she turned and ran quickly into the temple office. As soon as the cat vanished, a large woman with a very round head appeared, a green apron wrapped around her waist.

'You are lucky to have a cat,' said Joshua.

'We don't have a cat,' the woman replied, excusing herself, and walking down the steps to the entrance.

Joshua, a little surprised, wondering if his Japanese was not as good as he thought it was, walked down the corridor. The dark wooden floor continued until it reached an amazing portrait on the wall ahead, which reflected in the glass cabinets which hung on the left wall. Two faces looked at him, one in full color, the other reflected. To his left, the polished floor gave way to tatami mats which extended to the end of the corridor and a far wall. A few portraits hung on the wall and a red carpet had been laid on the edge. The tatami room had its sliding doors removed so the room was exposed to the elements and the veranda had no railing, so it was possible to view the garden without obstruction. The view was quite unexpected. Joshua had been to gardens in Kyoto before, but most of them were so crowded that the sense of peace attributed to them could only be attained in a metaphorical sense, but here, what a sight!

A large pond sat in the middle of neatly pruned shrubs and trees and beyond the path which encircled the pond was another larger pond. To the left, a small tea house stood resilient next to the swaying beams of a bamboo grove. Joshua remembered how he felt on that first day. This is the Japan he had so sought to find, and which had hitherto been so elusive. Kyoto was becoming overcrowded and the sights and sounds of an older, more dignified, refined, traditional Japan was fast evaporating amidst trinket shops with cheap imports, fake Japanese goods, and chain stores. The beautiful old machiya, the long wooden 'eel' houses were all being torn down for car parks. He had left vacuous American consumerism only to find it reborn in Japan.

From that first day, when he discovered the gate and found this delightful little temple, his life in Japan changed. For the last year, he lived in three places – his university office, his home, and the temple. He would spend as much time as possible in this little temple, off the tourist trail, away from the crowds, with the grumpy old priest, the temple cats, and serenity. At every opportunity, he would come, sip tea, and look at the garden. He visited it so often, that the old priest felt obliged to even say hello from time to time.

Joshua stopped thinking of the past and his experiences and returned to the present day. He looked up at the calendar on the wall. It was March 11, 2011. It was one year to the day Joshua arrived in Japan to study for his postgraduate degree in the discipline of International Relations at Ritsumeikan University. Joshua reflected on a year of memories. Most were good, except for times like last night when the young woman slapped him across the face. He laughed to himself and put down the cup.

'What do you think of the tea?' asked a man to his right in perfect Japanese.

Joshua turned and there was a man seated in the Japanese-style a few feet away from him, in the same position, waiting patiently for his tea and cake. He was in his mid-50s. He was not a thin man, and this was reflected in large cheeks that seemed to hang precariously on his face. His eyes were small but intense, and these eyes were on an unusually small head as if it did not belong to a much larger body. His ears stuck out and they held up a fragile wooden framed pair of glasses. His hands were large, and they were grasping each of his knees. He had little hair and was wearing a brown old-fashioned suit, with a waistcoat and bow tie, a cream shirt, and white socks.

'It is good tea,' replied Joshua 'The cake is nice too.'

'I will look forward to today's tea then,' said the man with a smile.

The man closed his eyes and let his hands rest on his knees. Joshua turned his eyes back to the garden. The pond was still except for the movement of colored carp in the water. In the corner of his eye, he spotted the cat once more. She was running along the path and disappeared behind some trees.

'There is always a cat in this temple,' said Joshua to himself in Japanese, but loud enough for the other man to hear him.

'The pond attracts them,' said the man. 'And the carp. What brings you here?'

'It is quiet, and I like the way the seasons change. I came here a few times this winter, it was freezing but beautiful.'

The man nodded to himself again but said nothing. Joshua let him be. He closed his eyes and soaked in the silence. The image of Michiko appeared but he dismissed her. He thought of his dissertation. He then, for some reason, thought of Masayoshi Kato. He had called Kato a few days before asking if he wanted to go for a drink, but Kato said that he was going to Matsushima on a business trip. The last time they met was at the end of the previous year when he spent the evening with Kato, Akiko, and Ai at their small home in one of the suburbs of west Kyoto. They ate soba, as well as some delicately prepared food made especially for New Year, and then watched an end-of-year concert on TV. Akiko and Ai went to bed around midnight, but Kato and Joshua Tree spent the rest of the morning drinking whiskey on the back veranda.

Joshua liked and admired Akiko. She was quintessentially a Japanese wife, or the wife Joshua imagined a Japanese woman to be. She was impeccably polite, the house was spotless, and she was, it seemed to Joshua, a good mother to Ai. Kato, for his part, must have been a difficult man to live with, especially after coming back from Iraq in 2006 after being dishonorably discharged from the Japanese military for gross subordination.

Akiko wasn't told the truth, nor was she allowed to know. Kato wouldn't have told her, and it would have been difficult for her to come to terms with the unexpected end of his military career. She expected he would rise through the ranks like her father did, bringing prestige and honor to the family name. Instead, he was kicked out in disgrace. Kato would have harbored resentment about it, even though it really was not his fault, and at the end of the day, what he did saved Joshua's life and that of his three colleagues. If Kato were American, he would have been decorated for bravery, but he was Japanese, and they were there ostensibly to aid humanitarian work, not get involved in fighting.

The Japanese took their Constitution seriously on this point and forbade military action, even for the army. Kato had crossed the line. Not only did he leave the base without permission, but he also took up arms against the enemy and killed quite a few of them in what the board of inquiry called 'actions under extreme duress.' Japanese government officials wanted to make an example of him, but the Americans intervened and ensured it was all swept under the carpet. It was better for everyone. Kato would have been angry, and Akiko would have been on the receiving end of his frustration, especially during the first year when Kato was forced to sell kimono.

Kato hated the family business. That was why he left and joined the army. His dislike of kimono was one of the first things he mentioned to Joshua when the two men were being held captive. He felt trapped in his family's chosen profession. He always felt that he was destined for another career. After his dishonorable discharge, he would be surrounded by kimono. He said he had nightmares that he would drown in a sea of kimono and be found one morning dead, surrounded by fabrics. Hidden behind the veil of marriage, any indication of the anger he must have felt or expressed was smothered by Akiko's politeness.

Only Joshua Tree, the three surviving marines under his command, and senior officials in Tokyo and Washington knew what really happened that fateful day in Southern Iraq. Joshua knew that he owed Kato his life and that he would have most certainly been shot in some shallow grave or beheaded if Kato had not rescued them all. There was nothing he would not do for Kato. His men felt the same. Joshua was thinking of contacting Kato when he returned from Matsushima when a noise irritated him. It was strong enough to break his meditation. It felt like part of his mind was being torn away and he had a rush of images pass by his eyes. He quickly opened them to see the cause of the rupture. The cat near the pond was hissing loudly, her ears sticking up straight, her fur all on end. It was as if the ground had suddenly become hot and the cat had nowhere to go. In the distance, dogs began to howl as if they had lost their masters. The bowl he had been handling began to tremble on the tatami. Joshua felt the ground beneath him move suddenly. Joshua felt that the walls of the temple had become fluid and seemed to be no longer wooden.

Then as suddenly as it began, the trembling ceased. Joshua found the tea bowl was resting on its side, so he pushed it back into place on the tatami. In the corner of his eye, the white cat had left the pond and was nowhere to be seen. He looked up at the bamboo forest to see the branches shivering despite the absence of any breeze. He was startled by a noise to his right. He turned to the man seated next to him. He had been knocked over and was getting himself upright.

'That was a strong earthquake,' he said. 'But it was far away.'

'I agree,' said Joshua. 'It's the strongest earthquake I have felt in Japan. I wonder where it was.'

At that moment, the lady who served the tea came rushing in, very apologetically. She was holding a red tray with a tea bowl and a small plate with a soft cake. 'I'm really sorry,' she said to the man. 'That was a big earthquake,' she said, more to herself. 'Did you hear the dogs?' asked the old woman excitedly.

The man nodded. She knelt and put the tea bowl in front of him and the little cake next to it. She bowed and stood up. 'It is amazing how the animals sense such things,' said the man but she was not really listening and quickly shuffled off. He drank his tea and ate the cake. Joshua tried to settle himself back into his meditative position when the man spoke to him again.

'Do you live in Kyoto?' he asked.

Joshua opened his eyes again and turned to him. 'Yes, I live near here.'

'What do you do for a living?'

'I am a graduate student at university.'

'Is that the one next to this temple?' asked the man. Joshua nodded.

'What is your area of specialization?'

'I am studying International Relations, with a focus on US-Japan history.'

'You would be uniquely suited to do that, given your background.' It was a surprising thing for the man to say.

'What background would that be?' asked Joshua.

'I refer to your employment, past or present in the U.S. armed forces. You are currently or have previously served, haven't you?'

'How did you work that out?'

'It is relatively easy young man,' he said. 'Looking at your posture and demeanor, the way you hold yourself. My guess is you have spent a few years in the service and are now doing further studies to keep your options open in the future?'

'Again, you are right,' replied Joshua. 'Two tours of duty in Iraq. I have the rank of Captain in the U.S. Marine Corps and am now taking some time to study in Japan.'

'Your Japanese is excellent. Did you study at university?'

'I grew up in Okinawa. My Mother is Japanese, and I lived there until I was twelve.'

'It is excellent, very impressive. You speak Japanese naturally, and it is good you have come back here, it will only reinforce your ability. Do you still have relatives in Japan?'

'Some of my mother's relatives are in Okinawa though I don't see them regularly. Where are you from?' asked Joshua turning the conversation back to the man.

He looked out to the garden and looked uncomfortable with the question as if no one had asked the question before. He didn't answer it. 'Well, I have two older brothers, but I have not seen them in a long time.' He stopped himself and paused.

'Listen, young man,' he said. 'I'm sorry for all my babbling. I did not introduce myself properly. My name is Honda.'

'There is no need to apologize,' replied Joshua. 'My name is Tree, Joshua Tree.'

'Tree?' asked Honda slightly surprised with a smile on his face. 'There is a national park in the U.S. with that name. Are you named after that?'

'Everyone asks me that question. The surname 'Tree' is an old one and my ancestors were in Pennsylvania in the nineteenth century. I am half Japanese and half native American and even that half is complicated as well. My Japanese name is Oshiro, but I have lived in the U.S. since I was twelve.'

'Well Captain Tree,' said Honda with a smile. He turned around to face Joshua, still on his knees, and bowed deeply to him. 'I am very pleased to meet you,' he said.

Joshua returned the polite bow with his own. 'I am pleased to meet you too, Honda-san. Have you been to this temple before?'

'Let me see. Well, it has been a long time, a long time,' he said. Honda tilted his head to the right and crumpled his face in a contorted squint.

'I'm thinking it must be at least five years. I was struck by the beauty of the temple, but it is the garden which attracts me,' said Honda.

'What do you like about the garden?' asked Joshua.

'That is a good question. There are several ponds here. But as you can see, looking from this point, the second pond is hidden by the trees. To view the second pond, one must get up and walk through the garden. I think in this garden, the place we are sitting – the viewing platform – gives us only a glimpse of the garden's secrets, a taste of the possible. To fully enjoy it, we must not sit here. We must put on our slippers and walk along one of the paths provided to fully understand this place. By walking, we can search our hearts and we can think deeply about the steps we take, not only here, but in life. In this way, this garden is unusual in Kyoto. Most traditional gardens can be seen fully from one vantage point, or at the very least, the best view can be seen from the veranda. They offer places of meditation, and you must sit still. That is one way. This is another. Perhaps, that is the reason this temple is not as popular as some of the others. Some other temples sometimes do the thinking for you, but here, you are left alone with your thoughts.'

'They are some profound observations Honda-san,' replied Joshua. 'Thank you. I think you are also commenting about life itself are you not? The path of meditation is not to sit still, but to walk along the path and in walking we truly see.'

Honda laughed out loud and pointed to Joshua. You are very Japanese!' he exclaimed. He continued to laugh to himself. He looked at Joshua who seemed to be increasingly uncomfortable in his traditional Japanese seated position. Honda moved to a cross-legged position on the floor.

'You know Joshua-san, you do not need to sit with your legs under you if you do not want to.'

'But isn't it the traditional way for Japanese?' asked Joshua.

'It is, in a fashion of course, but it is still just a form. Not all Japanese can do it. For some, it is physically impossible, and for others too difficult, but they are still Japanese. You must remember that not all Japanese eat sushi. Not all Japanese drink green tea or wear kimono. Some Japanese have never been to a temple, and some have never learned one of the martial arts.'

'I just want to fit in.'

'In some ways, you will, of course, Joshua-san, but in others, it is impossible. It is just the way it is. I would not take it to heart. The Japanese are a proud people and you, well, you are somewhat of an enigma. You are half-Japanese, half-American, as they say these days 'half-and-half,' I hate that expression but there we have it. To most, you will always be a gaijin, a foreigner, and you also work for the U.S. military. You need to remember that the memories of the war are still strong in the minds of most Japanese, and you need to tread carefully. America has lots of bases in Japan and Japan is, from one point of view, an occupied state, and there are many in Kyoto who resent that, including many members of your university faculty. When I look at you, a see a man sitting comfortably in three worlds but for most Japanese, you will always be an outsider.'

'I don't understand Honda-san,' said Joshua. 'What do you mean, 'three worlds'?'

'The three worlds are this: the world of Japan, the world outside Japan, and the world in between. The ones who live in between are few, but they are the ones who have the capacity to change the world for the better. Do not see your position as something negative, rather see it as a blessing and do not try to fit in, but just adapt, because that after all is what everyone does anyway. Use your time here to learn, but also filter what is useful without losing your identity.'

Joshua listened to Honda-san intently realizing that he made a lot of sense. He released his legs and sat cross-legged.

'It feels better, doesn't it?' reflected Honda.

Joshua nodded.

'It is just as common as the traditional position. In the old days, it was how many people sat on the floor before they introduced the relatively soft straw tatami mats.'

Honda and Joshua were interrupted by a phone. It was Honda's. He took it out.

'This is Honda', he said. His face suddenly went serious. 'When?' he asked. 'Where was it?' Honda's face went suddenly quite furious as he listened patiently. 'It's going to be higher, much higher!' he said abruptly, 'I don't care who said it, they are incompetent. It has happened before.'

He looked over to Joshua and hung up.

'What is it?' asked Joshua.

Honda looked very anxious. 'That was a friend in the Japanese Bureau of Meteorology. There has been a magnitude 9 earthquake off the coast of Tohoku. The official estimate is that a tsunami of three meters will strike the coast, but they have underestimated the potential height of the wave. I must get up there.'

Honda got to his feet and turned to leave. He then stopped and turned back to Joshua who himself was getting to his feet. 'When was the last time you went to Sendai?' asked Honda.

'I've never been, a friend of mine is in Matsushima at the moment.'

'Matsushima,' mused Honda. 'It is probably the best place to be on the entire eastern coastline. There are lots of islands and they will act to slow down the tsunami. It happened last time as well. Let us hope he stayed in Matsushima and didn't go to Sendai or somewhere else.'

'Are you going up to Sendai now?' asked Joshua.

'Yes, I am,' replied Honda, suddenly reverting to English. 'I will fly to Tokyo from Osaka. If my guess is correct, I will not be able to get to Sendai airport. I have a jet waiting for me there in Osaka. I am only supposed to be here for a few days and then I must go back to the States.'

The way he was starting to speak surprised Joshua. 'Your English is very good Honda-san.'

'Well, it should be. I was born in Connecticut.' He laughed.

'You are an American?' asked Joshua, who was convinced Honda was Japanese.

'Call me David, please. Like you, I live in the world between Japan and the West. My family has been in the U.S. since the 1890s.'

'I assumed you were Japanese.'

Honda laughed again. 'Like you, I try to fit in when I can,' replied Honda. 'I have enjoyed our conversation but if you are not doing anything today, I suggest that we continue it on the plane to Tokyo. We can contact the university on the way. I am sure they will give you some time off in the next few days.'

'What will we be doing?'

'Well,' said Honda, 'If I am not the only one worried about the earthquake in Tohoku, I suspect the U.S. military is already formulating a response. You may well be called up to help with the disaster relief.'

'Surely the tsunami will not be that severe?' asked Joshua.

'In 1896, there was an earthquake at Sanriku of about 8.5, and 38m waves destroyed the coastal villages. The earthquake today is about 9 and the government thinks there will be only waves of 3m.'

'Where is Sanriku?'

'In present-day Iwate Prefecture, just north of Sendai. If history is going to repeat itself, by the end of the day tens of thousands will be dead!'

5

Kato reached the red bridge at Matsushima when the tsunami struck. Under instructions from Abe the priest, he had returned to see if he could find Yamaguchi-san and get him to safety before the tsunami arrived. He knew that the old man, whoever he was, was last seen walking over to the island. Despite his unpleasant encounter with the man, he felt a connection with him. He didn't want him to be swept away by the wave. Whatever he claimed to be, that limp in his leg was real and he needed a cane to walk. He felt sympathy for the man. He could not put his finger on it. It was the kind of affection one has for an old friend or a distant relative. It was as if he knew Yamaguchi, even though he had only just met him, but he knew that their lives were in some way intertwined.

After the earthquake struck the town, Abe convinced everyone in the restaurant to take refuge on the hills behind his temple, Zuiganji. Kato carried the frail Mrs. Okuda in his arms to the gate of the temple where he gave her into the arms of the girl from Beijing whom he learned was called Lijuan. The two had developed a grudging respect for each other. The young Chinese boy had the surname of 'Wu,' but preferred to be called Peter. He was also from Beijing. They said they were cousins. Wu's mother was a businesswoman spending her time in China and Kyoto while he studied at university. Kato wondered if this was the woman his friend Miura was dating. Okuda was still quite weak from the scalding and so when they arrived at the temple, Wu and Lijuan took him to the temple office and administered first aid.

Abe had also called Ka-chan, the other priest, who said that he was on the outskirts of town and that he would try and return to the temple as soon as possible. It was Abe who mentioned the old man Yamaguchi to Kato. Kato volunteered to go and find him, but Abe warned him not to take any risks.

Kato had only made it to the bridge when he realized he was too late. One moment the ocean was still, and then it was not. Kato looked at the water. He watched mesmerized as the waves heaved towards the stone wall of the esplanade as if warning him to move back, but Kato could not move. He could sense something in the ocean as it stirred in turmoil. He had seen a tsunami before, mainly from a distance but not this close. It fascinated him. He needed to retreat, but his feet refused to move. He looked out to the island. There, somewhere was the old man Yamaguchi, and the body of his friend Kenji. He suddenly remembered Akiko and Ai and reached for his phone, hoping that they were already on the way to Sendai station, but when he pulled out his phone and looked at it, the battery had run out. He had forgotten to charge it the night before, so he put it back in his pocket.

Kato heard someone yell in the distance, and he looked back. People had seen and heard the ocean waves and were running away as fast as they could. He could see people fleeing down the street and calling to others to get to higher ground. Kato turned to run back to the temple. He had not gone far when he heard a noise behind him. It was the sound of a boat crashing into the stone wall, its hull cracked open like a hammer cracks a nut. Water quickly entered the boat and dragged it beneath the surface. It was an awful sound. Kato did not look back, but he could smell the ocean behind him. It was being driven along, almost against its own will, throwing itself at the small town of Matsushima, bursting the banks with increasing intensity and violence. Kato had almost reached the entrance to the temple. On the top of the tiled gate roof was the young boy Wu. He was perched comfortably on the tiles, but he stood up when he saw Kato.

'Kato-san!' he called out. 'Get up here!'

Wu pointed to the Temple wall as the way for Kato to climb up. There was a pile of old tiles next to the wall and so Kato scrambled up them frantically, but his feet dislodged a loose tile and it fell away, causing him to fall backward onto the path. Bruised and fearful, he got up quickly and looked at Wu who was motioning to him wildly and pointing at the ocean. Kato did not want to look behind him but took a few steps back and ran up the tiles quickly easily reaching the top. From there it was not difficult to ascend the gate. Wu offered his hand, but Kato did not take it, but he thanked him for offering it. Wu told him that he wanted to make sure Kato made it back to the temple safely along with the other priest. Kato nodded and sat on the tiles of the gate next to Wu with a sense of relief. They had a superb view of the temple to their rear and the town of Matsushima in front. Kato could see everything he needed to see.

The wave forced its way through the streets of the small town, overturning virtually everything in its path. Several small vessels moored in the harbor were lifted and turned on their side, one being thrust up onto the land. Houses and restaurants closest to the sea were inundated with water, the deluge bursting through the windows and doors, collecting the debris of life and experience, and throwing them back onto the relentless wave which carried them exposed through the town to its conclusion. All of life was taken up without distinction: books, clothes, memorabilia, ornaments, and heirlooms, carefully placed pottery and artifacts, picture frames, furniture, and plants. The force of the wave cracked the foundation of buildings and they groaned and creaked. Kato heard structures snapping like matchsticks, weighed down by the heaviness of the ocean which groaned audibly as if it was consuming the houses. Remarkably, the buildings stayed firm, but the mud and the debris and the water spewed through the doors and overcame the windows, spreading through the shops and the restaurants and everything in its path.

Kato looked with sadness at the town of Matsushima. Without a doubt, everything he saw was never to be the same again. This event, this day, and this moment would change this little town for generations. All the houses at the level of the sea were going to be swamped and in, them there might be too many who were too old to escape, those too young to know, and those caught unaware. This didn't dissuade him from looking, for he was yet hopeful to see the old man Yamaguchi, or even the priest running towards the Temple. His eyes darted from house to house, and saw cars being dragged unwillingly up the street and thrown against homes.

'I hope Ka-chan got to safety,' said Wu nervously perched on the tiles next to Kato. Kato looked at him but said nothing. He kept his eyes on the tsunami as it surged toward the temple.

'Where's your friend?' asked Kato.

'She is with the others on the hill near the temple.'

'I think Abe was right,' reflected Kato. 'The wave is not going to be as high as we thought it might be.'

'Even so, Matsushima is protected by the islands but what about the north and the south, they face the open sea, what about them?'

Kato turned and looked at him. Wu was right. The boy was going to speak again, and Kato suspected he was going to say something about Kato's family but chose not to. Ever since Kato told them that they were south of Matsushima along the coast near the city of Sendai, everyone had said the same things, such as 'I am sure they will be fine,' or 'Don't worry Kato, I am sure that they got to the station on time.' Kato knew they were only being polite as they did not know what to say. Abe also had many friends in Sendai and along the coast especially, but he kept quiet.

They were all thinking the same thing. They all knew that the coast of Japan had thousands of concrete buoys linked together as tsunami-breakers, but the waves were probably going to go right over the top of them and into dozens of little towns. Kato hoped that Akiko and Ai had made it to the train station at least or were on their way to Sendai. He hoped that they had found high ground or were safe. He had no way of knowing and he was relying entirely upon hope where in fact he was completely helpless.

'There!' shouted Wu, and Kato's eyes lit up. 'I don't believe it! Look!' he shouted and stood up. On a rooftop at the end of the street ran Ka-chan, completely wet and holding a long bamboo pole.

'What is he doing?' asked Kato, getting to his feet. He looked down at the tsunami. It had lingered for a few moments on the street, unsure of what to do, whether it needed permission to enter the temple precincts or not. Suddenly, Ka-chan lowered the pole onto the ground and used it to leap off the roof, landing effortlessly on the ground. He spun around to see the tsunami make its decision to roar into the temple, as if overcome with a temptation to consume the agile priest.

'Up here!' shouted Wu to Ka-chan, loudly in English. The priest had already seen them. He tossed aside his bamboo pole and ran towards the gate of the temple. Kato knew exactly what he was planning on doing, though he thought it would be impossible. Kato moved down carefully from the top of the gate to the lower edge. It was precarious but he was able to find a foothold and held onto some of the tiles with his left hand. Kato knew that he only had one chance and it was a slim one. Kato could not do anything to help Akiko or Ai, but he could help this man or certainly try. Kato could hear the groan of the waves and the loud thuds of human structures being twisted and buffeted by the worst of unrestrained creation, but Ka-chan was a step ahead and then he leapt off the ground into the air towards Kato, and he managed to grab hold of the edge of the roof.

Kato lent down quickly and grabbed his arms. He felt the tension as the weight of the man began to make its presence felt. Ka-chan slowly began to emerge from below as the waves burst through the temple gates and surged down the stone path toward the temple, invading the forest with impunity. Kato held onto the priest with every ounce of energy he had and slowly and surely, the man was able to pull himself up to his chest. The tiles pressed into his ribs and though his legs dangled helplessly above the torrent, Kato was able to rudely pull him up a little further until the man collapsed on the tiles virtually on top of him.

Both men were exhausted. The priest was out of breath and pulled himself away from Kato and held onto the tiles of the roof. Below them, the tsunami pushed past the row of Buddhist statues. The ocean with its fury had taken all things of ordinary life into the temple grounds as if in some strange offering to the gods. The wave of water bursting through the entrance to the temple carrying with it what seemed to be part of the town itself. There were the chairs from the outside of the souvenir shops, as well as much of their merchandise, pieces of wood and debris, flowerpots, and plants all smothered with mud from the ocean floor.

Kato did not look at the temple or the strange offering, but his eyes were fixed on the ocean. It looked as if it had claimed the land as its own territory. He had always liked the ocean, was drawn to it, and delighted in its company, but on this day, it filled him with a deep horror as if it had for so long deceived him, as if the ocean had pretended to be his friend, only to reveal its true nature when he least expected.

Wu had already gone over to Ka-chan and helped him further up the roof of the gate. For the first time, on the temple gate, Kato got a good look at the priest. He was in his mid-twenties, with dark flowing hair and two neatly trimmed eyebrows, and despite being soaking wet, he exuded a faint odor of incense, as if he bathed in temple perfumes. He was dressed like any ordinary priest would be for an official function except that he was wearing white gloves. Kato had not really noticed them before. The two men looked at each other. His face said all that needed to be said.

'I am so deeply grateful to you,' said the priest.

'There is no need,' said Kato panting and trying to get his breath back.

'I had one chance, and you were there to catch me. I will not forget this act of kindness. I am forever in your debt.'

'That was amazing!' interrupted Wu. 'What you did with the bamboo pole, it was like something out of a movie, I didn't think it was possible!'

Ka-chan turned to Wu and smiled. 'If you like I can teach you sometime. You need good muscles, good luck, and a lot of stupidity!'

Wu laughed and Kato smiled to himself. 'My mother would say I excel in stupidity and good luck, but my arms are too weak.'

'As I said,' repeated the priest. 'If you come to Kyoto one day, I will teach you and you will get those muscles, I can promise you that.' Wu bowed appreciatively.

Ka-chan turned to Kato. 'We have to go back as soon as possible,' he said.

'What do you mean?' asked Kato, surprised. 'The tsunami has just arrived.'

'Yes, I know, but there will be many trapped in their homes.'

'Surely, let's wait until the wave subsides and we should let Abe know what we are doing,' cautioned Kato. Ka-chan didn't seem convinced.

The men sat on the gate and watched the waves continue to surge under them. Ka-chan seemed anxious to move on and do something rather than just sitting on the roof and waiting out the tsunami.

'I am going to see Abe now,' he said and was about to jump off the gate into the water below. Wu held his arm, worried that he might be drowned by the wave.

'It's not deep enough to cause any danger,' said the priest. 'Abe was right. Matsushima was lucky.'

'Ok,' said Wu, releasing his arm. 'I'm sorry.'

'No need to be,' replied the priest. 'You were just being careful and that's good.'

The tsunami continued to surge beneath the gate, engulfing the forest and licking the edge of the temple itself. What the men saw surprised them. The tsunami had come to a halt somewhere at the end of the forest. The entire area was swamped with mud and debris and water but most in its path was still intact. The ferocity had not been there. In the distance, Yamaguchi, Kato, and the priest could see people scurrying around near the edges of the water, which while a few feet high at this stage was not nearly as high as it could or should have been. The ocean had stopped groaning and heaving, and it was replaced by something else, a deafening silence.

'I can hear nothing,' said the priest. 'It is like the whole world is silent.'

Kato looked out at the ocean and murmured assent. He rubbed his chin.

Wu looked out to the ocean as well. 'The ocean is indeed still Ka-chan,' he observed. 'Maybe this tsunami wasn't as bad as we thought it would be.'

'It is bad,' said the priest. 'But you are right, it seems like all is back to normal.'

Kato knew that nothing would be back to normal after today. He could feel it. The more he thought about it, the more he felt that Akiko was gone and so was Ai. He did not know for sure, but he felt their absence. He always had a warm glow in his heart since the day he first met Akiko during that tennis match when they were young. It seemed like an eternity ago. That glow was gone. It had been snuffed out by the tsunami. Nothing would be the same again.

'I am sure your family is safe,' said Wu trying to reassure him. Kato looked at the priest who looked back at him but said nothing. Kato knew that the priest probably shared his view. Yes, the tsunami was over, but nothing would be the same again.

'Well, I'm off to see Abe,' said the priest.

'By the way,' said Wu. 'I have been meaning to ask you, what does Ka-chan stand for?'

The priest looked over to Wu and then looked at Kato intently as if wanting him to know the answer as well. 'My name is Kawabata,' said the priest, and with that, he jumped off the gate into the water below.

6

Kawabata!

It was impossible.

Kato was astonished. The man he just saved is a man from Kyoto with the same name as the man who wanted him dead. It was no coincidence. He must be the grandson of Kawabata Koichiro. Is he the one who took over the family syndicate after his grandfather retired? Kawabata was indeed on the island. He was there with Abe. They were smoking cigarettes, but how long was Kawabata there? Did he meet Abe at the island or walk with him from the temple?

Ka-chan seemed intent on letting him know who he was but nothing more. Kato had spoken with him for a short time but during all that time, the man betrayed not even the slightest hint of being an assassin. He was simply a kind priest. He had given him his white cloth when he was ill and let him lean on his shoulder. Were these the acts of a killer? Kato himself had walked with him and talked with him. Strange fate indeed thought Kato that destiny would decree that the outstretched hand of friendship would be the invitation to end his own life. Kato had immediately regretted saving this man, of all men, from the clutches of the tsunami. Why didn't he let him drown to save him from the trouble he was now in? Better to save an enemy than let a stranger die alone, he thought. He was alive, but he had saved the man who had come to this small town to kill him.

Kato and Wu decided to make their way to the temple along the wall as best as possible and then up along the small ridge above the forest. They climbed down from the gate to the wall and crawled as best they could along the wall until they reached the ridge whereupon they both found themselves once again on solid ground. Both men walked along the ridge above the temple forest. Below them they could see the backs of the stone statues facing the mud-drenched forest, standing resolute as if they were holding back the deluge. Neither man said anything until they reached the end of the forest path and were able to find their way to the entrance of the temple. Mud, water, and debris had reached the steps of the temple itself but had been unable to ascend the stairs.

Kato saw Abe at once and acknowledged him. The priest was trying to comfort two small children who were in tears. 'What a relief,' he said, wiping his brow.

'What a relief! I am so glad to see you safe and well!'

He grabbed Kato by the shoulders and shook him happily, smiling broadly. 'You too Peter,' he said as he hugged the boy also. The priest greeted them as if they had returned from the dead. He told Kato that he had feared that he had sent him to his death. Kato told him that he could not find Yamaguchi. The priest nodded and thanked him for trying.

'What is the situation, Abe Sensei?' asked Kato.

The priest looked visibly upset when he was asked this question.

'Listen you two,' he said. 'I have just heard from my friends from Shiogama in the south and Ishinomaki in the north and both tell of unspeakable devastation following high waves. The tsunami is still destroying towns up and down the coast as we speak.'

'What would you like us to do?' asked Wu immediately.

Abe smiled and put his hand on his shoulder. 'Well, first, we need to move people away from the water and get them dry and then we should find a place for them to stay overnight.'

'Where should we put them?' asked Kato. 'What if this tsunami is not the only one.'

'That is a possibility,' replied the priest. They all looked around them. Quite a few people were sitting on the steps of the temple and others in various places in the courtyard. Their faces were all worried and few were speaking. The priest rubbed his mouth and breathed in deeply hissing. He shook his head.

'We have to decide where to put people,' he said. 'We cannot put them in the temple. That is impossible. It is too old and important.'

At that moment, Ka-chan appeared and stood next to Kato. 'Who cares about the temple Abe? It can be repaired, and the artifacts can be restored. People are not going to steal anything; they will be happy to just sleep dry tonight. It does not matter where you put them. I might suggest the temple hall. It is above ground, and it is not used very often.'

Kato thought that Ka-chan didn't sound like a priest. Why would a priest be so dismissive of the treasures of Zuiganji? Kato still could not believe that he wanted to leave the town to avoid meeting Kawabata Koichiro and ended up meeting the man's grandson.

Abe spoke. 'I think Ka-chan is right, we need to put them in the temple hall.'

'Where is it?' asked Wu.

'Over there' pointed Ka-chan, 'through the stone tunnel you see there and to your left. The entrance is at the front.' There was a little stone tunnel, more like a passageway, and beyond that the wooden structure of the temple hall.

At that moment, Lijuan appeared and hugged Wu. Kato said hello and she smiled at him. 'You decide to join us now?' she asked Ka-chan. 'Were you off sleeping somewhere?' she asked him playfully.

Ka-chan smiled but said nothing. He just looked at her, kind of mesmerized. Kato knew the look. It was the way he looked at Akiko the first time he really saw her. Ka-chan and Lijuan stared at each other for what seemed the longest time until Kato broke the silence.

'Let's encourage people to go to the temple hall, we can stare at each other later,' he said. Ka-chan and the woman turned their faces away, both embarrassed.

'What are you talking about?' asked Wu innocently.

'It's nothing,' said Lijuan and looked at Kato furiously.

At last, thought Kato, something real. He rubbed his chin. He might be an assassin, but he was still a man and that gave him a deeper insight into him.

'Not married then?' he asked Ka-chan.

'No,' he replied curtly.

Kato looked at Ka-chan's hands. The only thing which puzzled Kato about his appearance was that both of his hands were covered in white gloves which seemed to extend up and under the beginning of his long-sleeved shirt, which still clung tightly to his body.

'You are wet from head to toe,' said Kato. 'Why don't you change your gloves, as I am sure Abe Sensei would have some spare somewhere.'

'Why don't you mind your own business,' spat back Ka-chan, and walked off.

Kato was surprised at his rudeness. Abe came up to him.

'I think everyone is a little tense today,' he said. 'Even Ka-chan, who usually keeps his cool. I guess we are human.'

'Why are his hands covered?' asked Kato.

'I thought it would be obvious Kato-san,' said Abe.

Kato said nothing. He guessed that Ka-chan had some tattoos on his arms, as he had connections with the yakuza.

'He was in a house fire when he was a boy,' said Abe soberly. 'He suffered terrible burns on both his hands. His parents died in the fire.'

Kato was astonished again. Was Ka-chan the older version of the child he rescued from the burning house all those years ago? Had he forgotten the name of the family he tried to save? If the boy was the priest, then the parents he failed to save were his parents and his father was the son of Koichiro Kawabata. He never thought to remember the name of the child, nor did he ask at the time.

'I should not have mentioned it,' said Kato.

'Don't tell him I told you,' Abe replied. 'Ka-chan is touchy about his family. He doesn't get on well with them. He likes to say that he prefers coffee to tea.'

Kato said he would not mention it again. Abe moved away to talk to some people who needed his attention.

Kato stood stunned, thinking about what he had just been told. That night, the night his father died, he also rescued a small boy who was trapped in the burning house. He could not rescue the boy's parents. Rescuing the boy was a blur, but he remembered putting him down outside, and some kind neighbors took care of him. Kato went immediately to his father's side and was with him in those last, brief moments before he died in his arms. Why was his father at the house in the first place? He always assumed he was just at the wrong place at the wrong time. Kato knew the reason why details such as the name of the boy's father meant little to him that night and the following day. He wanted revenge for his father's death, and it consumed his life until he had it. Kato felt a sharp pain in his head and squeezed the top of his nose. When he breathed in again, he smelt smoke, but it was not his mind. The priests lit a fire to keep people warm. He sighed with relief.

For the rest of the evening, Kato helped Abe and other priests, including Ka-chan, move people under the stone walkway to the other side and to the temple hall. It was to be their home for the night, indeed, for several nights. It was a large structure, with a long open veranda and a courtyard and it was situated at the bottom of a small hill, at the top of which seemed to be a small temple or shrine of some kind. Kato had never been there before, as his visits to the temple had only ever included the main temple and the treasures within. The priests were, it seemed, ill-prepared for such an event, but made up for it with gentle and polite kindness to all who walked through their doors. Tea was prepared as was some soup and what meager food could be found was distributed to those present, first to those with the greatest need. Kato kept an ever-watchful eye on Ka-chan, never allowing him to move out of sight, while Ka-chan, for his part, found his eyes continually gazing in the direction of the beautiful Chinese woman who served tea and helped various people in need.

Throughout the night, the fire burned slowly, and the smoke rose into the sky. Kato felt tired and so began to rest against the wall of the temple hall. In his drowsiness, he lost sight of his nemesis, and when he realized Ka-chan was gone, he tried in vain to find him. He was able to locate Wu, who was on the veranda. He then saw Lijuan at the edge of the fire, standing close to the flames, warming herself. She was alone. Kato saw her a few feet away and watched her. She seemed sad, forlorn, as if lost, her eyes flickering in the hues of the flames which spat into the night sky. Kato sensed a sound behind him and turned around quickly to find Ka-chan standing there.

'Please,' he said, 'take this tea Kato, to warm yourself.'

Kato looked down and saw the man holding two cups of tea, the steam rising in the cold. Kato bowed in appreciation and took it, holding it in two hands. Ka-chan nodded and then took the other cup to the woman and then crouched in front of the fire. Kato encircled the small fire to the other side and saw them both staring into the embers. The woman and Ka-chan, were both mesmerized by the flames, both entranced by the colors of its beauty and yet just far enough away to avoid getting burnt. Both seemed as if they wanted to leap into the fire as one wants to leap into a hot bath on a cold night.

Kato stared at the man he had just met a few hours before. He found that there was something familiar about him. It was the eyes. He had seen those eyes before. The more he looked, the more he was certain that Ka-chan was indeed at one stage, the terrified child he pulled from the flames.

If so, Kato and this priest had at least one thing in common. They had both experienced tragedies in a house fire. Ka-chan lost his parents while Kato lost his father. He did not expect to be thinking about that night on the night following the tsunami. His mind usually focused on what happened after his father died, as the death was too painful to relive.

Maybe tonight, thought Kato, was a time to remember. It was a night he felt numb anyway. He had just lost his wife and daughter and the shock of it all was still lingering in the air. He could open that locked door in his heart. Maybe the embers were only smoldering, doused by the tragedy of the tsunami and all the lives touched by it. Maybe the ocean depths would drown any sparks that might ignite a fire in his mind. Maybe he could unchain that room in his heart. Kato looked at the sky. It was a night like this, he remembered, the night of the fire. The sky was dark, and it was cold.

He had been told by his mother that evening that his father needed to follow up with a customer at a certain address in Kyoto. That was unusual. He was always punctual and kept to a rigid timetable, making sure he didn't work late or start too early. The accepted practice was that the clients would come to the shop and all business would be conducted there. Looking back, that fact was itself, unusual.

His mother had not heard from her husband Shinya, often known to his friends as Shin-chan. She asked Kato to go and find out what was going on. She had prepared dinner and wanted to know what time he would be returning. Kato was staying with his parents at the time. He was preparing to get married to Akiko a few months later. He drove to the street where his father was supposed to be. He could already see the smoke. Kato remembered running down a narrow alleyway. People had come out of their homes and were tending to a man lying on the ground outside. Everyone was concerned because their houses were adjacent to the burning structure, and they were throwing water from buckets onto the blaze. In the distance, Kato could hear the sirens of the fire trucks approaching.

It was then that the elderly couple who lived next door pleaded with the onlookers to see if anyone had seen the young boy who lived there. At this news, Kato doused himself in water and kicked down the front door. He checked in the two front rooms. He found no one and so ran up the stairs into the upper part of the house. On the landing, he found two bodies, that of a man and a woman. The woman was still alive, barely, but the man was probably dead. He had been stabbed in the back several times, and he was lying in a pool of blood. Kato could not see a knife anywhere. He shook the woman, but she was unconscious. He was about to lift the woman onto his shoulders when he heard the sobbing of a child. It was from a small boy, about eight years old. He was in the corner of the landing, closest to safety but he was held down by a beam of wood. Kato was able to dislodge him and bring him down the stairs to safety and into the arms of neighbors. He had been burnt, held his hands together, and was crying. He turned to go back and rescue the woman, but there was a loud crash and the upper level collapsed onto the ground floor. It would have killed them both. Kato barely escaped with his life.

Kato had not thought about the boy he rescued for years. The police never followed up with him or asked him what he saw or what he did that night. He thought it odd at the time. Maybe nobody knew he rescued the boy. He never went forward. He did not look up the incident in the newspapers. Kato was focused on the funeral of his father and did not remember the name of anyone called Kawabata Koichiro. As far as he knew, this man didn't know his father. Why would he? He probably did not remember the child because he was more interested in responding to his father's death. As soon as he handed the child over, he realized that he knew the man lying on the ground. It was his father. He had also been stabbed. Kato was horrified. He was beside himself with grief. For years, he assumed the men who were responsible for his father's death were in the yakuza.

Kato held his father in his arms as his life ebbed away. The last words he spoke to him enabled Kato to find out who was responsible for his murder and take his revenge, which he did in the early hours of the next morning. His father gave him the name of the man who had stabbed him. It was someone called 'Saito,' and his father said that everyone in that house had blood on their hands. Kato went quickly to his father's office, took his sword, and then made his way to Takao and the address his father had given him. He knocked on the door politely asking for Saito. When a man answering that name came to the door, Kato pulled out his sword, and ran him through, entering the house and that's when the killing began. Kato killed everyone in that house at the address his father gave him and got away with it. No one ever suspected him or even guessed he was the killer. But he avenged the death of his father and felt his spirit could be at rest, knowing his son fulfilled his dying wish. That was sixteen years ago. The boy had grown into a man, now probably around his mid-20s, the same age Ka-chan appeared to be.

Kato looked at Ka-chan sitting in front of the fire near the temple hall in Matsushima and thought how strange life was to bring the past and present together on a day like this one. Maybe the old man Yamaguchi was right, maybe life is not a series of random events, but everything is intertwined. He followed the sparks flying upwards into the sky. He looked around and saw Wu, the young Chinese boy, sitting by himself on the veranda. He walked over.

'How are you?' he asked, sitting down next to him.

'I'm fine Kato-san, thank you.'

'Have you been able to contact your mother?'

'No, she is not answering, probably too busy.'

'She would certainly know about the tsunami by now.'

'She is too busy with her love life I think to actually care about me.'

'What's he like, the new guy?'

'I've never met him, probably rich, my mother likes that kind of man.'

Kato decided to change the subject. He felt uncomfortable talking about his friend Miura, especially if that came up in the conversation. The boy Wu was probably about a few years older than Ai, but Lijuan was much older, at least a decade or so.

'What's the story between you and Lijuan?' he asked.

'The story about Lijuan?'

Kato nodded.

'It is not a nice story, but ok, I can tell you I think,' said Wu. 'In Beijing, I had an older friend, he was about six years older than I am, I am twenty now. He was the kind of friend who is always there for you. Life was difficult growing up, especially when my father left us. Anyway, this friend of mine met Lijuan and they started a relationship. For a few years we were always together good friends, but then one day, he was diagnosed with cancer. He died slowly and painfully and

Lijuan was never really the same again. She used to smile and laugh, and nothing ever affected her. Now, she is grumpy and irritable. You saw what she was like at the restaurant, that silly contest about China and Japan. She was never like that.'

'Sometimes things happen in life that changes people,' replied Kato. He looked at the sky.

'Tell me about your wife,' said Wu.

'Akiko?'

'Yes, tell me about her. What is her best point?'

Kato smiled and nodded. He knew the answer to that question.

'Akiko,' he said. 'She was a very forgiving woman, she overlooked all my mistakes, of which they are many.'

Wu noticed that Kato was using the past tense. He didn't say anything about it.

'I cannot imagine you would be a man like that,' he said instead.

'You would be surprised. I have made many mistakes over the years, but Akiko was very forgiving. She was a Christian woman. When I was younger, I didn't think much of Christianity or her devotion to it. I thought she would have given it up, but over the years, I realized that it was her faith in God that kept her married to me. I am not a Christian, most Japanese are not these days, nor have ever been, but she lived her faith and was true to her God and she was true to her family, and that was her best point.'

Kato looked at Wu. 'What about your mother? What is her best point?'

Wu smiled. 'I knew you would ask me this. I think my mother is still sad because my father left her so long ago, and that is why she is so distant from me because I remind her of her husband. I have my father's face, his eyes, his nose, and his personality. But she is a hard worker and good at her job. In fact, she is ruthless, and even strong men are terrified of her.'

Kato laughed. 'She sounds like a good woman to have on your side,' said Kato. 'I think your mother and Akiko would've gotten on really well.'

'I think they would have as well Kato-san,' replied Wu.

Kato got up and patted Wu's shoulder. It was the first time he spoke of his wife as if she had already died. He went off to meet some other people huddled near the fire. From what Kato could gather in short conversations with others, the rest of the population in the town of

Matsushima had been forced to their roof tops or the upper stories of the buildings to escape the wave and destruction. Kato was deeply impressed with the behavior of the priests especially Abe and some others he had not met personally. They all had families in the local area and could well have left the temple in search of them, but they decided to stay and look after all the people who had taken shelter in their temple. Kato tried to rub himself warm.

It was then that he remembered Kenji's money. It was in his coat pocket. He had not counted it, nor did he want to. He had no need of it. It was blood money. He still felt that Kenji should never have given it to him. He left the crowded temple hall and walked around to Zuiganji itself, looking for a collection box.

He eventually found it. It had survived the tsunami unscathed. Worshippers normally placed coins of the lowest denominations in the box when they come to worship. Kato took out the envelope and opened it to see if there was only money there. He did not want anything to lead back to him or Kenji. There was only money. Kato looked around. He was the only one there. He put the envelope in the collection box and bowed deeply. 'You have a long road ahead of yourself,' he said to the temple. 'You will need it more than I will.'

He realized that he had not seen Abe for a while and asked after him. He discovered that he was up the hill at the old mausoleum. The walk was short but took him to the back of the temple hall. The further he walked the fewer sounds he heard, and even the fire was out of view. The path went up a steep incline and he found some steps. There was nothing to light his way, but Kato managed to avoid slipping and kept to the path. He soon found a series of stone steps that led him to the top of the hill and to the outline of a small temple building. There was a sign in front of it and he could faintly read the inscription that it was the mausoleum of the daughter of Date Masamune, the founder of Sendai. However, the priest was nowhere to be found. Kato looked around for him. He walked around to the side and at the back of the building, sitting down, was a figure hunched over. He could smell alcohol. The figure looked up at him.

'Ah! It is you, Kato,' exclaimed Abe.

Kato walked over and sat down next to him. Both men looked out into the void. The priest handed him the bottle and Kato drank deeply, handing it back.

'I was going to cut grass after I dropped you at Sendai,' said Abe.

'When?'

'Just after we met on the bridge. I was going to take you to the station, pick up the incense and come back here and cut some grass before dusk. It was a quiet day; it was going to be a normal day.'

'You did your best,' Kato said reassuringly. 'No one could have prepared for a day like this. It has been a difficult day.'

'How can you prepare for a day like this?' protested the priest angrily. 'In the morning, my most pressing concern was grass, and in the evening, I am weighing life and death. I cannot eat even if I want to.'

He drank from the bottle and wiped his mouth. 'The night is dark Kato, very dark and quiet. Tonight, there is much darkness and too much silence. I fear across Japan, voices are silent.'

'We seemed to have little damage here. Perhaps it was the case in other places.'

The priest drank some more and wiped his mouth. 'No Kato,' he said soberly. 'Quite the opposite.'

'What have you heard?'

The priest refused to say more, but threw his bottle down on the ground, stood up, and brushed himself with his hands. He breathed in deeply. 'We have to go and look for survivors now,' he said. 'I just have never done anything like this before Kato. I don't know where to start.'

'Well,' said Kato, 'you are a good man, and you are surrounded by good people. You need to delegate responsibility. I can give you advice. I am sure it will all be fine.'

'I'm sorry Kato-san, I truly am,' said the priest. 'I have been drinking up here not knowing how to tell you, or even having the confidence to broach the subject. Everything is a wasteland to the north and to the south, there is complete destruction everywhere. I cannot say with any certainty that your wife and child are alive. I am truly sorry.'

He put his hands on Kato's shoulders. Kato looked at him.

'Thank you,' he said. 'I sensed it when I was on the gate with Wu and Ka-chan. They are most certainly dead. I feel it. I have done the calculations. Her friend lived right on the coast. It is highly unlikely they survived. It has not sunk in yet. But now, you and I must get as many survivors to safety as possible. There will be a time for tears, but not tonight.'

7

Masayoshi Kato knew in his head that his wife and daughter were most likely dead on March 11, 2011, at around four in the afternoon, while he was on the roof of the gate in front of the long path that led to Zuiganji temple at Matsushima. His heart didn't want to accept what that meant. It would mean he would be alone, truly alone. He didn't want to go home, certainly not to his actual home, where he lived with Akiko and Ai. They would not be there, and his heart would be full of despair. He could not walk into an empty house. How wonderful it would be if she were there to meet him. It was not to be. She died, along with everyone else that day. Kato survived, as did Wu, Lijuan, Abe, and Ka-chan, but they were never the same again.

Early on March 12, a local man, Onishi had returned to the history museum on the edge of town. It was much closer to the ocean than the temple. He did not work there, but he lived nearby. He saw that the tsunami had caused considerable damage to the lower floor of the property. He had already taken everyone to safety before the tsunami struck, but he felt a deep sense of unease and wanted to search there again. He was wise enough not to go by himself in case the building collapsed, and so he went to the temple for help. His appeals had been politely ignored in favor of more pressing concerns. A few people had been rescued from other places and Onishi was left standing alone. He saw that Abe was busy and did not want to disturb him because he felt that others needed the priest more than he did. But dawn was approaching, and he was unable to get rid of the sense of unease. Abe had disappeared and Onishi could not find him and so he was just about to give up and search the museum by himself when he saw the priest and another man walking down from the mausoleum. When he saw Abe, Onishi ran up to him.

'Abe Sensei,' he pleaded with the priest. 'I am trying to get men to go back to the museum. I think there might still be people trapped there.'

Abe looked at him disapprovingly. He felt that Onishi was just trying to make a name for himself. He had seen him wandering around the temple rather aimlessly and thought that while he had helped to bring people from the museum at the beginning of the crisis, he was being a burden more than anything else. He decided to compliment him in the hope that he would go away.

'Onishi-san, you took everyone out this afternoon and did a splendid job, everyone was impressed, but you said it yourself: you don't think there is anyone left there. Tomorrow the army will probably be here, and they can attend to your investigation.'

Onishi looked dejected and he put his hands on his hips and looked downwards. That was the end of it, and Abe turned back to talk to Kato.

'Don't be so hasty Abe Sensei,' interrupted Ka-chan, who emerged out of the darkness with Lijuan by his side. 'Lijuan, she felt something was wrong just before the tsunami struck, a sense of foreboding, I felt it too when I was with you when we were smoking cigarettes on the island. You did too, do you remember you said to me earlier in the day, that 'today didn't feel right.' Do you remember saying that?'

Abe nodded.

'I don't think you are wrong,' continued Ka-chan. 'On any other day maybe we could dismiss it, but today is not an ordinary day, it is an exceptionally awful day and for some reason, we all seem to have our minds tuned on a higher level of awareness.'

Ka-chan looked at the pathetic figure of Onishi. He had been wearing a suit, but it was caked with dry mud and debris. He realized that no one asked the man if he was ok or that he lost anyone in the tsunami. 'I know you probably won't approve,' said Ka-chan. 'But let me take Lijuan, Wu, and Kato-san with me to the museum with Onishi here. If we find anyone, then that is good, but if not, then we have not wasted valuable resources. That is if the others agree?'

Lijuan said that she would go, and she also said Wu would certainly want to help. Abe looked at Kato who nodded to him. Kato looked over to Ka-chan, who looked very angelic next to his new Chinese friend. He reminded himself that he should be careful and not be left alone in the same room with Ka-Chan in case the man tried to kill him. When the small group finally set out to the museum, it was early on the morning of March 12. The group gathered in front of Abe. Everyone looked at him.

'Listen everyone,' he said. 'For some reason our town has been spared the worst of the wrath of the tsunami. Zuiganji has been damaged, and we have lost some trees, and some of the temple is damaged, but thankfully that is about it. We know that most of the town has been damaged by the tsunami and many of the houses are now unsafe. There are dangers associated with electrical cables and wires. The streets are dark and there is mud everywhere. If you do find a survivor and they can be taken out safely from a house, then do so, but if not, wait for assistance. Your objective is to get to the museum, but do not hurry. On the way, check the places you pass for signs of life, don't talk unless you need to, walk slowly, and use your torches. I suspect, given the state of the town that it will take you about twenty minutes to find the museum. Use common sense and take no unnecessary risks. The other rescue parties have found that it is easy to get injured by broken glass, and splinters of wood. The mud is everywhere, so be careful please be careful. Ka-chan is in charge. Follow his advice and take no risks. Good luck!'

With that, Abe bowed deeply in front of everyone, turned around and went back to Zuiganji. Onishi, Wu, Lijuan, Kato, and Ka-chan took the path along the ridge which Kato had taken earlier that afternoon, along the side of the temple park, overlooking the Buddhist statues, holding their torches to light their path. The group descended from the ridge down towards the gate and entered the mud, which went up to their knees. To Kato's surprise, most of the structures had survived, but the mud had flushed through every possible entrance. Reaching the main street, the group looked in either direction and saw destruction as far as the eye could see, meters of mud and debris, cars overturned and pressed up against each other and there was a foul stench in the air.

As they walked along the main street, Kato remembered he was near the restaurant he had been to earlier in the day, and he stopped, shining his torch down the alleyway.

'What are you looking for?' called out Ka-chan, who was wading through the mud and the debris ahead of him. The entire town was caked in mud and sludge and the refuse of the ocean floor. Gone were the footpaths and the roads, replaced by a highway of mud oozing through doors, around corners and in houses. Cars were overturned and thrown around the town as if they were made of paper, boats in the harbor had been tossed aside, one resting right up against the wharf.

Kato's foot touched something in the mud, so he stooped down to see what it was. The head of a wooden kokeshi doll was sticking out of the mud, dirtied and grey. Kato lifted it up and looked at it. The face of the doll continued to smile even though its gaze was obscured. Kato rubbed the doll against his coat until all the mud was removed. He then reached into his jacket and pulled out a handkerchief and rubbed the doll all over until it looked as reasonable as it could be under the circumstances. He then looked at the doll. Her face continued to stare into space, seemingly unchanged by the experience of the tsunami.

Kato realized that he had found a doll for his daughter, but it was too late, she would never see it. When he looked up, he saw that he was in front of the restaurant he had stopped at earlier. He shone his torch on the sign. It was still there, but the windows were all blown out, the door was unhinged and gone and most of the tables and chairs in the restaurant had been smashed up. He waded through the mud and came to the kitchen peering inside. There was nothing much left there either. The stairs to the second level of the house had gone and the floor in the room above had crashed into the kitchen, its foundation snapped in two. Various household items were now lying everywhere.

A flashlight shone on his face. He heard the voice of Ka-chan. 'What is it?' he asked. Kato told him that this was the place where they had lunch earlier in the day.

'I don't think this house will stay up much longer,' cautioned Ka-chan. 'It will be torn down I would think. Thankfully, no one was here when the tsunami struck.'

He noticed Kato holding something. He asked what it was, and Kato showed it to him. 'You wanted to get a kokeshi doll for your daughter, I remember,' he said quietly. 'I am sure that you can take this one if you wish, I don't think anyone would deny you that.'

Kato held the doll in his hands and then left the doll on one of the remaining tables. He shone his torch at the doll and her face smiled back at him. He found he could not smile in return. Kato turned to leave when he heard Ka-chan praying.

'Be careful how you go little doll,' he said. 'Watch over this place and over us.' He bowed to the doll and joined Kato in the doorway.

'The water is still now,' said Kato.

'The sea is never still. It is always raging,' countered Ka-chan.

'Like the human heart. Deceptively quiet,' replied Kato.

Ka-chan ignored him. They left the restaurant together and walked slowly through the mud until they reached the others, who were waiting for them.

Kato said nothing until they reached the museum. As they were walking along, Kato's mind instead turned away from thoughts of his daughter to Kenji, whose body was, presumably still on the island, unless the tsunami had picked it up and tossed it into the sea. If that happened, the body would no longer be surrounded by a pool of blood and if it were found at all, then it might be mistaken for another drowned victim. It was unlikely that the police would pay much attention to it given the enormity of the disaster. The original plan was that if anyone asked, he would say he was going to meet Kenji at Matsushima. He waited for his old friend, but Kenji failed to show.

Kato's thoughts turned to the question of Ka-chan. Perhaps he had made a mistake. Kawabata was a common name. Who knows, this priest might simply just have the same name as Kawabata Koichiro. He was certainly not the only boy to be in a house fire. He had known a few in his time. If Kato was the one who rescued him, why not say anything to him about it? Why keep it secret? Maybe this Ka-chan was innocent. He had not seen anything so far to confirm his fears. Quite the contrary. Ka-chan seemed to have great empathy and compassion for people, hardly the traits one would expect to find in an assassin. He was being very tender to the Chinese girl, and it was obvious that he liked her. Ka-chan seemed to be a genuine priest and he found it hard to believe that a man who devoted himself to the life of Buddha would also be a killer.

On the other hand, thought Kato, he was a killer, and he was able to hide behind the façade of politeness. Maybe it was simply that Ka-chan shared with Kato the ability to entirely cloak his personal feelings. Kato kept his true feelings to himself and even from his family as best he could. This was his way. Perhaps Ka-chan was the same. He could not make up his mind.

His anxiety over Kenji and Ka-chan was superficial next to the bigger problem that he needed to confront. These concerns stood on a thick sponge soaked in regret and this centered on one single question: how did he come to be here? One week ago, he was happily living in Kyoto. He was not planning on visiting Matsushima. He had no plan to visit the north for quite some time. His life went on its mundane routine. One week flowed seamlessly into another, as if threaded neatly through a needle. Every week weaved the same tapestry. Ai went to university. She was involved in some new club at school and was talking about it all the time. It was something traditional. He overheard her talking with her friends on the phone about it. She liked mathematics and science and was an average, but hardworking student. Kato paid little attention to the details, encouraged her when he could, but the nurturing and the daily support, that was Akiko's domain. Akiko caught up with her friends almost every day, visiting cafes and museums and concerts. She would always invite Kato and he would always come up with the same excuse, that he was too busy.

Kato, for his part, was absorbed in his work. He was the owner of a very respected establishment that made top-end silk kimonos in the city of Kyoto. It was in the centre of Kyoto, on the corner of one of the busiest streets. He inherited the company from his older brother, after he died of a heart attack. His brother inherited it from his father.

Kato left most of the day-to-day work with a trustworthy manager. His manager's name was Tamura Ichiro. He was a very able and polite man who had run the shop from about the same time his older brother inherited it from their father. It was this connection with his late brother which compelled Kato to keep Tamura on, as he knew everything there was to know about kimono. Tamura lived alone. He had nonetheless peculiar and somewhat perverse habits which made Kato uncomfortable. He nibbled his fingers when was anxious. He licked his lips when he had not eaten anything. He would spend a long time in the mirror looking at himself and pulling strange faces, grooming his hair. It was like he had borrowed someone else's face and was trying it on for size.

Tamura also spent too long looking at female customers. Tamura was employed by Kato's father a few years before his own death. He was married then but had since divorced. He never spoke of his young son. Kato never asked. It was not his place. His wife took the child with her. Tamura, for his part, threw all his energy into making the business successful, building good relationships with clients, and continuing good accounting. This delicate balancing act came unstuck only once, when the shop lost one its finest employees, a talented girl by the name of Maya. Her disappearance shook Tamura greatly as he obviously liked her. One day she was there, the next day she was gone. Kato was so anxious about her that he contacted a detective from Kyoto's special crime bureau, a man by the name of Goro Fujita. Fujita's investigations turned up a letter from Maya which she had sent to her mother. The letter stated that she had fallen in love with a man and had moved to Hokkaido.

Tamura was assisted by Ms. Sasaki, a very capable former artisan and designer in her late thirties, and a few other people who acted on behalf of the company. His work was his world. Kato had few friends. Kato spent most of his day inspecting the shop, welcoming clients, talking with Tamura and his assistants, and having a regular lunch time at his favourite café from one in the afternoon until two. He would always order beef curry and white rice with hot black coffee and a side of salad. He would always have a reserved seat at the café and was never late and made sure that Tamura kept that hour clear of appointments. After work, he would always visit a local public bath owned by a delightful couple he had known for the last few years, the Itoh family. Mr Itoh was a good family friend and he and his wife were both entertaining and harmless. He loved the evening banter. The Itoh family had only recently come to Kyoto where they bought and restored a decrepit public bath in Kyoto, turning it from an old building to a popular bathing spot for locals.

His life was forever changed the day his lunch schedule was interrupted by a sudden appointment. The potential client must have known Kato's movements, since he insisted on an appointment at one in the afternoon. Mr. Tamura protested, but the client persisted. Tamura would have politely ended the conversation had it not been for the tone of voice. Tamura told Kato the man's voice seemed desperate and unnatural. Kato rang the café and cancelled his lunch appointment and caught a taxi to the south side of Kyoto station, to an old alley way and a disused, derelict restaurant.

When Kato arrived, the restaurant was boarded up and closed and he thought at first that someone had wasted his time. But curiosity got the better of him and he found that there was a thin alley at the back of the restaurant, and he squeezed through until he found a back door that was slightly ajar and entered. The restaurant was old, and smelt of dust and mold, and was dark. A light was visible in a room next to the kitchen and Kato went straight in.

In the corner huddled up against the wall, with a grey blanket over him, was the figure of a man, or at least, he looked like a man. He was hunched over and muttering to himself incoherently. He did not appear to notice Kato, who had just appeared at the doorway. Kato cleared his throat and the figure turned around suddenly and advanced menacingly, straightening up, letting the blanket fall off him onto the ground. He appeared to be holding a thin walking cane which he held up into the air with his left hand waving it furiously. With the right hand he held onto the wall and let out a deep unnatural groan. In the light, Kato could see an emaciated face, gaunt and hollow, as if his life had been sucked out of him. His body was clothed in a nice suit and tie, but it longer fitted him, but hung loosely on what was left of his skeletal frame. Kato looked into his eyes with horror, for he knew him. He was his oldest school friend Kenji Nomura.

Kenji told him a story about a man who through a series of poor decisions, lost his family, friends and job, and ended up with working for someone who seemed to have all the wrong connections with all the worst people in Kyoto. This man had entrusted him with a piece of information that people would kill for. He did not know why he was told. He was soon kidnapped by someone who tortured him for information about this important document. He only knew that there was such a document and that it was located on the grounds of a temple in Kyoto. That was all. He didn't know anything else. His interrogators did not believe him. They gave him some tea. He thought it was just tea, but it contained poison. They boasted to him that he had been given the poison known as Polonium 2-10. Somehow, he escaped. That was two days ago. Kenji estimated that he had days left before an excruciating and painful death.

But Kenji didn't know anything beyond what he told those who tortured him. He was telling the truth. Kato could see that his old friend was in terrible pain. He had read about radiation poisoning while he trained in the army. He could tell that Kenji wanted to take his own life but was too afraid to do it. He wanted to die, and he wanted Kato to kill him, but it had to be in a location of his choosing, and it needed to be soon.

Kenji told him that he believed the one who poisoned him was from the yakuza in Kyoto, a group led by a man whom Kato knew, Miura. Kato knew Miura and so he protested, telling Kenji that Miura was a true yakuza but would not resort to methods so horrible. Miura was a man of the sword, who would face his enemies head on, not from behind. How would he get his hands on something as deadly as polonium? Why would he need it? He had an army of thugs who would, with their own crude methods, obtain any information they needed from anyone who dared to cross them. After pressing him further, Kenji conceded that the order might have come from another man, but he needed to make contact again with his former employer in secret, to ask him. But Kenji was convinced that the man behind everything was Miura Hajime.

Kato asked him where he wanted to die, and Kenji suggested that they meet in a small town in the north of Japan, in the city of Sendai, a town called Matsushima. There was a little island there connected to the mainland by a bridge. Kenji had been there when he was young and loved it. There was a lookout on the far end of the island with a perfect view of a tree that sat on top of another island in the distance. The lookout was surrounded by pampas grass. It was a place he associated with happy memories. He wanted to die as soon as was possible but allowed a three-day window for Kato to arrange things so it would not look too out of character.

Kato asked why it was his favourite place in all Japan. Kenji replied that he used to go there when he was a boy and it was where he took his first girlfriend on a day trip from Sendai, where he lived in those days. Kenji did not say so, but Kato was sure that the girl he was talking about was Akiko. Kenji told him that years later, he returned to Matsushima and accepted for the first time that someone had asked this girl to marry him and that he lost her forever. Kato could still see, beneath the wrinkled brow and pain, that his old friend had never forgiven him for marrying Akiko. It was Kenji's last revenge in a way, a final rebuke for Kato who stole the love of his life. It was there, at Matsushima, that Kenji wanted to gaze one last time upon the islands and there at the end for Kato to kill him, a mercy killing, and a final act of friendship.

They agreed on the time of 1.30 pm on March 11, 2011. Kenji produced a gun with a silencer and some bullets. He asked where his friend got the weapon, but Kenji refused to tell him. Perhaps he should have asked more questions, thought Kato. Perhaps he should have just talked his friend out of it. Fujita would have been able to help. He was an honest officer of the law. Looking back, it would have gone according to plan if the tsunami did not come, but it did come and changed everything. Kato agreed to one last request from an old friend and now his entire family were dead. He was now alone. He did not even have the name of the temple that was at the centre of everything. Kenji never told him. What a mess, thought Kato, what a complete and pointless mess.

At that moment, Kato realized they had reached what seemed to be the museum, though with all the mud and debris, the building looked like any other and whatever beauty and character it once had, was washed away. Onishi had run up to him and thanked him for being able to help him find anyone who had been overlooked during the first rescue attempt.

'Was this really a museum?' asked Wu, summing up Kato's thoughts exactly.

Onishi nodded furiously.

'It is in honour of the great Date Masamune,' Onishi said. Kato rolled his eyes. He had heard that name mentioned so many times in association with this place, it just felt nauseous on a day like this.

'Who was he?' asked Wu innocently. Onishi seemed shocked.

'You don't know Date Masamune?' he asked. 'Why, he is the most famous samurai in all Japan. Sendai was his domain and Zuiganji, where you were before, was his temple and his daughter is buried up on the hill. The Lord Date was one of the first samurai to build a link with the Western world and sent an embassy to Europe to meet the Pope.'

Ka-chan interrupted him.

'Lord Date was a minor figure Wu-san, overshadowed by the three men who made Japan what it is today: Oda Nobunaga, Toyotomi Hideyoshi and Ieyasu Tokugawa. Date Masamune knew all these men and his exploits took place during perhaps one of the most important political shifts in Japan, the end of the Warring-States period and the unification of the country.'

'He was far from a minor figure,' protested Onishi. 'He was an important samurai warlord, and he is very important in Japan.'

'It's all very interesting,' interrupted Lijuan. 'But you boys can discuss history later. I think Kato-san has already gone into the museum. Are we going to stand outside here talking?'

The four of them looked around. They were alone outside the museum. Kato had indeed gone in without them. He was not interested in talking about Date Masamune, even though he was indeed a fascinating figure in Japanese history. Ka-chan, Lijuan and Wu were all lucky and had been spared the worst of what was a horrific tsunami. They all lived and enjoyed quite privileged lives, and this day was just one big adventure for them. Today was anything but an adventure. Once the sun rose, all would be revealed. He hoped they understood what was really going on. Their frivolity and eagerness to argue about who was the best samurai was further evidence for Kato that Kenji was wrong about Ka-chan. This man seemed to be a typical Japanese Buddhist priest, nice enough, but not a killer. Why would he bother arguing over something as silly as which samurai was the best? With each step forward, Kato was becoming more relaxed.

He was thinking this when he found a set of stairs, but as he shone the torch upwards, the light was lost in a thick, dark fog. It was black and it was swirling down the stairs and around him. Kato had not seen fog like this before. He had often seen fog rising across the fields in Kyoto when he was a boy and it was pleasant and beautiful and expectant, and he always felt his heart lifting towards the heavens. This fog was different. With each swirl, he seemed to be sinking into the mud. He started to ascend the stairs, but the fog thickened and then, when he was three steps up, his torch flickered and stopped, plunging him into darkness. He reached for the wall and found it, running his hands along until he reached the top of the stairs. He looked down and thought for a moment that he saw a figure in the fog running past him. He thought he heard the tender voices of children playing but dismissed it out of his mind.

'Hey!' he called out to whoever might be there, but there was no response.

He started to walk when he tripped over something hard on the floor. He fell heavily to the ground. When he got up, he turned around and felt for whatever made him fall and his hands found a body. From what he could discern from her shape, she was a woman, and she was alive. He shook her gently, but she did not move. His hands suddenly felt wet, and they were not wet with water, but blood. He could not tell where it was coming from.

'Oi!' he called out. 'I am up on the stairs! I cannot see anything! Where are you? There is a woman up here and she has been injured.'

There was no response. He was completely alone, with the injured woman on the top of the stairs. He stared out into the fog which seemed to envelop him. It was then that he heard the bird. Its cry was haunting, and it reached into the deep recesses of his heart with notes of despair and loss. Kato realized that this was the first bird call he had heard since the tsunami. He had never heard such a sad bird call. It made him feel helpless and hopeless inside. The sound of the bird seemed to come from down the corridor. Kato thought it strange that a bird would be caught in the museum, but it was not impossible. Maybe it came in to escape the waves or maybe it was injured. He crawled on his knees towards the source of the sound, and it was as if the bird was just around the corner.

It was then he heard the scream. He had never heard anyone scream like that before. It was the scream of an innocent person who had suddenly faced the horrors of life with no preparation. It sounded like Lijuan, but he could not be certain. It was followed by silence.

A few minutes earlier, Onishi led the others into the Museum after Kato, but did not go up the stairs, nor were they confronted with any fog. Onishi had already told them that most of the ground floor had been destroyed by the tsunami and he was upset about it, weeping as he spoke, as most of the exhibits had been irrevocably destroyed. The rooms were dark, and they were all knee deep in water and mud. Wu and Lijuan had begun to complain about the mud when the young woman shone her torch towards the wall and thought she saw something. She reached down and pulled up an arm, severed from its body. The light of the torch revealed a figure up against the wall, with its head face down in the mud, its other arms and legs twisted and contorted. She dropped the arm into the mud and screamed. She did not stop screaming until Ka-chan ran up and held her and her screams were muffled into his chest. He held her close until she stopped. Wu was soon by her side and began shining his torch around the room. It was full of bodies, all floating in the mud, some with arms and legs missing, others severed at the hips and all their eyes were vacant, staring into space.

'What is this place?' asked Wu. 'It is like a slaughterhouse!'

Onishi came running up very apologetic, bowing profusely. 'I am so sorry,' he said. 'I thought you all knew. This museum is mainly mannequins and wax models, all ruined now.'

He reached down to pick up the arm that Lijuan had dropped. He looked at it intently and smiled. 'We were talking about him just outside,' he said. 'This is Date Masamune, or his arm, or the model of him. I am really, I am so sorry.'

Meanwhile, Kato kept following the sound of the bird. It was indeed coming from around the corner. Kato felt with his hands and found himself in another room. The floor was surprisingly dry. It was then he heard the voice. It was that of a young girl.

'Is there someone there?' she cried out.

'Help us! Please help us, my grandfather needs help!'

Kato crawled over towards the voice.

'I am coming!' he shouted. 'Keep talking. I don't have a torch and can't see anything. Let your voice bring me to you. Do you understand?'

'Yes!' cried the girl, 'Please hurry, my grandfather is injured. He is under the wall. It fell. I cannot lift it.'

Kato had reached the girl. He stretched out his hands and found the frightened figure of a young girl, maybe ten or eleven. She grabbed his arms, and they held each other. They could hardly see each other. Kato could only discern a faint outline in the mist of the girl with whom he was speaking.

'Where are your parents?' asked Kato.

'My parents?' she asked confused.

'My mother went to get help when the wall fell. That was about an hour ago. I cannot leave my grandfather. He is very weak now. The wall fell and he pushed me out of the way, after the noise began.'

'You mean the tsunami?' checked Kato. This meant the little girl and her grandfather had been stuck in the room all night. He was probably dead.

'No, about an hour ago, the noise, there was so much noise,' she insisted.

'What kind of noise?' asked Kato.

'Screaming. Something was screaming and throwing things around and that's when the wall fell,' said the girl.

'Did you see anything?' asked Kato.

The girl squeezed Kato's arms as if he had just said something silly.

'I am blind,' she said. 'I *saw* nothing. But when the screaming started, I covered my ears and then when I opened them, my mother was gone, and grandfather was stuck under the wall. Have you come with my mother? Is she with you?'

Kato realized that the woman in the corridor was probably this child's mother. At that moment, the room was full of light, as Ka-chan, Wu, Lijuan and Onishi arrived.

'What is this fog? Where did it come from?' asked the priest.

Kato stood up. 'Lijuan, take the child please,' he said. He went to the wall that had fallen over. It was as if the entire side of the room had collapsed. He turned to the men.

'There is an old man under here. I do not know if he is alive or dead. Wu and Ka-chan take the edges and see if you can lift it and I will get the old man out. I just need you to hold it up until I can move him. Do you understand?'

The men nodded.

'If we cannot hold it Kato, you will be squashed underneath,' said Wu.

'Then don't drop it!' shouted Kato sharply.

The three men took the edges of the wall and began to lift it. Kato climbed under the wall and reached for anything he could find. He did not have a torch and didn't want one. He knew that the man if he was alive could easily be dragged out. Kato reached out his hand and to his surprise, the old man grabbed it. He held Kato's hand firmly and strongly and this gave Kato enough confidence to pull the man quickly out from under the fallen wall. He released the hand and reached for the man's chest, dragging him out until he was safely in the middle of the room. When the others saw that the old man was safe, they dropped the wall and leapt away. It crashed to the floor with an awful thud.

'I cannot imagine anyone surviving this,' said Ka-chan. 'That wall is terribly heavy. That he is even breathing is remarkable.'

'Give me a torch!' said Kato and Wu handed his over. He turned it on, turned over the body of the old man he had pulled out from under the wall.

It was Yamaguchi.

He grabbed hold of Kato and stared into his eyes. 'Ah, Ichinosuke!' said the old man, 'we meet again. I tried to stop it, I did, I really did, I tried to stop it, but I couldn't.'

Yamaguchi seemed visibly and emotionally shaken, but unhurt. Kato felt a warm and strong man holding his arms and looking into his eyes, but Yamaguchi's eyes were full of tears. He began to weep, and tears ran down his cheeks.

'I was given two to look after, and I have done my best Kato, you must understand, I tried my best. He let me take care of two of Yoshitune's children. He was kind, especially after what I did to him, all those years ago, you know, when I met Ichinosuke. We escaped the tsunami and took refuge here, but it followed us. It wanted to kill us. I tried my best. I could not stop it!'

8

After Yamaguchi blurted this out to Kato, he collapsed. Ka-chan offered to carry Yamaguchi out of the museum on his back. He remarked that the old man seemed to have no major injuries as the result of being hemmed in under the fallen wall. Indeed, Yamaguchi didn't appear to have any visible injuries to speak of. He was just exhausted, shaken, and dehydrated. The young child also turned out to be Yamaguchi's next-door neighbour, not an actual relative, though she often referred to him as 'Grandpa,' but her mother was indeed her mother, and her wounds, were quite unusual. Onishi said he had not seen anything like it. She was not in a good shape, and it was if she had been tossed around like a rag doll in the jaws of a large dog. The window near where she fell had blown out during the earthquake and there was little glass on the floor.

Lijuan tended to her, gave her some water and was able to bandage some of her wounds to staunch the blood loss. She told Kato and Onishi that if she received proper medical attention then she should pull through but said that the woman was rambling and speaking in a language she could not understand. No one could understand what she was saying. Kato said it was obviously Japanese, but Lijuan insisted that it was not. Wu agreed and said that it sounded like she was speaking a language that was both Chinese and Japanese mixed together in a dialect of some sort. They rummaged through the museum until Wu found a stretcher in one of the storerooms, along with some medicines and bandages.

'This is probably a prop for one of the exhibits,' said Onishi. 'I am not sure if it will hold the woman, but we will take her as far as we can.'

Wu and Lijuan offered to carry the woman back to Zuiganji, so everyone helped move her onto the stretcher and slowly took her down the stairs. Kato was glad to be out of the building, as he had the terrible feeling that they were not alone. What Onishi said next confirmed his fears. When the stretcher had reached the bottom of the stairs, Onishi pulled him aside and tugged on his arm.

'It makes no sense, Kato-san, no sense at all, I don't understand it,' he said.

'What are you talking about?' asked Kato.

'There is something I wanted to show you,' he said quietly and nervously. 'I didn't want to tell the others, they are too young and the priest, well, he has enough on his mind.'

Onishi pulled him back to the end of the corridor and to the stairs. The mist was lingering but it was quickly vanishing into the air. The hall was still dark, so Onishi took out his torch and shone it on the wall. Kato's eyes widened when he saw the unmistakable tears in the cement of four deep lines running from the bottom of the steps to the top. The lines were not even but moved ever so slightly with every step, but real they were, and they were deep. They looked like claw marks. Kato grabbed the torch and shone it onto the other side of the wall. There were four deep lines deeply cut into the cement on that side as well.

'What are they?' whispered Onishi loudly to Kato, holding onto his arm 'Are we in Hell or in some afterlife?'

'There wouldn't be so many unanswered questions if we were,' replied Kato, but he told Onishi to help the others take the injured woman out of the museum safely. They made good progress and passed all the dismembered figures in the rooms until they were outside. It was only then Kato sighed with relief.

In his mind, he remembered what he saw at the red bridge at Matsushima. That creature had claws, huge claws, hugging the railing of the bridge, and the very sight of that creature made him physically ill. Did Yamaguchi transform into this creature, and come up the stairs, scratching the wall as he went? Was he responsible for what happened to the woman, but if so, why did he save the little girl and what was he doing trapped under the wall? If Yamaguchi did not make those claw marks on the wall and didn't hurt the woman and if he was as strong and as powerful as Kato's vision suggested, then something more powerful than Yamaguchi had been here and maybe it still was. Maybe it was still in the fog listening and watching in the dark.

Kato was thinking this when he saw Ka-chan put the old man down just outside the museum. He was able to walk as he had regained his strength. They were all surprised that he was able to stand up straight or walk without the aid of his cane. Ka-chan tried to protest, but the old man would have none of it. He was very polite and kept bowing to the priest and thanked him for his consideration. He immediately came back to Kato who had taken one handle of the back of the stretcher, with Lijuan on the other side and Wu on the front. The young blind girl was walking next to her mother, on the left side, holding her left hand. In the museum, Lijuan had managed to bandage the mother's wounds with some of the medical cloth she brought with her, but they needed to get the woman to a doctor as soon as possible.

Yamaguchi patted the little girl on the head and held her mother's right hand. He asked Lijuan how the woman was faring, and the Chinese girl told her the truth, that she had been badly hurt and needed immediate attention. The old man held her hand tightly, closed his eyes and prayed for her. Kato was the only one to notice that the woman immediately opened her eyes when the old man prayed and looked up at Yamaguchi standing there.

'Everything will be fine, my child,' said Yamaguchi. 'You will be safe soon. Your daughter is well, and we will be out of danger soon.'

The woman looked at Yamaguchi and then around at Lijuan, Kato, Wu and Onishi. She seemed uncomfortable and asked the old man who they were.

'They are friends,' said Yamaguchi. 'They rescued you from the museum.'

'I don't remember anything,' replied the woman, speaking normal Japanese with a distinct local dialect, and then she lost consciousness again. At that moment, the group began to be aware that the light in Matsushima was changing. The night was over, and the dawn had come. Kato realized that it was no longer March 11, but the next day. The sun's rays began to seep across the horizon and bathe the entire town with light. Everything seemed to be covered with rays of warmth.

It seemed like an eternity, but they eventually returned to the main street and had made it back to where they started hours earlier. Kato looked over and at the end of the street were men running towards them. They must have come from the temple. Yamaguchi recognized one of them as a man named Keisuke. Yamaguchi was mumbling something about a boat and going home. The men took hold of the stretcher and took the woman to the temple. The small and weary rescue party followed them at a distance, but Yamaguchi and the young child stayed close to the woman.

When they approached the entrance to the temple, there was already a lot of activity. Kato noticed that there was a young girl from Zuiganji, one of the acolytes, standing in the knee-deep mud looking out to sea. The mud seemed to be oozing out of the ground itself, enveloping her legs. In her left hand she clutched her phone. A little toy figure dangled by a slender string, hanging still below the phone as if hovering above the mud like a levitated Buddha. She seemed desolate and must have lived in a town north or south of Matsushima. She must have been told what happened there and was in disbelief. Death had come elsewhere and taken its fill of human life. The people of Matsushima had been spared a swathe of tragedies, but the rest of the east coast had not. The little girl had survived and stood knee deep in the aftermath of a wave that no doubt had removed her town from the map of human existence. No doubt she was not the only one who was thinking that this morning.

Kato turned and there was Yamaguchi.

'The young girl and her mother will be taken care of,' he said. 'I cannot thank you all enough for rescuing them from the museum, they were in great danger due to the earthquake and tsunami.'

'I am sure the earthquake and tsunami had their part to play, but you didn't need rescuing Yamaguchi-san,' replied Kato. 'I pulled you out easily and there was not a scratch on you. In fact, you seem completely healthy.'

'I was, in fact, completely exhausted,' said the old man. 'You seem to think Kato, that you have all the answers and know everything that is going on, but you don't. I was exhausted and could not move and the weight on my back was indeed heavy. I did what I had to do to survive, and we did survive.'

'I have lots of questions,' said Kato.

'What are they?' asked the old man, clearly irritated. 'But know this Kato, that not all questions should be asked and once asked, you might not like what you hear.'

Kato ignored him and continued. 'When we were in the museum, Onishi showed me scratch marks on the walls going up the stairs that seemed remarkably like those made by claws, and those talons were enormous, at least each the size of a man's arm. Your friend, the young woman was tossed around like a rag doll by some large creature, but not killed and when I climbed the stairs, I encountered deep fog and the cries of a bird that still haunts my mind.

'That is not all. When I pulled you out, you told me that you rescued two of Yoshitune's children, but only two. Now, I know, as everyone does, that Yoshitune, the medieval samurai warrior, did not have any children, so that made no sense to me. Furthermore, when I left you on the red bridge, I looked back and saw you and you had transformed into a huge monster with terrible claws clutching the railing of the bridge. I could see a man who looked much like myself staring back at me in terror as if he were about to die and he was surrounded by hundreds and hundreds of decaying bodies, all rotting in the sun. When we were in the museum, those claws were real and so were the injuries of that poor woman, but the life of the child was spared. I have been thinking about it since we met you there. Why did you spare the life of the child and not the mother?'

Yamaguchi looked at Kato and turned away, walking a few steps towards Matsushima Bay. The sun had burst into full view and Yamaguchi was looking directly at it, but then he closed his eyes.

'I never get tired of the rising sun in the morning,' he said to Kato, who could hear him. 'The moment when the sky is hovering between two worlds, one the world of the night and that of the day. The sun hesitates, as if it is unsure of what to do, it tentatively allows a stray beam to creep through as if gingerly tiptoeing on the sky, and then, when it is fully confident of being welcome, it bursts through, ending the darkness, at least for another day.

'I have not always lived in Matsushima. I arrived here after the war, got married, had children, and settled down. That young woman you rescued from the museum is one of my adopted children and she lived with us, my wife and I, along with our daughter and two sons, who died yesterday in the tsunami. I am not completely sure they are dead, but I feel in my heart that they have gone. Each night, my dear wife and I would often sit on the veranda and watch the sun rise.

'Yesterday, in the afternoon, I went for my walk. I saw you and I immediately began to think of my old life, a life that I lived a long time ago. I was a different man then, a different man entirely. At the end of that life was a battle, and it decided the future of Japan and certainly the future of my family. I was betrayed by my closest and dearest friend. But his betrayal meant nothing. We both lost. In that battle, just before I was about to destroy the man I had come to kill, a young samurai retainer of the emperor stood in my way. His name was Ichinosuke. He was your ancestor. Those who triumphed over us were merciful and let us live. Maybe that was our greatest punishment, living in a world where our failure was a constant reminder. We accepted defeat and I returned to the shadows, taking what was left of my family with me. We have lived as hidden refugees in a nation that would most certainly kill us, if they knew who or what we are, so we stay in the shadows, out of sight and we wear the clothes of humanity such as they are. We are bound by our ancient oaths never to reveal our true face and whatever I am, I keep my word. Time took its toll on us. What time didn't kill, the bombings during the last war killed most of the rest. Deprived of light, many of us simply died, or disappeared until there was only a handful of us. Now, in Matsushima, there are only three remaining, including myself.'

Yamaguchi turned to Kato.

'You and Onishi were absolutely right,' said Yamaguchi. 'As fate would have it, the girl and her mother were here in town while I walked across the bridge. I love that old island and I was going for a walk along a familiar path. After the earthquake I knew a tsunami was coming so we went to higher ground and stayed there last night. I couldn't get home to my wife and family, and I could not save them from the tsunami. We were making our way to Zuiganji this morning when we had to hide. We took refuge in the wax museum.'

'To hide from whom?' asked Kato.

'I have no idea. I have not seen it before, nor did I expect it, nor have I ever encountered it before. The Japanese used to call me the strongest of them all, but not even I was a match for whatever tried to kill us last night. It was someone who hates my people, even more than the Japanese do. It was not one of us. It tried to kill the little one and her mother. I stopped it and it retreated, but it is still out there, in the dark, lurking, waiting, until we are weak or asleep or unprepared. Then it will strike again.

'When I saw you on the bridge Kato yesterday, I did not change into my natural form. By our laws, I am forbidden to show myself as I really am, and I know well the consequences for my children if I do. Somehow seeing me triggered an ancient memory buried deep in your subconscious, a genetic warning, if you like, should you or any of your descendants encounter me. Maybe it was the mention of the name 'Ichinosuke' which triggered the memory. I do not know. We, that is my people and I, believe in the ancient faith of Shinto. We are not Buddhists. We believe that when we die, we do not come back but become what you might call gods or kami. There are no second chances. There is no reincarnation. But we also believe that our lives and our experiences can be passed on to our children, not all the memories and not all the experiences, but some of them. It depends on someone's sense of character and purpose in life. You obviously remembered something of your ancestor Ichinosuke because it was deeply embedded in your being of what makes you, you.

'But I have kept my promise to my old enemy. I did not change my form yesterday when I met you or when I fought the creature who tried to kill us. I fought the creature as a man, and it threw a wall at me. I have a few old tricks up my sleeve that I remember from the old days. I can teach you to fight if you like. My methods seemed to daze it or stupefy it. It eventually retreated. I admit I relied upon my powers to sustain myself during the night and the fog came from me, because I did not want the child to die. The creature was waiting for us when we arrived, and I was too late to help the mother. Since that battle with Ichinosuke, I have kept my word, I kept my promise. I can promise you this Kato, if you ever see me take my original and natural form, then the old order had died, and we will be at the end.'

'The end of what?' asked Kato.

'The last day of old Japan,' replied Yamaguchi. 'The last battle against the forces that conspire to put Amaterasu back into the cave and plunge the world into darkness.'

'I know the story,' said Kato. 'That the goddess Amaterasu was in the cave and the other gods enticed her to come out to bring light into the world.'

'It is the heart of the Shinto faith, but my dear Kato, it is the battle we all face, each day. Think of those little statues at Zuiganji, the stone statues on the edge of the path, relatively undisturbed by the events of the day before. Long ago, men came here and found the caves and from them hewed rocks and statues. What do they know of what we have experienced yesterday?

'You and I both lost our families. We will never be the same. You will not feel it now Kato, but soon there will be a rage, an inconsolable rage and it may never leave you. I have harboured rage in my heart for years, and it has been a constant companion. I will now have to bury another wife and more children. You asked me about Yoshitune's children, and you were adamant that Yoshitune never had any. He lived 1159-1189 and he a wife and a child. How do you know they were no more?'

'I am sorry about the death of your family,' said Kato. 'But as for Yoshitune's children, it didn't happen. He didn't have any, it wasn't historical. Some say there may have been a child, but the records are unclear and even if he did, then the child died,' replied Kato.

'History is written by those who were there Kato, and sometimes history is written in a different way to cover up mistakes or to present things in a different light, and sometimes history is rewritten to protect people. What if I told you that your understanding of Japanese history is all wrong?'

'Then I would say that you are crazy,' said Kato. The old man laughed.

'When you get back to Kyoto today, you might run into a man who has a deep understanding of history, Japanese history. I will not tell you his name, but he will be able to tell you more about Yoshitune's children.'

'How do you know that I am going back to Kyoto today?' asked Kato, surprised.

'It is because the reason for your visit to Matsushima is fulfilled,' said the old man.

'What reason was that?'

'To meet me of course! And now that we have met, I will be keeping a close eye on you, my old friend. The memory of me is lodged deep in your subconscious. It is a starting point. If you have seen me in my true form, then I am sure that this memory will return to you more strongly in the future. Hopefully, we will see much more of each other in the weeks ahead,' said Yamaguchi with a strange smile. He turned aside and walked back to Zuiganji.

Kato stayed where he was and pondered what he had been told. Kato was a rationalist. He did not believe in the supernatural world, but only what he could see or touch or smell. The more he spoke to Yamaguchi, the more questions were posed and the more confused he became. He found a chair that had been tossed around by the tsunami and so he put it upright, and in the middle of the street, he sat on it. He closed his eyes and tried to sleep. Much to his surprise, he fell asleep.

Kato woke up with a start a few moments later.

'I like the chair,' said Lijuan. 'I hope you have one for all of us.'

Kato looked up and saw he was surrounded by Ka-chan, Wu and Lijuan. Kato rose to his feet and handed Lijuan the chair. She smiled and sat down. Wu told him that Yamaguchi had been given the use of a small outboard motorboat by his friend Keisuke, so he could take them all to north Matsushima.

'Why would I want to go to north Matsushima?' asked Kato. He had no intention of going anywhere. He was exhausted and wanted to spend some time resting at Zuiganji. He looked at the Chinese kids. They both wanted to go, and Ka-chan would go wherever Lijuan went. Kato reluctantly agreed.

'We should spend more time getting to know each other Kato,' said Yamaguchi who had appeared again. 'I think you would all benefit from seeing what has happened up there. Keisuke's boat was undamaged by the tsunami by some miracle, probably because he never uses it, but it will fit us comfortably. It does mean going out into the open sea. Will that be a problem for anyone?'

No one said anything.

It did not take them long to find Keisuke waiting for them with the motorboat and they all felt a sigh of relief when the motor finally spurted into life and the little boat edged out into the bay. They passed the island where Kato had been only a day before and where he stood and took the life of his best friend. He tried not to look at the island or pay it much attention. But Yamaguchi pointed it out to everyone and told them that it was normally a beautiful place to visit and where all the good look out places were. He smiled knowingly at Kato.

The sea was quiet. It said nothing, but all their hearts were in turmoil. Wu had tried calling his mother, but the phone lines were either busy or down. He was anxious about her and even though he did not think she cared about him he was worried about her. Wu sat looking back at the port city of Matsushima and Ka-chan and Kato huddled at the front of the boat, squashed together, not speaking, and not looking at each other. Yamaguchi sat next to Keisuke at the back of the small boat and only Lijuan stood, her hand on Ka-chan's back, her long black hair blowing in the breeze.

It did not take the little party long to discover how fortunate they had been. The boat began to bang against floating wood and pieces of furniture and housing and the effects of life, and the more the motor churned, the more the boat struck debris in its path. Soon it became too difficult to move and it seemed as if the boat had reached the edge of a floating city. The roofs of houses sat half submerged on the water, surrounded by fencing, windows, walls that had been surgically spliced, and the houses were all bumping into each other. No bodies could be seen.

'We must get to the land and go the rest of the way on foot if that is possible,' said Yamaguchi. Keisuke nodded. It took Yamaguchi a while to moor the boat safely on a small beach or what seemed to be a beach further up the coast. Ka-chan and Kato jumped out first. Ka-chan offered his hand to Lijuan, followed by Wu and Yamaguchi. Keisuke stayed with the boat. The little beach edged upwards so no one could see what was on the other side.

The small party walked to the top of the beach and stopped. They were all speechless. Wu fell to his knees and Lijuan turned her face away, walking off down the beach towards the boat until she sat down putting her head in her hands.

'How many people died here?' she asked.

Kato stood by Ka-chan and just stared towards the town. He pushed his way past Ka-chan and walked onwards. The town however was no longer there. Instead of houses, there were empty spaces, and instead of roads there was mud and the remains of houses, all but their foundations gone. Entire streets were absent. There were a few buildings left standing, but they were older concrete structures but those too looked as though life had been sucked out of them.

'Let me show you around,' said Yamaguchi, walking towards the town. 'Come with me, all of your, including Lijuan.'

He walked back and knelt before the Chinese woman.

'Take my arm,' he said. 'I am an old man and I need your support.' She looked up and smiled and stood up, taking his arm in hers.

Let us walk awhile,' he said to them all. 'I will show you all my home.'

As they walked, Yamaguchi continued to talk. Nobody else spoke, indeed, there was nothing anyone could say.

'I was in Matsushima when the tsunami came. Most of my family were in this town. They are all dead now, including my wife and children. I was not here to help them. Like you, I didn't know there would be a tsunami. We have had so many earthquakes over the years, and I assumed it was just like all the others.' He sighed.

'The waves would have breached the sea barriers designed to prevent tsunami, by only several meters. Our town had long prepared for tsunami, but no one believed that any tsunami would be sufficiently high to overcome the sea walls. When the earthquake hit, the sirens rang out and the community announcements would have told everyone to go to higher ground, but many would have ignored the warning while others, especially the elderly, were in no condition to move anyway. After all, this is a land where earthquakes are relatively common and not every quake is followed by tsunami.

'When the wall of water surged over the embankments and onto the road, many motorists would have been caught unawares, as were those in the shops, restaurants, and businesses closest to the ocean. They would not have stood a chance. They would have had nowhere to hide. Those who managed to reach the second floor of houses nearest the water would have discovered that their well-constructed, earthquake-proof homes were no match for the might of the tsunami, crushing them like eggs and tossing the debris onto the surging water. Schools, hospitals, clinics, homes, businesses, the waves would have stopped for no one and nothing. The elderly, the young, the infirmed, the strong, the wealthy and the poor, all picked up, smothered, and thrown into the waves.

'Some of those who perished would have been driving, only to be picked up by the waves, unable to get out and unable to drive, waiting for the windows to crack or smash to be followed by a slow, agonizing death. Boats in the harbor would have been picked up and thrown at the port to be dismembered or tossed at one another to be mangled. Some would have lifted by the waves and carried into the town to collide with some of the taller buildings, and to find a resting place hundreds of meters inland.

'Those who did survive would have found the tops of small hills or the tallest buildings and would have been able to watch the complete destruction of their town. I do not know why I survived to be honest with you all. I am an old man and I have had a long and full life, whereas many of the dead in this town were children. I do not know why we were in Matsushima that afternoon and we were saved, and everyone here was killed. Some would have been saved because they pushed and shoved and climbed over the backs of others while, yet others would have been just fortunate to be in the right place at the right time. Yesterday, was a day when many never said goodbye, where conversations were left unfinished, relationships unfulfilled, controversies unresolved. This was a day were everything normal didn't seem to matter anymore, when all the pressing concerns of the day and the week and the year seemed to melt away in irrelevance.'

They had been walking through the desolation for about half an hour when Yamaguchi and Lijuan had reached what seemed to be an intersection. He stopped and turned to all of them, letting Lijuan go.

'Let me introduce you to my street,' said Yamaguchi. 'It is always good to put a face to a tragedy. I don't know how many lived here, but I have lived in this town for a long time, and I knew many people in this street.'

Yamaguchi began to point to vacant spaces on the road where houses used to stand.

'I knew the couple who lived in this house. They were elderly, like me, a nice couple, Mr, and Mrs. Kubota. She had a little garden in the front of her home, modest, not like the ones you would find in rural areas, but about a dozen little pots full of little flowers. Next to them was a man who lived alone. His name was Tetsuo. His wife left him long ago because he had a gambling problem. He worked as a manager in a clothing store. He kept to himself, but he would always greet me in the street. Next to him lived his sister Taka and her husband, Koji. They were retired, he used to work in a factory. She was a hoarder and would collect anything she could find. Koji and I would sometimes go for a coffee down the road at an interesting old place where they used to play Jazz in the evenings. Next to Koji's place was a larger house that had recently been built, for a family that had just moved to the area from Tokyo. The father had been given a promotion to a retail outlet. He only came a few weeks ago and was telling me how excited he was to escape the frantic life in Tokyo. His wife was a small lady, much younger than he was, very pleasant. Her name was Kiku-san if I remember correctly. They had two children who went to the local school which was about five blocks away. It was supposed to be an emergency shelter in the event of a tsunami, but it has been washed away along with all the children and teachers.

'Next to the new house was another house owned by a man in Tokyo by the name of Abe. He was a distant relative of the priest Abe and that is why I know him so well. He owned a machinery business in Mito Prefecture and had inherited the house when his father died last year. He did not know what to do with it. Next to his house was a small playground for the children. It was popular a long time ago when there were more children, but in more recent years it had fallen into disrepair.'

Yamaguchi turned to the small group who had listened to him patiently.

'I will not show you where I lived. The memories are too painful to share. Allow me the privacy to mourn for my family in my own way. Thank you for not asking me. I don't know how many died, but I remember their names and I will not forget them. I hope that when you go home to your comfortable beds wherever they are, and wash off the mud, and get on with your life, that you will not forget them. Oh, I neglected to tell you, look over there, in the distance, can you see it?'

Everyone looked back at the ocean. It was still.

'Yesterday the sun rose over there and it rose again today, and it will rise again tomorrow. I enjoy watching the sun rise as I told Kato-san earlier. The Japanese have the sun on their flag. It is because the rising sun is important to them. The sun brings light into darkness.

'Sometimes, the sun is not enough. Yesterday we witnessed a tsunami, which is simply a large wave, and it has swept away my home, but there were other tsunamis in the past you cannot forget. The first was at the cusp of a new dawn for Japan. One day, the sun rose on a nation ruled not by political power, but by the emperor, something that had not happened for centuries. The second tsunami was brought about by Japan's war against her neighbours. I know Lijuan that you Chinese still are angry with us Japanese for what happened during that time. I went to Nanking many years ago, and I spoke to survivors. Their stories have haunted me for years. I cannot speak for them Ka-chan, they must speak for themselves, if we care to listen. If either of you see a future with the other, and I believe you do, then listening to each other is a good place to start.

'I have also been to Hiroshima and Nagasaki. Kato-san, you asked me about monsters. If you want to know about monsters, look within yourself, or go to one of those three places. There is enough horror there to fill one hundred lifetimes. You do not need to find monsters on red bridges or in museums because the real monsters are people. If monsters do exist, then they are spending most of their time trying to escape the anger of humanity.'

'Do you think there will ever be peace between China and Japan?' asked Wu.

The old man turned to the young man and smiled.

'I don't think it is as simple as that. That struggle is a symptom of a deeper malaise of the human condition. I do know that another tsunami is coming, a third tsunami, and it will be the last. It will be Japan's last test as a nation, and it will mark the last days of old Japan.'

'There is no hope then?' asked Ka-chan. Yamaguchi shook his head.

'There is always hope, young priest,' he said. 'But people need to choose the world they wish to live in.'

Yamaguchi looked up into the sky and smiled. He turned to the little group.

'And now, you are all going to go home, for your transport has arrived. Abe Sensei told me before we left that he received a call from the Japanese Self-Defence Force this morning asking for the whereabouts of one Masayoshi Kato. I did not know you had so much influence Kato-san. I told him I was taking all of you to my town today, so the army knows where to find you, in fact, here they are.'

Suddenly, there was a rush of wind and a helicopter appeared over the ocean. It was a military helicopter. Everyone was astonished. The noise broke the silence, and everyone felt uneasy because it reminded them of the way the tsunami roared the day before. The helicopter reached their position quickly and landed a safe distance away. A few soldiers and medical personnel jumped out. One of them Kato recognized as Joshua Tree. Joshua ran up to them and Kato warmly shook his hands.

'It is good to see you alive Masa,' he said. Kato nodded.

'It is good to be alive,' said Kato and then quickly introduced the American to all who were present. Joshua introduced Mr Honda, who was with him.

'This is Mr. Honda,' said Joshua to everyone. 'He is here to take you to Tokyo and then onto Kyoto.'

'What is the urgency?' asked Ka-chan. 'We are all happy to help here with the rescue effort.' Wu and Lijuan agreed. They had no desire to leave.

'I cannot force you to leave of course,' replied Honda. 'But there has been a major accident at a nuclear reactor in Fukushima, south of Sendai, and we don't know the extent of the damage. It could be another Chernobyl. If I am wrong, then you can all come back here in a few days. We need to get to Tokyo and there I can speak with people who would know what is going on.'

'I suggest you all go with this gentleman,' insisted Yamaguchi. 'As he said, you can always come back, and you would be most welcome. I will stay here with Keisuke, and we will go back to Zuiganji this evening.'

They all said their farewells to Yamaguchi, including Kato, who bowed politely and said that he hoped to continue their conversation another time. Honda ushered everyone towards the helicopter quickly. He was the last to leave, looking at Yamaguchi who was walking back towards the boat.

The helicopter took them to the southern tip of Fukushima Prefecture, where they exchanged the helicopter for two comfortable cars. Honda drove one with Ka-chan, Lijuan and Wu in the back, while Joshua drove the other one and spent the entire trip talking with Kato. Lijuan fell asleep on Ka-chan's shoulder. Honda helped Wu so he was able finally to speak to his mother. Wu asked why he could not get through. She said that she had been shopping and didn't want to be disturbed.

9

The two cars stopped in front of Omiya station, north of Tokyo, in the Prefecture of Saitama late in the evening on March 12. Only Kato was awake when the cars pulled into the taxi stand. He had been thinking about Akiko and Ai. He found it difficult to accept their deaths, even though his mind was telling him otherwise. He kept playing the events of the last day over again and again in his head. He also pondered the strange events in connection with the elderly man Yamaguchi and wondered if they were all part of his imagination. His rationalist disposition was carefully and gradually dispelling every unusual aspect of his encounter. Maybe he exaggerated the mist in the museum. Maybe he became overexcited when he saw the scratch marks on the wall. Maybe they were examples of the wall buckling under the stress of the earthquake. Maybe the old man had just played with his paranoia and stress on the red bridge at Matsushima and that strange vision was a product of his psychological manipulation.

The idea of a monster, a real monster, like the ones he read about as a child, were stories invented by ancient and superstitious people who tried to understand and explain a dangerous and complex world around them. He had read of the yokai, the monsters of old Japan who haunted, tormented, and manipulated people such as the Tengu who lived on the top of Mount Kurama in Kyoto, a huge red-faced being with a long nose, who walked on huge wooden sandals and had wings.

The creature he saw in his strange vision on the bridge resembled his recollection of another yokai, the famous Nue, a foul and evil fiend, that was often indescribable but possessed enormous claws. But they were not real, only legends, creative but fictional types invented by scholars who wanted to tell stories about society in a way that could easily be understood. They were morality plays, nothing more, parts of Japanese culture, but to suggest these creatures were real was stretching credulity.

His mind had convinced him that Yamaguchi must have manipulated him psychologically that day on the bridge and that he was an expert in mind control. He was good, almost as good as some terrorists he encountered in Iraq. Kato, along with his comrades in the Japanese Self-Defence Force, had been warned to be aware of the role psychology plays in war and the challenges they might face on the battlefield. He learnt that the mind is a fragile creation and that healthy respect of the mind as well as careful boundaries were needed just as much as fighting ability, to survive.

Kato also knew that he lost his mind in Iraq where he was captured by the terrorists and tortured. During those few days of misery, his mind went to places he did not think possible, he imagined, and he wrestled with demons that were not there and conversed with people long dead until he finally snapped under the pressure. When he began to rethink his time in Iraq, he started to believe that something that the old man had said on the bridge must have triggered a memory of trauma that he experienced in Iraq and that led to his violent physical reaction and collapse. He reminded himself that there was no such thing as yokai or ghosts, they were for children and the superstitious.

As the cars pulled into the taxi stand, he accepted that the old man did say some profound things and the one thing that he really liked was what he mentioned towards the end of their strange encounter: the real monsters are people. He knew that to be true. He did not need to go to Iraq to realize that. It was obvious. If there really were monsters in the world, then the best thing they could do would be to stay out of the way of humanity.

Kato and Honda woke everyone up, and they all groggily climbed out of the cars. The doors were closed and as they slammed, everyone was more awake. Mr. Honda was speaking English with someone in the shadows. Both men laughed a few times. When Honda emerged, he did so with a tall man dressed impeccably in a grey suit. He was thin, with large hands, neatly trimmed hair, and intense eyes. He was Indian.

'This is Mr. Solomon,' said Honda. 'He is an old friend of mine and he will take you to an apartment. You can rest there for as long as you like and tomorrow decide what you would like to do, whether go onto Kyoto or back to Matsushima. We will also know more about the nuclear accident by then.'

Kato walked over to Honda and bowed. 'I deeply appreciate your kindness to us all,' he said. 'I am surprised that you sent a helicopter to fetch me. I am not that important.'

'On the contrary,' replied Honda. 'You are important to your friend Joshua Tree, whom I met just yesterday in Kyoto. As is the priest Ka-chan. On our way to Tokyo, I received a personal call from his grandfather, an old friend of mine, who told me his grandson was in Matsushima. He pleaded with me to take him home if possible.'

'You know the Kawabata family?' asked Lijuan.

'Yes, I do,' replied Honda. 'Kawabata Koichiro is a Tea Master of singular importance in Japan. He is the leader of an important tea ceremony school in Kyoto. Imagine my surprise when you were both together. It saved me two trips.'

Well, thought Kato, that settled it. Ka-chan was the grandson of Kawabata Koichiro and if Miura's information was correct, he had taken over from his grandfather the secretive and deadly profession of assassination. He might be a priest, but he is also an assassin. Kenji was right and he had every reason to be cautious.

Honda and Joshua Tree said goodbye to everyone and got back in their cars. Mr. Solomon came over to Kato and extended his hand. While shaking hands, they introduced each other. The Indian spoke with a very polished upper-class English accent. As Kato found out, he would never speak Japanese in their presence, only English. Mr. Solomon showed Kato to the front seat. Already in the back seat were Wu, Lijuan and Ka-chan.

'I would like to welcome you all to the Kobayashi Corporation,' said Mr. Solomon. 'I am Mr. Kobayashi's personal assistant and tonight I am taking you to one of his apartments in Aoyama, in Tokyo. There you can take a Japanese bath, have some food, and enjoy a good night's sleep.'

'You work for Kiyoshi Kobayashi?' asked Lijuan. 'He is one of Japan's richest men.'

'Allow me to correct you, Ms. Lijuan, he is one of the world's richest men, but yes, I work for Mr. Kobayashi.'

'Solomon-san,' asked Wu. 'How long have you worked for Mr. Kobayashi.'

'Young Mr. Wu, please do not refer to me as Solomon-san, my correct title is Mr. Solomon, only Mr. Solomon. You may of course refer to Mr. Kobayashi as Kobayashi-san.'

'I've heard about you,' said Ka-chan.

'I am surprised that you have,' replied Mr. Solomon. 'I hope you have heard only positive things about me.'

Turning to Wu and Lijuan, Ka-chan said, 'let me introduce you to Mr. Solomon properly. He is perhaps one of the most interesting men you are ever likely to meet in Japan. He is fluent in most languages, including both Cantonese and Mandarin, as well as Japanese and Korean. He holds a black belt in karate among several other martial arts and has written the definite account of the life of the Indian National Army and its leader Subhas Chandra Bose.'

'What was the Indian National Army?' asked Wu.

'They were the army of India on the side of Japan during the war,' interjected Kato. 'They numbered over forty thousand and saw active service from 1942 until the end of the war. Scholars today say that they were partly responsible for the British pulling out of India in 1947.'

'Kato-san is right, and so is Kawabata-san,' said Mr. Solomon. 'It is one of those episodes in the Japan that has been neglected and hopefully, my little treatise might go some way to rebalancing focus. It is more a personal story than a political one, as my grandfather was friends with Subhas Chandra Bose and served in the Indian National Army.'

'Do you have a copy of your book I could borrow?' asked the priest.

'Absolutely,' said Mr. Solomon, quite elated. 'I can certainly give you one if you wish.'

'Where are we heading tonight?' asked Lijuan. 'I don't know Tokyo very well. Wu and I have spent most of our time in Sendai.'

'We are going to Mr Kobayashi's personal apartments in Aoyama in Tokyo, which is near the city of Shibuya. We call it the 'Summer Palace.' It is our little joke. He bought it a few years ago as an investment and to entertain guests in Tokyo. It is near the prestigious United Nations University and Aoyama Gakuin University, Mr.

Kobayashi studied there when he was younger, so he has a sense of nostalgia whenever he visits it.'

'I am actually really quite hungry,' said Lijuan. 'I am sorry, but we have not eaten anything today. I didn't want to mention it.'

'I will prepare something for you. It will not be anything too grandiose I must apologize for that, Mr. Honda only informed me of your visit a few hours ago,'

'I am sure anything will be fine,' said Lijuan.

'How do you know Honda-san?' asked Wu.

'Mr. Honda and Mr. Kobayashi are members of a business committee in Tokyo that provides advice to the Japanese Government from time to time, but he is also very active in what I call the 'Diaspora Community Network,' which is a group of important people who work to improve the position of minorities in Japan. Japan is full of minorities. I am one. I am from India, but more significantly, there are the Korean Japanese, the Ainu, the Burakumin, the so-called 'people of the hamlets,' or the people called the Eta, or the Hinin people, the non-humans. Our group is mainly focused on education. We are concerned that the nuclear radiation from the Fukushima reactor leak might lead to more discrimination, towards people who live near the reactor.'

'Like Hiroshima and Nagasaki in the war,' said Wu.

'Yes, that is right,' replied Mr. Solomon. 'These are all the kinds of issues the Diaspora Community Network looks at. If you are going to stay in Japan, maybe you should visit one of our events.'

'I have never heard of it,' replied Kato.

'It is probably because we do not promote it very well. It was started last year by Mr. Honda.'

'I see,' said Kato, 'Is there a branch of the network in Kyoto?'

'I don't believe so,' said Mr. Solomon, disappointingly. 'Maybe you could start one. There are many people involved in various community organizations interested in helping, but we do not yet, have a coordinator. The position is vacant. Maybe it is something for you to consider Kato-san.'

They soon arrived at the building in Aoyama and Mr. Solomon parked the car underneath in the basement carpark. The little party went to the elevator and got off at the top floor. The doors opened to a lavishly decorated hallway, with a selection of Japanese woodblock prints, or 'ukiyo-e' framed on the wall. At the bottom of the wall was a narrow strip of pebbles that extended from one end of the hall to the other and at regular intervals there were paper lanterns. Mr. Solomon introduced them to a lady in a bright pink kimono, whose name was Takano. Kato was impressed by the cut of the kimono. It was beautifully made. Tamura would have known the brand, he thought to himself.

Mrs Takano explained to them the location of the bathing facilities. There was an indoor pool and an outdoor hot spring on the roof. Mr. Solomon apologized that the water was not actually water from a hot spring, but it did have a beautiful view over Tokyo. Lijuan and Wu said that they had never actually been to a public bath before, so Mrs. Takano explained to them the etiquette of bathing in Japan. They both seem very embarrassed at the idea of bathing together until Lijuan realized that the male and female facilities were separate. She expressed great relief.

When Kato entered the changeroom, he realized he had not bathed in three days. When they arrived in Matsushima on the tenth of March, they arrived late in the afternoon and the hotel they booked in Sendai did not have a hot spring or public bath, so he didn't bathe but took a shower in his room. He let Akiko take his meagre luggage with her to visit her friend as they were planning to check into a nicer hotel on the evening of the following day. He suddenly felt quite filthy and quickly tore off his clothes. Then he wondered what he would change into, but Ka-chan told him that Mrs. Takano was going to provide them with appropriate evening wear for dinner.

Kato walked out into the bath area, found a little wooden stool, and sat down, turning on the hot water from the tap into a round plastic bucket. He did not check the temperature of the water but lifted the bucket and poured it over his back and arms. He let out a loud sigh. The last time he bathed, he had a family. Now, he did not. This large bathhouse made his little bathroom in Kyoto seem incredibly small. He wondered whether he should not have bought a larger place for his family. The bathroom size was the main reason he spent so many visiting the public bath owned by the Itoh family. His wife often went there as well. The only one to really use the bathroom at home was Ai, who, as a young woman was very self-conscious about her appearance and refused to go to the public bath with her mother.

Kato heard Ka-chan slide into the pool behind him and say how wonderful it was. Kato turned to the soap and lathered himself all over, until he was thoroughly covered in white foam. He then turned to the shower tap and soaked himself, including his hair. He then washed his hair keeping his eyes closed, cleaning behind his ears and face until he felt completely purged of sweat, grime, and dirt. He then joined Ka-chan in the pool. It was hot for a public bath and so Kato slid slowly downwards until only his head was above the water. He sensed his body absorbing the heat of the water until he felt incredibly exhilarated. He closed his eyes but saw Akiko's face staring back at him in the void, smiling, so he opened his eyes again and saw the mist rising from the surface. Ka-chan had climbed out of the pool and walked outside onto the roof of the building to the outside baths. There were three large wooden tubs on the roof for the men. Mr. Solomon was right. It afforded a beautiful view of the Tokyo skyline.

When Kato went to join Ka-chan outside, he marvelled at the sights of Tokyo. It did not seem real. He was looking over a bustling, moving, city, full of people, even late at night. Earlier, when the helicopter flew over south Matsushima to the edge of Miyagi Prefecture, Kato could see firsthand the absolute devastation that the tsunami had wrought. They passed over the place where his wife and daughter probably died, and Kato did not feel anything, no sadness or guilt or shame, just a resounding numbness, as if it weren't real. It did not seem possible that the entire city was gone, all those houses and streets and schools and shops and cars. Now, overlooking Aoyama in the late evening, it all seemed too surreal, as if the last two days never happened and that he would wake up the next morning and everything would be back to normal. The wind began to cool him down and so he climbed into the tub next to Ka-chan. They sat in the tubs quietly as the noise of Tokyo could be heard below them.

'Where's the kid?' asked Kato.

'He has gone to bed,' replied Ka-chan. 'He is embarrassed by the idea of men bathing together.'

'I see,' said Kato. Wu was a lot like Ai. She was always very self-conscious about her appearance and did not like the company of too many people. Ai and Wu would have probably got on quite well as friends. They were both intelligent, socially awkward, with intense curiosity for life. Thinking about Ai reminded him that he still had his phone in his coat pocket. The battery had run out but if he could recharge it, then he might be able to find out if his wife or daughter contacted him on the day of the tsunami. He convinced himself that

Mr. Solomon would probably not have the right charger. He dismissed it out of his mind.

'Have you been to China?' asked Ka-chan.

'A few times,' replied Kato. 'Mainly business. Shanghai, Beijing, also Taiwan and Hong Kong.'

'I've never been there.'

'Well, you should take the girl. She obviously likes you, that much is clear.'

Ka-chan got up and lent on the edge of the wooden tub, looking out over Tokyo.

'My grandfather would oppose our marriage,' he said.

'Marriage?' asked Kato, surprised. 'You just met her yesterday; you are not ready to even think about marriage. Why would your grandfather oppose you? Is it because she is Chinese?'

Ka-chan laughed. 'That might be how he would say it, to avoid a real argument, but no, it is because he wants to arrange a marriage for me to the right kind of person, someone who agrees with his world of view, someone to carry on the family business, the tea ceremony.'

Kato had assumed that Ka-chan had a good relationship with his grandfather despite what Abe had said, but the more the man spoke, the more complex their relationship seemed to be.

'My father died when I was young,' said the priest. 'He died in a house fire and the scars I have on my arms and hands, a constant reminder to me of my Father's shame.' He wiped his head with a towel and continued.

'Grandfather always saw my sister and me as a burden and he regretted the death of his own son, my father. He did not really care for my mother. She was from Sendai originally. I am surprised he allowed them to marry in the first place. I suspect grandfather was much more mellow in the past and he has just hardened with age. When my parents died, he was upset that he had to raise two more children. My sister was with friends the night my parents died, but I was there. I did not see what happened to my parents. I was asleep and the first thing I saw was the fire and they were lying nearby, dead. You can imagine what memories I would have as a child. As I result, I was always fighting with the other kids, stealing things and so on.'

'What changed?' asked Kato. 'You are a priest now, and well respected.'

'It was Buddhism that made a real difference to me, gave me purpose and peace when I needed it the most. My grandfather believes in nothing. Well, he believes in himself, and keeps up the appearance of a good Buddhist and a faithful worshipper of Shinto, but it is only on the surface. In practice he is an atheist. What matters is appearance and form, not heart and substance. My sister is like he is, and she, not me, now runs the Tea School. He sees me as too compromised by the world, by which grandfather means Buddhism and compassion for others.

'I had an experience in Arashiyama, at Tenryuji when I was fifteen, around springtime, when the cherry blossoms began to bloom. I was on a hard path at the time, I was always angry, and I had this rage deep within me. It was very self-destructive. I remember sitting on the veranda of the temple looking at the garden. It was quiet in those days. I saw an old man walking slowly along the veranda. He had a cane but even so, it was hard going. He came over to me, sat down and looked at me. He smiled and we looked at the garden together. After a long while, he told me he was a retired priest from around Sendai, and we talked about everything.

'He listened to me, did not judge me, or criticize me. I felt I could tell him anything. I do not know his name and never asked. We said our farewells and he went on his way. We never met again, but when he left, I knew I wanted to be a priest and carry on the work he started. My grandfather opposed my going into the priesthood. My grandfather and I never speak, except to argue or fight over something and he never listened to the cries of pain from a young boy.'

Kato knew that Ka-chan had disclosed very personal details to him, quite unusual for a Japanese man, but they had just lived through the tsunami together and for some reason, Kato felt a closeness to the man as he did with Wu and his friend. They survived tragedy together, just like he had with Joshua Tree, bonds were formed, inexplicable bonds that transcended time. He also felt that Ka-chan was still basically a boy, still in the house fire, lamenting his parents and craving good father figures like the old priest in lieu of poor role models like his grandfather. He was almost certainly the boy he rescued from the house fire. Kato was surprised that Ka-chan had not come out and said it.

'That's why you were in Matsushima,' said Kato. Ka-chan nodded.

'I run a meditation session for some priests in Sendai every year around this time, and that's why I was in Matsushima with Abe. My mother's family are still in the city.'

Ka-chan slid back into the tub.

'Are they ok?' asked Kato.

Ka-chan nodded. 'They live in the mountains,' he said. 'They were fine.'

He lay in the water looking up at the ceiling. 'I think I will go to China with Lijuan,' he blurted out. 'But my grandfather will be angry with me. Lijuan has had difficult years and I think I can help her.'

'It is not a good reason to marry someone,' objected Kato. 'Don't marry her simply to save her. Sometimes people need to save themselves.'

'You sound just like my grandfather,' replied Ka-chan rudely. 'I have made up my mind. Lijuan and I are leaving, just as soon as I can get my visa organized.'

'When will you tell your grandfather?' asked Kato.

'When I am in China,' said Ka-chan.

'Who knows the future?' Kato said. 'Regardless of how bad your relationship is, running away is not the best option, you might not see him again.'

Kato was thinking of his own situation and the fact that his family had died without the chance to say goodbye. But he was genuinely surprised with how cavalier Ka-chan was towards his family, or what was left of it.

'I am not running away, and I don't need a lecture,' said the priest and with that he climbed out of the tub and went back inside. Kato remained in the tub for a long time, thinking. He then got out and wandered to the edge of the balcony and looked out over Tokyo. The sounds had quietened down, but there were still many cars on the road.

Kato went back inside and found that Mr. Solomon had laid out an evening gown or yukata for him to wear and it fit him perfectly. There was also a note from the man which said that if he wished for something to eat, then there would be some food left in a bento box in the dining room. Mr. Solomon had included a little map so Kato would be able to find his way. He felt quite hungry and so he used the map to find the dining room. There were twin doors elaborately designed with flowers and birds which he opened and there was a room from wall to wall with brand-new tatami mats. There were a few tables in the room and three bento boxes in front of three chairs. Lijuan was sitting at one chair waiting for Kato. She looked up at him and smiled. She was wearing a similar evening gown that seemed to fit her perfectly as well.

'I asked how he knew what our size would be?' she said with a smile. 'He said that he had worked out all the measurements as soon as he met us.'

'I am not surprised,' said Kato sitting down. 'I don't think there is anything that escapes that man.'

Lijuan clasped her hands together and picked up her chopsticks.

'I waited for you,' she said, taking off the lid of the bento box. She squealed with delight.

'Oh my,' she said, 'what a beautiful collection of delicacies.'

Kato was not expecting much but what he saw even surprised him. It was almost midnight, but Mr. Solomon had prepared nine neat, separate little morsels of food, each with their own texture, taste, and flavour. The man himself suddenly appeared still wearing his fine suit.

'I apologize for the lack of choice,' he said. 'But I didn't have much time to prepare.'

'No, no, that's perfectly fine,' protested Kato. Lijuan said the same.

'Would you like some beer or wine?' asked Mr. Solomon. They both said they would like some beer. Lijuan waited until Mr. Solomon had left the room and closed the screen doors.

'He wants me to take him to China,' she said suddenly, her eyes hesitant.

Kato put down his chopsticks. 'Do you want to go back with him?'

'I don't know Kato-san, I really don't. I think I love him. He certainly said he loves me. I do not know. Has he said anything to you?'

'You met him yesterday didn't you, at the temple? What do you like about him?'

Lijuan picked up a piece of fish. 'What is this?' she asked.

Kato looked at his small piece of fish still in its little wooden cubicle. 'I think its sea bream actually, with a little batter, like a tempura.'

Lijuan popped it in her mouth. 'He's strong, kind, gentle, very intelligent and he listens to me.'

Kato ate some of his rice, a small pocket of red rice tucked together. 'I really don't know you, or Ka-chan, I don't think it is my place to give you advice on relationships.'

'He really respects you though,' said Lijuan.

'How can he, we only just met,' protested Kato.

'No, he told me that he remembers you, because you were the man who pulled him out of the fire the night his parents died. He recognized you at the temple. He told me that when you met on the bridge, he partly recognized you but couldn't place you anywhere but after the tsunami, in front of the fire, he was looking at me and he told me that it was at this time his mind went back to that night and he remembered your face. It is amazing to think that you saved a young boy from a fire like that Kato-san, it is very impressive.'

Ah, thought Kato, all the pieces of the puzzle have fallen into place. Ka-chan was the young boy he pulled from the flames, and he is the grandson of Kawabata Koichiro. But Ka-chan said that his sister runs the Tea School now and that he and his grandfather are not on speaking terms, so much so that the priest wants to leave Japan with his fiancé and get married in China. Maybe the granddaughter is running the syndicate now, with her grandfather pulling the strings from behind the scenes. It seemed unlikely. It all just seemed too complicated to be true. That man, whom he thought had come to Matsushima to kill him was there for a meditation retreat and to see his mother's relatives and was only alive because Kato had pulled him from a burning house. What possible connection could there be between Kenji and the Kawabata family? There was none. Kenji must have got it wrong.

Kato looked up from his food and at the wall in front of him. The more Kato thought about it, the more he realized that maybe Kenji had been playing him or someone had manipulated his old friend. If Kawabata was hired to do the job of taking out Kenji and killing him, then someone needed to hire him, and that meant someone else was involved, not Miura, not Kawabata, but another party, in the shadows. Kenji did not know about the tsunami. He did not know that Kato would meet Ka-chan. He simply supplied the name Kawabata, and this would have been enough to drive Kato to take revenge for the death of his friend on Kenji's behalf. Driven by anger at the poisoning of his old friend, Kato was going to return to Kyoto and work with his old friend Miura the gangster boss, to take down Kawabata. But Kawabata, even if he was trying to kill him, was only a hired gun and needed to be hired by someone else.

Kato gasped audibly. There was another group out there, or another person, even more secretive, even more in the shadows. That is the group Kenji was involved with and their motives, whatever they were, included wiping out the Kawabata family for their own reasons. Kenji did not ask Kato to help him perform an act of mercy. He was preparing him to be a weapon.

'What are you thinking about?' asked Lijuan noticing that Kato was deep in thought.

Kato smiled. 'I think you should go and visit Kyoto, visit his temple, meet his sister and grandfather, and friends, and gauge how he is with all of them. Then make up your mind about China. You have plenty of time.'

Lijuan looked at him seriously.

'Thank you, Kato-san' she said finally. 'I think that is good advice.'

'Call me Masa,' he said to her. She said that she would. They did not say much for the next half an hour but ate their food quietly. Mr. Solomon came in with some beer and he joined them at the table for a while until Lijuan made her excuses and went to sleep. Kato mentioned to Mr. Solomon about his phone, and so he took the phone and promised that he would get it recharged as soon as possible. He also asked Kato if he wanted to drink some whiskey later. Kato said that would be good and Mr. Solomon drew him a little map so he could easily find the room where they were going to drink whiskey.

Kato had finished his meal and looked around the room. There was a large suit of a samurai warrior in the corner and a vase with some flowers. There was also a hanging scroll with some indecipherable ancient Japanese script on it. There was also a small bookshelf. Kato went over and found Mr. Solomon's book, titled *'Subhas Chandra Bose and early Indian nationalism.'* He took it back to the table and opened it up. It was quite a long book, over four hundred pages and went into detail about the rise and fall of the Indian National Army and its relationship with Japan. He flicked through the text and found that someone had underlined a few passages here and there. The first one caught his eye in the introduction. It read:

'My family's history was the history of the Indian National Army and a desire for independence. They did not hide their allegiance to Japan. After the war, everyone knew their history, everyone knew that allegiance, but it was never spoken about, it was never mentioned, but right to their end, they always believed they were right.'

For some reason, these words seem to make a lot of sense to Kato, but he could not put his finger on it. He thought to ask Mr. Solomon when they had a drink later in the evening. Kato persisted with the book and had reached the fifth chapter when Mr. Solomon arrived with Kato's phone fully charged. He thanked Solomon and then went out of the room and to the roof to get some privacy.

The first message was the one he dreaded. It was from his wife, Akiko. She had called him at 3.35 pm on March 11. He listened to the message. There was only static, some background sounds but nothing more, then silence. He listened to the message again and again. He put the phone on the edge of one of the outdoor wooden bathtubs and went to the railing, looking out over Tokyo. The night was still but many of the buildings still had lights on in their many apartments and businesses. He saw lots of little people doing whatever they did late at night, each with their own lives to lead, their own priorities and aspirations and dreams, their own families, and their own friends. They all lived as if one day merged into the other and little seemed to upset their world. For Kato, his world was over. His family was gone. He was now alone.

He went back to the phone and listened to the other messages. The rest were from his business manager Tamura, who was concerned for his welfare and current whereabouts. He had not thought about his business for a few days. When he left Kyoto, he was aware that his kimono enterprise was in a fragile state, as the demand for high quality kimono had declined dramatically, as people favoured the newer styles and cheaper products. Tamura had urged him for the last few years to incorporate a new line of cheaper kimono, but he had steadfastly refused.

Kato went to the room marked on the map and met Mr Solomon who had just poured two glasses of whiskey. The two men talked long into the early hours of the morning, mainly about Solomon's book, which Kato continued to read long after the Indian had retired for the night. It was about five in the morning when Kato's eyelids finally felt quite heavy, and he fell asleep briefly with his head on the table.

In Kato's dream, he found himself at home, sitting at the small table in his kitchen. His wife was sitting across from him, with her Bible open, next to a half-empty cup of coffee. Kato was surprised to see her.

'What are you doing here?' he asked her. Akiko laughed.

'What am I doing here? I live here!' she said in a loud voice. 'Husband!' she called out. Kato turned around on his chair and saw

Kenji standing in the entrance, next to Ai, his daughter. Both their faces were stern.

'What is he doing here?' asked his daughter, pointing at Kato. Kenji shrugged his shoulders.

'You don't belong here!' his daughter accused him. 'Look!' she said and pointed to his legs. Kato looked and he was still wearing his shoes. They were covered with mud. He had not taken them off when he entered the house. Kato bowed to them apologizing profusely.

'He did not even take off his shoes!' said his daughter.

'He did not even take off his shoes!' repeated his wife.

When she came forward, Kato looked down and saw that she had no feet. He stood up and looked at Kenji. He had no feet either. He turned around to see his wife rising off her seat and hover above the table. Her body seemed to disappear around the waist and her hair had grown longer, dangling over her thin shoulders. Her face faded and became a lantern in the dark, with long gaping eyes. The lantern split near the bottom and this split became a mouth with teeth.

Kato pushed his way past them and into the corridor, trying to find the front door. He reached the entrance, stepped down and opened the door. Suddenly, a wall of mud burst into the entrance of the home, spilling into the hallway, knocking Kato off his feet. He fell back onto the floor.

'He brought the mud with him,' he heard his wife say from behind.

'How thoughtless of him,' Kenji added.

'Such selfishness!' murmured his daughter.

Kato closed the door as best he could and in so doing preventing mud from entering the house. He returned and pushed his way past the spectres of his family and Kenji who were waiting for him in the kitchen, and he staggered outside to the courtyard. It too was deep in mud. Ka-chan was playing cards on the veranda but every time he threw down a card it vanished underneath the mud. Kato turned around to see Abe the priest.

'Would you like some death?' he asked, holding up an iron pot. 'I just brewed some.'

Ka-chan called out to him. 'Death for me!' he said. 'Kenji wants death too. In fact, death for everyone!' Kenji smiled and waved to Kato.

Behind him, Kato sensed something dark and sinister. It was the sound of a man clapping slowly. He peered around the entrance of his house to see an old man standing on the other side of the fence. It was Yamaguchi. His skin was pale, and he had long hair down to his ankles.

'Don't stand out there,' insisted Kato. 'Please come in.'

'I am already here Kato,' said the man. 'I will not be leaving for a long time.'

'I don't remember inviting you,' said Kato.

'You didn't,' said the man. Kato looked and Yamaguchi's eyes turned jet black.

The old man opened the gate and then put his hands onto Kato's shoulders. He looked down and realized the hands had become huge claws and the talons were digging into his skin. His teeth grew sharp, and Kato could smell rotting flesh. A voice told him that he would soon find that hidden room deep in his mind, the one with the chains and all he needed was a key.

Kato woke up from his nightmare to find Lijuan shaking him. Wu was with her. He was telling everyone how wonderful the outside baths were on the roof of the building. Solomon and Ka-chan were enjoying a cup of coffee on another table. He rubbed his eyes and realized that it was morning.

10

Kato looked out of the window in the carriage of the bullet train from Tokyo to Kyoto. He looked out at the landscape whizzing past, all blurred, images caught in his mind only to be replaced by others. The further he looked away, the clearer his vision became. He could see rice fields in the distance, cut in half by thin roads crisscrossing the landscape. A young boy on a bicycle rode off towards the hill and he could see a small stone statue, covered by a wooden roof. The train went past small villages tucked between hills, passed in an instant, lives lived out of sight, through narrow mountain ravines, only gaining a glimpse of mountains few climb and deep forests, darkened by the canopy. Kato glanced at the man in the seat beside him, fast asleep, his head back on the seat and snoring. It was Ka-chan, or Kawabata's grandson. Next to him, at the window seat was young woman, fast asleep.

Earlier in the day both men decided that they needed to return to Kyoto. Kato had to return to work and Ka-chan was needed back at his temple. Solomon had kindly offered to take Wu and Lijuan around Tokyo for a day or two and they happily agreed. Solomon told Kato and Ka-chan privately that both Wu and Lijuan had suffered a traumatic experience in Matsushima and that a positive time in Tokyo would do them a lot of good. Ka-chan and Lijuan had agreed to meet up again in Kyoto in a few days and she insisted on meeting

Kawabata's family. Ka-chan, for his part would not elope from Japan but would face his grandfather and introduce Lijuan to him. Kato was glad that Lijuan would be respected in this way.

After listening to the empty phone message from Akiko the night before, Kato was more certain that his family was dead. It still did not feel real to him, even though his mind told him that it was. He would not be seeing them again. He kept his personal feelings about the matter hidden from view. A more pressing matter, one that was on the minds of everyone, was the fallout from the nuclear accident at the reactor in Fukushima. The explosion had shocked everyone, comfortable in their extensive reliance on nuclear power as the basis for the nation's energy supply. The media and the general population quickly made parallels with the atomic blasts of Hiroshima and Nagasaki.

Japan feared a radiation cloud that would mix with the rain, people feared association with anyone who might have lived near the reactor, people feared further explosions at the reactor, and they feared the impact of the radiation on their national food supply. Had the tsunami only destroyed towns and villages along the northern coast of Japan, it might have been different. There would have been an outpouring of grief and support for those who died, those who survived and those who were left homeless. The tsunami and earthquake triggered a meltdown at a large nuclear facility and this catastrophic event threatened the entire nation and future of Japan.

It was difficult to get a seat to Kyoto because the trains were full of families trying to head as far south as they could, in fear of the radiation spewing from the Fukushima reactor. Despite government assurances that all would be well, foreign experts and the response of foreign embassies said otherwise. Foreign nationals were fleeing northern Japan as quickly as possible, and some embassies encouraged pulling their entire presence out of the country altogether. The Prime Minister of Japan had made a hasty trip to the site of the accident dressed in overalls and a flimsy dust mask along with chants of reassurance, but this meant little to the Japanese, fed up with decades of deceit and deception from the national government. With the nuclear disaster, thousands of people were on the move, most heading south to Tokyo. It was only March 13 but already fear was beginning to grip Tokyo's middle classes, and many began to believe that they could catch radiation from those who might have been exposed to it.

Most of the people on the train were from parts of Tokyo, mainly women with small children and older couples. The men had stayed behind. Kato and Ka-chan were just two more faces in the crowd of anxious people. Each had the same fears simmering in their hearts while striving to stay calm. Kato could see the strain in their faces, with their tired children asleep in their arms. More people seemed irritable and anxious, more aggressive, and less polite. Few spoke, but most were thinking the same thing.

Kato had bathed several times in Kobayashi's outdoor wooden tubs but did not feel completely clean. He could not understand why he felt this. He was deeply disturbed that he did. His mind kept taking him to the dirty kokeshi doll he found in the mud and how he tried to clean her face, leaving her on the table. He wondered whether rescuers in Sendai would find his wife and daughter in the mud and be forced to lift them up and wipe the mud from their faces or were they washed out to sea? He scrubbed every part of his body and washed his hair several times. He filed his nails and cleaned them, washed his ears, and shaved until he removed the last bristle from his chin and showered several times before he felt able to sit in the public bath and soak his body. But even then, he still felt filthy, as if he stank of death. He didn't think that it was because he killed Kenji. Rather, it was because he had survived, and he felt shame that he did.

Kato and Ka-chan boarded the train with only moments to spare. Kato looked outside. The platform was full of people, and it was quite unlike anything he had ever seen. Tokyo trains were known to be very crowded around New Years, but this was different. He had never seen so many people. Mr Solomon had bought two tickets for them in one of the reserved cars, for which they were grateful. They would not have found a seat otherwise.

On the way to the train, Kato bought a rice ball wrapped in dried seaweed, which he tucked into his pocket. By habit his eyes began to search the souvenir stalls lined along the railway corridor for his wife's favourite sweet from Tokyo, *'Tokyo Banana.'* He had even reached into his pocket for cash when he stopped himself. He let the cash fall out of his fingers back into the depths of his pocket and politely apologized to the vendor. He usually bought a large can of beer and some nuts but could not bring himself to buy them on this occasion. One rice ball would be enough for the journey.

Kato fell asleep briefly, his mouth opening but he found himself snoring and woke up suddenly, bumping Ka-chan who woke up as well. Kato rubbed his eyes and stared up. A face of a child looked down at him, peering over from the seat in front of him. His little eyes opened and closed quickly as if he had just woken up and wanted to eat. The boy said nothing. Kato reached into his pocket, pulled out the rice ball and offered it to him. The boy smiled, took it, and disappeared.

'You are kind,' said the child's mother who turned around to see Kato. She took the rice ball and unwrapped it for her son. Seated next to her on the aisle seat was an older woman, obviously her mother or mother-in-law.

'Where are you heading?' asked Kato.

'Kyushu' said the older lady. 'We want to get as far as possible away from Fukushima. We already have radiation poisoning.'

'Were you at the reactor?'

'No, of course not, we live in Tokyo but now the poison is in the air, and we have to get away.'

'I think you will be fine,' piped up Ka-chan who overheard what she said.

'Don't be ridiculous!' retorted the woman. 'Everyone in Tokyo has been contaminated, the food, the water, the trees, everything.'

Kato was surprised at her aggressive voice. He didn't know what to say.

'Spare a thought for those poor people who live near the reactor,' insisted Ka-chan, 'Imagine how they are feeling.'

'Don't get me started on those people,' said the woman.

'It was an accident,' said Kato.

'It doesn't matter,' she said. 'Those people are contaminated. They should have stayed up there to die. Instead, they travel everywhere and bring their poison with them.'

'I don't understand,' said Kato. 'They cannot stay near the reactor – they must move.'

'Yes. But as I said, they are all contaminated with radiation poisoning so they should be forced to stay there. Instead, they bring their diseased bodies to Tokyo so they can kill us too.'

'You cannot catch 'radiation,'' insisted Ka-chan. 'It might get into the food supply due to the ground water or rain but if a person from Fukushima turned up in this carriage, we would not catch radiation from them.'

'Rubbish!' retorted the woman. 'Don't you remember after the war. There were those people from Hiroshima and Nagasaki: they were poisoned, and they contaminated people.'

'That is not true,' interjected a man from across the aisle.

'Rubbish!' insisted the woman, speaking more loudly. 'They will pollute Japan. If they have any sense of honour, they should stay up in Fukushima and die quietly.'

The man across the aisle spoke again. 'There are children here woman – you are scaring them – please be quiet.'

This surprised her. She felt embarrassed. Even her daughter told her to be quiet and she apologised to everyone, saying that her mother was just upset. Everyone in the carriage was looking at them. Most of the faces were angry, sad, and upset. The woman began to slip back to her seat when an older man came in from the next carriage.

'What is going on here?' he asked.

'Are you alright?' he asked the woman.

'My husband,' she indicated to everyone in the carriage.

'Please tell your wife to calm down,' said the man across the aisle. 'She is scaring the children with her talk of radiation.'

The man looked at him angrily as if he were about to start a fight. His brow was furrowed, and he did not want to stand there and hear people criticize his wife. His stare began to make people feel anxious.

'Just sit down please,' said Kato quietly. 'Let us have some peace.'

'No one tells me what to do,' retorted the man. 'My wife has a right to express her opinion.'

'Your wife is a fool,' said Kato. 'If you agree with her, so are you.'

'How dare you!' said the man pushing past Ka-chan and grabbing Kato by the collar. Kato brought his arms up between the man's hands and freed himself. Kato rose from his seat and punched the man in the face. The man stumbled back across the legs of the priest and onto a crumpled heap in the aisle, his nose broken, and bloodied. Trying to get up, he knocked into the man seated on the other side of the aisle, his coffee spilling onto his lap and his open bento box was thrown onto the floor. The seated man angrily pushed the old man off him and onto the floor of the train and cursed him.

Ka-chan got up and pushed past Kato offering the man some assistance, which he declined. It was clear that the nose had been broken and he had blood all over his shirt. Everyone in the carriage saw what had happened and were just stunned by the turn of events.

Whatever bravado the grandfather had was gone but he felt ashamed and left the carriage as soon as possible, quickly followed by his wife who kept calling after him. She turned around and looked at Kato in disgust. Kato turned his face away. He looked at the young mother holding her child who was quietly eating the rice ball. He fell back into his seat and covered his face with his hands.

It was not long before one of the train guards came and asked Kato to leave the carriage and spend the rest of the trip standing up between the carriages with those who could not get a seat. Ka-chan decided to join him. They said nothing to each other the rest of the journey. When the train pulled into Kyoto, the guard came out and looked seriously at Kato and then spoke to the priest probably because he was dressed like one and looked respectable.

'Tell your friend to stay out of trouble. It is a difficult time, and many people are suffering. That is why we need people to stay calm.'

'I understand,' said Ka-chan, as the door opened. Kato said nothing. On the platform, there were two uniformed officers waiting for him. Kato bowed to the train officer and alighted. The door closed behind Ka-chan.

'This way please,' said one of the officers and they walked to the centre of the platform as the train departed.

'Your wallet please,' said one of the officers. Kato reached into his pocket and pulled it out and handed it over. The officer found a few credit cards and a business card. He was about to hand it over when another man turned up and grabbed it from the officer's hand. The uniformed officer turned and bowed deeply to the new man. Kato recognised him immediately. It was Fujita. He was smoking a pipe. He flicked through the wallet and then turned to Kato.

'Please wait over here,' he said to Kato and Ka-chan and continued to talk with the uniformed officers. They treated the man with sincere deference, bowing frequently. Kato was unsure of what was happening, but it seemed that he may have been in considerable trouble, and he felt embarrassed for striking the passenger and he was ashamed of his entire behaviour.

But Kato could not abide her attitude and was shocked that she held to it. Within days of the reactor accident, people would be turned away from hotels because they came from Fukushima. Hotels would throw away towels and night kimonos used by these people out of fear, and rooms fumigated after their departure. People would leave restaurants when they heard the distinctive dialect from Fukushima.

Kato was appalled by this irrational prejudice, though he had his own. He was quintessentially Japanese. He was a rationalist, but if he had any faith, he was devoted to Shintoism, often seen as the native religion of the Japanese. He had little time for Buddhism, though he respected the priests and their devotion. He held a deep and abiding dislike of the United States because of the carpet bombing of civilian targets during the War, and the atomic bombs dropped on Nagasaki and Hiroshima. At the same time, he respected and admired Joshua Tree. He thought it strange that the U.S. marines were willing to walk into harm's way to help the Japanese, but so many Japanese it seemed, were so afraid to even touch those who lived in the north. Kato glanced at the clock on the wall. It was almost midnight. Fewer and fewer passengers were on the platforms, though the arriving trains spilled out with more and more people their faces drained and tired.

Suddenly, the three police officers laughed out loud and the two uniformed officers left leaving Fujita behind. There was a reason he was the most respected detective in the region. He played the part perfectly. He looked dismissively at Ka-chan who had sat on the bench quietly reading Solomon's book while Kato fidgeted and worried.

'Ah, Mr. Kato,' said Fujita. 'You have wasted so much of our time today. You should be ashamed of yourself, especially during this time, with so many more important things going on around here.'

'We know each other,' said Kato. 'I have spoken with you before.'

The detective just looked at him with no expression on his face. 'And that means what exactly? Who cares?'

Kato tried to stand up, but the man told him to stay seated. He continued. 'As you know, everyone is very emotional. It is a difficult time. All we ask is that people respect each other and avoid disagreement. The arguments only start because of the events in Tohoku. Today we have had to respond to many issues related to this and everywhere it is the same. People are on edge. People are tired. People are upset. People do not have all the information they need and so they rely on hearsay and rumour. This is unacceptable but what do you expect?'

He sighed and put his hands in his coat pocket. 'Do you have a cigarette?'

'I don't smoke.'

'Well, if you did, maybe you would not be so stressed and maybe we wouldn't be here having this conversation.'

Kato said nothing.

The officer scratched the back of his head and readjusted his glasses. 'We don't have an official complaint yet, but this may yet come through tomorrow or the next day. If it does, we may have to pursue this matter further. It is unfortunate as you know because we are so busy with other more pressing matters.'

Kato tried to speak, but the officer cut him short.

'Don't say anything, I'm not finished.'

Kato was silent.

'Don't punch anyone else.'

'I'm truly sorry,' replied Kato, standing, and bowing deeply.

'I doubt it,' retorted Fujita. 'You probably feel pleased with yourself for striking the other man. No doubt he deserved it, but you crossed the line. Our society is based on rules. They are there for a reason. Sometimes children make mistakes because they are too young to know the rules. You are not. You are an adult. Behave like one. You say you know me. I do not recall the occasion. Were you busy hitting someone else that time as well?'

He did not give Kato any time to respond.

'My name is Fujita, and I am a senior detective inspector in Kyoto. I have much more important things to do than attend to adults who behave like spoilt children. Don't waste my time again.'

The man looked at Ka-chan who was still politely reading Solomon's book.

'A good read?' asked the detective. Ka-chan nodded. He walked off puffing on his pipe.

'Well,' said Ka-chan. 'I'm off home. It has been fun Kato-san,' he murmured sarcastically.

Kato felt embarrassed. 'At least you got to read Solomon's book.'

Ka-chan looked at it. 'I think I will hold onto it for a while if that is alright,' he said. 'Lijuan and Peter are coming to Kyoto in two days so I will drop it at your shop if that suits you.'

Kato nodded. Both men walked down the steps to the ticket area and the entrance. To his amazement, Tamura his manager, was waiting for him.

'Tamura!' he exclaimed. 'It is after midnight. What are you doing here?'

Tamura ran forward and bowed. 'It is very good to see you again boss,' said Tamura, bowing repeatedly.

'There is no need for that,' implored Kato, grabbing his shoulder and pulling him over for a hug. Kato turned to Ka-chan.

'This is Ka-chan, or Kawabata Sensei,' said Kato.

Tamura bowed deeply.

'I am Tamura,' he said.

'Nice to meet you Tamura-san,' said Ka-chan. 'Well Kato, it seems you are in good hands. I will return to my temple. No doubt we will meet again.'

He bowed to Kato and Kato reciprocated. The priest walked off. Kato turned to Tamura.

'It is good to be back in Kyoto,' he said.

'I will get you home,' insisted Tamura.

'I cannot go home,' said Kato. 'Don't take me home.'

Tamura looked at him not entirely sure of his reasoning, but he consented.

'Alright, I will take you to the office. It is not comfortable, but it is the best I can do at such short notice.'

'It will be fine Tamura.'

'We will get a taxi,' indicated Tamura and led the way to the left, down the escalator.

'Do you know a detective by the name of Fujita?' asked Kato.

'Fujita? Yes, he is a detective. He investigated us when young Maya disappeared.'

'I thought so.'

'Why do you ask about Fujita?' asked Tamura, just as the next available taxi pulled into the curb, its door opening wide.

'I met him on the platform tonight.'

'Oh, I see. By the way, where are your family? Are they on a different train?'

'They are dead. They were killed in the tsunami.'

Tamura did not say anything and struggled with the right words but could not come up with any and so remained silent.

11

It was about one in the morning of March 13 when the taxi arrived at Kato's kimono shop on the corner of one of Kyoto's busiest streets. Tamura gave Kato the keys to the shop while he went to buy some food from the convenience store. At that time in the night, there were still a few people on the streets going home from work. It was just another night for them. They might have known about the tsunami and the earthquake, but it did not affect them. He heard a couple arguing with each other about the meal they had just eaten, and an old man walked past with his dog, out for an evening stroll. It just seemed too surreal. Kato looked up and down the wide streets. They were immaculate and free from rubbish and debris, straight and long, fading off into the distance.

Kato opened the door and entered his shop. It seemed strange to walk through the door. The room was dark, but he could sense the kimono in the windows and in the frames and on the shelves, a myriad of colours all welcoming him back again. Oh, how he had missed them! He was surprised that he felt this way. When he left to go to see Kenji, the shop was just a shop, and the business was simply a business. It was not that he was disinterested in his work. It just held no real passion for him. He had inherited the kimonos but had inherited no love for them. He worked out of a sense of obligation, first not only for his brother's relatives and the other members of the family but also for the honour of his family name. He fell back into the kimono business only after he was forced out of the army. He left the business under a cloud, returned under a cloud, and tried to make up for lost time in the only profession that would take him.

Tamura always kept the lights dimmed and never put the shutters down like most shops did. It was his decision. He was like that. It was one of his strange and peculiar habits. He said that the kimono was part of a person, and that to treat the kimono as an object was to do them some damage. He said that just as a woman goes to bed and turns out the light so the kimonos should rest at night and not be disturbed. When night fell, Tamura would dim the lights slightly and as the night progressed towards closing time his assistant would gradually turn out all the lights until darkness consumed the shop. He treated the kimono with such reverence that Kato felt that he might have been having a love affair with them. He refused to roll down the shutters at night because he said that the kimono needed something to look out on at night and they would need the sun to wake up in the morning.

Kato tip-toed through the shop and out to the back rooms. Tamura left most of the establishment immaculate, except for a few storerooms. Behind the shop front and desks and change rooms was a long corridor floored with tatami mats and walled with wooden beams, dating back a few centuries. Kato's office was on the right and behind that was a small kitchen. On the left were several rooms that were used to store kimonos and other items. Towards the back of the property were a few other, older rooms, including a few family rooms that housed the family memorial tablets, an old bathroom and a rarely used storeroom that Kato used to put old fabrics, tools, and old stock.

The corridor continued until it reached the end which was a final room that led out to the older part of the building and an access road. A toilet and another bathroom were at the back next to a small garden which had long fallen into disuse. Most of the merchandise was brought through the front of the shop so the back rooms were rarely used. The shop was not the only property owned by the Kato family. They had other buildings in the textile district of Kyoto, a museum that was open to the public and several warehouses and workshops all over Japan but most of them were unused.

Kato was still standing in the dimmed light with the kimono when Tamura arrived. 'Don't they look beautiful tonight?' he asked, running his fingers gently up one of the silk kimonos in the front window.

He smiled at the kimono, gently caressing it. Then he stopped and smiled his embarrassingly creepy smile and told Kato that he had already made preparation in an event his boss wanted to stay overnight. In the third room to the right, behind the shop front, in one of the rooms for hanging kimono a futon bed was laid out on the floor. Tamura motioned to the cupboard and Kato saw that he had placed some extra shirts and a suit. This thoughtfulness touched Kato, and he found a tear rising in his eye. Tamura went and boiled a pot for some tea and told him that he would prepare some rice and miso soup if he wanted it. After he did this, he bowed politely to his boss and left for the night, leaving Kato alone in the room surrounded by the hanging kimono.

Kato could smell the rice in the rice cooker and the miso soup was still warm, though he could heat it up if he wanted. The rice had a good aroma. He returned to the room with the futon, his new bedroom and put the straw pillow in place. He turned on the heater on the wall, took off his coat, tie and shirt and lay down on the futon. He suddenly felt exhausted and fell asleep.

He woke up shortly afterwards in a hot sweat. His mind was a jumble. He could not remember any nightmares, but he felt queasy. He looked at the clock on the wall. He had barely been asleep for an hour. It seemed like an eternity. He pulled himself off the futon and onto his feet. He went into the kitchen and washed his face, drying it with a towel. The miso soup had gone cold, but the rice was still warm.

He had a craving for a bottle of sake even though it was about 2 am. Akiko would not have approved, and she didn't allow alcohol in the house. She wanted to set a good example for Ai-chan. Kato usually kept a supply in the shop. He opened the cupboard and tried to find one of the many glass jars of sake that Tamura usually kept there. They were gone. He reached down over to some other cupboards as he thought that he kept at least one bottle of rice wine there, but there was nothing.

Kato decided to go to the convenience store down the street, so he put on his shirt again, grabbed his jacket, put on some wooden sandals, walked into the shop front again past the silent kimono and left the store. He locked the door. The evening was cool, and his feet felt the chill, but he turned right and began to walk down the street.

There was no one on the street that night as it was three o'clock in the morning. He reached the first cross street and walked across the road when the light was red. As soon as his feet touched the other side of the footpath, he realized someone else was walking on the street with him, a few feet behind. He turned around instinctively, and it was a man. He was middle aged, dressed quite normally as if he had also just stepped out of his house or apartment. Kato paid him no more attention and continued to walk to the store.

When he arrived, the light of the convenience store almost blinded him as did the many colours of the processed food, magazines, and drinks. He pushed through the door and greeted the store clerk, who was an overweight, pimpled man in his forties wearing glasses. He was sweeping the floor with a mop. A few moments later the other man also entered the shop and mumbled a greeting to the clerk, walking over to the fresh food and bento box section of the store on the far wall, right past Kato who was eyeing the selection of cup noodles nearest the counter.

There was a time in his life when he lived on cup noodles, thought Kato. In those days, while he was a student, there was far less selection than there was now. His wife had told him to stop eating them because she read of a man who died after eating only cup noodles for a month. Kato responded by saying that if you ate only one thing for a month, anything at all, it would probably kill you. His eyes scanned, tomato flavour, chili flavour, seafood flavour, curry flavour and he settled on curry. He had suddenly lost all taste for sake and just wanted to have some cup noodles. He went to the counter and put down the exact number of coins for the cup noodles, ripped off the wrapping, tore back the paper lid, added the powder, placed the container under the hot water jug and filled it to the brim.

The clerk who had returned to the counter, pointed to the disposable chopsticks and Kato took a pair, pressed it out of its wrapping, snapped it in two and shoved them violently into the boiling soup, stirring vigorously. He tossed away the wrappings into the nearest bin and stepped outside, standing in front of the store bins, on the small driveway behind the footpath. As he began to slurp in the noodles, he turned around to see what had happened to the other man.

On the train from Tokyo to Kyoto he had finally put to rest the final remnant of Kenji's theory, that the Kawabata family were responsible for his old friend's poisoning. There had been plenty of opportunities for Ka-chan the priest to strike but he didn't, and he gave very credible reasons for being in Matsushima. It couldn't be

Miura, but it could also not be Ka-chan or his grandfather. The one behind everything must be someone else.

While he was thinking this, it occurred to him that it was strange for this man to appear from nowhere and follow him to the convenience store. As he gazed into the store, the man was gone. He was nowhere to be seen. Perhaps he was out of view or using the facilities, so Kato felt a little more reassured. He finished his noodle soup and tossed it into the bin from where he was standing. The remainder of the noodles and soup splattered on the lid of the bin as it crashed through.

He was about to leave when the man appeared in the window reading a magazine. Kato swore to himself that this man had been staring in his direction, watching him. He of course was incredibly tired, and it could well have been a typical man in Kyoto out for a stroll at three in the morning wanting to read a magazine. It was quite possible. Tamura was not the only one with unusual habits. Japan was full of men like Tamura. But it still made him feel uneasy and so he decided to leave. Instead of walking back to his shop the same way, Kato decided to take a different route. He crossed the main street which was at this time devoid of any cars and walked to the other side of the road. When he got to the other side of the road, he heard the doors of the convenience store open and turned to see the man walk to the edge of the road looking both ways. He began to take up a position behind Kato.

There was no doubt about it. He was being followed. Kato began to walk along the main street towards his shop. He was about three minutes away on foot. The man was behind him and getting closer. He had two choices. He could make a run for it, or he could confront the man and see what he wanted. Kato did not run from anyone, so he turned around to face the man. This surprised the other man who stopped in his tracks looking at Kato.

Neither man said anything. The night was still. There were no cars, no pedestrians, and no sounds.

'What do you want?' Kato called out roughly.

The man said nothing but reached into his jacket and pulled out a knife.

'Who sent you?' Kato called out.

The man said nothing but ran towards him lunging with his knife. Kato did not move until the last moment and then stepped aside, letting the man rush past. Using his right elbow, he brought it down hard on the man's back as he passed, forcing him to the ground. Kato did not let him get up but kicked him in the stomach, forcing him to drop his knife and curl up in pain.

'Who sent you?' shouted Kato again.

By this stage, the door to the convenience store had opened and the clerk had come out looking over in concern. Kato said nothing to him. It looked from that distance that Kato may have knocked over the man and was responsible for this incident. Kato looked furiously in the direction of the clerk and hoped that the man would do nothing. As suspected, the man, turned around, distracted by something in the store and disappeared. Kato walked over to his attacker who was staggering to his feet and knocked him down again, kicking him violently in the stomach. The man groaned loudly in pain and began to vomit.

'If you want to live, don't follow me,' said Kato, who turned his back on the man and walked back to his shop. When he arrived, he made sure to lock the door. He sat down near the entrance, behind one of the desks and waited. It seemed like a long time had passed and there was no sound at the door which must have meant that the person who followed him had decided to give up, or it was possible, quite possible that he lay in wait for Kato just outside or that he lurked at the back of the store.

When he thought this, Kato decided to go and to check the back door and see if it had been disturbed. He went to the desk and pulled out a small torch. He passed the hallway and the rooms for kimono storage, the offices, and finally the other rooms of the shop until he came to a small, almost insignificant room at the end of the corridor. The sliding door was closed, and dust covered the handle. Kato stopped there for a moment and continued to the end of the store, walked down onto the dirt floor, and put on some sandals and went to the old wooden door. Fortunately, it was also locked. It had not been open for some time, the bolts and chain still intact but gathering dust and rust. It was sometimes used, but not often.

He sat down on the veranda. As a boy, he remembered playing on the veranda among the boxes as his father and grandfather discussed kimono with other merchants. He could still recall the smell of new kimonos and the smell of fabrics. It was all quiet now. Kato looked back down the corridor. The shop seemed secure.

For some reason, he thought it might be time to look at what was in the room of junk. He could not sleep and so it made sense to do some cleaning. It was in fact his father's old office. Kato turned on the light. It was very bright. He had not been into this room for a long time. It was full of old boxes, unwanted silks, frayed sashes, discoloured cloth, and torn kimono. The air smelt slightly damp and musty. Not even Tamura with his dedicated efficiency went into this room. It had not always been this way. When Kato was young, it was his father's meeting room. His brother, Ryo, inherited the room when he took over the business from their parents and until his death it was where the kimono was sorted. Beneath the boxes, the pile of old kimono and beyond the smell was a long, polished desk made of the best cedar. On the desk everything lay intact the day his brother died. Kato left it as it was: his watch, his diary, his coffee cup, and his pencils. Nothing was disturbed.

Kato was sitting by the river that ran through the heart of Kyoto the day he received news of his brother's heart attack. He ran to the kimono shop only to find the ambulance taking out the body. He had dropped dead due to stress, death by overwork, pulled down by generations of extreme dedication, a fragile economy and stiff competition. Out of respect, Kato felt that he could not move into this office and so kept it as he found it, except for one drawer where he placed a few items from his old life from time to time.

Unlike the rest of his family, Kato was not a hoarder. The only thing he valued was family and they were gone. There were the many associated relatives, but he rarely saw them. Beyond his family, the rest of his life was found hidden away in one drawer in his father's old desk. He had forgotten about his old life, those days, those friends, those experiences. He had been a soldier until 2006, and then a kimono merchant. Kato bent down and lifted a wooden box. It was light and soft to touch, and it seemed to contain a kimono. Kato threw it over his shoulder and the box cracked against the door, falling to the ground. Kato reached for another box and then another. Each went over his shoulder, some landing in the hallway, some bashed against the wall and others landing just behind him.

Perspiration began to appear on his brow but still he continued relentlessly. He was soon knee deep in kimono, silk, and sashes, their many colours tangled between his ankles, as if awash in a sea of clothes. It was then that he could see the edge of the cedar desk and his heart lifted. He lent forward and with great effort pushed an entire pile of boxes to the floor until he could reach the drawers. He pulled out the top drawer but it was empty and so it ended up on top of the kimono. The second drawer was more promising. As he pulled it out, a sigh of relief washed over him, and tears came to his eyes.

He pulled the drawer out entirely and placed it on the top of the desk. His eyes had sighted something familiar: a small wooden box, ornately carved with small animals. He had picked it up when he was in Thailand with his two oldest school friends, Kenji, and Masao Okubo a few months following their graduation from university. He had made it his box of special and precious things and therein were secrets he had hidden even from his wife.

He opened the box. On top were some papers which he gently placed to one side along with some envelopes. Underneath them were some photographs. He held the first up to the light. The scene was a younger Kato surrounded by his comrades in his army unit posted to Iraq. There was Sakae, the manga maniac from Komatsu in Kanazawa, Kono the fisherman from Yamanashi, Katsu, the actor from Kyoto, Satake the musician from Sendai and of course Masayoshi Kato. They were all dressed in military uniform with the harsh Iraqi climate behind them. He realized this photo was taken a month before he was forced to leave the Self-Defence Force. The smile which had appeared on his face soon evaporated. Kato wondered what had happened to all his old friends, the men who knew him the most. He had heard Sakae returned to Komatsu and Satake was pursuing a career as a saxophonist, but he had lost touch with the others. Kato sighed deeply and placed the photo on the desk.

Kato tried to disentangle himself from the kimono, but he tripped and fell headlong into the sea of silks. With great difficulty he managed to pull himself free from the knots and ties and grabbing the frame of the door, pulled himself out into the corridor.

When Kato woke, he was back on the futon and there were people in the shop. Tamura must have disentangled him from the kimono and somehow dragged him back to the futon while he was half asleep. It was March 14. He could hear their voices down the corridor. Close to the edge of his bed was a polished saucer made from the bark of a cherry tree with a thin white ceramic cup of hot green tea. Nestled next to the cup were two cinnamon cakes. Kato was touched by Tamura's devotion. He sipped the tea. Tucked up under the saucer of cherry bark was a schedule for the day's activities, some of them past. He placed down the schedule and the next thing he knew was that it was after five in the afternoon. He had not slept well but continued to toss and turn. He woke up staring at the ceiling. He rummaged in his pockets and found a few coins amounting to one thousand yen. Tamura appeared at the doorway.

'I can make some tea if you like,' he said politely. Kato said he did not need any but would be going out for dinner down the street. He got to his feet, gathered the small change and then realized he needed more money. Tamura was happy to oblige and in total he ended up with about ten thousand yen. He stuffed this into his pockets and after finding a coat in the cupboard made his way out of the store.

'Excuse me sir, before you go,' spoke Tamura gently. Kato looked back his face drained.

'Tomorrow morning first thing we have a few important clients coming in. Everything is arranged but it would be nice if you dropped in for some words of welcome. We also need to have a talk about the finances.'

Kato nodded and walked out of the shop onto the street, leaving Tamura behind holding the inventory. He passed Ms. Sasaki, his secretary, who was closing for the day. She bowed and said goodnight, but Kato said nothing.

Sasaki looked anxious. 'Do you think he will be alright?' she asked.

Tamura's expression was strained, and he did not reply. Instead, he tucked the inventory under his arm and returned to his office. He walked down the hall to the end of the corridor and his eyes widened in horror when he remembered the mess Kato had made the night before. He sighed deeply, mumbling to himself about how much time it would take to put everything away.

12

Kato did not notice the crowds of people walking past him or the bright lights of the department store across the street. He turned right and kept walking until he saw the sign of his favourite bar. There was a mask of the mountain yokai or monster on the door, the Tengu, with his bulging eyes and huge red nose. He looked at the mask for a moment and laughed. He was right. These yokai belonged on the walls of pubs and in children's stories, but nowhere else. They were figments of the imagination, invented by powerful people to ensure compliance to their rigorous religious rules. Kato descended the steps, each foot bringing him deeper into the traditional inn that was sunken between buildings on either side. If you were walking past and blinked you would miss the entrance, but this unusual feature attracted Kato the first time he visited it long ago.

The further he walked he could sense the tightening of the air, but this was brushed away by the churning of a breeze when he slid open the door. As the wind tickled his ears, the calls of welcome rang out loudly. A small, thin girl with long hair rushed over and guided him to one of the seats of the bar between two businessmen. He could not see the one on the left because his back was turned, and he must have been talking to a woman because Kato could smell perfume. The other had just ordered some sake and was wiping his hands with a napkin. He tossed it to one side and when he saw Kato take his seat, he bowed to him politely. Kato nodded his head politely and took his seat. He ordered a glass of beer from the waitress walking past. He reached for the napkin, tore open the packet and wiped his hands thoroughly, tossing it to one side, reaching for the menu.

'They have good sashimi here,' said the man to his right.

'The best,' agreed Kato. He of course always ordered the raw fish. He beckoned to the chef, who was busy preparing food on the other side of the counter. He served Kato several times a week, so he knew him well.

'What's tonight's special?' he asked casually.

'Sea bream,' said the chef. 'We also have a few bottles of sake from Kyushu that came in yesterday, would you like one?'

'Ah, it is tempting,' said Kato with a smile. 'What town are they from?' he asked.

'I have a few from Kagoshima and one from Ureshino, the hot spring town. My brother-in-law brought them up.'

'Is he from there?'

'Yes, he is from near there, Sasebo.'

'The naval base, there are lots of American sailors stationed there. right?'

'My brother-in-law runs an Italian restaurant down there. Lots of foreigners like his cooking.'

'There are lots of foreigners in Kyoto these days too,' said the man to Kato's right, who decided to join the conversation. He was eating from a plate of sea bream, salmon, and tuna, and had a small wooden rice box cube full of sake.

'What sake is he drinking?' Kato asked the chef.

'Ureshino sake.'

'What do you think of it?' Kato asked the man. He nodded with a smile.

'It is very good, it goes well with the fish,' he said.

'Ok,' replied Kato to the chef. 'Give me one bottle of hot sake from Ureshino and a plate of sea bream with a few other pieces, you know what I like.'

The chef laughed. 'Of course, I do, Kato-san. By the way, my wife has something for your wife. I think it might be some pickles or something.'

'For Akiko?' asked Kato. He politely bowed and thanked him. He forgot that the chef's wife and his wife were friends, or acquaintances and were involved in different social activities together. He left the chef go and prepare the meal and he would talk about Akiko later. He sat down. He turned to the man on his right.

'There are indeed lots of foreigners in Kyoto,' said Kato. 'I met two foreigners this week, one is studying in Kyoto, a very smart boy from China.'

'What is he studying?'

'History or culture I think, at Kyoto University.'

'I know it well. It is my university.'

Kato looked at him. At first glance, the man did not look Japanese but slightly Western with a roundish clear face and round eyes, which hid behind thick glasses. His ears were large, and his face wrinkled. He looked to be in his mid to late 50s. He wore a very smart suit from what Kato could see, it looked expensive. He had a neatly trimmed beard.

'What do you teach?' asked Kato.

'I am a Professor of Japanese history.'

At that moment, the chef politely interrupted and passed over to Kato a beautifully presented plate of sea bream, tuna, and salmon.

'Kato-san,' he inquired. 'Have you met Professor Watanabe from Kyoto University?'

Kato politely bowed to the man. Watanabe bowed politely in return.

'Sensei,' said the chef to the Professor,.'This is Kato-san, of whom I spoke before. He owns the kimono shop up on the corner, near the department store.'

The Professor bowed again.

'It is very good to meet you,' said the Professor.

'Likewise,' said Kato. The chef leaned across and gave him the bottle of sake and a cup. Kato unscrewed the cap on the bottle and turned to the Professor. 'Let me pour you a glass,' he offered.

The Professor bowed his head slightly. 'It is very kind of you.' He lifted his wooden cup and Kato half-filled it. The man thanked him and sipped.

'Ah, that is good sake,' he said.

'I told you so,' said the chef from behind the counter.

'I met a historian only a few days ago, in Tokyo,' said Kato. 'He has just published a book on India's involvement in the war.'

'You don't mean Mr Solomon's book, do you? It is causing quite a stir in some circles.'

'Have you read it? What do you think of it?'

'I don't know. Sometimes things are best forgotten, but then again, it is refreshing to see the same events from a different perspective.'

'It is interesting,' said Kato. 'The mention of your name made me think of something from my work. One of my employees was a young girl who was studying at Kyoto University. She worked part time for me to make some extra money and so on. She mentioned a book written by you, something about Japan's myths and legends, the history of the yokai or Japanese monsters. I remember she kept talking about Watanabe's book on yokai and Japanese monsters, how to identify them and recognise them and so on.'

'I wrote that a long time ago,' replied the Professor. 'It was just a basic introduction on the types of monsters, demons, goblins, and devils in Japanese folklore. It was a bit tongue-in-cheek as well, it had a section on how to identify them and recognise them and so on. It was not reprinted, but I use it in my classes.'

The Professor looked at Kato. 'Her name was Maya-chan, wasn't it?' he asked. 'She was a very bright student, very curious. If I remember correctly, she was interested in the book you mentioned, especially the section on Japanese shape-shifting animals, like the fox or the racoon-dog, the tanuki. She seemed to think that she saw one of them in Kyoto, which is of course impossible. She wanted to know how to identify them by their mannerisms and behaviour.'

'One day she didn't show up for work and never returned,' said Kato. 'The police were involved, and they were able to find a letter she sent from Hokkaido and that was it. But she never wrote to me or said goodbye. It was all very strange.'

'I heard that she worked for a kimono firm,' said the Professor. 'I had my assistant write to her family in Hokkaido. They did not reply. I remember it was a busy time for me, around exam time. Her departure was disappointing. She was a good student. Far too many women give up and leave for various reasons, and they are often the best students.'

'She was impossible to replace at the shop,' continued Kato. 'She was a natural. She loved kimono. She knew everything. She learned quickly. She was well liked. After she left, the shop was not the same.

I have Ms Sasaki and a business manager, but Maya-chan brought a kind of positive energy to work and she seemed so radiant.'

'We are both talking about her as if she is dead,' said the Professor.

'I hope not,' said Kato. 'I assumed she was still in Hokkaido.'

There was a pause in the conversation while both men ate their sushi and drank their sake.

'I remember something she said,' continued Kato. 'She was talking about you, I would assume, since you wrote the book. We were all in the office having a party for Tamura, my business manager and she said that you wrote like you lived in the past, like you were born hundreds of years ago, like you were an immortal being. That is basically what she said.'

'It is interesting you remember that night,' said the Professor. 'Did anything happen?'

Kato rubbed his chin. 'As a matter of fact, yes there was something. It is interesting that I am remembering it all now. I had forgotten it all. At that little party, Maya-chan and her friend Tamura, my business manager fell out. I think it was a case of unrequited love on Tamura's part. He was besotted by her. I did not overhear the exact conversation, but she came back the next day. I pulled Tamura aside and asked him if everything was ok and he said that they had a disagreement over something he said, and he was very apologetic. I suggested that he patch things up with her and apparently, they talked and resolved their differences. Maya-chan kept coming to work until the end of that week and then she suddenly left.'

Kato and Watanabe were interrupted by the chef's wife who was standing behind him with a white plastic bag full of pickles. She slapped Kato on the back. He turned around and apologised and bowed to her. 'I am sorry, I did not see you there,' he said.

The woman laughed. 'It is alright Kato-san, I am used to being ignored. That monkey-faced husband of mine is too busy to pay any attention to me!' She poked her tongue out at the chef who was smiling at her. She gave Kato the bag.

'This is for Akiko, she knows what it is,' she said. Kato took the bag in both hands and bowed respectfully.

'Thank you,' said Kato. He looked up at the woman. She was smiling. Kato knew that she needed to know the truth. 'I have something to tell you. You might want to sit down.'

'What?' said the woman, 'Akiko has found a younger man?'

Kato laughed. 'No, nothing like that,' he said. The woman pulled a chair over and sat down close to Kato.

'I don't know how to say this, so I will just tell you.' He looked up to face the chef and then he glanced at Watanabe, before he looked at the woman.

'Akiko and my daughter Ai-chan, both died in the tsunami on March 11,' he said slowly.

The woman grabbed Kato's arm and gipped it tightly. 'Kato-san,' said the chef sympathetically.

'I didn't know you were in the north of Japan,' said the woman.

'It was a last-minute business trip,' replied Kato. 'It was only a few days ago and Akiko and Ai-chan came with me. I was at Matsushima when the tsunami struck, but they were visiting friends on the coast.'

'Are you sure they died?' asked the woman, her eyes full of tears. 'I spoke to her only last week. She asked me to get her some pickles from the market so she could use for her cooking. I said I was too busy, but I would make time later in the week for her.' She used her other hand to cover her eyes.

'I am very sorry to hear this news Kato-san,' said the chef. He looked stunned and did not know what to say. He looked at his wife, who felt the same.

'I am also very sorry Kato-san,' said Watanabe.

Kato looked over to him. Watanabe's face looked very sincere. Kato thanked everyone for their kind words and wiped his eyes and breathed out heavily. 'I am sorry,' he said, 'it is still very fresh in my mind,' rubbing his eyes again.

The four of them talked some more together, until the call of other customers became too frequent, and the woman made her excuses and left, and the chef returned to cutting sushi. He kept looking over in Kato's direction, often about to say something, but then stopping himself. The Professor however stayed with him, ordering more sushi and sashimi and other delicacies and plates as well as more sake.

They continued to talk, and the more they did, the more distant the deaths of his wife and daughter seemed to be, at least that night. It was one of those conversations which was not only interesting to both men, but also of such high quality that in the words spoken, and the subjects covered that a bond was formed. Watanabe learnt a lot about Kato that evening.

Kato was truly Japanese, a man who, despite the loss of his wife and only child, was able to shield his emotions and thoughts to such a degree that the emotion was all but hidden except for some twitches of the eyes and some facial expressions and for the occasional tear. Watanabe didn't mention the earthquake or tsunami and Kato was grateful for this. He just wanted a conversation where the events of the last few days were not part of it. He wanted to pretend as if life was going on normally. He fought with every effort of his heart to resist thoughts of his family and why he could not sleep properly, and he hoped with every glass of sake that there would be sufficient momentum to force his body to shutdown eventually and give him at least a few hours of uninterrupted sleep.

Kato was fascinated by Professor Watanabe's historical obsessions and Watanabe for his part, had not enjoyed such an in-depth conversation about his field for quite some time. Kato was well-educated and held an interest in Japanese history, indeed it was one thing his wife appreciated as well, but he had little time for it, as he spent most of his life in his work. It was very refreshing for Watanabe that Kato's questions were penetrating and mature.

Kato was particularly interested in the yokai, the Japanese monsters of folklore, especially the ones who could change their appearance, such as the mountain monster the Tengu, the Nue and the racoon-dog, the tanuki. Kato did not say anything about his strange encounter with Yamaguchi at Matsushima or the disturbing vision he experienced on the red bridge, but he felt that he needed to know more about these strange creatures. Watanabe was amazed that a man who was imbibing such large amounts of sake was able to retain such activity in his brain but talk they did. They talked about the life and times of Yoshitune, the eleventh century samurai general, Bushido, the way of the samurai, the Pacific War, the history of sashimi and of course, the brewing of sake. Both men continued to talk long into the night until they had both drunk several bottles of sake from different regions of Japan.

'It must be a busy time of year for you Kato-san,' said Watanabe. Kato turned his head to one side and hissed in the air. He nodded.

'Aside from Tamura, how many people work for you?' asked the Professor.

'Well, let me see,' replied Kato. 'Not many these days. My grandfather rebuilt the business after the war and never retired. He died at in the late 1950s and my father took over. He hired a few more people, but the numbers have gone up and down over the years. We have artisans, accountants, salespeople and so on. The Kyoto shop is quite small. Everyone is very loyal and has been with the Kato family for a long time.'

'Your kimono has a good reputation in Kyoto and all over Japan I would think,' said Watanabe.

'I owe that to my brother of course. He rescued the company from bankruptcy in 1995 after the death of my father. My brother took the decision to diversify beyond textiles into a few other kinds of investments. Without those more profitable businesses it would be hard to break even. Those businesses are a buffer to allow me to continue to sell the absolute best kimonos to our clients.' said Kato.

'You must be lucky to have someone like Tamura-san,' said Watanabe.

Kato nodded and picked up some tuna sashimi and tucked it into his mouth.

'Yes, yes of course. Tamura is one of a kind you know. He is the last link to my father's time. He began working for him a few years before he died. He does all the finances and was responsible for diversifying the business. He is invaluable but he is not perfect.'

'What do you mean?' asked the Professor.

'Well, his wife divorced him about ten years ago and took her son with her to Akita Prefecture. He never remarried but devoted himself to the work.'

Kato sipped the sake. The bottle they had been drinking from was empty and so he called out for another from the chef, who continued to keep his eye on Kato, and was happy to see that his mood had improved.

'He has unusual habits,' added Kato cautiously.

'Tamura?'

'Yes, he talks to the kimono late at night.'

'Talks to them?' asked the Professor with a puzzled look on his face.

Kato nodded. 'Yes, he thinks they are alive. He chats with them, like you and I are talking now. I have heard him. They answer back to him even though they are just fabrics and cloth. He is always licking his lips when he is not eating. I sometimes think that I conceded far too much power to him.'

'Maybe you have,' said Watanabe.

Kato nodded. 'He loves incense and makes sure our shop is stocked well with various kinds. I sometimes think he is trying to hide some foul odour from the street or maybe the drains, but he told me that he just likes the smell.'

'It might be something ritualistic,' said Watanabe. 'Maybe it reminds him of the past or some past religious duty or experience, or maybe it reminds him of his wife. People often perform the most elaborate daily rituals to keep the past alive in their own mind.'

Kato turned his head to one side and scratched his chin. 'I had not thought about that,' he said, drinking his sake.

'What is his relationship with women?' asked Watanabe.

Kato looked surprised. 'It is interesting you ask me that,' replied Kato. 'Tamura is obsessed with what he calls 'pretty girls,' and is often off in search of them in Kyoto. I had to admonish him a few times because he was scaring away some of the daughters of our prestigious clients. He just was being very creepy around them.

'It all stopped when Maya-chan came along. She and Tamura seemed to get on very well. There was real chemistry between them. She flirted with him, and he flirted with her, all very innocent if you ask me, and I sometimes thought he might have wanted to have a relationship with her. When you meet Tamura, you think he is a young man, but the more you talk with him, his maturity becomes clearer. His eyes are old, and he is not as young as you might think. Sometimes I think he might have borrowed someone's face and put it on to hide to real appearance.'

'What an interesting thing to say,' said the Professor.

'I know,' replied Kato. 'Someone else in Matsushima was talking about masks and taking faces the other day, and I just thought of it then. He was an old man I met. He was like Tamura, his eyes seemed old and did not go with his body. He said that someone who borrows faces is the most dangerous kind of person you are ever likely to meet.'

'What was his name?' asked the Professor.

The name of Yamaguchi suddenly vanished from Kato's mind as he was about to say it. He rubbed his chin. 'His name was on the tip of my tongue. I cannot remember now. He was an old man. I met him on a bridge, and then I think I met him again somewhere else, after the tsunami. You know Professor, it is very strange. I cannot remember.'

Kato rubbed his chin again. He could not understand why he was not able to remember. The more he tried to think about Yamaguchi, the more indistinct the memories of the man became. He turned to his sake and drank it. The Professor looked at him with a puzzled expression. He asked the chef for another bottle.

'How old was Ai-chan,' asked the Professor. Kato's eyes lit up. The memory of his daughter brought light back into his heart like the bursting of sun through open curtains at midday. He turned to the Professor.

'I remember now,' he said. 'I don't know why I forgot, but when you mentioned Ai-chan, it all came back to me. His name was Yamaguchi and he kept talking about Yoshitune's children.'

'Yoshitune's children?' asked the chef listening in. 'I don't think he had any kids, did he?'

'His wife had a child,' replied the Professor. 'Or so the story goes, but who knows what really happened so long ago? But Yoshitune's 'children' rather than Yoshitune's 'child,' it is a big difference. He said the former did he, this Yamaguchi?'

'Who?' asked Kato, who had forgotten Yamaguchi's name again. Again, it was on his mind, but he could not form the words. It was as if the memory of Yamaguchi had been deleted from his head and the two men had never met.

'The man you were just talking about,' insisted the Professor.

Kato shrugged his shoulders. He had completely forgotten what Watanabe asked him. The two men drank some more and after some time, the chef closed the restaurant early and he and his wife moved Kato to a larger table and they all sat together and talked about old times, about Akiko and Ai. Kato suddenly remembered Yamaguchi again and wondered why he had forgotten about him. Whenever he talked about his family, he could remember Yamaguchi, but whenever the conversation moved elsewhere, his memory of the old man seemed to evaporate. The chef cooked some of his popular delicacies for them and they opened an old bottle of whiskey he had been saving for an important occasion.

Kato really did not know the chef and his wife all that well, but from that night on, they became firm friends, and he never forgot their kindness to him. It was early morning when the chef and Watanabe carried Kato up the stairs to the road. Kato had passed out at the table, and he was immovable. Watanabe asked the chef to help him carry Kato back to the kimono shop, which was quite close. Watanabe paid the bill. Getting Kato up the stairs was the most difficult part, but the street was virtually empty. Kato was able to walk when they got to the top of the stairs and so Watanabe said goodbye to the chef who went home with his wife.

When they arrived at the shop, Watanabe saw that the light was still on. There were figures inside the shop. He peered into the dim lights and saw Tamura gently stroking the kimono talking to it and smiling. Watanabe rang the bell. It shook Tamura and he came running to the front door. He was horrified to see his employer in such a state. He apologized profusely and opened the door, ushering them to bring Kato out to the back of the shop and into the storeroom where the futon was located. There they laid Kato on the futon and Tamura brought another blanket for him. When they were finished, Watanabe breathed in deeply.

'There is a strange smell in here,' he said to Tamura. 'What is it?'

Tamura breathed in.

'Maybe Kato,' said Tamura. He smiled a little.

'I smell the forest,' said Watanabe.

'I smell the incense,' countered Tamura. 'Maybe it is the incense that you smell tonight. I started burning some new sticks.'

'No,' said the Professor. 'You have tried hard to mask it Tamura, but it is still there – the smell of the forest.'

Tamura ignored him. 'I'm so deeply sorry for causing so much trouble for you to bring Kato-san back tonight,' said Tamura.

Watanabe shook his head.

'It is no trouble at all,' said Watanabe, walking to the door.

Tamura hurried past him and opened it.

'Do you keep in contact with that young girl who used to work here?' asked Watanabe.

'Who?'

'I think her name was 'Maya,''

Tamura's face was expressionless.

'Ah!' he said finally and smiled. 'No, she is in Hokkaido.'

'Yes, I know. That is what the letter said.'

'What letter?'

'The letter she apparently sent from Hokkaido to her mother.'

'How do you know about the letter?'

'Inspector Goro Fujita told me, from the Kyoto Police. She was a student in my seminar class at university.'

'You are Professor Watanabe, from Kyoto University, you wrote that book on yokai. You made many mistakes in that book. I don't think you know much about yokai.'

'Maybe you could enlighten me,' said the Professor. 'I am always looking for material for my next book.'

'Are you writing another book?' asked Tamura.

The Professor changed the subject. 'I went to the address in Hokkaido last week. I was following up loose ends. I know it has taken me some time, but I like to be thorough. The address the letter cited led me to a boarding house in Hakodate city, near the coast,' said the Professor.

'Then she sent the letter from there,' smiled Tamura.

'Well, strangely enough, you are known to the owners, because you went there with a woman called Maya-chan, apparently as a couple,' said the Professor.

'We were together for a short while,' said Tamura, beginning to fidget with his fingers.

'The letter her mother received was dated the same day as the last time you were seen there at the boarding house. But the last time you went to Hokkaido, you went alone. Maya-chan was not there. The owners can confirm that the young woman was not there the last time you were there and in fact, you never went there with her. I showed the owners a photo of Maya and it is not the women you were seen with. They said they only saw a woman in a kimono, but never her face.'

'You really do try to tie up loose ends, don't you Professor,' said Tamura, licking his lips.

'My theory is that the letter Maya's mother received was a fake. I have compared the writing style from the letter she wrote with some of her essays, and they are virtually the same, but not quite.'

Tamura's face remained without any expression.

'Why don't you come drinking with us next time?' said Watanabe.

'I don't drink alcohol,' said Tamura.

'Really?' asked Watanabe. 'That's a real change for you. I heard you used to drink a lot when you were young. Last week I spoke to your old friends from when you were married. They all told me that Tamura-san loved to drink. When did you stop drinking?'

'I don't remember exactly,' said Tamura.

'Maybe it was about ten years ago when your wife divorced you and left you alone.'

'It might have been then,' said Tamura. 'I don't remember exactly.'

'I don't blame them for leaving you,' continued Watanabe. After all, you seem obsessed by every young woman who passes by you. You are famous in Kyoto for being a creepy man who chases young girls regardless of their age. Speaking of children, I cannot find your son, or your ex-wife for that matter.'

Tamura still said nothing but looked emotionless at Watanabe.

'Your family have vanished. No one has seen them. They do not live at their official address. I have been there also. It has not been lived in for some time.'

'Of course, I am sad to hear that you cannot find them, but they didn't tell me where they were going,' replied Tamura.

Watanabe sighed and smiled.

'What are you going to do about May-chan?' asked Tamura.

'I am not a police officer Tamura, I am just a humble University Professor who misses a good student,' said the Professor. 'I have no power over the lives of humans in this city,' he added. 'Even if I would like to.'

Watanabe stepped out of the door and turned around. 'By the way, please give this note to Mr. Kato. I have asked him to meet me tomorrow for an important engagement at 11am.'

Tamura nodded and took the note. He started at Watanabe and stopped fidgeting. His face became expressionless, and he bowed.

Watanabe nodded and left.

Tamura closed the door behind him and locked it.

13

Kato woke early. His sleep was punctuated by a nightmare. He dreamt he was being pursued through a forest by a huge creature with claws and sharp teeth that hid from view deep in a soup-like mist. It looked like a demon from one of the old legends his father had spoken about. The demon came close a few times and lunged at him, and Kato cried up in his sleep several times trying to escape the clutches of this hideous creature. In his dream he managed somehow to escape from the demon and make his way up a mountain slope. It seemed familiar but he could not remember the name of the place. As he ran up the slope, he could see dark figures hiding behind the trees or flying across the branches.

When he reached the top of the mountain, he took refuge in the temple, and met a man who claimed to be the emperor's cousin. He did not recognise the face, but the man said he was part of Japan's royal family. Kato looked at the man and he was dressed in white robes, as if preparing to commit ritual suicide. Kato protested, but the man insisted that he needed to die on behalf of the nation to stop the madness. If by his death he could make peace with the ghosts of the past, then he would do so.

Kato told him that he would not allow the man to face the demon himself, because there is no way he would survive. The emperor's cousin pushed his way past, but Kato knocked him out, undressed the man and put on his white robes. He then hid the man out of sight in a safe place with the priests who were also hiding there.

Kato found a sword in the temple and walked to the entrance of the temple hall. He pulled open the door, standing on the top of the stairs looking down to the courtyard. It was a sea of black, men dressed in dark clothes, the costumes of assassins. He stepped down onto the next wooden step and the sea of men parted, drawing their swords. Kato reached for his sword but it was gone.

He suddenly woke up in a hot sweat, crying out in fear. He looked at the clock on the wall. It was six in the morning. When he sat up, he noticed on the side table that Tamura must have provided him with some tea and coffee, and a jug of hot water, with an assortment of small cakes. He made himself a cup of coffee and ate the cakes. Next to the cakes was Watanabe's business card and a note from Tamura saying that Professor Watanabe had invited him to a meeting that morning at 11 am. Kato could not remember the reason for the meeting, and he was even less sure about arranging it. He thought back to the night before but could not remember much of the conversation. He rubbed his forehead and he felt queasy. He had a hangover. He realized that he must have drunk a river of sake the night before, and it was still coursing through his veins.

He stood up and went into the kitchen. Tamura had prepared a few rice balls and some pickles. He realised these were from the pickles the lady gave him the night before. He looked in the small fridge and discovered that Tamura bought some beer and spirits. The fridge was well-stocked with Kato's favourite brands and glass cups of sake. He found a can of beer, opened it, and drank some. He took the rice balls and the pickles back to his makeshift bedroom and sat down on the futon. After he ate the rice balls and the crunched on the pickles, he finished his beer, got up and dressed, putting on some wooden sandals and walked into the shop. Tamura and Ms. Sasaki were opening for the day. They both politely bowed to Kato as he left. He had decided to have a bath. He had not washed since he arrived back in Kyoto. He was going to go to the Itoh bathhouse.

It was a quiet morning and aside from a few people walking their dogs, the side streets of Kyoto were calm and motionless. A few shopkeepers were preparing for the day, and Kato received the occasional muffled greeting. He was still thinking about the appointment as he stumbled into the bath house. He took off his sandals at the door, and his clothes he put casually in one of the baskets in the change room. He realised he had forgotten his towel and so picked up one of the complimentary towels that were in a neat pile at the entrance to the public bath. He slid open the door and was met by hot air, steam, and the smell of recycled water. He washed himself on a plastic stool and then sat in the hot pool for about ten minutes.

There were a few others there at that time and Kato engaged in conversation with them. The main topics were the tsunami, the earthquake, and the nuclear accident. After his bath, he dressed and met the owner's wife in the lobby of the bathhouse. She, like her husband, was in her eighties, but still had strength and a strong personality. She managed the bath house with calculating efficiency and often cleaned the bathhouse while the male clients were still in there. She paid no attention to Kato's nakedness. After all, she had seen hundreds of naked men in her bathhouse, and she was seeing nothing new.

Kato used to go to another bathhouse when he was fired from the army in 2006. But that closed a year later. From a competitor in the kimono trade, he heard that an old bathhouse that was dilapidated had been restored by an older couple from the town of Tono in Iwate, a city to the north of Sendai. It was famous for the ancient mythical being called the Kappa, which, according to legend, was a thin, slimy monster that lived in rivers and would sometimes emerge to live among people. The owners of the restored bathhouse had brought in some artists to paint some interesting murals over the walls of the bathhouse with their impressions of the Kappa doing ordinary human tasks. It gave the clients something to look at and talk about when they visited. Kato and the Itoh family got on very well when they first met. They were from the north as they had a similar dialect to his wife Akiko, as she came from the city south of Iwate, Sendai, as did the late Kenji Nomura.

Just before he left the bathhouse that morning, Mrs Itoh told him that Tamura had told her about the tragic death of his family in the tsunami. She expressed her deepest condolences to him and apologized that her husband Mr. Itoh was out on business but would meet Kato when he returned. Kato thanked her for her remarks. He noted that since she also came from the north of Japan, she too must have lost people she knew. She said that was certainly the case and that she had heard of at least two families who could not be accounted for.

She asked about the funeral arrangements for Akiko and Ai. Kato had not even thought about it. He rubbed his chin and apologised. Mrs Itoh told him that if he needed any help with the funeral, then they would both make themselves available if he needed them. He politely bowed, thanked her, and left.

Kato returned to the shop, went to his bedroom, and changed into a new suit, laid out for him by Tamura. He looked at his watch and it was only about 10 am and so he wandered around the shop, greeting customers. He remembered that Tamura wanted to talk to him about the finances of the business. He looked at his business manager who was talking with a client. Pleasantries were exchanged and Tamura conducted the affairs with his usual elegance and charm, paying attention to the minutest detail and answering every question posed. Kato waited at the back of the store behind the entrance and came out again a few times only briefly as if he were occupied with some tasks and surprised to find customers in his shop. He then retreated to the back room and wandered around in the kitchen, making himself a cup of green tea. After he drank a few sips, he went back into the shop as if he were still busy. He said goodbye to the client who had decided on buying an expensive kimono. He stood at the door, bowing deeply to them as they left. He turned to Tamura.

'I have that appointment,' he said to Tamura. Tamura nodded politely.

Kato left for the meeting, hailing a taxi from the street outside going south. The topic of conversation with the taxi driver for the entire journey was the tsunami. Kato pleaded ignorance on all matters regarding the earthquake and tsunami. The taxi driver was very anxious about the nuclear accident in Fukushima. The taxi driver was angry that the Prime Minister had visited the reactor the day after the accident and his presence had prevented critical repairs to the site and that he did not visit the coastal regions which were destroyed by the tsunami, but that he returned to Tokyo by helicopter. The driver said that politicians were all the same and could never be trusted. He also echoed the concerns of the man whom Kato struck on the train about the contaminated people from Tohoku, but this time Kato held his tongue.

Kato had arrived at his destination. He was at the entrance to the garden called Shosei-en, part of the huge Higashi Honganji Buddhist temple complex. Standing at the entrance to the garden, Kato nervously held Watanabe's business card in his hand. A thin man in a black suit approached and introduced himself as one of the temple officials. He was to escort Kato to the gathering. Along the way, Kato sought to elicit further information about this meeting, but the official insisted that his role was just to bring Kato to the tea house, and he denied knowing anything more.

Kato did not persist with his questions but allowed his eyes to take in the surroundings. The garden was, to his mind, not as splendid as some of the more famous places in Kyoto but realized that it was perhaps his first visit. The ponds were delicate and the garden itself was spacious considering it was so close to Kyoto Station. Kato had visited the temple many times and he knew some priests who worked in the precincts, but his visits never took him to the garden. They had arrived at the tea house and the thin man in the black suit departed. Kato took off his shoes and ascended the rock which acted as the entrance step to the tea house. The sliding doors to the house had been removed and the tatami floor extended across the entire floor.

Five people sitting in a line looked up to Kato when he arrived, the first Kato recognizing as Professor Watanabe. The Professor was wearing a traditional yukata made from purple cloth with a faint green belt wrapped around his waist. He arose and walked over to Kato bowing deeply.

'Welcome Kato-san,' said Watanabe. 'Thank you for agreeing to come.'

Kato smiled and bowed.

He walked over to greet the other four guests. Three of the guests he recognized. The first was Mrs Murakami, the former head of a famous tea ceremony school in Kyoto. Mrs. Murakami was in her early nineties. Her school was very exclusive and only the extremely wealthy could afford to join her company, but she had an impeccable reputation. Mrs. Murakami was in a simple sense, the essence of Kyoto culture herself, and many people looked up to her as a role model. The other member of this party known to Kato was Mr. Sato, a senior official in Kyoto City Hall. Sato was in effect, the most powerful bureaucrat in the city, with extensive ties to political, business, and cultural circles. The third member of the party Kato also knew, and the man jumped to his feet when he saw Kato enter the tea house and was standing there politely while Kato spoke to the others.

'I don't stand on ceremony,' he said and held Kato's hand warmly and shook it.

It was Mr. Honda. 'How are you Kato-san?' asked Honda in English. Kato said he was well and asked about Joshua Tree.

'He is still up in Sendai,' said Honda. 'He is working with the U.S. military who are working with the Self-Defence Force.'

'Thank you for getting us out of Matsushima,' replied Kato. He politely bowed.

'It was no trouble at all,' replied Honda. 'You should thank your friend Joshua Tree. He told me you were up there.' Honda turned around and motioned to the last man who stood up and was standing next to him. 'Let me introduce you to the final member of our little committee.'

The man was well-built and with a round face and round eyes, a receding hairline, and large ears. His name was Seiji Oda, a member of Japan's Air Self-Defence Force. Kato politely bowed to him as well. He had exchanged all his pleasantries and assumed his prepared position on the floor.

Mrs. Murakami led the tea ceremony. As she prepared the tea for each person, Watanabe reflected on the history of tea and its significance for the people of Kyoto. He explained to everyone present each aspect of the tea ceremony, the meaning of each utensil and each movement, so everyone understood the meaning. Kato was a little puzzled by this because everyone present was Japanese, until he realised that Watanabe was giving his lecture for the benefit of Honda-san. For some reason, Kato had naturally assumed he was Japanese, even though he spoke English. His manner, his bearing, all pointed to a deep understanding of the Japanese spirit.

The cup eventually made its way to Kato, who was seated next to Oda. Mrs Murakami placed the bowl in front of him. Kato took the cup and drank. He felt for some reason, a lifting of his spirit and he sighed, placing the bowl on the tatami. He looked out to the garden. A plum tree shook slightly in the breeze.

After Mrs Murakami had concluded the tea ceremony, she returned to her seat and Watanabe took her place, sitting opposite everyone. They all looked at him.

'I wish to thank all of you for attending today on this special occasion. Today we can be thankful that all of you were able to come, despite your busy schedules and difficult circumstances. We especially remember what happened on the 11th of March. We have all been affected in different ways, some of us personally.'

Watanabe glanced in the direction of Kato and bowed slightly. He continued. 'This committee has its origins in a proposal by Mr Honda, which he presented to me three years ago. His proposal was to create a committee that would look at practical ways to help the minorities who live in Japan. I am not just speaking about foreigners who live here, but also the various Japanese minorities who have lived with discrimination and other obstacles to a happy, healthy, and productive life. The events of the last few days have challenged all of us and we ask ourselves: what can we do to help? The issue for us is to think about what we might do as a city to prepare for some of the consequences of these events.

'I do not pretend to know the answers. I am a student of history, and I am aware, as are you, of similar tragedies in our nation's past. The memories of Hiroshima and Nagasaki are both still fresh in the minds of the people of Japan. Japan suffered not only defeat at the hands of America but was the only nation in history to suffer the terrible effects of an atomic bomb on a populated area. Young people in Japan are losing their appreciation of our history as well as the sacrifices that were made to make Japan what it is today. Is this disaster in Fukushima an opportunity for us to move forward, or will it hold us back as a nation? These are some questions to ponder. I will now ask Mr. Sato to make some remarks.'

Sato bowed to everyone and thanked them for coming. He gave a long and detailed talk on the large influx of temporary residents fleeing from the north of Japan to Kyoto and the surrounding area and the pressures this would place on the current inn and hotel accommodation. He stressed that the problems facing the now defunct nuclear reactor in Fukushima had implications for the entire country in terms of effectively relocating the hundreds of thousands of Japanese now forcibly displaced. He ended his talk by pleading with all of those present to work together to come up with effective measures to help mitigate the effect of this demographic shift.

The next person to speak was Honda. He was brief and to the point. He spoke in Japanese.

'I want to thank everyone for coming today so we could enjoy this beautiful tea ceremony from Mrs. Murakami. I have not had the pleasure of hearing her play before, but I am told that it is a real window into the life of the Kyoto cultural community. I am looking forward to her playing the shamisen later.

'As Mr. Sato has said, the challenge we face is an enormous one. The nuclear reactor explosions and meltdown at Fukushima has certainly brought about the largest movement of internal refugees in Japan since the end of the Pacific War. The city of Kyoto needs to think seriously about the implications of this movement of people for our infrastructure and facilities.

'I was speaking with Professor Watanabe before, and we both agreed that the events of March 11 bear many similarities to the terrible 1894 Sanriku earthquake and tsunami to strike the east coast of Japan. Sadly, we will have thousands dead and thousands missing, and I have been told that the Japanese Government is establishing a special missing persons bureau in the heart of the Tokyo police bureaucracy. I hear that the man who is going to lead this new committee is a senior police executive called Mr. Okubo.'

This caught Kato's attention and he motioned an interruption. 'Excuse me Honda-san. Did you say Okubo?'

Honda nodded. 'Masao Okubo, yes, Kato-san, do you know him?'

Kato nodded. 'We went to school together, high school, in Kyoto.'

'Is he originally from Kyoto?' asked Watanabe.

'Yes, he was born here,' replied Kato. 'But his family moved around a fair bit.'

'This is really fortuitous,' said Sato. 'If you know him, please do all you can to have him communicate with us and keep us informed.'

'I will try and contact him,' replied Kato.

Honda continued. 'For those of you who do not know, Kato-san was in Matsushima the day of the tsunami and witnessed first-hand the ferocity of the tsunami and the earthquake. He was involved in the clean-up and rescue effort on the 11th and 12th of March. I am also told reliably that his wife and child are still recorded as missing as of today, along with over three thousand people along the east coast of Japan.'

Kato felt the eyes of everyone look at him and he stared steadily at the tatami mats in front of him.

'I am amazed that Kato-san has been able to return to work and focus on anything given this tragic news,' continued Honda. 'Kato leads us by his example. We need to keep moving forward, while dealing with the pain of the last few days. We have all lost those whom we have known. It reinforces the imperative of the Japanese Government to do all it can to bring relief to those who lost homes and loved ones during this terrible experience.'

There was a long silence.

Watanabe thought Kato might want to say something, but he stayed silent. Watanabe motioned to the tea master, who took up her instrument, the Japanese shamisen and she begun to pluck a tune. It was melancholy, with each note piercing the morning silence at the garden, sharp and direct, and each note with purpose, step by step as if each note took off into the air like ascending incense. Kato listened to Mrs. Murakami play, looking out across the open green field which was in the foreground of the pond. He recalled the melody, but could not place it, the chords reminded him of earlier days and for the first time since the tsunami, he toyed with the idea of releasing the memories of his wife and daughter from the box in which they were tightly imprisoned. He did not want the feeling of desolation to overwhelm him. That time would come when he realised that was completely alone, but he didn't want it to be today.

In the company of such esteemed individuals, he did not wish to show any sign of weakness, lest they used that as a means of empathy with him and besides, he protected his heart all the time and especially now. But in his inner being, he yearned to release such thoughts, even for a moment and as the song continued along its course, he found his fingers relaxing and he sighed deeply. But in the corner of his eye, he noticed the watchful gaze of Professor Watanabe, so he quickly put out of his mind any thought of his family and returned to the day's events.

When she had finished playing, Kato volunteered to walk with her and Professor Watanabe to a waiting taxi to return her to her home. Along the way, he expressed his deep appreciation of her playing and commented how much he had enjoyed listening to it. It was a rare treat, thought Kato, even for him, to walk in the presence of such an esteemed woman. Watanabe allowed him to speak and aside from some words of thanks and farewell, said nothing on the way to the taxi. When the car left the garden precincts, Watanabe turned to Kato.

'Walk with me Kato,' he said and led the way back along the path to the pond. Kato thanked him again for the invitation and the tea ceremony, which Watanabe cordially accepted.

'What do you think of Mrs. Murakami?' he asked. 'Is she not the very essence of traditional Kyoto culture?'

Kato nodded. 'She is Kyoto in every way,' he said.

'She was born in Hiroshima and survived the atomic blast,' said Watanabe.

'Hiroshima?' asked Kato, surprised.

Watanabe nodded. 'She was only young when the Americans dropped the atomic bomb on the city. Her parents were killed, but she was far enough away from the blast to avoid the worst of the radiation. Nonetheless, as you know, she and most of her friends were shunned by our nation. People viewed them as contaminated.'

'It was an ignorant time,' Kato replied.

'No,' disagreed Watanabe. 'It was unacceptable.'

He paused and then spoke again.

'I heard a story long ago that there was a family in Japan who made it their business to move people from one place to another, those who were outcasts of one form or another. In our language we called them the 'non-humans,' for that is what they are. We deem them unworthy to receive any rights normally granted to everyone else. The bombs at Hiroshima and Nagasaki simply added more to their number, more outsiders. These people had no future, no hope in a nation already burnt by the war.'

'Surely the government would have found out about it. Their accents would have also given them away. As soon as they opened their mouths people would have realized that they came from a different part of Japan.'

'It is incredible the capacity of people to change when faced with very few options Kato-san,' continued Watanabe.

'This family began their work at the beginning of modern Japan in the late 1860s. There was a man by the name of Sakamoto Ryoma. He was a samurai from the southern island of Shikoku, and he held to the belief in democracy, the idea that everyone had a voice. It was why the government of the time sent a man by the name of Sasaki Tadasaburo to murder him in 1867. Two powerful clans, the Satsuma in modern day Kagoshima and the Choshu in modern day Yamaguchi, seized control of the young emperor, who largely did what he was told. This emperor, Meiji led a largely autocratic state until the military grew tired of being sidelined and took over in the 1930s. A military-style government led Japan to war with China, Korea and then later with

America. The Americans gave us a constitution that resembles something of the democratic vision Ryoma spoke of in the 1860s.

'From the 1860s until the madness of the war, there were still some families, like Sakamoto, who believed that all Japanese, regardless of their situation, deserved equality under the law, a fair treatment. One family, a very wealthy merchant family, decided to promote the interests of the non-humans secretly, by giving them new identities. Large numbers of people were moved between the 1860s and 1930s. As luck would have it, tragically, two common destinations for these non-humans were the cities of Hiroshima and Nagasaki. Most of them died in the atomic blasts, along with the other Japanese.'

Watanabe sighed and continued to walk slowly.

'After the war, it was relatively easy to move people. Most government records were lost or destroyed during the air raids, and there were so many dying from disease and starvation, who would notice a few misplaced people. In those days, when the Americans were here, they discovered that a similar highway was in place during the American civil war, when a group of people needed protection in a world that did not tolerate them. In the nineteenth century, many African Americans escaped slavery through what they called an 'underground railroad' from the Southern states where they faced terrible bondage to the northern states. This Japanese family learnt all it could about the American experience and adapted it to the Japanese situation. As a result, thousands were able to enjoy a new life.'

'If it is true, it is a fascinating story,' replied Kato. Watanabe agreed.

'I have heard the story from time to time," said Watanabe. "I only mention it because we as a nation are heading back to familiar territory. We both know that the Fukushima reactor disaster is mirroring the bombing of Japanese cities in the war, and it is only a matter of time before these people become another member in the rank of Japan's neglected minorities.'

Kato thought of the prejudice he encountered on the train and in the taxi. There was a revival of the idea of the 'non-human' to increasingly mean people who lived near or around Fukushima.

'You are talking about a significant enterprise here,' said Kato, 'Giving people new identities, new lives, and new homes. What about their families and their friends?' Kato asked.

'It is not a plan without problems, I grant you that,' said the Professor. 'There needs to be a trade-off. In the case of Mrs.

Murakami, her family was all wiped out, so she could start anew. Let us not forget there were many orphans due to the war as well, so many children were given to other families to raise,' said Watanabe.

'Do you believe the stories?' asked Kato. 'Is such a thing possible?'

'If it is true, then it has existed in Japan in absolute secrecy for over a hundred years and has moved thousands of people. The logistics alone would require significant activity and secrecy. It is highly unlikely to be true,' replied Watanabe.

'Why not simply push Japanese to change their minds?' asked Kato.

'Do you think the Japanese people would change their minds about the minorities in their midst?' asked Watanabe. 'The Japanese are resolute in their love for their country and for their culture. They change only when met with impossible personalities who appear at significant junctures in their history. These personalities are magnetic and powerful and charismatic, and they change the course of the nation, men like Oda Nobunaga or Yoshitune. I think it is better to use prejudice against Japan, until another leader emerges to lead Japan to its new future.'

At this moment, the conversation was brought to a halt because Watanabe was called back to the tea house and Kato needed to leave as well. He saw on his phone that Tanura had called him over ten times. When he heard the messages on the phone in the taxi on the way back to the shop, he knew something was terribly wrong. Tamura had urgency and fear in his voice and would not tell Kato over the phone but wanted him to return to the shop as soon as possible.

When Kato reached the shop, Tamura was waiting for him. His face was white, and in his hand, he held a collection of documents. He bowed deeply when Kato walked in the door. He ushered Kato into the back office and forced him to sit down. He laid the documents in front of him and apologized profusely. Kato had no idea what he was talking about. This made Tamura even more upset, and he then produced a large map of Japan which covered the entire desk. It contained a series of concentric circles around the coast. Kato looked and realized that the circles emanated from the Prefecture of Fukushima.

'What is going on Tamura?'

'We are on the edge of complete bankruptcy,' blurted out the business manager and fell to his knees.

'What on earth are you talking about?'

'Five years ago, you asked me to diversify our business. Do you remember?'

'Yes, Tamura. My Father trusted you and my brother and so I trusted them for their trust in you. I asked you to diversify and I have been happy with the results. So, what is the problem?'

'Originally, everything was fine,' replied Tamura. 'In Kyoto, it was becoming harder to find weavers to make the kimono and so I went further and further to find the best artisans in Japan. This took me everywhere and soon our orders were being completed by skilled weavers and artisans all over the country.

'Then, two years ago, three of our best artisans retired, they were good, and I naturally passed on the orders to two kimono artisans in the Prefecture of Fukushima, one of them in the town of Naraha and the other in the town of Soma. We also had two of our best people visiting the east coast with their families, like you went to Matsushima. The town of Naraha is now being evacuated and we have lost all our stock there. The town of Soma was flooded, and our artisans are missing, as are three artisans who were visiting the east coast. Together, they represent almost half of our workforce in Japan. We were busy fulfilling three large orders from that area and unfortunately, we will not be able to cover our costs.'

Kato sat back in the chair. 'Those poor people, how horrible, it really was a terrible thing for all of them,' he said. 'The tsunami and earthquake were not your fault Tamura-san.'

'But I have led the company into bankruptcy!'

Kato was philosophical. 'We will pull through,' he said. 'We are all experiencing the same thing. It is a terrible time. No doubt our competitors will find similar constraints on their business. I must admit from a strictly business point of view it is not a good situation but from a human point of view, I have lost some wonderful people. I really must get their names and send letters of condolence to their families. I also want the families to receive the income that they would normally receive for at least the next two years.'

'We don't have the funds Kato-san,' protested Tamura.

'Then we will have to sell the shop,' said Kato abruptly. 'If we need to sell, then we must sell. I will not see people destitute or on the street or be responsible for putting people through misery. Those workers worked hard for us, and we must support their families.'

He looked up at Tamura. His face was expressionless, but Kato could see the look of fear in his eyes. He obviously felt full of shame. He burst into tears, turned around and ran out of the office, not even looking at the kimono. Kato never saw him again.

14

Meanwhile, Professor Watanabe had finished his time at the tea house and said goodbye to all the guests. It was late afternoon when the event was over, and he wandered around the garden by himself afterwards. As was his custom, he decided to visit the Inari Shrine at dusk, which is located a few miles south of Kyoto station. He caught a taxi to Kyoto station and then the train to Fushimi Inari station and walked to the entrance of the shrine. Watanabe always felt comfortable in shrine precincts, wherever they happened to be. He was more at home there than in his own home in the north of Kyoto. The more he went to the shrines, the more he bathed in the mystery that was the Shinto faith, the faith of the shrine, the native faith of the Japanese people steeped in tradition, folklore, and nature. Watanabe never made a distinction between these three, seeing the tradition as a link to the past, the folklore the spirit of the people and nature as the home for the spirits.

There was a time long ago when the shrines were free and independent, but in the late nineteenth century, the government forced a process of elimination and amalgamation to promote the new religion of emperor worship. Watanabe accepted that but he still loved the mystery and magic of places like Fushimi, that seemed to have a wildness and raw beauty that could not be controlled by any human.

At Fushimi, nature's shadow continued to be cast over the modern city of Kyoto.

Inari Shrine is a shrine connected to the fox, and there are little Inari shrines all over the country often identified by little stone statues of foxes found at the entrance. Kyoto's Inari Shrine is unusual in the sense that it is in fact many little shrines connected by paths which were cut into the mountain and hills which surround the area. But the uniqueness does not stop there. It is normally the case that a red wooden gate stands at the entrance to a Japanese shrine, comprising of two round poles with a third piece laid on top of them at the with the edges sticking out. The Inari shrine in Kyoto has thousands of red gates, called Torii, which have been erected side by side like dominos following some of the paths, creating an effect which is never lost on those who walk through them.

Watanabe knew that the people of Kyoto tended to stay away from Inari Shrine at this time of day. It remained one of the strangest locations in the city. There is an air about Inari which is both enticing but oppressive, a sense of a darkness hidden, hiding, and waiting, and one never feels quite alone in that place. Forests are often the places where people go to relax, to breathe in the air, to sit back and delight in the birds and the sights and the smells, but not so Inari. One cannot breathe deeply there, nor does one feel able to linger or reflect. Rather, one is compelled to walk quickly, ever with the feeling that one is being watched or to be more correct, studied. Thousands of foxes lie in Inari, often collected on mounds of dirt, piled together, like a graveyard of souls.

Sightings of ghosts and other strange beings are commonplace there and many have a deep sense of foreboding as they walk the paths covered by the vermillion painted red Shinto gates. Watanabe regularly encouraged his students to join him on his evening visits to Inari but most declined. Most of his colleagues were disturbed that Watanabe visited Inari Shrine so often and some expected that one night he might not return at all.

University rumour suggested theories for Watanabe's visits. Some thought him to be just a strange old academic, while others expected that the Inari visits were convenient excuses for illicit rendezvous with female students. Watanabe was single and never showed interest in romance, but this only fuelled the gossip because he had a presence about him that many found enchanting. After lectures, many gathered around him to listen to his tales of old Japan, most of them young women. He did not see any of them as romantic opportunities. He saw them more like his children.

Those who knew Watanabe more than casually had suspected that there may have been a more personal reason for his visit. They had heard that he was once married and walked through life with another. Nobody dared to pry, but his friends suspected pain lodged deep in his past. Perhaps Inari was a place of significance for the young Professor and his wife. Whatever the truth was, Watanabe made a regular visit to Inari only at night at dusk, returning to his car in the morning. He only decided to go to the shrine after the tea ceremony. He felt the tragic events of the earthquake and tsunami heavily upon his heart and lingered long at the garden before taking his leave. He wondered about Kato and his response to their conversation, but more importantly, his heart wept for the thousands of people who were swept away to their deaths less only a few days ago. While he was thinking this, Tachibana-san, the local priest of the Shrine appeared, saw him, and walked over, bowing deeply.

'Good evening, Sensei!' he said. Watanabe reciprocated.

'It's quite cold this evening. Are you sure you are going to walk the track tonight?'

Watanabe nodded.

'No students?' asked Tachibana.

Watanabe shook his head.

'Well,' said Watanabe. 'Good night,' and turned to leave.

'Before you go Sensei,' said Tachibana, moving closer, running his hand through his hair.

'What is it?'

'We have had two more sightings since your last visit.'

'Tell me, what happened?'

'Yesterday, a group of women told us that they were convinced they saw two fox spirits dressed as young women in kimono.'

'Really? Tell me more.'

'It happened in the usual place, deep in the mountain, along the path. The women were walking together, chatting about life and they met two young women in kimono. They looked emaciated but friendly. The two women spoke to the group for a few minutes and turned to leave. As you know, the path in that section of the shrine is open, one can see the entire field on both sides and there is nowhere to hide. The group of women turned to leave but one turned back suddenly and to her surprise the two women had vanished. They all huddled together and then one spotted a fox hiding in the undergrowth.'

'Mm. It is the usual story it seems…'

'But that is not all,' said the priest.

'What?' he asked, his curiously stimulated.

'On the footpath, the women found something which disturbed them greatly and they immediately came back to the office.'

'What did they find?'

'They found a Kokeshi.'

'A wooden doll?'

'It was a doll from Fukushima, I am sure of it. It had its head ripped off, torn off and I found it further down the track in the bushes. A pilgrim must have left it there to remember their loved one, but the foxes didn't appreciate it and threw it away. I checked some other sites where pilgrims often visit and found similar destruction.'

'They are responding with malice and anger,' replied Watanabe.

'But against whom?' asked the priest.

'It is hard to say Tachibana-san,' replied Watanabe. 'The tsunami has wrecked the east coast of Japan, thousands are gone, maybe they feel the anguished cries of the dead and feel especially the loss of the children, taken away just before they could enjoy their lives. The tsunami has sent ripples across the nation. The foxes are restless, upset, uncertain, and this is not good, not good at all.'

'Are they seeking a sacrifice? Should we perform some rites? Maybe we should close off the track and say we need to do some urgent repairs,' suggested the priest.

Watanabe disagreed. 'That would enrage them. It would provoke them further and that is the last thing we need. The public would also get suspicious and the last thing we need is more people looking for the foxes in Inari, especially foreigners who seem to know more about Japanese folklore than the Japanese.'

'You are referring to that French Professor, always looking into our traditions and customs of the yokai.'

'Absolutely,' replied Watanabe. 'He is brilliant and underrated in his field, if we had a dozen Japanese like him then they may be his equal, but the sad thing about today is that most Japanese are losing interest in their traditions and the past.'

The priest nodded. 'I was thinking of inviting him to some of our gatherings, opening the door to him so to speak.'

'I think that's a good idea,' replied Watanabe. 'He is a good man. We need more people like him, who revive an interest in our nation's culture. As for Inari, make sure he doesn't go walking late at night. We do not want him to disappear. It would be a shame. Make sure you tell your people as well. Tourists are welcome up to dusk but after that, the mountain belongs to the foxes.'

'Inari is the last place the foxes walk openly in all Japan,' said the priest.

'I had better be going,' said Watanabe with a smile and the two men parted company, with Tachibana walking off into the dusk leaving Watanabe alone. He walked around the main shrine building, past the closed souvenir shops and up the steps to the beginning of the track. Watanabe reflected on the conversation. Tachibana was one of the few priests who believed in the myths of old Japan. For both men, they were not fictional stories, but real. As for Tachibana, he did not just stand as priest over Inari but custodian and guardian of the creatures which were protected within its walls and boundaries. Watanabe lamented that fewer and fewer people believed such things because as Japan became more and more Western, belief in the old ways waned.

As he walked, his mind continued to move from one subject to another, from one thought to another, weaving a fabric of images and ideas together, drawing from the ancient past to the contemporary present, from the depths of uncertainties to scientific experience, from vague memories of the past to the clear and vivid thoughts of the last few days. It was true – Inari did have great significance for him. He came here when he first set eyes on Kyoto. It was different then. Fewer people. Mainly pilgrims. More foxes. There were a lot more foxes. They roamed the hills and scurried with confidence through the corridors of vermillion red gates like it was their home. Now, they hid out of sight, fearful of humanity. Watanabe came to Inari to remind himself of the past and friends long gone, both humans and non-humans.

As soon as he walked beneath the first red gate however, Watanabe knew without a doubt that he was not alone. He had walked long enough with his own shadow at dusk to tell the difference between his solitary strolling and the presence of another, even one trained to hide in the darkness. There was most certainly someone behind him. It was not Tachibana. The priest always smelt of smoke because he tended one of the fires in the shrine and the smoke was ingrained in his clothes. He usually wore old sandals made of tough hardened straw and they creaked as he paced up and down the shrine. His presence brought a light air to any room, a word from his voice the aspirations to hope on even the dreariest day.

No, this was someone else entirely. There were two paths ahead of him, each going under a long corridor of red wooden gates into the darkness. Watanabe took the left path, but he was sure that the one following him had taken the right path, perhaps to stay out of sight. Perhaps it was another, like he, who delighted in an evening stroll through Fushimi Inari Shrine. It was possible, but unlikely. No one came here at night, not anymore.

Watanabe stopped. He listened behind him but could hear nothing. The last rays of dusk were filtering through the vermillion pillars of wood around him, and the forest was still. The cold of mid-March began to creep out of the shadows and slip around his neck and dance on his fingers, penetrating down his arms. Watanabe tilted his head to one side and breathed in deeply, holding his breath. He stretched out his arms and his fingers, embracing the evening and listened. Beneath the silence of the forest path, beyond the whispers of the night, Watanabe's ears could discern the faint breathing of another, lurking on the path beside him. The unknown figure breathed erratically, uncertain of his surroundings and perhaps unclear as to his purpose. Watanabe could sense a degree of fear in his breath, and a certain amount of fidgeting, notably the flicking of the fingers on one of his hands together.

Watanabe immediately began to walk quickly along the path to the end of the tunnel, and the man shadowing him began to follow, quietly but quickly behind him. Watanabe reached the Shrine building at the end of the tunnel. It was closed and the lights were off. The benches where pilgrims could write prayers stood across the path and the small shrine sat in the middle of the clearing, with the fox statues standing resolutely in the dusk. It was in front of the Shrine that Watanabe waited for his pursuer. He closed his eyes and clasped his hands together. The sound of footsteps came closer until they seemed to be at the very end of the tunnel. It was then that Watanabe spoke.

'Is it not a beautiful evening!' he exclaimed loudly.

Watanabe opened his eyes but turned his face away as if about to pray before the shrine. The other figure stopped, and the fidgeting began. His fingers had found a few loose coins in his pocket to rub together as he stood still. The voice of the stranger began to dribble out of his mouth cautiously.

'Why yes, it is,' said the voice somewhat surprised with the question, but a few words were enough. Watanabe recognised the voice. He was not at all surprised. It was Tamura, Kato's assistant.

'Is it not a perfect evening to stroll in Fushimi?' reflected Watanabe.

'Yes, it is,' said Tamura. 'How strange it is to find another on this path, at this time.'

'Yes,' replied Watanabe. 'It is strange, especially at this time of night, that we should meet again so quickly after our last encounter. I walk this path often in the dark. I have never met you here before.'

Watanabe turned around. He could see Tamura only slightly, his shadow resting against the faint light of dusk which fell upon the wooden tunnel. The figure crouched as if looking for something and his head twisted slightly in Watanabe's direction.

'Am I right in assuming that I am addressing Professor Watanabe?' asked Tamura.

Watanabe nodded, to which Tamura replied with a squeal of delight and clasped his hands together. 'What a wonderful coincidence!' he exclaimed. 'We were only talking last night in Kato's office.'

'Yes, we were,' replied Watanabe. 'It is a coincidence indeed.'

'Well, you know,' said Tamura. 'I was only thinking this morning over breakfast, that it would be splendid to meet you again.'

Tamura began to giggle to himself, and Watanabe could hear him rubbing his hands together loudly.

'You seem such a clever person and so interested in the history of our esteemed Kimono establishment. When you mentioned Maya-chan, to me yesterday it brought back such sweet memories. What a lovely girl she was, always polite, always courteous, and respectful, and hard working. It is such a shame that she disappeared the way she did. I do not know what happened to her. One day she was there, the next day she was gone, just like that. I explained this to Kato and to the police and they all accepted my explanation.'

'Yes,' replied Watanabe. 'You told me much the same last night.'

'Yes, I did,' said Tamura. He continued to fidget and then began to bite his fingernails, licking his lips loudly.

'That's the thing really. I have my own reputation to think of. I have given my explanation to the Police, and they accepted it too, you understand?'

'Of course, I do,' replied the Professor.

'It was a painful memory for me – not being trusted, not being believed. I could see it in their eyes – in the eyes of the Police I knew, especially that fat Goro Fujita, the one who smoked those awful cigars and blew smoke in my face. The Police, they did not trust me, nor did they believe me, even when I showed them the letter. Why would I write it for her? They questioned my reputation. I know I like the pretty girls and I like to look at them, but I only look, I do not do anything with them, I stand at a distance and look, that is all, and it was the same as Maya-chan, sweet Maya, such a delicious person, so full of life and vitality and energy, she exuded it with every step she took. Yes, I salivated after her, but that was all. As for Kato, I need to consider my reputation with him. He trusts me, of course he does. He cannot do without me – I have become indispensable to him – he tolerates my… what shall I call them – my foibles, my habits, but I do the work – yes, I do, I work well and hard and have made a life for myself in Kyoto and I do not want any of it to change. Do you understand?'

'Yes, I understand,' said the Professor. He stood while Tamura, obviously agitated, breathed deeply on the forest path, fidgeting with his fingers.

'Tamura-san,' said Professor Watanabe. 'Did you follow me here tonight?'

'Certainly not,' protested Tamura. 'Why would I follow you? I did not even know that you were here. No, no, no – I was eating noodles in the city, and I thought to myself, why not go for a walk in the forest, yes, why not –it is a good night, and I needed to clear my head. It was a complete coincidence.'

'I find it hard to believe,' replied Watanabe. 'I know this path like the back of my hand. I have walked it hundreds of times. I know every step and every corner and every stop. This is not the place to come for a casual stroll. Even during the day, it is mysterious and strange. At night, this place is desolate.'

'It is strange, I freely admit,' said Tamura, feeling more uncertain and continuing to fidget. 'But it is still a good place to walk without distractions.'

'But it is not just desolate,' said the Professor. 'The priests of this Shrine leave early so they can return to their families because they are too afraid to be here after dark. People come to this place to commit murder Tamura, to kill, to disembowel to dispose of bodies. This is a place of death – I smell it every night I come here. It reminds me of the darkness of the human heart, how men so easily think they can escape the consequences of their actions, that they think the past cannot catch up to them, that they think that the tricks and the deceptions of yesterday can be so easily forgotten and that their real murderous, viciousness and malice can be covered up by politeness.'

Tamura seemed quite agitated that he shuffled on the spot. 'You are not answering my question,' replied Tamura, quite irritated.

'What was your question?'

'Do you wish me harm or not?'

'Harm? Do I wish you harm?'

He scratched his chin. 'That is a very good question to ask Tamura,' said Watanabe.

He looked at the man in the dark. His eyes could see the outline of a small, crouching man, as if he were trying hard to stay together. He was shaking, and obviously wrestling with emotions deep inside him.

'Let me talk about the definition of 'harm' for a moment,' said Watanabe. 'Your wife has never been found, nor has Maya. The last person to see either of them alive was you. The reason you have never been convicted is because the Police did not have enough evidence to convict you, but in both cases, you have been their chief suspect.'

'But why would I kill my wife?' protested Tamura. 'Of course, we got divorced - yes – she didn't like my foibles – but why did she marry me – nobody is perfect are they? She did not like the man I became, but I like the man I became, he has good qualities. Kato also likes the man I became. It is good to be accepted. Yes, it is! Our divorce was amicable and pleasant.'

Tamura paused and his voice became more aggressive.

'Why would I kill Maya? I liked Maya. I liked her very much – she liked me, she said so – yes, of course she did – she liked me – who would not? I am a nice man – I have no reason to kill her – where is my motive Professor - Surely with any murder, there needs to be a motive and where is mine?'

'I know a few things about justice from my experience,' said the Professor. 'Goro may be fat, and he may smoke those awful cigars and strut around Kyoto like he is one of those old Hollywood actors from America, but he follows the law, he lives by the law, and if anything is true in this world, he has made a commitment to doing things right, even when the rest of the world is telling him to do the opposite. That is Goro Fujita. If they could, the rest of the Police in Kyoto would lock you in a cell and beat a confession out of you, they would thump you until you bled from every possible part of your body. But not Fujita. I will not have anyone say anything bad about Goro Fujita.

'We were talking about you. Everyone knows how you look at women, the way your eyes follow them around a room, the way you lick you lips and bit your nails, the way you smile at them and follow them down the street, looking at them innocently but with darkness in your heart. You killed Maya because she refused to love you, and you killed your wife because she fell out of love with you. I can understand those motives. I have seen them so many times before. I could perhaps find it in my heart to see why you did it – the heart is deeply wicked and predictable – but it was your child, a child, I cannot accept that – I have dealt with murderers before, and no matter how far gone they are, there is always the possibility that they can turn around and return to the right path, but you were not content with adults, you killed a child as well. You murdered a child! I would do a deal with the god of the dead to save one child from death, but you killed your own child!'

There was silence at the shrine. Tamura stopped fidgeting, and in the darkness, Watanabe saw a slimmer figure before him. The suit jacket was gone, tossed aside.

'Is not clarity a beautiful thing Professor,' said Tamura.

His voice had changed. It was deeper and rougher, and much older, as if under his skin was someone different. Tamura walked forward and came right up to the Professor, standing only a few metres away.

'I see that my time as Tamura has run its course. I am old now. When I took his face, I was young, and my life was just beginning. Now I am elderly, like you Professor. It is time to find a new face. I will be out of a job anyway since Kato has driven our shop to bankruptcy. But I could take your job Professor and retire early and spend my days reading and walking and eating. You have few friends and no family to speak of, and when I take your face, we can continue our search for poor old Tamura, but we will not find him will we?'

There was a sucking sound, like water draining down the sink but getting clogged and before Watanabe's eyes Tamura's face was absorbed into his skin, so that instead of a protruding nose, sockets for the eyes and cheek bones, his face became flat, shiny, whitish with no features whatsoever. It was round and lifeless, and Watanabe stepped back when he saw it, to see the man Tamura completely gone except for his clothes to be replaced by a creature with no expression, no features, and no mouth.

'I will take your face now,' said Tamura, laughing mischievously in the dark. He stepped forward towards the shape of Professor Watanabe. Tamura was salivating and muttering words of joy to himself. He began talking to himself. His last victim was poor Maya. He was sure that this meddling Professor would be particularly tasty and eating him would compensate for the irritation he caused. Tamura chuckled. Maybe he would hide the bones where he kept the others, under the floorboards in his house in Kyoto. No one ever thought to look there. Maybe he would just tuck into the old Professor and scatter his bones here in the shrine. Oh, how he relished the thought of a good feast, now that Watanabe was all alone in the dark. He thought he might start with the feet and work his way up, keeping the old man alive, but then again, why have all that screaming? It was better to finish him off quickly so he could enjoy himself without any distractions. Tamura decided he would just overpower the Professor, kill him, and eat him slowly at his leisure, undisturbed on the mountain.

But in his excitement to devour the Professor, he took his eyes off the man and fell into his vivid imagination as to how he would cut up and consume him. He was ecstatic and realized that he could escape into a new, a safe life, away from the prying eyes of the police and the stress of working for Kato. He turned his eyes away from the Professor only for a few moments, a brief fragment in time, but when his eyes searched for the Professor, he found it hard to focus on him, and he tried to find the tall, thin shadow the man cast in the dark. Maybe his eyes were playing up on him, for Watanabe seemed much taller than before. Tamura's eyes followed the figure upwards and outwards and instead of a human figure on the path in front of him cowering in the dark with the white of his eyes shivering in the night he saw instead a figure that stood at least nine feet tall. Two dark red eyes glowed in the night sky, and they peered down at him from above.

Then Tamura heard the laughter. It began silently in the deepest recesses of the forest and whispered through the trees until like a brush of wind it hit his face and knocked him back. His blank face returned to the features of Tamura, and he fell to the ground. The laughter grew louder until Tamura felt he must hold his hands to his head in pain as the peals echoed in his brain. Then almost as soon as it began, it stopped.

'What are you doing playing the fool in Kyoto?' demanded a voice from above.

'Who are you?' asked Tamura, looking around frantically. 'Where is Professor Watanabe?'

'Professor Watanabe?' said the voice. 'Who is he?'

This made Tamura gulp audibly. It occurred to him that it was he, not Professor Watanabe who had walked into a trap. He stepped back to hide himself in the darkness, looking around for a place to run to. The voice laughed.

'You have taken the face of Tamura for far too long,' said the voice. 'Why did you take his face?'

'Please forgive me,' begged Tamura. 'When I was young, I desperately wanted to escape my family and take human form,' protested Tamura honestly. 'My mother told me stories of the ancient warriors who walked among humans, and I lusted after that way of life. I was tired of living in the shadows.'

'Living in the shadows is what we do young one. We cannot walk in the light. You know our ways: we walk in the corner of the eye, the moments after dusk and the early hours of the morning. Your mother would have taught you about the treaty with the emperor: in return for his protection, we do not walk openly among the humans, that includes the taking of faces, such actions are forbidden. Why did you take the form of Tamura?'

'He was not using it at the time,' protested Tamura. 'I was playing on the edge of Kyoto as a young tanuki when Tamura drove past in his car. He collapsed at the wheel and drove into the forest. When I found him, he had died I promise you. I did not kill him. His heart failed him, and he was white. I took his face because I wanted to be human.'

'But that must have been years ago,' said the voice. 'I do not know how long you have had Tamura's face, but it is quite likely that your relatives are probably long dead, you have no one left to remember you or bury you when you are gone. Loneliness will be your constant companion. Why stay so long as Tamura?'

'I found that I enjoyed the life of Tamura. He had a family and responsibility. I enjoyed working in the kimono shop. I discovered that Tamura had such an enjoyable life, busy of course, but one of schedules and meetings and appointments and tasks and methods. I adapted to it very quickly.'

'Kato trusted you, yes that is true. But you didn't allow your new position as a human to change your ways. Your perverse interest in young women and your idiotic obsessions continued,' said the creature.

'Kato never saw me as I truly am. He never suspected me. He was the same as his father and brother. They did not suspect me either. Kato does not believe in the supernatural. He was too busy with his own affairs and left me to run things as I saw fit,' replied Tamura.

'But Tamura's family began to suspect you, yes?'

Tamura nodded frantically.

'I showed no interest in the wife. Tamura was affectionate but she was old and plump and unattractive. The little things that Tamura did I could not copy. She picked up on them and noticed them. So did her child. In fact, the little child was the first to see beyond my face and the child never believed me, no matter what I said or what I did.'

'So, you killed them?'

'I did yes,' said Tamura. 'I ate them and scattered their bones under my house in Kyoto.'

'And why did you kill Maya, Tamura?'

'She refused to love me. All I asked was for her affection. I wanted her but she rejected me. I killed and ate her as well and went to Hokkaido, writing a letter to her mother to put everyone off the scent. I wrote that Maya did not want to be contacted by anyone and just wanted to start a new life. I was also writing about me. Now, Kato trusts me as his faithful servant Tamura.'

'But you are not Tamura,' said the figure. 'You are nothing of the sort. You are a mujina, a shape-changer, and a clever one from the depths of the forest. I knew the moment I stepped into the shop. Your thick incense tried to hide the smell, your scent as a tanuki, you could not hide it. Fujita had his eye on you, but he has spent so long among the humans that he now thinks like them, along rational lines of deduction. He closed his mind to our world, the world of the yokai and spirits and demons long ago. He is like Kato now, a rationalist. But as soon as we met, I suspected you. You have a rare gift young one, to hide yourself among the humans with relative ease. It is a difficult thing to trick me.

'If you simply took Tamura's face, then I would forgive you and let you scurry off into the forest to find your relatives, if they are still alive, but you have committed the worse offence imaginable among our people, you have committed murder, and that included the murder of a child. There is no forgiveness for you, no place of refuge and no second chances. You have also tried to kill me and that happens very rarely.'

Tamura continued to fidget, staring up into the sky.

'If you will not give me your name, please tell me at least where you are from?' insisted Tamura.

'Where am I from?' asked the enormous creature. 'I came from a cave, a dark cave long ago and a young woman guided me out of it and brought light into the world. I was in the cave with two others, who dwell in the mountains to the east in a faraway land. I do not know why I was there, nor where I came from. But I can tell you where I live now, my home is not far from here. Maybe you know it. It is the mountain of Kurama.'

'Mount Kurama?'

Tamura fell to his knees in fear.

'It is impossible!' exclaimed Tamura absolutely terrified. 'It cannot be, you died in Hiroshima, in the war, with all the others. You cannot be alive.'

Tamura looked up into the sky. The creature laughed.

'I am very much alive,' he replied looking down on the cowering Tamura.

'I am the Tengu, the first of us and the last of us, the leader of the yokai in this great land and the protector of their descendants, all who live in the darkness. Yes, I survived Hiroshima, unlike most of our people, and I spent long in solitude reflecting over our defeat, but I did not die. For over a thousand years I have protected my people, the children of Yoshitune as I call them, as I trained him and failed to protect him, I have protected them, my children with the same spirit of devotion. You are one of the 'non-humans,' one of the yokai, Tamura.

'There are so few of us left now and you want to go and jeopardize what we have achieved these last many years. The Imperial House pledges your safety and protection under two conditions. First, you are not permitted to reveal yourself to humans and second, I am not allowed to be seen unless I am directly saving the emperor himself or the Imperial Household.'

The Tengu looked down at Tamura.

'But now, the time for small talk is over – it is time for you to die.'

'Please have mercy!' Tamura pleaded.

'Mercy?' asked the Tengu. 'Did you give mercy to Maya or Tamura or his wife or his son? Did you ignore their calls for mercy?'

'Forgive me!' pleaded Tamura. 'I will amend my life – I will go back to the forest and never disturb anyone again.'

'It is too late Tamura. Your fate was decided by your own hand. You tried to kill me and add me to a long list of your victims. You know the rules, no one alive can see me in my true form and live, or else the treaty is void.'

'So, death awaits me?'

'Tamura is already dead.'

Tamura could see the Tengu more clearly now. His face was red, ablaze with anger, and a long nose protruded from his face, his nostrils flared. He was wearing armour and clothes of a warrior and a giant sword hung at his waist and in his right hand he held a long halberd, with its blade glittering in the dark. His wings were outstretched, and his feet were clawed like a wolf.

'When the police search your home tomorrow, they will find the bones of all your victims under the floorboards. I am sure you didn't move them. You wanted the bones nearby so you could salivate over them, pile them in your room during those lonely nights and relive every morsel and mouthful. This will of course puzzle them because if Mr. Tamura has been dead for years, then who was he who took his place? Your story will go into a file which is kept in the Kyoto police headquarters which contains dozens of strange and unexplained stories and unsolved crimes. Fujita has the file, and your sad story is by no means the first, nor shall it be the last, but I can guarantee you one thing. Your story will receive no attention, your existence will be only as an entry in a report, no one will be weeping for you and since you have died long ago, no one will remember you.'

'Kato will remember me,' protested Tamura. 'I have been indispensable to him.'

The creature laughed coldly.

'Yes, he will remember you Tamura, that he most certainly will. But Kato belongs to no one,' said the Tengu.

It was Tamura's time to laugh and laugh he did, albeit nervously.

'Then you don't know Mr. Kato, you do not know what has happened to him.'

'What has happened to him?'

'You should just kill me now.'

The Tengu was silent.

'Hurry up and kill me!' pleaded Tamura, stretching out his arms. He knew he was trying to blackmail the most powerful yokai in all Japan, if not Asia, as the legends go. But he was gambling for his life. He fully expected his life to end at any moment, but the Tengu relented and hovered in the air, his giant wings holding him in flight until he sat in the bough of a nearby tree, from there he could look down upon the creature cowering in front of him.

'Tell me what you know of Kato,' said the Tengu. 'I promise I will not kill you tonight.'

Tamura collapsed with relief to the ground. He took a few moments to compose himself and after he breathed deeply, he told the Tengu all that he knew, every detail, every piece of information he gave voluntarily.

'When Kato was in Matsushima, he saw something, something from our world. I believe that Kato has been touched by one of us.'

'One of us?' asked the Tengu.

'A yokai yes,' said Tamura. 'Since returning from Matsushima he has had terrible nightmares. I have listened to his cries in the night, his anguish of the soul. I cannot describe it or even put it into words, but the feeling is there. It is elusive, just on the tip of my tongue but then gone again, the remnants of last night's dream during the early hours of the morning, when reality bursts in and takes away the thoughts made in the dark. He is never alone in his thoughts. It is as if someone else is with him and this presence haunts his every step and only comes out in the night.'

'Are you suggesting possession? It is impossible to contemplate today, there are so few of us who have that ability. I have not encountered possession for over a hundred years. It is a vile wickedness among our people. It is forbidden and punishable by death.'

'The old legends talk of a creature, more malevolent than even you O Tengu,' said Tamura. 'He used his powerful mind to control and manipulate people so they would do what he wanted. My father taught me the story, as did his father before him. He told us that this creature swayed most of our people, including you. They all stood behind him ready for battle. But the day that the emperor was to die, you appeared on the battlefield changed and free from his power. You stood between the emperor and the hordes of our people bent on killing him, you and three samurai whom you had enlisted to your cause. You protected the emperor that day and in return he granted you your freedom in return for your silence and departure to the shadows.

'The one in the legend is the one that Kato speaks of during his nightmares: Nue,' said Tamura, 'He keeps using the word 'Nue.''

At the mention of the Nue, the Tengu let go a terrible hiss that sounded like the ferocity of a snake.

'That meddling fool, at every opportunity he seeks to usurp my authority,' said the Tengu angrily. 'He is trying to shape history and force things along the path of destiny but that is not our way. He obviously thinks Kato is a sign of the new age. He tried the same thing with one of his ancestors. Destiny doesn't work like that. We cannot force people to change. We cannot force events. We must give humans the freedom and enable them to choose wisely. I suspected possession when I met Kato the other night. Yamaguchi is the Nue, and he has come out of hiding. He is trying to repeat history once more and force events to occur instead of letting them unfold naturally. Kato needs to choose from his own free will.'

'So,' said Tamura, 'you promised not to kill me, can I leave now? I promise to amend my ways.'

'Oh, little badger,' said the Tengu. 'You were so wrong to leave the sanctuary of the forest. You do not have to convince me. I promised not to take your life. They did not.'

Tamura looked around him. He was no longer alone with the Tengu. Tamura could see small eyes coming towards him. They were not the eyes of foxes, but young women, all in kimonos, brightly coloured, of different hues. They crept out of the forest on their knees, looking at each other, with their faces painted white and black teeth. Tamura could smell the forest on them, leaves and undergrowth, and a cool breeze.

'Ah,' thought Tamura, 'They are all so beautiful.'

'Little tanuki,' said the Tengu, 'Now you have all the women you could possibly want.'

One of the women climbed to her feet and turned her head to the sky. The Tengu looked at her intently. 'You have your sacrifice. This one murdered your sisters. He ate some young ones, and without mercy. Show him none in return. After tonight, return to your homes. No more violence please, no more upsetting Tachibana and the others. Don't eat anyone else. The people who visit you here only want what is best for you. You do not know how fortunate you are.'

The Tengu leapt into the sky and flew into the darkness of the mountains.

The woman bowed deeply and then suddenly turned to Tamura, returning to the ground, and joined the others who all surrounded him in the dark. Tamura, eyes wide, began to breathe deeply and could not speak but tried to escape. But one of the women grabbed his legs and pulled him down to the ground. He was soon enveloped in kimono. Tamura knew he was about to suffer the same fate he had dealt to Maya, and Tamura's family. He could feel their teeth tearing him apart and he began to scream. In a few moments, Tamura was gone, carried off into the dark, and all fell still beneath the moon.

15

When Tamura left, Kato realized that it was only a matter of days before he would have to shut the shop and go into an early retirement. Perhaps it was for the best. He would always associate the business with Akiko and Ai, and they were gone. He never really had much time for the business anyway. He would however make adequate provision for the families of his staff members and ensure they were well taken care of. In a way he was relieved, as the shop had too many memories of his wife and child and the death of his brother and father. Maybe it was time for a new beginning. He went to the front and back doors and made sure all were locked. He had no intention of sleeping, even if he could sleep. He went to the room that held the memorial tablets of his family. This room had lots of the memories he preferred to forget.

The room was simple and traditional. A Buddhist shrine sat on the far wall, reserved for his parents and brother. The floor was covered by tatami mats over a much older wooden floor. In the cupboards along the walls were old files, kimono, paper, and an assortment of memories stretching back generations including some of his parent's belongings stored there after their deaths. Tamura kept it swept from time to time and replaced the flowers in the altar as well as the vase which sat on a raised wooden table at the far wall, under a scroll painting.

Kato went and sat down in front of the shrine in the dark. He looked at the shrine. There, in the dark, were the memorial tablets of his father, mother, brother, and the rest of his relatives who had died. Tablets for his grandfather and great-grandfather were also there. He sat there for a long time before he realised that the candles were not lit, and that he had not attended to it for a while. He bowed deeply to his ancestors and apologised to them that he had neglected them for so long. He promised to make things right.

He went to the kitchen and found a cloth and some polish. He took a few mandarins from the counter, and a few blocks of rice cake in a package and unwrapped them. He found some matches and took some cups of sake from the fridge. Finally, he found some incense sticks. His Father had enjoyed drinking sake. He placed all the things he found on a wooden tray made of exquisite cherry bark and took them into the room.

Kato took each of the memorial tablets off the shrine one by one, placed them in front of him, bowed deeply, with his face to the floor, then proceeded to clean them. Once he had dusted all of them, he bowed to them all gathered on the tatami mat and polished the wood of the shrine, making sure not to miss a spot. Once convinced he had cleaned everything, Kato bowed to the memorial tablets once more and put each of them dutifully and carefully back in the shrine. He lit the candles, and placed the mandarins, rice cakes and bottles of sake in front of them. He opened the box of incense sticks, placed a few in the incense burner, and lit them. He then cleaned up the room, taking everything out to the kitchen and disposing of the rubbish. He then returned to the room, bowing politely to the ground, with his face almost touching the tatami mats. He then sat quietly for a while.

While he sat there in the quietness, he remembered his strange dream from the night before. He could not remember all of it in detail. The image that came back to him was of walking down the steps of the huge temple on the top of the mountain and standing before him a sea of black figures waiting to kill him. He remembered in his dream, that he reached for his sword only to find that it was not there. Kato only owned one sword. One was enough. It was a gift from his father when he became a man. He had only drawn it once. Kato had trained with wooden swords since he was a boy. He was adept in kendo, or the fighting discipline of donning armour and fighting with wooden sticks. He had grown tired of such disciplines. They did nothing for him, and he was only doing what his father wanted him to do. What he really wanted to do as a young man was to buy a motorcycle and ride all over Japan, but his father refused to let him have one.

When he turned twenty, his father took him to a famous swordsmith in Kyoto and asked him to choose a sword from among his collection. He protested to his father that he had no interest in swords and would never use one in real life. He told his father that he knew kendo and stick fighting and reminded him of some of the great samurai from the past who never took up a sword against their enemies. He said that he wanted to be like them, never to be in a position where the sword would need to be used against anyone. His father was exasperated and so he asked for some time to talk to the swordsmith. He could hear them laughing and smoking cigarettes together, while he wandered around the entrance to the shop, leafing through the pamphlets.

His father emerged from the cigarette smoke about twenty minutes later smelling of sake and told Kato that he had decided to order a special present, one that would be both beautiful and practical, one with which he could remember his father. He told Kato that the emblem of the sword would be the dragon. Kato's father chose this because Masayoshi had loved dragons since the first time they went as father and son to the temple complex in Myoshinji, when Kato was a teenager. On the ceiling of one of the huge wooden halls was the beautiful painting of a dragon looking down on everyone with his all-seeing eyes. No matter where he stood, the dragon was looking at him. He could not escape his gaze.

Kato's father also loved that temple, and it was a rare moment both loved the same thing. He placed his hands on his son's shoulders and stared at him in the eyes.

'This sword will be part of you and part of me, it will be a bond between us, an extension of our spirits, so that we will be together for all time, no matter what happens in the future.'

The day Kato received his sword, he was speechless. It did not look like a sword. It was a cane, a wooden cane, lacquered in vermillion red and carved from the top to the tip in a beautiful dragon that weaved and flowed around the shaft. The head of the dragon was clearly visible at the top of the cane, with his eyes, teeth and ears, and his body extended down the frame of the walking stick until his tail disappeared into clouds at the bottom. Kato could not see where the sheath began so his father showed him, and so Kato pulled it off slowly to reveal the sharpest and brightest blade he had ever seen.

'This is the sharpest blade you will ever find in Kyoto,' said his father. 'I made sure it is the best, and the strongest.'

Kato looked at the sword in amazement. He bowed deeply to his father and thanked him. He had never seen such craftmanship. He found out later that the swordsmith had never made a swordstick before, but made it as a gift for his father, whom he knew quite well. It was not made in secret, but it was also not commonly known, for obvious reasons. It looked like a walking stick and could be used as such but could also become a deadly weapon if used as a sword. Kato was always appreciative of the skill of the swordsmith.

After Kato's father died, Kato would pop into the shop every few months with a bottle of sake for the old man, who had now passed the craft onto his eldest son. A few years later, the sword maker died, and the son decided to broaden his business as the demand for swords declined more and more rapidly as time went on.

Kato had not seen his sword since that night in 1995, the only time he used it. He felt a desire to see it again. He went to the far-left corner, the furthest from the Buddhist altar and crouched down. He placed his fingers between the tatami mats and pulled up the one in the corner. It smelt of wood and dust. He laid the tatami gently behind him and stared at the wooden floor underneath. He rubbed his chin which was no longer clean-shaven but rough with stubble. The wooden floor looked innocent enough. A casual observer would see nothing amiss in this whatsoever.

He bent down and ran his left index finger along the edge of the wooden floor up against the corner of the room where the floor met the edge of the wall. His finger reached the middle of the exposed wood between the tatami mats. He pressed downwards with his finger until he heard a snap in the wood. The plank of wood became loose, and he pulled it towards him with all his fingers until the end stuck out. He lifted it up carefully and put it on top of the exposed tatami mat. He stared into the cavity under the floor. It was long and narrow and held only one item. This item seemed cylindrical in form, was covered in purple cloth, and tied with an orange cord.

He sat there for a moment before pulling it out into the open. His ears listened to sound but could hear nothing. The room and the shop were completely silent. He reached into the wooden cavity and pulled out the item wrapped in the purple cloth. He held it up and shook it, to remove any dust and laid it to one side. He then took the plank of wood and replaced it in its original position, clicking it into place. He lent back and with both hands, lifted the tatami mat and restored it to its original resting place, tucking all the edges down until it formed a seamless edge.

The room looked as if it had been untouched and undisturbed. Kato took the item he removed from the hidden cavity in the floor, stood up and left the room, after turning off the light. Before returning to the room which was his new bedroom, he realized that the rooms and the entire shop no longer smelt of incense. He made it a point of burning joss sticks through the premises every day in part because he liked the smell but also because it made customers feel at ease. Tamura had insisted upon it as well, but for some reason, there was no smell of incense at all.

Kato took the covered item to his futon and put it beside his pillow. Exhausted, he tried to fall asleep. That night Kato continued to have the same recurring nightmare about his family and could not sleep. He left the futon in the storeroom and decided to sit in the empty room. He brought with him the cylindrical item wrapped in the purple cloth and the orange cord and sat down in front of the family altar. It was dark. He did not turn on the light but lent forward and lit a small candle in the Buddhist altar in front of him, as the previous one had melted and extinguished the flame. He sat for a few moments, and then leaned forward and touched the edge of a metallic cup with a wooden stick. The sound rang out in the silent room and Kato sat back down staring at the portrait of his parents in front of him. He bowed to them, sat cross-legged, and placed the item on his lap and began to unwrap it.

He put the cloth to one side and lifted what was hidden inside. It was his swordstick. Kato held it up to the light of the candle. Behind the candle was the faint picture of his parents in the dark. All was silent. Kato held the wooden stick with his right hand and let it hang vertically, his left hand grasping the top of the stick and wrapping his fingers around it, pulling it apart so that the apparently seamless wooden stick separated into two parts. In the night, lit by the gaze of the candle, Kato pulled the metallic blade from its sheath. It had come out easily without much fuss, despite being dormant for so long under the floor. Kato pulled out the sword until the blade was completely exposed and held it up to the light. He looked over to the portrait of his parents and looked straight into the eyes of his Father.

He then returned the blade to its sheath and lent forward, placing it behind the portrait on the altar. He wrapped up the purple cloth with the orange cord and placed it next to the altar. He stood up and went into the kimono shop. He found a seat close to the door and decided to sit down. He stared into the dark until his eyes became accustomed to it and remained there, staring into oblivion until the first rays of light appeared and streamed into the shop windows from the street.

On the morning of the 16th of March, he heard the first cars on the streets of Kyoto and went to the public bath owned by Itoh and his wife. He shaved and bathed and returned to his shop. Itoh was still away so he could not see him. He went to his new bedroom, and put on a new suit, shirt, and tie, prepared some tea, and called Tamura, who should have already arrived for work. It was most unusual for him to be late. There was no answer on the phone. Kato searched the entire shop, the back rooms, the kitchen, and the storeroom. He returned to the kitchen and to his tea when he glanced at his watch. Tamura was an hour late. He was thinking of calling him again to see if he was home when the bell to the shop rang. Kato hurried to the entrance and pulled it open. A tall man in a grey suit introduced himself.

'I have an appointment with Tamura.'

Kato bowed. 'Welcome to my shop,' he said politely.

'Oh, are you Kato-san?' Kato nodded.

'Well, it is indeed an honour Mr. Kato. Tamura speaks very highly of you. It is through his recommendation that I decided to choose your shop to design our festival kimono for this Year's summer festival.'

'Summer festival?' asked Kato. The visitor nodded.

'We don't usually design festival clothes,' said Kato. 'I can recommend some good businesses in Kyoto that specialize in such things.'

'I think perhaps you misunderstand me Mr. Kato,' said the man. 'I don't require any typical festival clothes, though I am sure that the shops you will recommend will be of the highest quality. No, I wish to take my daughter to a festival in Tokyo and it is a special event for her. Mrs. Murakami recommended your shop and gave me the name of Tamura as the person to contact.'

'Ah, Murakami,' said Kato. 'It is indeed a great honour that she recommended us. I had the good fortune of taking tea ceremony with her only this week. It was such a special occasion.'

Kato looked around the office and then back at the visitor. At that moment, Mrs Sasaki entered the store. Kato sighed with relief.

'Please come this way,' he said, motioning with his hand for the client to move to the back of the store and sit down. He did so and Kato went out back to provide some tea for his guest.

'Where is Tamura?' asked Sasaki. Kato said he had no idea.

'Can you look after the client?' he asked. She nodded and went out first, bowing to the guest and finding out more about their requirements for the kimono. Kato prepared a cup of tea and a small cake.

'I would like to apologise to you,' Kato began. 'I must tell you that Mr. Tamura, who is always on time and always such a great help to me, has not turned up for work this morning. I am sure that if he knew you were coming, he would not have missed this appointment.'

'Tamura did seem to be a very particular and efficient individual,' replied the visitor. 'But I am in no hurry. This young lady is doing a great job and I am very happy with her, so let us get down the preliminary information and I can come back to the store tomorrow morning and talk to Mr. Tamura in person.'

'I am of course happy to be of assistance to you in any way I can,' said Kato. 'I am sure that by then Tamura will be back at work.'

Kato walked away and scratched his head. 'Where is Tamura?' he thought to himself. He looked up and saw the door to the shop opening again. It was old Mr. Itoh dressed in a traditional blue kimono and wearing wooden sandals. Itoh was also holding some persimmons in a paper bag.

'Here you are,' he said to Kato casually and gave him the persimmons. Kato was surprised to see them. They were bright orange and plump.

'Where did you get them?' he asked.

'There is a tree at the temple called Kozanji on the western part of Kyoto. The priest gives a few to me from time to time. I often go there to think about my wild youth. It is amazing what you can find near temples.'

Kato laughed. 'I cannot imagine that you had a wild youth. But thank you.' He bowed deeply in appreciation.

'The last time I was in was in your shop was about a month ago,' said Itoh. 'You were not there, but Tamura showed me around. We had been talking about the past and Tamura mentioned that there were some interesting architectural features in the old house, so he gave me a personal guided tour of the back rooms. Those rooms are fascinating Kato-san, there are so many interesting things in there.'

'I didn't know,' replied Kato, distracted, and barely paying attention. 'Tamura never mentioned it.'

Itoh looked around the shop. 'Where is Tamura today anyway? I had something to ask him.'

'He hasn't turned up today.'

'That is unusual for him. I wonder what happened to him.'

'Would you like some tea?' asked Kato. The old man nodded in appreciation.

Kato went into the back room and brought out two cups of tea and some small sweets. The old man hissed in loudly.

'It's always amazing to walk in here Kato,' he called out.

'Why?'

'Such beautiful fabrics for such beautiful bodies!' said Itoh with a sly laugh.

'Including Mrs. Itoh too, no doubt,' said Kato.

The old man laughed. 'Do you think so?'

'Of course! She still turns heads wherever she goes in Kyoto.'

'But for all the wrong reasons!'

Kato smiled politely but did not laugh. He often played down Akiko's character as was quite normal, but Itoh often went too far.

'She is a good woman of course, I could not have survived without her,' he said. 'But I have to put up with her nagging every day, about this and about that, about everything really. It has got to the stage that she is driving me crazy every day so that is why I am never there.'

'Yes, you were not there the last two times,' said Kato.

The old man took a teacup and warmed his hands. 'I am sorry to hear about Akiko and Ai.'

'Thank you. I was stuck in the town of Matsushima but unfortunately, Akiko and Ai were near the coast. They probably drowned. We spent the night at the local temple. There were lots of kind and compassionate people there.'

'It was truly a tragedy of epic proportions,' added the old man. 'I remember you telling me that your wife and daughter were going with you to Sendai. When we heard about the earthquake and tsunami, the first thing I thought about was whether Kato and his family were all right. I am sorry my old friend. How long have we known each other? A few years I think, but it feels much longer.'

Their conversation was interrupted when the phone of the shop rang. Kato answered it. It was a Mrs. Sugimoto from Tokyo. She rang to tell him that she was cancelling her orders for three kimonos due to the tsunami. They had discovered that one of their daughter's husbands had died in the earthquake and they were cancelling the wedding. Kato passed on his condolences and hung up.

'We have to close the shop,' said Kato to Itoh.

'Are you in that much trouble?'

'It is inevitable,' said Kato. 'We just cannot pay our staff and with the tsunami, we have lost too many customers.'

At this point, Mizuno-san, who owned a café three doors down from Kato's shop, strolled in. Like Kato, he put the running of his business into the hands of others and spent most of his time wandering around visiting his friends and drinking coffee in cafes.

'Don't you serve tea here?' he called out.

'Make it yourself!' said Kato in jest.

'Ok, I will!' replied Mizuno and he walked off to the back of the shop. He returned with a cup of coffee.

'Where is Tamura?' he asked.

'No idea. He didn't come into work today,' replied Kato.

'That is not like him at all,' said Mizuno.

'Have you called him?'

Kato said he had called several times.

'Very strange,' said Mizuno, shaking his head. 'Tamura hasn't missed a day since you lost that girl, whose name I cannot remember.'

'Maya,' said Itoh.

'I will go over to his house and see what is going on. You certainly need some help today, with so many customers,' proposed Mizuno.

'You don't have to do that,' said Kato.

'I insist,' said Mizuno, drinking his coffee with loud slurps. He put down the cup and left without saying anything else. Itoh also decided to return to the bathhouse and said goodbye to Kato.

It was mid-afternoon when Mizuno returned. Kato was alone in the store. Ms Sasaki had left for the day. Three more clients had rung to cancel their orders. Ms Sasaki had found out about Tamura's mysterious client. He was a local man, a Japanese of Korean descent, a local bus driver, who wanted to surprise his daughter with a kimono. Ms Sasaki had convinced him to bring his daughter in for a fitting. He agreed and had said he would book in an appointment in a week or so. Kato had never noticed that Ms Sasaki was better at her job than Tamura was at his. Tamura was polite, but Sasaki appeared genuine.

He was exhausted. He had not worked this hard in years. He did not know how Tamura or Sasaki could have worked under these conditions. He should have hired more staff members. He felt like a complete fraud and was astounded no one ever raised it with him. This feeling of continual tiredness and the calls from clients that they wanted to cancel orders convinced him that afternoon to arrange the sale of the shop as soon as possible. It was at this moment that Mizuno returned. He looked visibly shaken.

'What is it?' asked Kato, concerned.

'Have you anything strong?' asked Mizuno.

'Strong?' asked Kato, 'At this time of day?'

Kato shrugged and went off in search of some alcohol, finding a few small glass cups of sake in the kitchen. He brought two cups of sake out, pushed through the curtain and gave one to Mizuno, who pulled off the lid and tossed it aside, drinking the cup in a matter of moments. He looked at Kato and then at the second cup of sake which Kato had not even begun to drink. Kato handed it over and this too was consumed quickly. Mizuno placed the second cup on the counter as gently as he could and turned to Kato, his eyes red.

'I went to see Tamura,' he said.

'Is he unwell?' asked Kato.

'Tamura is gone,' he said, looking at Kato, his face strained.

Kato grasped the edge of the counter until the joints on his fingers were white. He closed his eyes as tightly as he could and breathed in deeply.

'Gone?' asked Kato in disbelief. 'What do you mean? Gone for good or gone away?'

He turned away from Mizuno and sat down on the seat behind the counter. He looked up to Mizuno who was visibly distressed and shaking, holding onto the counter not only for comfort but stability. He looked as if he were about to fall.

'When I arrived at his house, the police were already there. I spoke to an officer by the name of Noguchi who said that the owner of the house is wanted for murder and has fled. Forensic investigators are everywhere. The entire house is cordoned off.'

'Murder?' asked Kato, surprised. 'I don't believe it. I spoke to him just last night. I thought he might have been ill or might have decided to take the day off work for some reason.'

'I am sorry Kato,' said Mizuno. 'But this is all too much. I really do not want to talk anymore about it. I have seen enough death on the television and the internet with thousands washed away into the ocean, completely out of their control and I look at it every time I turn on the TV or hear about it when I turn on the radio. Now, they think Tamura is a murderer.'

He turned to the sake cups lying on the counter empty.

'I need more of these,' he said to himself and not saying a word to Kato, he left. Kato watched him go and said nothing. He picked up the cups and returned them to the kitchen and then collapsed himself down on one of the seats near the door. Poor Tamura. He was so upset the night before about the finances. He did not know that he was so on edge. If he even had some indication, then he would have tried to help him. He must have gone out and argued with someone and in a sea of anger and frustration, lashed out and killed someone by accident.

Kato had barely sat down when the front door to the shop opened. Two men walked in and called out to him. Kato stood up and went out into the showroom and saw detective Goro Fujita standing there, smoking his pipe, next to a younger detective, whom he did not know. The younger one was perhaps in his mid-twenties, and he was tall, thin with large eyes. Fujita did not say hello immediately but surveyed the room carefully. He looked at the silks and kimono on display and even browsed through one of the catalogues which were on the counter.

'Is it the season for kimono?' asked Fujita looking at the catalogue.

Kato was surprised at the question. 'Not really,' he said. 'But most of my customers are careful planners so they think months ahead, to prepare for special occasions.'

Kato could not think of anything else to say, after all, of course it was a quiet season, but his store was always popular in Kyoto and he always had several customers coming in and out, some to browse and some to buy.

'Are you also a careful planner?' asked Fujita, not looking up from the catalogue.

'I have to be,' replied Kato. 'In my business, I have to be exact, with the measurements, the expectations and the service. People who want the best come to me, and I am careful in everything I do.'

Fujita tossed the catalogue to his colleague. 'Except on trains apparently. Have you punched anyone else?'

Kato did not say anything.

'Do you know a Mr. Tamura,' asked the younger detective.

'Yes, he has worked here in the shop for a decade,' replied Kato.

'How did he seem to you?' asked Fujita.

'Well, he seemed quite normal until yesterday,' said Kato. 'Until he told me about the finances of the shop. We are, you see, going under. The tsunami will bring us to bankruptcy. Tamura was upset the last time we spoke.'

'You don't seem upset.'

'It is only a shop. I was told that you suspect him of murder. Is that true?'

Noguchi put the catalogue on a table. 'We suspect he took his own life. He left a suicide note,' he said. 'Gave some reasons why he wanted to die.'

'What were those reasons?' asked Kato, deeply shocked.

'We are not able to tell you at this time,' interrupted Fujita.

'I will be frank Kato,' he said. 'Given what we know about you – and we do know a great deal – I am convinced that whatever you did, you had your reasons.'

Kato said nothing and was unsure what he should say in reply.

'But' continued Fujita. 'There are lots of unanswered questions. We have not found his body so he may yet be alive, but we doubt that very much. You are a suspect.'

'Why would I kill Tamura? He was indispensable. I could not run this store without him.'

'Any number of reasons,' said the younger detective. 'It could be jealousy, it could be fear that he would expose your business practices, who knows? We must investigate every possibility.'

'That is all possible,' said Fujita. 'But there is also another theory I would like to run past you if I may.'

Kato nodded his assent.

'You had a secretary by the name of Maya, didn't you?' said Fujita. Kato nodded.

The detective continued to speak, looking around at the kimono.

'We had a letter written purportedly from her from Hokkaido. That is the last we heard from her. Since that letter, her parents have received nothing. She is now officially a missing person. We suspected that Tamura murdered her because she rebuffed his advances. We could not find enough evidence and never made an arrest, but we suspected he was somehow involved. It is quite possible he went to Hokkaido and wrote the letter as well, to fool her parents and us. We have yet to examine Tamura's house to see if there is any evidence to incriminate Tamura or anyone else. We are busy in Kyoto now. We are overwhelmed by cases related to the tsunami, so we might not have any information for a while. I encourage you to think it all over and let us know later if you come up with any more information you could give us which might help us with our investigation.'

'Does your suspicion of Tamura extend beyond Maya?' asked Kato. 'I thought your investigation was over, but I was told Tamura's house is cordoned off and there are investigators everywhere.'

Fujita looked at his junior officer. 'You should know the truth Kato,' said Fujita. 'We suspect Tamura murdered his ex-wife and child as well.'

Kato sat down on a chair shocked. He could not believe what he was hearing.

'You have had quite a week,' Fujita said. 'You deserve a good rest. Maybe take some time off. You are going to sell the shop. It is probably a good idea, especially if we end up finding that any of this sordid affair ends up being traced back to you.'

Kato nodded and both officers left the shop. He locked up after them, even though it was early. He felt exhausted but he had no desire to sleep. Indeed, he did not think it possible because he was sure to have some more nightmares. Kato sat in the chair behind the desk in the showroom. He could not believe that Tamura was a murderer. He had known Tanura for years and could not believe that he was a murderer. He was strange and had perverse habits, but Kato could not believe the allegations. He looked at the kimono standing around him. He felt their gaze. Perhaps they were glad he was gone, thought Kato, or perhaps they will miss him.

16

Goro Fujita sighed heavily when he stood on the footpath in front of the kimono shop. He looked out across the busy intersection and over to the bustling department store in the final minutes before closing time. He turned to Noguchi whose face looked drained and weary.

'I need a drink,' said Fujita, looking at his watch. 'Tell Ueno we will be late getting back to the office.'

Noguchi pulled out his phone. Meanwhile Fujita searched the street for somewhere to drink. It had been a while since he had been on the main street, he thought to himself. Most of his drinking occurred in the backstreets of Kyoto, in small, cramped places, next to people he knew. He felt out of place here in the open, close to the tourist routes and souvenir shops. But it could not be helped. He needed a drink as much as he needed to breathe and so did Noguchi. He turned back to Noguchi who did not look pleased. Ueno, the police superintendent was probably irritated as usual. They quickly found a place to drink at a local restaurant that served beer, wine, and spirits, and started talking.

'Why didn't you tell him that we found the skeletons under the floorboards?' asked Noguchi.

'There is no reason for him to know. The less he knows the better. We still don't know how many there are, or who they are.'

'I think there might be at least half a dozen, some going back years,' said Noguchi.

'I think you would be right.'

'Today was bleak. Was it the worst you have ever seen?'

Noguchi had only been a detective for a year. He came from a family of accountants, and they were not pleased with his choice of profession, but he displayed an unusually analytical mind and the inability to follow a crowd. Fujita had immediately taken the young detective under his wing and tried to teach him as best he could. Most of his early cases were as complicated as they were tedious, but Noguchi relished them as a child would a roomful of toys. There had been a few moments of excitement, but this was Kyoto. Not much happened here except for the odd extortion, run-ins with the yakuza, and the occasional murder. Detectives from Osaka said that Fujita and his men did more tourist work than police work which was not, on a typical day, far from the truth.

'There was one other time which was worse than today,' Fujita admitted. He put the small sake cup to one side and taking the much larger empty beer glass, filled it to the brim with the sake. He wrapped his hands around the cup and continued.

'It was a few years after I came to Kyoto. Takahashi – you know him – the grumpy old officer in the records room – he and I were posted here at the same time. He was from Kyushu while I came from Ise where the emperor's shrine is. Ueno joined the same year we did but he was more eager to promote himself as well you know, so he rose through the ranks. Now he is our boss. Takahashi and I preferred the streets to the office. I still do. In those days we were eager to prove ourselves. They were good days. Takahashi married and he tried to find a woman for me. His first wife was a real beauty. We were all jealous of him. Life was good, policing was easy, and we rarely had much trouble. In 1995, the honeymoon was over. Tokyo subways were flooded with poison gas, a real day of terror.'

Noguchi nodded. 'Asahara, the cult leader.'

Fujita nodded, 'That man was a real monster. On that day, March 20, 1995, Takahashi's sister was one of the victims. She also had just married her childhood sweetheart and was going to Tokyo for some shopping. It was a spur of the moment thing and she happened to be there on the wrong day at the wrong place. When you meet Takahashi all you see is the bitter and twisted version, all full of bile and nastiness.

Take it from me, he was not always like that. The dead woman's husband took Takahashi to task and even blamed him for his wife's death. It was not his fault, but he took it hard. He was close to his sister. He took it badly and felt responsible that he was not there at the time to help. The fact that we did not find all those responsible until much later really affected him and it was not long until he was a new man.

'We were busy in Kyoto as well. There was a house fire in Kyoto that night, and a stabbing. The fire was quite early in the evening, at dusk. Takahashi was the detective put in charge of the case. I was running an investigation into a fraud case at the time, up to my neck in paperwork and a dozen accountants from Tokyo working with me. I tried to get involved with the house fire investigation, so I could help Takahashi as he was struggling, but the order came down from on high, that I was to focus on the accounting case and leave the house fire and stabbing to Takahashi. His final report ended up a real mess and that is why he has been stuck in records ever since.'

Fujita drank some more of his sake.

'But that wasn't the worst of it,' he said. 'The following morning, March 21, Takahashi was called to a house near Takao. He asked me to come along. I needed a break from the fraud case to clear my head. We arrived at dawn. A neighbour was suspicious about people coming and going and so it was a routine visit. It really was a job for one of the junior officers, but they had all busy. The door was open and when I entered the house the first thing, I could smell was the strong scent of a woman's perfume. It was odd. It was as if a woman stood at the door for a while and did not go in. While I was thinking about this, I could see the crumpled form of a body in the hallway. When I came closer, I realized the head was missing and the wall was covered in blood.

'Takahashi found the head in the next room where we found three more bodies. It was then that Takahashi found a phone and called for assistance. While he went outside to vomit, I went upstairs. Each room contained more corpses. Upon closer inspection they had all been run through with a blade, which immediately I thought was unusual because it is usually a weapon used by the yakuza. I checked a few of the bodies, but none of them had any tattoo marks. They all looked very much like they were ordinary members of the public. I immediately thought that there might be a connection with the events in Tokyo but then we noticed that they were all men, of varying ages, no women, and no children. It was like they had gathered for a meeting.'

Noguchi poured more sake into Fujita's beer glass which was now empty. His boss was appreciative.

'It was a horrific sight. In all my years as a police officer I have never seen such a thing. In one room, some characters were written in blood on the tatami floor.'

'What did they say?' asked Noguchi.

'Only one word: dragon.'

'Dragon?' asked Noguchi surprised.

Fujita nodded.

'To this day, we don't know what it meant. It could have meant that the killer was a dragon or was known by this name or was wearing a kimono with a dragon on it. We have no idea. While I was examining the blood on the tatami, we were disturbed by two men who had apparently gone out to buy some provisions for their evening 'party.' They were both hysterical with grief. They were not related to any of the victims, but they confirmed my suspicion. They were all members of a club. They had an interest in photography. We found lots of cameras in one of the rooms. Our superiors at the time said that the crime would not be publicized because it might create hysteria with the thought that what occurred all the way in Tokyo was also taking place in Kyoto, and so, after much thought, we were to investigate as quietly as we could. We covered it all up.'

'Who were the men that survived?' asked Noguchi.

'At the time, I didn't ask them for their names. I assumed that they were waiting outside for me. I was only gone for a moment, but when I came out, they had fled. We never saw them again. We searched for them throughout Kyoto, but we never found them.'

'Were the victims killed with a samurai sword?' asked Noguchi.

Fujita dismissed this with his hand. 'No, we had our people investigate it. The run of the blade through the flesh was all wrong. It was an unusual blade. We settled on the proposition that it had to be a swordstick.'

'There would have hundreds out there in the city,' protested Noguchi.

'There are indeed lots of them, but I had a feeling that there might have been some sort of carving or emblem on the sword or on the clothes of the assassin. I dismissed the latter. Who wears traditional kimono every day? It is very unusual, especially for men. No, there was something about the sword. Takahashi was on sick leave and Ueno was working his way up the ladder. I was told by the head of our division that we were to bury the case. I had been told off the record by our superiors that they did not think that the members were involved in a camera club, but they might have been involved in some criminal enterprise. I was surprised at the pressure I was under to drop the case.

'This all changed when we looked at the house again. A closer examination of the house revealed some hidden compartments full of swords and guns as well as detailed maps of government buildings in Tokyo and the Imperial Palace. The view was formed that believed there might have been some connection between this group and the terrorist organization that flooded the subway with gas, but we were not sure. This was something specific. They had photos of the emperor and members of the royal family. It was clear to me and to our masters in Tokyo that these guys were planning on assassinating the emperor, as incredible as it seems. I met an investigator in Tokyo who told me that officially I was not allowed to investigate. The matter was to be sent to Japanese national security, but unofficially, I was to find out what I could, but it would have to be in my own time.

'I undertook my own investigation and went to every sword maker in Kyoto, to see if anyone had made a sword with an engraved dragon. It took months. In my spare time I would go to a sword maker and get client lists and then visit each of them individually to see the swords. I created in my mind the image that I thought would have been what the victim saw when he was looking up at the man who had just stabbed him. It would not have been a simple engraving, it had to be prominent, it had to be beautiful, and it had to be visible from several feet.'

'Did you find it?' asked Noguchi.

Noguchi was fascinated by the story, staring at the older officer with deep curiosity. He had presented two intriguing puzzles, both unsolved but Fujita could see Noguchi's furrowed brow in search of answers. Fujita could see that already the young officer was forgetting the day's events and focusing on something completely different.

'There would not be many suspects though,' added Noguchi. 'It wouldn't be the yakuza. There would have been some talk about it before or subsequently. They run gambling, prostitution and extortion, the usual things, the odd killing, but none of these men were yakuza. This was skilful and clever, calculated, and swift. It is doubtful that any of them knew what was happening until it was too late. He or she had to be a master swordsman.'

'You are absolutely right,' continued Fujita. 'My investigation led me to a man called Ogaki, whose daughter runs a tofu restaurant, but he came from a family of swordsmiths. They are expensive items these days and most craftsmen cannot make a living from them. Ogaki made one or two a year and spends months carving things not only on the handle but on the entire sword stick itself. They are lacquered and polished, ornate, and beautiful. They are also incredibly expensive. I almost missed him because he was at the time very elderly. He had a son who now sells kitchen knives. He does not make swords anymore.

'He has a beautiful daughter who married a man by the name of Tsuda who has taken over the tofu shop, and they have a physically handicapped young son, whom they keep at home. He has a strange deformity, nothing horrible but they are deeply ashamed about it and have kept him at home. Tsuda does not make swords, he only knows about tofu. I often buy tofu from Tsuda, it is good tofu. One day he told me about his father-in-law and so I went to see him. He made a sword like the one I described, but only one, with the image of a dragon that wrapped itself around the handle of the sword and the scabbard seamlessly. He showed me photos of it. He said it was his finest work. I asked him who he sold it to, and you would never guess who that was.'

Noguchi shrugged. He had no clue.

'It was Kato Shinya, Masayoshi Kato's father, who was murdered the night before at the scene of the house fire,' said Fujita.

'He was the stabbing victim?' asked Noguchi. Fujita nodded.

'This is how I think it all played out,' said the seasoned officer. 'Kato's father is killed on March 20, 1995. Kato Masayoshi, his son gets his father's sword and goes to Takao, taking his revenge on the morning of March 21. By accident he wipes out a group of terrorists who are planning to murder the emperor.'

Both men paused and drank sake for a while silently.

'Are you going to arrest Kato?' asked an eager Noguchi.

'On what evidence?' asked Fujita, drinking the last of his sake and looking at his watch.

'I asked Kato about it when he came back from his honeymoon to Matsushima, and he said that he had a sword given to him as a present from his father, but he could not locate it. I did my research. Kato was still in the Self-Defence Force in those days. He was officially in Osaka on the night in question. But I have an eyewitness who admitted to seeing him or a man matching his description in Takao on the night of the massacre. I am convinced Kato is the 'dragon,' and however long it takes, I will bring him to justice. That's why this Tamura business is a blessing. I will use it to tear his life apart until I get to the truth, because that man is a killer, a cold-blooded killer, I stake all my years as a detective on it.'

He turned to the young officer.

'Listen to me son, if you learn anything on this job it is this, we Japanese might have invented the best monsters such as the Tengu and the Nue, but the worst monsters in this world are people, ordinary people who do terrible things. So, if you want to be head of division one day, you need to catch a dragon or two. I think Kato is the dragon, all my years on the police force and every intuition of my heart tells me that he is the man we have been looking for. We know that one of his employees disappeared under mysterious circumstances and now his business manager has apparently committed suicide and we found a dozen bodies under his floorboards. Death seems to be a constant companion to Masayoshi Kato. It really is a mystery to me. Let us use the death of Tamura as a wedge to tear his life apart and maybe we can catch this dragon.'

Noguchi agreed and they drank sake till late. It was the end of the evening of March 16th. Noguchi carried his drunken boss to a waiting taxi and then called his fiancé. He stepped out onto the road and looked at the sky. The moon was shining.

At the same time, much further north in Japan, Joshua Tree was looking up at the same moon, at the end of his fifth day in Sendai. He was sitting outside on the ruins of another town. He did not bother to remember the name as there were so many of them, and they all looked alike, destroyed, towns of the dead. He ate the second half of a rice ball that he kept squashed in one of his pockets and drank some water. As he drank, two helicopters flew overhead towards the coast. The last time Captain Joshua Tree heard so many military helicopters he was in Iraq, just before he returned to the United States. He went to Iraq with five close friends, two returned with him wrapped in American flags.

The other three went their separate ways. One returned to Virginia, another was stationed in Okinawa and the third left the military and moved to northern Japan with his wife.

After he met up with Kato in Matsushima, Tree joined many other marines as part of the U.S. response to the tsunami. It seemed to be one of the largest mobilizations in the region for decades. The days had been busy. Along with other marines, he helped to clear the debris from around Sendai Airport before moving on to assisting a variety of towns along the northeast coast. There was complete desolation everywhere, like building estates just before foundations are laid, except strewn around the streets were all the indications of once flourishing communities.

He had seen more discarded school bags, toys, and clothes than he cared to remember. The first school bag he found brought the tears welling up and he struggled to compose himself, but then next to the first he found the second and the third and the horror of the moment began to numb his senses. It seemed that the teachers and students ran from their school building to the ovals during the earthquake but were swept away by the tsunami. The bodies were nowhere to be found.

Aside from the military personnel from the U.S., the Japanese Self-Defence Force and some local officials from Sendai, the towns were relatively deserted. But it wasn't just the tsunami. The Fukushima Number 1 reactor, operated by TEPCO, the Tokyo Electric Power Company, had experienced a series of explosions because of the earthquake. This nuclear disaster, on par with some of the world's most horrific nuclear accidents, spewed radioactive poisons across Fukushima and the surrounding area, contaminating entire villages and towns, and exposing hundreds of thousands of people to radiation.

This was on the back of the minds of all those who were involved in the rescue and recovery operations. For the people of Fukushima, this was intimately connected with their individual and collective survival and another terrible burden to bear. For those in Tokyo, this event filled them with dread and fear. Many refused to go out when it rained, resisted eating locally sourced food, but more ominously, became acutely interested in where people came from.

People who lived next to or near the nuclear plant were being shunned and ignored by others in the population. Some had travelled beyond Fukushima, further south to Ibaraki, Chiba, and Tokyo, only to be turned away at restaurants, or refused entry to hotels. Relatives were closing doors and friends terminating relationships. Joshua felt helpless in his position. At least in Iraq he could see the enemy and kill him but here, the enemy was nature itself and it could not be subdued, let alone mastered.

That day, March 16 had been particularly difficult. The soldiers with some civilians had removed bodies from the remains of several houses. Joshua had been doing this for several days and he began to feel the weight of emotional exhaustion and so he spoke to his superiors and was granted a few days leave in Kyoto. He was due to fly out the next day. But it was not just the tsunami and earthquake that bothered him. He had been visited that morning by an old friend of Masayoshi Kato and he was not the bearer of good news. Joshua felt that he had said too much and wondered if anything he had said might have contravened the agreement he made under oath to his own government and the Japanese regarding the incidents involving Kato in Iraq. He hoped not and so he kept playing the conversation over and over in his mind.

He had been paid a visit by one Okubo, the newly appointed head of the Missing Persons Bureau. He asked for Joshua Tree by name. He had not met the officer before. Okubo appeared out of nowhere with a few assistants and some rice balls and bento boxes for Joshua's men. They were in the middle of taking out some bodies, three in fact, from the wreckage of a house. They were laid respectfully on stretchers on what was once the road. The morning had not brought much hope for any of the rescuers. Little was said and they kept their views to themselves. Most of them ate their lunch in silence, sitting on planks of wood or remnants of the houses. Most sat by themselves so they could be alone with their thoughts.

Okubo came over to Joshua and introduced himself. After the pleasantries and a discussion about the tsunami and its terrible consequences, Okubo's tone changed.

'I will come to the point,' he said. 'I do not wish to take up much of your time. As you might know, I am now in charge of the Missing Person's Bureau. I am also investigating an incident that occurred in Matsushima on March 11, the day of the tsunami.'

'What kind of incident?'

'A murder.'

'A murder? At Matsushima?'

'Yes, the man was shot in the head on a small island that is a botanical garden in Matsushima Bay.'

'Actually, Okubo-san, I am not surprised,' replied Tree.

'Not surprised?' Okubo looked shocked.

'The tsunami would be the perfect time to kill someone or to take an identity. I would not be surprised to find that at least a few people on March 11 were deliberately murdered. I would also investigate theft- it is a common practice after tragedies.'

'We are not Americans,' responded Okubo.

'I am not saying you are Okubo-san, but it has been my experience that most people when confronted with the choice to commit a crime, choose not to do so. There are others however who do. Most people do not commit murder on a whim or an impulse. Most do it in a calculated fashion. For them, the question is not if, but how. On any given day, many murders are committed in both our countries. This is the same for the U.S. as it is for Japan. Tsunami or not – if a man wants to kill, he will do so.'

'Of course, you are right,' said Okubo. 'As you say, it is not the 'if' but the 'how' and in this case, it is not the 'how' but the 'who.' I am concerned with the murder of a single individual.'

'Are you sure it is not suicide?' asked Joshua quite sincerely. 'I mean that day was pretty terrible for everyone. Maybe the man was distraught at the loss of his family in the tsunami. It would be enough for any man to take his own life.'

Okubo paused and scratched his head. 'A local police officer thought that as well when he found the body on March 13. The victim's hand held a gun that had recently been fired. It is possible of course, and we cannot rule that out, but I think there is more to it.'

'So, you are sure it was an execution-style death. A bullet to the head sounds like the yakuza. Was there anything else unusual about his death?' asked Joshua.

'Very interesting you should ask that,' replied Okubo. 'We checked his body and found an unusually high dosage of nuclear radiation. He had been poisoned with Polonium.'

'Radiation?' replied an astonished Tree, 'You must be joking!' Joshua looked at the man. 'What else do you have? How does it concern me?'

'I received a phone call from someone in Kyoto yesterday. The man said that the victim, whom we now know as Kenji Nomura was due to meet a friend on March 11 in Matsushima. The anonymous person said that Nomura's friend needed a great deal of money to help in his business and was pressuring Nomura to help him. He places this man at the scene of the crime.'

Okubo paused. Joshua still had no idea why the official was speaking with him.

'The man whom Kenji Nomura met was someone you know, and someone I know because Nomura, he and I went to school together. His name is Masayoshi Kato.'

Joshua Tree seemed surprised.

'I met Kato on March 12. He was indeed in Matsushima, or north of the town. We did not get the chance to talk much. You cannot possibly think he had anything to do with the murder of your school friend, can you?'

'I have spoken to the priest in charge of Zuiganji, a man by the name of Abe,' said Okubo. 'He told me that he first met Kato leaving the island where Kenji Nomura was found, and this statement was also backed up by an old man by the name of Yamaguchi who said he was talking with Kato for some time on that red bridge and that he seemed very anxious and distracted.'

'He might have been there, but it is no proof that he killed the man. Have you spoken with Kato?' asked Joshua.

'No,' replied Okubo. 'He is in Kyoto now. I know already that his family are dead, so he must be in mourning. Tragedy seems to haunt his steps. He is a 'walking disaster' as you Americans say. He seems to attract chaos and strife wherever he goes, as you know.'

'But he doesn't fit the profile of a killer,' said Tree quickly.

'What I know is that he is no longer in the Japanese Self-Defence Force. He was discharged and no official reason was given, but Kato is no longer with them and has no association with the army whatsoever now. I have heard mention of an incident in Iraq and the presence of some American officers during this incident.'

Tree looked at Okubo. 'I cannot talk about any event that took place in Iraq while I was there, Okubo-san, you know that.'

'Not even an event that involves Kato?' asked Okubo.

'I can neither confirm, nor deny the presence or involvement of Kato during any or all of my time in Iraq,' replied Joshua. He stood up. 'Have you seen this town? There is death everywhere. Tens of thousands of your people have been washed out to sea; almost a million homes destroyed or damaged, thousands made orphans and childless, not to mention the Fukushima debacle.'

Okubo was also irritated, and he felt offended.

'I have seen towns like this every day since March 11 Captain Tree, but a murder was committed under the cover of a natural disaster. It was a very clever scheme, but even if a million were dead, this is still murder and despite the clean-up, despite the destruction, despite the orphans, there is still a killer out there who thinks he has escaped justice. I find it hard to believe in my heart that the murderer might be my old college friend Masayoshi Kato, but I cannot let personal feelings get in the way of duty – you of all people must know that.'

'I am sorry Okubo-san,' said Tree. 'You are absolutely right; we all have our duties to perform.'

'Don't worry about it!' he insisted. 'I thought I had seen it all. I never thought to live long enough to see this destruction. I was told that you are returning to Kyoto tomorrow. Maybe you could visit Kato and say hello.'

'Do you want me to keep my eyes on him? Like a spy?'

'You will do that, anyway, isn't that your occupation?'

'I'm just a student.'

'Of course, just a student, of course you are, at a university faculty known for its anti-American sentiment and beliefs hostile to the United States and her interests.'

'Believing in peace is not a crime Okubo-san, nor is hating America or its foreign policy.'

Okubo smiled and turned to leave but he hesitated and turned back to face Joshua one last time. 'You Americans are very strange you know.'

'How?' asked Tree.

'You bomb us with atomic bombs, and then help us rebuild and all we do is complain about you. Now, you are still here and still helping us. I do not understand it,' said Okubo.

'Then perhaps we Americans are just as inscrutable as you Japanese,' smiled Joshua.

'Perhaps,' replied Okubo. 'Or perhaps you are better liars than we are.'

17

Early the next morning, March 17, 2011, around seven, Kato decided to go to the public bath. He had not slept well. His nights were spent as if there was something under his eyelids that prevented him from falling asleep. He only drank green tea or coffee sparingly and did not take any energy supplements, so he was amazed that he still could not sleep properly since March 11.

He was in a constant state of weariness, that seemed to drag him downwards as each hour passed. As he scrubbed himself in the bathhouse, he realized that it was one week since the earthquake and tsunami and one week since his wife and daughter perished. He sat on the wooden stool and looked at the mirror in front of him. He suddenly felt old and traced the wrinkles on his forehead as the beads of sweat rolled downwards. He also tapped his stomach and noted that he had also lost a fair bit of weight since he last looked, since he went to Matsushima. He had not been eating. He was not alone in the bathhouse, there were a few other locals, but he did not see Itoh or his wife.

On his return to the shop, he passed by his favourite local restaurant that sold curry and coffee. To his disappointment the door was closed and there was a little sign to say that the owners were on holidays. He went off in search of another place that was open. He walked back to his shop and on the way noticed that a tofu merchant had opened for the day. He gave a cursory greeting to the owner, a thin old man in a singlet and long pants, his chin unshaven, thick glasses, and a high forehead. The tofu blocks were sitting in a large tank of water, like white bricks in a fishpond. Kato bought one and the thin man wrapped it up for him. Kato went a little further and found a greengrocer. He bought some fresh spring onions, a dozen eggs, some shaved bonito flakes, soy sauce and some wheat noodles. The spring onions smelt fresh, and he was salivating at the thought of some boiled tofu.

As he approached his shop, he thought he saw a woman leave and walk in the opposite direction. She looked familiar. As he walked inside, he was hit by a wall of perfume. There were fresh flowers in a few vases that had long been empty and sitting in a cupboard out the back. The colours were vibrant, and the scent wafted through the showroom. Tamura's assistant, Ms. Sasaki told Kato there was something for him on the desk. It was a huge box of *'Tokyo Bananas,'* complete with note addressed to him. It read:

'To our dear friend Masayoshi, with love, Lijuan and Ka-chan.'

'It is very nice of her,' said Ms. Sasaki. 'What a beautiful woman that girl is, she brought all the flowers while you were away. She said that she will be back this afternoon about three and hoped to catch you then.'

Kato went to one of the nearest vases and smelt the flowers.

'They smell wonderful,' he said. 'Sasaki-san, let us have fresh flowers here more often.' She nodded and smiled.

Kato wondered whether he should tell her about the disappearance of Tamura, but he decided to let her know another time as he did not want to ruin the atmosphere. It was the first day since the tsunami that he felt little rays of happiness in his heart. It was the last rays of joy he was to feel for the next three days.

He heard a voice behind him. Someone was standing at the door. It was Seiji Oda.

'Are you busy?' he asked. Kato said that he was not.

'Professor Watanabe wants to have lunch with you if that is convenient for you,' said Oda. His large eyes, remained opened, staring at Kato waiting for a response. Kato agreed to go with him. He put the food he had bought in the kitchen and then went outside the shop again. A black car was parked in front. Oda drove.

'Where are we going?' he asked.

'Kurama,' replied Oda.

Oda said virtually nothing the entire journey. Kato thought it was odd that this member of the Japanese Self-Defence Force would act as chauffeur to a Professor of History from Kyoto University. Maybe it was Oda's part time job. The car left the busy streets of Kyoto and began to wind its way up to Mount Kurama. He found it more and more difficult to stay awake but while he wanted to doze off, the bumps on the road and the many turns kept him awake until the car ground to a halt on the mountain. Oda had pulled the car into a parking spot behind a restaurant.

Kato struggled to get out of the car and followed Oda around to the front of the restaurant, up a set of stairs and through the door. They were greeted by the proprietor who showed them through some curtains into a special traditional room reserved for important guests. It had a view over the valley, a tatami floor and two small tables, already full of an assortment of dishes. Behind one of the tables, sat Professor Watanabe, whose eyes lit up when he saw Kato.

Watanabe was dressed in a grey suit and a grey scarf wrapped around his neck. He wore black gloves. He rose to his feet and told Kato that he could put his coat on the wall behind him if he desired. Kato did so and returned to the tatami floor, slipping off his shoes and bowing to the Professor.

'I'm so glad you could make it,' said the Professor, bowing in return. The room was floored with new tatami mats and a beautiful screen painting adorned the wall behind a small vase. Kato could not recognize the style or language of the script. Two small, lacquered tables sat in the middle of the room full of an assortment of small bowls and each with a small ceramic bottle of sake. For Kato, the whole atmosphere of the room seemed old fashioned. Watanabe motioned for him to be seated and when he did, an older lady in a kimono appeared and brought in several bowls of soup and some appetizers. Watanabe sat furthest from the door, next to the window and opposite the screen painting, while Oda was seated in front of him. Kato was placed closest to the door on the right side of Oda.

'I did not expect this at all,' said Kato quite surprised. 'What is the special occasion?' he asked.

Watanabe laughed. 'I eat like this all the time,' he said. 'Nothing special at all Kato-san.'

'I don't recall ever being here before,' said Kato politely. 'It seems a lovely establishment.'

'My family have owned it since the Meiji period, in the 1870s,' he said. 'It used to be a house for some merchants, but they converted it into this guest house and restaurant in the 1920s.'

'I suppose your family must have places like this all over Kyoto,' said Kato jokingly.

Watanabe did not smile but took the comment quite seriously. He nodded.

'I own a few. And you Kato-san, I think you have more than a kimono shop.'

'Yes, I do. Most of them outside Kyoto. All over the country. Most of them empty.'

'We are both fortunate men,' said the Professor.

'We are most fortunate,' said Kato in agreement. The Professor lent over to Kato and with a bottle of sake poured him a drink. Kato was grateful. The Professor looked out through the window. The city of Kyoto lay in the distance.

He turned back to Kato. 'I invited you here today, so we could continue a conversation we began at the garden, when Mrs. Murakami played the shamisen for us. I was hoping to ask you to consider a business opportunity.'

'What kind of business opportunity?' asked Kato.

'I would put it to you if it were not for some other information about you that has come to light,' said Professor Watanabe.

'What kind of information?' asked Kato.

'Let me speak plainly. Someone is out to destroy your reputation. Were you aware of that?'

Kato put down his cup on the table gently. He did not look up. 'How are they planning on doing that?' asked Kato cautiously.

'This is the right question to ask. On March 11, the day of the tsunami, you were on a red bridge at Matsushima where you met a man by the name of Abe, who is a priest at Zuiganji. You also had a long conversation with another man by the name of Yamaguchi. Both men have given sworn testimony to place you at that island at that precise time. It is around this time that forensic investigators from Tokyo believe a certain Kenji Nomura was shot in the head. It has come to my attention that the Kyoto Police have received a written statement from a man by the name of Sugawara. Do you know him?'

'I know no one by this name,' replied Kato nervously.

'This Sugawara-san has sworn a statement that he saw you meet Nomura, argue with him, threaten him and then shoot him in the head.'

Kato was about to speak when the Professor hushed him.

'It gets worse, Kato-san. This Sugawara has come forward and told the Police that a few days before you went to Matsushima, you met with Kenji Nomura and sought to extort a large sum of money from a very ill man and arranged to meet in Matsushima for the money to change hands.'

'What would my motive be?' asked Kato.

'Well, maybe you are facing financial difficulties,' said the Professor.

'Due to the tsunami,' replied Kato. 'The shop will have to close so I can pay the income for the families of all employees killed by the events of last week.'

'That may be enough for the police to make an arrest,' said the Professor.

Kato looked at the Professor carefully. 'Why are you telling me this? You could keep quiet.'

'Of course, I could,' said Watanabe. 'But I prefer to give you a chance to see what you will do with this information. If you ask me for my opinion, I believe that there is someone out there with a plan to destroy you. It is a kind of criminal contract. There are two types of contracts. You probably already know but let me remind you. The first is your standard run of the mill contract. I have had several taken out on me over the years. Once you develop the right method of response, then you can take them in your stride. You probably might glean from my writings and from my public statements, that I believe deeply in the role of the emperor in Japan. I am a devout supporter of the emperor, the imperial House, and its position in Japan. I do not deny the controversial history involving our imperial family, but regardless of these events, I still hold the position that the emperor is descended from the goddess Amaterasu herself and is the heart and soul of the nation of Japan. This position has made me unpopular in some circles. There have been several attempts on my life over the years, mainly from communists and socialists, but as I said, I have developed a method of response and that has resolved the situation.'

Kato looked up at Oda who was sitting opposite him. Kato then realized that Oda was in fact Professor Watanabe's personal bodyguard. He smiled to himself. He thought it was odd for a harmless history Professor to have such a man follow him around.

The Professor continued. 'The second type is the contract you have to worry about. It is the more difficult one to handle. Someone is out to destroy you, not just your reputation, but you. They want you dead. Killing you would be too easy; they want to destroy everything of value in your life and bring you to a place where you take your own life. They probably have two contracts out on you and those you care about, one is the feint, and the other is the real goal, your complete and absolute destruction. Has someone tried to kill you recently?'

Kato nodded.

'Expect more of that in the next few days. If you own a gun or a sword, I recommend carrying it everywhere you go. I would be surprised if you did not have enemies of some sort. I really do not want to associate with someone who has no enemies. I simply cannot afford to trust such a man. But equally, I do not trust a man who cannot keep such affairs in check. Attention drawn to you will be attention drawn to me and I cannot afford that.'

Kato sipped from his tea again and put it down on the table. 'Oda-san is your method for dealing with assassins,' said Kato looking at Oda who was silent.

Watanabe nodded at Oda. 'Oda and his family have been with me for a while. Oda curtails scrutiny into my life from others. He is effective. You should have a man like Oda. I would have a much more complicated life if it were not for him.'

An older woman in a bright kimono appeared with two trays of food. There were four bowls each, one of rice, one of soup, one of pickles and one which seemed to be slightly raw pieces of steak marinated in sauce.

'You should try this meat Kato-san, it is delicious. I have been craving for meat since last night. I prefer my meat undercooked. I don't know about you.'

Kato looked at the food in front of him. He bit into the steak. It was very undercooked, and the blood mingled with the grease and fat. It had an odd taste. It did not taste like beef. 'What is it?' he asked.

Watanabe looked at him and smiled. 'I am not sure. I think a wild meat, wild boar, badger, or something, I can ask the chef, he does all the cooking. Do you like it?'

Kato tried it. It was good, but a little chewy.

'It is an unusual taste,' he said. 'But well marinated, aged and yes, it is quite good.'

Professor Watanabe looked at him intently while he ate and chatted with Oda. Yamaguchi was right. He looked exactly like Ichinosuke. The Tengu knew Ichinosuke as well. He was the sole retainer that stood protecting the emperor that terrible day, when the Nue unfurled his claws and tore through the royal bodyguard like a knife through butter, leaving one solitary man, his sword wavering, his eyes full of the fear of certain death. If the Tengu had not appeared at that very moment, Japanese history would have been completely different.

Uncanny, thought Watanabe. Kato's father's face was rounder, his grandfather's face was more angular and none of the others looked quite the same either. Maybe the appearance of Kato was more than a simple providential event. Maybe his appearance signalled something more significant.

Professor Watanabe and his 'ancestors' were one and the same. He had lived in Japan from the time he stepped out of that dark cave, given the sole task of protecting the young nation of Yamato, which became Japan. He was there at the beginning. He was there before it began, in the days when light began to shine out of the cave and words were spoken into being. He had done his best to ensure that the real story of the Tengu and the yokai remained consistently hidden. There were times that the real and fictitious story of the yokai intersected, but the Tengu needed to protect his people and to do that, he revised Japanese history to hide certain facts about himself and the others.

He loved Japan and the emperor, perhaps more than most. He had seen all of them grow, flourish, and die. He knew all their names. He knew all their secrets, especially the dark secrets from the beginning, and all the secrets along the way, and he made sure they all stayed hidden. He protected them from harm. He only started interfering in Japan when he was given the young boy Yoshitune to train around 1169. This caused the death of the young man a few years later and the Tengu retreated from view, content only to watch over his children. He did not know how long the Nue lay in the shadows but when he emerged, he had a different agenda. In was in his nature to interfere and manipulate, whereas the Tengu learned to give people the freedoms to choose.

In an effort to become more like the West, the young emperor Meiji and his associates began to merge all the little shrines throughout the nation of Japan, as well as wipe out aspects of Japanese culture that were viewed as obstacles to the future such as the samurai and castles. The yokai were also swept up in this purge to become western. It was then that the Nue convinced the Tengu to resist the emperor and so they stood together to destroy Meiji in revenge. At the last moment, the Tengu changed sides, and submitted himself to the emperor, fully expecting to be killed for his actions. The only reason he changed sides was that he believed that he met the goddess Amaterasu in the forest who pleaded with him to keep his ancient vows.

Instead, the young emperor made a secret bargain with the yokai, or those who were left. In return for secrecy, the Imperial House would permit the yokai to exist. The people of the Tengu, 'Yoshitune's children,' as he called them were in effect all those who claimed ancestry from yokai. They were not necessarily yokai themselves, but their families, children, and descendants. Like the Ainu, the Korean Japanese and Japan's so-called untouchables, the yokai were a minority, and they were hidden out of sight under the protection of the Imperial Throne. The Tengu tried to give them the freedoms allowed to all Japanese using the underground railroad, but this could only benefit a few without drawing attention. Most of the yokai kept to themselves on the edges of towns and villages and lived next to each other. Sometimes they made friends with the locals, but it was always precarious.

On March 12, Yamaguchi reported that he been attacked by something from across the ocean, something that tried to kill the two yokai he was protecting. Watanabe knew who it was and where it came from. He knew she was bound to turn up sooner or later. What Yamaguchi did not tell the Tengu was that he met Kato and had taken it upon himself to train Kato by using his trademark mind abuse, because he believed that meeting Kato had some kind of fortuitous ring to it, and he needed to make sure Kato made the right decisions. The Tengu knew this was the worst possible path forward as it would turn Kato into a puppet.

The fact that Kato was calling out to the Nue in his sleep told the Tengu that an insidious mind control was already taking effect. During their conversation in the pub, he could only remember the name of Yamaguchi when he thought of the death of his daughter, which was indicative of further mind control. Kato, eating the raw meat in front of him, looked exhausted as if he had not slept for days. Again, this was a further sign of psychological manipulation.

The Tengu needed to break the hold the Nue had on him as it was bordering on possession, and he did not want to perform an exorcism. He wanted Kato to help him with the underground railroad and he could not do that with Kato in the state he was. He needed to go to a shrine and pray, especially at a powerful shrine which held the spirit of a powerful deity. If he could do that, the memories of his family might be enough to break the power of the Nue and set Kato free.

The rest of the story was immaterial. None of it mattered if Kato became the puppet of his old nemesis the Nue. There were indeed premonitions around this Masayoshi Kato. The news from the Nue and then the sudden appearance of the face-stealing shapeshifter Tamura. The earthquake and tsunami were signs from heaven, but what did they mean? For the second time in almost as many days, he had thought of his birth, in the dark cave, with two other children.

But the way forward for Masayoshi Kato was precarious. The Tengu knew that the mind was precious but fragile. It could not be abused but cultivated and cherished. Kato needed all his wits about him to clear his name and be freed from the pernicious influence of the Nue. The Nue in battle was the best ally one could ask for, but without a war to fight, he simply went around causing trouble. That is why the Tengu banished him to Tohoku, where he settled down, had a family and until March 11, 2011, sent regular reports on his quiet life to Kyoto. That is why Kato needed to go and pray at a shrine. If there was any undue influence, his time there would expel it and Kato would be free. He would not be free from his past, that he would have to carry with him, but as the Tengu knew, the past cannot be changed, only learnt from.

Professor Watanabe interrupted Kato who was talking politely with Oda about jazz music. He had discovered that Oda owned a jazz bar in Kyoto and was a member of a band. They were deep in conversation about the schedule for the next concert and who might be playing.

'In two days, Kato, I would like to meet you again, this time at the Kitano-Tenmangu Shrine in Kyoto, say two in the afternoon. I am sure that the situation you are in will be resolved either today or tomorrow. If you are still with us, I would like to discuss a business proposition with you.'

Kato said that he would be there and the three of them ate in silence for the rest of the meal except for pleasantries. Kato was keen to leave but he was appreciative that the Professor had in fact probably saved his life. When the meal was over, he returned to the car with Oda. Kato realised that Oda was, beneath that rough exterior, quite a gentle person. He reminded Kato of his father and as he looked at him wondered if they had known each other in the past.

Back in the car, Kato looked through the window as they retraced their steps from the mountain restaurant to the city of Kyoto in the valley below. As they descended, Kato felt more and more confined. He saw the mountains behind him disappear only to be replaced by concrete and tall buildings and the noise of traffic. But it was the smell, the odour of civilization which hung in his nostrils. He longed for the open space at Matsushima and wished that he were back in the open space, not in the claustrophobic Kyoto.

He had been watched and followed wherever he went, first openly at the convenience store, then silently from a distance, until he feared to go out at all. He felt trapped and there in the car, surrounded by rising buildings and city smells, he began to feel a tightening of his throat right up to his chin, a squeezing which seemed to force out the air. He tried to breathe deeply but he could only get out shallow breaths and so he rolled down the window and let the air of Kyoto rush into his face. Kato felt his world closing in around him. He was full of questions, and he had no answers. His stomach rumbled and he rubbed it. He felt ill and realized what the Professor had said was true – the meat was almost raw.

When Kato arrived back at his shop, he went straight into the office area and to the room which contained the sword he had hidden away. But, to his surprise, it was gone. It was no longer where he had left it. He was wondering who might have moved it. It might have been Ms. Sasaki and he thought to ask her when he heard a familiar voice in the shop. It was Lijuan. She introduced herself to Ms. Sasaki and they were chattering away in Japanese. When Kato stood in the doorway, he could see she was radiant. She ran up to Kato and threw her arms around him and hugged him. He was taken aback but he was happy to see her. Lijuan was the only person he had met in the last week who had no hidden agenda. She was abrupt and slightly irritating, but she was genuine and open.

'Look at the ring he gave me,' she said, putting out her left hand.

'I didn't ask for one, but he bought one in Kyoto.' She was incredibly happy and had a smile from ear to ear.

'Did he propose to you?'

'On his knee last night.'

'Let us go and have a coffee and you can tell me all about it.'

'I would like that,' said Lijuan and arm in arm they left the shop.

'Where's Wu?' he asked.

'Oh, Peter has gone back to Sendai to help the victims of the tsunami.'

'That's something Ai would have done,' said Kato. Lijuan smiled. 'He said he will be back in a week or so. He is staying with Abe Sensei.'

Kato had forgotten that the curry shop would be closed but his mind was on other things and by the time he realized it, they were almost there.

'Oh, my goodness,' he confessed. 'I forgot they are closed. I was just so happy to hear the good news. Let us find another coffee place. Kyoto had hundreds. I am sure there is another one down this road.' Lijuan smiled and they continued walking.

Their path took them around the corner to a quieter street. Kato looked both ways and realized there were no shopfronts, only tightly packed buildings, apartments, and the backs of offices. He then realized there was a nice café a few blocks away that served cakes and pastries. There was also a Starbucks nearby so at least there would be a choice. He apologized to Lijuan, and they turned around and started to walk back to the corner. As they reached the end of the street, the bustling main road of Kyoto could be seen up the road, and Kato felt a sigh of relief. The side streets seemed too desolate and quiet.

'You want a cup noodle?' said a voice behind them.

Kato turned his head around. A group of men stood menacingly behind him who had appeared out of nowhere.

'Masa!' exclaimed Lijuan. Kato turned and saw three other men encircling them on the other side blocking their escape to the main street of Kyoto.

'Let the woman go,' said Kato. 'It is me you want.'

The man who had spoken pulled out a knife. So did the other men.

'You are Kawabata's girl, aren't you,' scoffed the man.

'I am nobody's girl,' replied Lijuan, who stepped forward towards the man who seemed to be their leader, pulled a canister out of her handbag, and sprayed him directly into his eyes. He cried out in pain and dropped his knife. Kato knocked his two companions to the ground quickly and while he was picking up one of the knives, the other men rushed them. Lijuan sprayed one of them in the face, and Kato turned the knife and threw it, striking another man in the chest. The man held the knife and staggered backwards onto the road, only to be thrown over the front of a black car that appeared out of nowhere.

Oda got out of the driver's seat. 'Get in!' he ordered.

Kato and Lijuan got into the back seat of the car. As it sped off, Oda deliberately ran over two of the assailants and crushed another against the wall of an apartment building.

'It is just like the old days,' he said with a smile. 'Kyoto is so boring!'

'Who were those men?' asked Lijuan. Kato said he did not know.

'I am not allowed to tell you this,' said Oda. 'Don't tell Professor Watanabe I told you, but these were probably Itoh's men.'

Kato was speechless. 'You don't mean Itoh, my friend Itoh?'

Oda nodded, 'The one and the same!'

'Who is Itoh,' asked Lijuan.

'He runs a public bath in Kyoto,' said Kato.

'Obviously, he runs more than that,' she said angrily.

'Nice work with the pepper spray,' congratulated Oda.

Lijuan smiled. 'I have never used it before,' she said.

'What is Itoh doing trying to kill me?' interrupted Kato, deeply shocked that Itoh would be trying to take his life.

'Itoh is a terrorist. You know someone who worked for him: Kenji Nomura.'

'Nomura and Itoh knew each other?' asked Kato, deeply shocked.

Oda continued. 'Sugawara, the one who made the complaint against you is one of Itoh's men.'

'But Itoh is a friend in Kyoto,' complained Kato. 'He and his wife run a bathhouse and I go there every day. I have been there for about a couple of years now. He is just a harmless old man.'

'Kato,' said Oda. 'Nobody is harmless. Everyone has their secrets. Maybe you were friends, but something has changed. You need to find out what that is.'

As they drove through the back streets of Kyoto, Kato tried to think of something that was different, something said or something missing. Aside from the disappearance of Tamura, he could not think of anything. Then, suddenly, he remembered that his sword was gone.

Maybe Itoh had something to do with it, but what? What would he want with it?

'Where are we going?' asked Lijuan.

'I am taking you to your fiancé Ms. Lijuan, at the Myoshinji Temple complex. You will be safe there with him,' said Oda.

'What do you know of Itoh before he arrived in Kyoto?' Oda asked Kato.

'I never thought about it,' replied Kato. 'I had no reason to ask.'

Oda seemed about to say something, but he stayed quiet. 'I have already said too much,' he said.

The car past a row of grey and off-coloured beige apartments lining both sides of the street, and he turned left, just as the road ended. Kato was familiar with the street. The road was full of people lining up in front of a place called 'Jumbo', an old and small, but extremely popular okonomiyaki restaurant. Oda turned left and drove up the road which passed over a small bridge, past a few shops and then came to the edge of the northern wall of the Myoshinji temple complex. He took the taxi right up along the tall white wall with the grey tiled roof until he came to the enormous wooden gate on his left and its cobbled entrance. He pulled up in front and Kato's door opened. As he stepped out of the car, he noticed that it had begun to rain.

'Do you have an umbrella?' he asked.

'In the back,' motioned Oda. Kato went to the back of the car and the boot popped open revealing a solitary umbrella. Kato gave it to Lijuan. 'We can both huddle under here,' she said.

She went to the driver's window. Oda wound it down.

'Thank you,' she said, 'I will not forget your kindness today.'

Oda smiled and drove off.

Kato and Lijuan stood under the tall wooden gate at the entrance to Myoshinji. The road forked, with one lane continuing down the length of the compound while the other went to the right, up towards Ninnaji, a giant temple on the edge of the mountain with late blooming cherry trees. It was also the road to the river. Kato watched as the car speed away until all he could see were the tail lights in the distance. Soon they were left alone. All was quiet. He looked up at the huge temple door. The door to the temple complex was closed, but a small side-door remained open and would do so all night.

An old man walked past on his evening walk and bowed with the obligatory evening remarks. The sounds of the raindrops on the umbrella were the only sound he could hear. They walked through the small door and down the path a little to see if Ka-chan was waiting down there. When Kato and Lijuan stepped through the door, the rain began to fall more heavily.

The path was cobbled in parts with gravel as well and on both sides of the path were hedges that protected the walls on either side. Behind the walls were the various temples of the complex. Elaborately carved tiles were on the roofs, some reaching up into the sky, some with dragons and monsters peering down, many built so long ago. Many people had walked this path, thought Kato, many lives had been lived out on these streets.

As Kato and Lijuan walked, his mind was full of questions concerning the warnings of Professor Watanabe, and the involvement of Itoh. He pieced together what he knew. Itoh was the leader of a gang, and the one responsible for framing him. He was the one in the shadows and the one behind Kenji. It wasn't Kawabata Koichiro. But who was he and what did he have against him for wanting him dead? It was all a mystery.

Kato and Lijuan both saw the bicycle appear at the end of the path, turning the corner from what seemed to be the other side of the temple. From a distance, she looked like a student on her way home from school, but it could equally have been an older woman. Kato was surprised she rode without an umbrella, even on a night like this. The woman had scarcely turned the corner when the bicycle slipped on the pebbles in the rain, forcing the bike and the rider down onto the path. The bicycle crashed into the hedge at the edge of the path. Kato and Lijuan saw the entire thing and instinctively ran down to her aid. By the time they had arrived, the girl was still trying to disentangle herself from the bicycle and seemed to have injured herself.

'Are you all right?' Kato asked, moving to lift the bicycle off the young lady who seemed to be trapped underneath.

'Leave her alone old man,' said a voice from the darkness further down the path.

'She has been hurt,' replied Kato. 'Can you not see for yourself? Help me get this bicycle off her.'

'You pushed her over and now you are taking advantage of her,' said the voice in the shadow.

'Don't be ridiculous,' said Lijuan who helped the girl to her feet, while Kato moved the bicycle away. She pushed Lijuan away so forcefully that she fell back onto a hedge and dropped the umbrella.

'What is your problem?' said Lijuan. 'I was only trying to help you,'

'They pushed me over,' accused the girl. 'They obviously work together!'

'Then we should teach them a lesson,' said the voice. The source of the voice emerged from the darkness. It was not one but three men, all hiding in the shadows.

'This is a huge overreaction to one bicycle,' said Kato. 'We didn't push the girl over, she fell over.'

'This isn't about the bicycle Kato,' warned Lijuan. 'This is the same gang as before.'

The woman who fell with the bicycle took out a knife and attacked Kato. He pulled back at the last moment and the knife cut through his coat but not his shirt, but it forced him backwards onto the hedge. The woman climbed over the bicycle and lunged at him again, but Kato pulled Lijuan behind him and they moved up along the stone path. Lijuan pulled out her canister of pepper spray but one of the men saw it and wrestled it out of her hand, throwing her against the hedge. She fell to the ground and grabbed two handfuls of pebbles throwing them into the man's face. He dropped the canister and fell back.

The bicycle and the woman had fallen in front of a gate to a small sub-temple. They were now all in front of the temple. A little door swung open with a loud bang. A priest emerged, wearing a gown and wooden sandals. He was holding a traditional umbrella and a walking stick.

'Thank you so much!' he said to someone in the temple. 'I had a wonderful time.'

He bowed. He seemed to be in conversation with another priest who was hidden behind the door. He also seemed to be slightly drunk for he seemed to slur his words. Nobody could see his face, for it was turned away. The priest turned around and put up his umbrella. He began to walk toward Kato, Lijuan, and the four assassins. Nobody moved. The priest reached Kato first.

'What's going on here?' asked the priest rudely in a voice that Kato did not recognize.

'Mind your own business,' said one of the men.

'What do you mean 'mind your own business?'' asked the priest. 'This is my temple! This is my driveway!' he tried to point to the ground but realized both his hands were holding something.

'Amazing!' he exclaimed. 'This hand has my umbrella, and this hand has my walking stick. I have only two hands. How can I explain this to you properly?'

With that, the priest threw his umbrella up into the air, followed by the eyes of all present. What they did not see was that with his left hand, he held the bottom of his walking stick and slid off the top, revealing a sharp blade. He immediately cut the blade across the chest of the woman, killing her, and then down across the closest man. With an upward sweep, the sword gutted the third and fourth man before they could say anything and just as quickly, he returned the sword to its resting place.

Kato's eyes watched as the umbrella fell effortlessly into the priest's hands again and only then, did he notice that the four assailants were lying dead on the ground. He looked up at the priest. It was only in the moonlight he could see the outline of a face he had come to know.

'Ka-chan!' cried Lijuan, running up to him. Kato stood stunned.

'We need to get out of here quickly,' said Ka-chan. 'Others will come soon. We need to hide over the wall across the path.'

Ka-chan pointed to the wall behind the hedge on the other side of the path. He stepped over the bodies lying motionless on the ground, leaped across the hedge, and disappeared in the ditch for a moment but then remarkably, leapt up into the air until he landed on top of the wall. He spun around to Kato and Lijuan who were standing still on the path. Ka-chan held out his hand.

'Take my hand,' he said to Lijuan. She took it and he pulled her up and over the wall. He turned to Kato and held out his hand. Kato grabbed it and climbed up and over as well. When he landed on the ground, Kato found himself in another world. It was as if, with one jump, he had left the world of the living and entered the world of dreams. He was in an ancient garden, at the edge, amid a few small trees which gave way to two stone lanterns on his immediate right, set in a sea of moss and waves of greyish-white gravel all neatly shoveled in patterns. To his far right was the outline of a temple with a veranda. The sliding doors were all closed, and the only light was from a lamp in the corner.

He turned to Ka-chan who crouched next to him. He motioned for Kato and Lijuan to be quiet. It was then that they heard the rapid movement of people down the path from the north gate. Kato could hear their feet crunching on the gravel. They also heard others coming from the other direction, up from the south of the temple. They all seemed to gather where the bodies lay.

Nobody spoke, but the sounds of movement on the pebbles could be heard as if decisions were being made in the dark. Soon, the feet scattered once more and they went off in various directions until it seemed, none were left. But even then, Ka-chan motioned for Kato and Lijuan to stay perfectly still. Kato breathed only shallowly. Sure enough, in the dark a final set of footsteps could be heard on the gravel. Ka-chan sighed and turned to Kato. He was about to speak when the sounds of others running could be heard. He waited until they had gone.

The three of them waited in the garden for what seemed like an eternity. Kato was trying to understand what had just happened. Ka-chan, the priest, had just slain four people with a sword in a matter of seconds which made him not only a good swordsman but perhaps the best he had ever seen. Who was this man? Was he a priest? An assassin? Both?

'I did not know that you are adept with the sword,' said Kato.

'There are a lot of things about me you don't know Kato-san,' replied Ka-chan. 'Oda told me you were coming, and I was going out to meet you when I discovered two men on my veranda. My sword was the closest, it is usually ceremonial and hangs on the wall in one of the rooms, but it is a real sword. I cut down the two men and then heard more hurrying around outside, so I found an umbrella and feigned drunkenness.'

'Why do they want to kill me?' whispered Kato.

'I am not sure that they do,' replied Ka-chan. 'It is complicated. It is always complicated with my family,' he turned to his fiancé. 'But at least you brought my Lijuan back to me.'

She smiled, but her face displayed great anxiety.

'My home here is now compromised; we must return to my grandfather's house in Arashiyama. There is a car waiting for us on the road.'

'I asked Seiji Oda to keep an eye on you both,' said Ka-chan.

'How do you know him?' asked Lijuan. Ka-chan's face went red, though she could not see it in the dark.

'Oda and I are drinking buddies,' he said. 'There is a bar we go to in downtown Kyoto.'

There was an awkward pause as Ka-chan did not want to say anything else.

'Now you are getting married,' said Lijuan. 'There is no need for you to go there anymore, is there Ka-chan?'

Kato smiled to himself. He could read between the lines. Ka-chan and Oda were in fact frequent customers of a hostess bar, which was a bar where male clients would pay a lot of money for women to serve them drinks and listen to their stories. Ka-chan took this silence as the opportunity for them to leave. They walked through the garden, along the edge of the temple hall which led out to the main walkway through the gate which took them to the path they had been on before. They walked all the way back to the gate through which they had entered only a short while ago.

There was a car waiting for them on the side of the road near the bus stop. A young woman stepped out. She was wearing a business suit. She was in her mid-30s and looked remarkably like Ka-chan.

'This is my sister Michiko,' he said.

'Introductions later,' she said, 'Saito's men will be back soon in greater numbers.'

'Who is Saito?' asked Kato, but he was told to get in the car.

Nothing was said as they drove through the city of Kyoto to Arashiyama.

'You will be safe here sister,' said Michiko to Lijuan. 'This is my grandfather's mansion. It is like a fortress, so you will be safe.'

'Who is Saito?' asked Kato again, not having the slightest idea who the man was.

'Saito, Itoh, same person,' said Ka-chan, as they got out of the taxi, 'One of the most dangerous men in Japan. His full name is Saito Yoshimura. In 1995 he planned to kill the emperor, but someone stopped him, that's all I know.'

Kato fell back into the seat next to Lijuan.

Saito. He knew the name now. It all came back to him. It cannot be him, thought Kato. He was dead. He was killed, along with all the others. He was the one he beheaded that night in the town of Takao. He called Saito's name when he entered the house and a man said that he was Saito and Kato killed him instantly. Kato was speechless. He killed the wrong man.

18

The car entered a large, open gate, the only entrance, hemmed in on either side by a high stone wall that encircled the property, and drove along a driveway surrounded by neatly trimmed plants and shrubs. A series of smooth stones paved the way away from the driveway to a tea house hidden in the garden. Kato could see the tops of trees and in the distance the sound of a bamboo water fountain echoed in the silence of the night. They soon arrived at the end of the driveway.

A large man met them. He was wearing a blue kimono tightened by a yellow sash around his waist and wooden sandals. His head was completely bald, his eyes set deep in his skull and a pair of glasses sat on his nose. He bowed to Kato and held out his hand to welcome him in. Michiko took Lijuan with her and disappeared down a stone path while Ka-chan bowed and introduced the small man to Kato as his grandfather's assistant. The man asked him to stretch out his arms which he did, and the man proceeded to search Kato, presumably for weapons. Satisfied, he apologized and ushered Kato to the stone path which left the driveway and disappeared into the garden. Kato was asked to remove his shoes and put on some wooden sandals which he did. They fitted perfectly.

The first stone step was slightly further away than normal, and Kato had to stretch his gait a little further to reach the next one. The path had been neatly and recently swept, and the faint light of a lantern guided his steps forward. Each step brought him into a different part of the garden, through plants dormant waiting for the right season to blossom and others in full bloom, their petals on the moss and their energy spent, their extremities turning green. The last of the cherry blossoms were sprouting, small, stocky trees with their roots confused and exposed as if uncertain when to flower, embarrassed at their nakedness. Every possible Japanese tree was represented here, mused Kato, and he wished he could see it in the daytime when he might appreciate it more fully.

On the last step, Kato saw the tea house. It stood in the middle of the garden, sitting on stone pillars. Kato saw the small entrance where guests were to make their appearance, but he looked around for somewhere to wash his hands. His eyes found the stone basin tucked away under a camellia bush. He took the bamboo ladle and gently washed his hands, placing it gently down on the edge and shaking his hands three times. He turned, stepped up onto the stone, removed his wooden sandals and slid open the door and climbed into the tea house. He turned around and arranged his shoes for his departure.

He slid the door closed, turned around and sat in the traditional manner, waiting for his host to appear. He observed the room. It was plain, with wooden walls and tatami floor mats all recently replaced. A faint scent of incense wafted by his nose, and he noticed at the far corner near the other entrance was a hanging scroll on the wall, and underneath a simply decorated flower. He could not remember the name of the flower, and this irritated him. The hanging scroll contained some delicately written script, but he could not read it from that distance, but it also held two small green birds sitting on the branch of a plum tree, their white eyes gleaming. In the middle of the room was a square-shaped hole in the floor and sitting in the cavity was a circular cast iron pot with a lid on it. Steam issued out of a hole on the side. Beside the cavity was a small, polished piece of wood from a cherry tree and a small bamboo ladle sat precariously on the edge.

Kato sat comfortably on his legs and pondered his situation. He had too many questions and he did not know where to start. He knew only one thing of importance. He had failed to kill Saito Yoshimura in 1995, the man who had stabbed his father at the house of Kawabata's son. But what relationship did Saito have with Kenji? How did they know each other? He shot Kenji because he was dying and because he was asked to, as a dying wish from an old friend. Why did Saito claim that he and Kenji argued at Matsushima over money? Also, no one saw him kill those men in Takao in 1995. He was sure of it.

As he was thinking this, the door slid open and a woman in kimono appeared. Her kimono was striking. It was a mixture of orange, white and red, with a bright red sash around her waist. The pattern was of cranes of different colors in flight across the fabric, and Kato could see that it was made from the finest silk. Her hair was long and black but tied on the top of her head and through the hair was a gold hairpin, which sparkled in the light. It was Michiko, Ka-chan's sister, whom he had met earlier.

The woman was on her knees and slid the door closed, turning around. She did not look at him, but her eyes were on the floor, and she bowed deeply before him, her delicate hands placed together in front of her, pressing the tatami. Kato, realizing his mistake, reciprocated, bowing as deep as he could to the floor. The young lady approached and sat before him, holding in her hands a thin wooden bowl with a small soft sweet made of soybeans and sugar. It was slightly colored and was in the shape of a plum blossom. Next to the sweet was a thin, small knife made from a shard of bamboo. Kato accepted the sweet gracefully and bowed deeply. When he heard the door close once more, he lifted his gaze. She was gone.

Kato looked at the sweet in front of him, took the shard of bamboo and spliced it in half, cutting the sweet, revealing a heart of red bean paste. He took the shard and stabbed it gently, pushing it through until he felt that he touched the plate and then lifted it to his mouth. It was indeed sweet to taste, and he swallowed it whole, relishing the softness and sweetness of the variety of flavours.

He looked over at the two birds on the scroll. They both seemed quite content on the branch, but he wondered how happy they would be if they stayed there for too long. The little green birds of Kyoto are not content to sit anywhere for any length of time, but dart from branch to branch as the moment passes to moment, their little heads moving from side to side in search of their food and each other.

Kato quickly devoured the last morsel of his sweet and then placed the shard of bamboo in his pocket as a token of memory. Just as he did this, the sliding door opened once more but his eyes deceived him. He thought he saw Ka-chan in front of him. The man entered the room and turning, closed the door behind him. Turning to Kato, he was wearing a white kimono and a white sash around his waist. Looking at him, Kato realized that it could not be Ka-chan at all, for he was in his eighties, but the face, the eyes, the nose, and even the ears, were all familiar to him. It was an older version of Ka-chan, with the same eyes. The old man smiled.

'He looks like me, doesn't he?' he asked, moving to the center of the room bringing with him a tray containing a ceramic tea bowl, a tea whisk, a tea caddy, and a small purple cloth.

'Yes,' replied Kato.

The old man turned to face Kato directly and bowed deeply, pressing his frail hands on the tatami mat in front of him. Kato did the same. When both men sat upright, they looked at each other. The man Kato saw was very much an older version of Ka-chan, but there was a lot more to this face. Family is one thing but there is also life and experience. Looking at this man, Kato could see a lot of life and a lot of experience, not all of it positive. The old man looked at the two birds on the plum branch.

'You have met the two people most important in my life. You also saved the life of my grandson twice, first in Kyoto in 1995 and second at Matsushima when you pulled him from the tsunami. For this I am in your debt.'

He bowed sincerely to the floor his hands pressed on the tatami. Kato also bowed politely. The older Kawabata turned to the tray in front of him which was covered by a silk cloth. He took the cloth gently in both hands and lifted it off, folding the cloth until it was put down on the edge of the tray. He took up the tea caddy in his left hand and proceeded to wipe the small container silently and returned the polished lacquered container to its original position. He then took up the thin, delicate bamboo utensil for collecting the tea and wiped and brushed this carefully and neatly, returning it to its original place. He paused.

Time passed. Kato could see in the immovable face the glimpse of deep emotion but with enormous willpower, the man forced it back down into the turmoil of his heart.

'It was during this part of the ceremony many years ago that I heard of the death of my son.'

He turned his head and fought to hold back the tears.

'I feel each day as if it were yesterday. I was asked to do a tea ceremony in Kyushu. When I heard the news, I was so upset, I broke all etiquette, and in my fear, I dropped the host's tea bowl. It was very precious to him, priceless and it was chipped. I allowed my personal feelings to interfere with the solemnity of the ceremony.'

He looked at Kato.

'It was the most intense moment of my life.'

The old man put the silk cloth back on the edge of the tray gently and looked up at the two birds on the plum branch. 'I have the same emotions at this very moment,' he said, 'but today, I will not disturb the occasion with my anger.'

He looked at Kato again. 'As I said before, I am completely in your debt for saving my grandson's life. If that kindness were not part of my thinking, whether to kill you or let you live would not be a troubling question for me.'

Kato sat still but uncomfortably, not sure what was implied with this comment. The old man continued. 'Michiko tells me that you rescued her future sister-in-law from Saito's men twice today. Once again, I am in your debt. My grandson has found someone he wants to be with and that is good. I would have preferred if he married a Japanese girl, but Ka-chan is his own man. He is a priest. He can do what he likes. I had hoped Michiko would have found someone by now, but that's life. We all make choices.'

Once again, the old man bent over and bowed deeply.

'Nonetheless,' said Kawabata. 'It was all because of your impulsion, acting without thinking, that so much of this could have been prevented.'

Kato now had no idea what Ka-chan's grandfather was speaking about, so he asked for further explanation.

'You don't deserve an explanation Kato,' shouted the old man, now very irritated. The sliding door opened and the bald head of the man who frisked Kato in the driveway appeared.

'Is everything all right?' he asked Kawabata. The old man dismissed him.

'See!' said the old man. 'I have not yet made the tea and I am already upset.'

He shook his head and turning to the ladle, he lifted the lid to the cast iron pot and using the ladle, scooped some water and poured it into the tea bowl. He took up the tea whisk and began to gently clean the bowl. Once this was completed, he tipped out the water into a waste container and holding the tea bowl in his left hand, proceeded to clean the bowl with a second cloth.

'If only life was as simple as the tea ceremony,' he said. 'But it is not. I should go back to the beginning. It is probably the best place to begin. You might be surprised but it does not concern you at all. You do not appear in this story until the very end, which for all concerned is a great blessing.

'Our story begins in the dying days of the Second World War. In August 1945, the emperor of Japan decided to surrender unconditionally to the US. There were some high-ranking officers in the army who did not wish to surrender. They wanted to keep on fighting. They staged a coup in the grounds of the Imperial Palace on the 14th and 15th of August of that year. It failed. When the war ended, General MacArthur came and led the Occupation of Japan, imposing many changes to our society. The emperor, instead of being removed and punished for his war crimes, remained.

'MacArthur, the ruler of Japan, abolished the titles and influence of the Japanese royalty, beyond the immediate royal family. These were families of prominent birth and distinction. He removed and punished the heads of industry. The Americans also forced upon us a Constitution written by them that would compel us to repudiate war. The emperor survived intact. The Imperial Household survived unscathed. This is the official story.

'Some of those who died in the coup had relatives who also believed that the emperor betrayed our nation to the Americans. Showa, as he is now known, was exonerated but important figures in the government and industry, who followed his orders, were put to death after the Tokyo War Crimes Tribunal. Even today, we struggle with this as a nation. Some believed that the then Prime Minister of Japan and others were sacrificed to cover up the responsibility of the emperor. The occupation by the Americans hid a secret, one that is not known today. There was a second coup attempt.

'The details of the plot are not well known beyond a few diary entries of some of those who survived and a scroll detailing the plan, the plot, and the names of those involved. It was in the early weeks of 1951. The coup plot was conceived and orchestrated by families associated with those who were executed and those who died in the first coup. The plan was to overthrow the emperor and replace him with one of his relatives, purge the Imperial Household of those who had departed from our traditions and values, and expel the Americans. There was conflict in Korea, and the Communists were active abroad in Asia. People were still suffering the effects of the war. The plotters felt that if there ever was a time to act, it was then.

'They wanted revenge for what they saw as the emperor's culpability in defeat. But as is often the case, someone talked. Nobody knew who it was. The Americans and those who were in the first units of the Self-Defence Force acted swiftly. All but 5 of the plotters were rounded up and killed. Those who died refused to give the names of their brothers to the government.

'Those who escaped the net decided to bide their time. In the 1970s, the Americans lost the Vietnam War and Japan realized that our future could not be guaranteed entirely by supporting the US. The plotters themselves by then had passed the torch to their children, to their eldest sons. The plotting continued but nothing was decided. The group became more of a social gathering of like-minded people, nothing more. We met together every year, often by the sea, at a hot spring, and we talked and drank, we longed for the old days, and lamented the present. But all we did was talk.

'This all changed by the end of 1994. There was a split in the group. Two members decided to leave. They changed their thinking on the nature of the vendetta and wanted to pursue the path of non-violence. They wanted a restoration of pre-war Imperial titles by democratic means, expulsion of the US and the creation of a new Constitution. The conservative wing of this group remained extremist. They wanted the removal or replacement of the Japanese Imperial House, by force if necessary. They were out for blood. You are probably wondering why I am telling you all this Kato.'

'Your family was one of the plotters,' guessed Kato.

The old man laughed.

'To my shame, yes,' replied Kawabata. 'To my shame.'

'I like my father, was committed to the cause. Looking back, I do not know why. I guess, my father was a very influential and powerful man and I lived under his shadow. But the more I did the Tea Ceremony, the more my mind saw in life beauty that would be destroyed by the path I had chosen. This decision to break ranks did not sit well with three members of the group, especially the leader, a man in Iwate by the name of Saito Yoshimura. He had in his possession and still does, the scroll with my family name on it. It is one of the great secret documents in Japan. People have died for it, including your friend Kenji, whom he kidnapped and poisoned.'

The old man picked up the tea scoop with his right hand and with the left, the tea container and then scooped up some rich ground green tea and placed it in the bowl. He hesitated and took one more scoop and did the same, tapping the wooden spoon on the edge of the tea bowl.

'It was the day of the Tokyo subway attack when that religious lunatic killed all those people. I informed Saito of my intention to leave the vendetta. While I was in Kyushu, it all went terribly wrong. The other man who joined me in breaking away from the vendetta went to talk with Saito at my son's place. That man was your father. To this day, I do not know all the details, but he argued with Saito, and Saito stabbed him in the back. Your father was smoking a cigar as he often did and started a fire in one of the rooms. In the resulting melee, my son and his wife died. The son however was rescued by someone who pulled him from the fire. I did not know who that was until March 11 when Ka-chan identified you at the bridge at Matsushima. He was there in the town visiting his friend Abe. Fate brought you together, a simple accident of events. He called me and told me just before the earthquake struck.'

Kawabata looked at Kato. 'You do know what I am telling you?'

Kato knew.

The old man continued. 'It is hard to hear that about your father, that he was involved in the plot, that he changed his mind, only to be killed by his old friend Saito Yoshimura.'

'I was there too late,' said Kato. 'He was already dying. He had moments to live.'

Kawabata sighed. 'It must have been an awful experience.'

Kato stared at Kawabata.

Kawabata stared at him and then at the tatami floor. 'If your father had not gone there that night, my son would still be alive. That night, Saito called me. He told me what happened, that your father and he met at my son's place, that there was a heated argument that led to the tragic house fire, but that it was caused by your father's cigar smoke. He tried to rescue my son, but he was overcome by the smoke. He has suffered from asthma for years, so I believe that he tried his best to save them. I believed him. He had no reason to lie.

'I was beside myself with grief. I did not blame Saito at the time. He was not to blame. He did not start the fire. He admitted to killing your father, but only in self-defense. The conservation ended amicably, and we agreed to meet up in Kyoto the following week when I returned from Kyushu. But then something happened that changed everything. That night, someone went to Saito's hideout in Takao, and in one night killed every member of his organization, except for Saito Yoshimura and his lieutenant, who were out buying groceries. The only clue the Police had was the character for a dragon, written in blood on the floor, by one of the victims before he died. Saito naturally accused me of hiring someone in the yakuza. The ferocity and brutality of the attack horrified him. All the men involved in the vendetta in Kyoto were killed that night. Saito went into hiding and disappeared.

'A week before the recent tsunami, I prepared tea for a man in this very tea house. He came highly recommended. It was Saito. He had returned to Kyoto secretly calling himself Itoh. He had opened a bathhouse a while ago and kept a very low profile. He apologized to me profusely and told me that he had discovered the identity of the man who wiped out his organization.'

Kato was silent.

The old man placed the lid back on the tea container and the bamboo scoop on the edge of the tray. He looked at the scroll on the wall.

'Saito believes that you are the one who killed his friends. He went to your shop before you went to Matsushima. Your manager Tamura showed him around. He knew about the sword you kept under the floorboards and took it out to show Saito. Saito knew what it was immediately, for at the base of the sword handle was the ornately carved red dragon. I think you know the rest.'

The old man reached over to the cast iron pot and taking the ladle dipped it deep into the boiling water, bringing it over the tea bowl, tipping it up so the water fell into the cup, mixing with the green tea powder, pushing it to the edges of the bowl, with froth beginning to surface, whitening the dark green liquid. He returned the ladle to its place and taking the whisk, whipped the tea back and forth until the froth emerged triumphantly, settling on the surface. He placed the whisk back onto the tray and then, taking the tea put it in front of Kato.

Kato bowed deeply to the old man, his hands pressing onto the tatami mat. He took the cup in his hands and turned the bowl one and a half times, then lifted it to his mouth. He tilted the cup towards him gently, the green liquid rushing toward his open mouth. The bitterness of the tea touched his lips, mingling in his teeth and his mouth, bitter to taste, he tilted the bowl again and a third time until he had spent all that could be found, he placed the tea bowl onto the tatami mat.

Kato did not say anything for a long time but sat in silence with the tea bowl in front of him. He did not notice Kawabata remove the tea utensils or the tea bowl or place the lid back on the cast iron pot or leave the room. Instead, his eyes were fixed on the tatami mat in front of him and he was lost in thought. He did not really know how he felt. He certainly felt numb, not physically, but emotionally, a numbness that ran up and down his inner being. It made him freeze to the point of not breathing at all, shocked to his core. His actions were known. What he had long sought to hide, was now in the open.

He turned his gaze away from the floor and his eyes fell on the scroll on the wall. The incense had burned itself out and the odors were now faint, competing with the stronger smell of new wood. He did not know how long he looked at the scroll, but when he turned his face away, it was only then that he noticed that he was alone in the room, and it was cold. He got to his feet. His legs were cramped and so he spent a while massaging them, but eventually he crawled to the small entrance door and left, sticking his feet down onto the waiting wooden sandals and he retraced his steps on the path. At the end of the path, he met the bald man once more who had his shoes ready. He took off the sandals and replaced them with his own shoes. He turned to thank the bald man but from the garden emerged Ka-chan's grandfather. He motioned for Kato to come closer, which he did.

'Why did you tell me all of this?' asked Kato.

The old man looked at him with a puzzled expression.

'It is quite simple Kato-san, I told you because I am in your debt. You are an important person in the lives of my grandson and his fiancé. Saito-san believes you are the man responsible for single-handedly wiping out his organization that night in 1995. From that day until a week ago, Saito-san has been in hiding, under the false name of Itoh and has lived in absolute fear of me, that I killed his organization because I thought that he killed my son, but he didn't. Your father did that.'

Kato knew that Kawabata was not telling him everything, and he was holding back some importance pieces of information. 'What do you want me to do?' asked Kato.

'If you did do what Saito alleges, then you did a great thing for Japan that night. He was planning to put his coup into action later that year. By killing his people, what you did Kato was to save Japan from an act of unspeakable horror.

'I want you to get the scroll from Itoh. If you can do that, then maybe I can use this as leverage against him and we can patch things up between us. We can end this vendetta like men. We are both too old now and we should move on from the past. But, be careful Kato, because Saito is like a fox, he is cunning and manipulative. He weaves a good story, and he is very persuasive. He will probably accuse me of killing my own son and even your father. He is spiteful and full of vengeance. He has tried to kill you a few times, but I want you safe and well, especially for the sake of my grandson and his fiancé. My grandson is preparing for his marriage, and you are of course welcome to attend.'

He looked at the night sky.

'The sky is beautiful tonight,' said Kawabata.

'Yes, it is,' said Kato, bowing to the old man. He turned around and walked into the darkness. Lijuan ran up to Kawabata.

'Where is Kato-san?' she asked.

'He has gone,' replied the old man.

'Will I see him again?' she asked.

Kawabata said nothing, turned and walked away.

Kato walked out of the Kawabata compound and started walking back to Arashiyama tram station. He had not walked far when he received a phone call from Joshua Tree. He had arrived back in Kyoto and wanted to meet him to tell him something important. Kato asked what it was.

'When I was in Sendai,' began Joshua. 'We had a visit from an old friend of yours by the name of Okubo. Do you know him?'

'Yes, he and I went to school together and he now works in Tokyo for the police. Why?'

'He wanted to know what happened in Iraq. I did not tell him of course. But he believes that you killed a man at Matsushima by the name of Kenji Nomura.'

Kato did not say anything.

'Masa,' said Joshua. 'Are you still there?'

'I will talk to you later,' said Kato and ended the conversation. He put the phone in his pocket and walked through Arashiyama until he came to the bridge by the river. He found a seat which overlooked the water and sat down. The night was still. There was little movement on the river and almost no breeze, but it was cool.

His conversation with Kawabata had shocked him but it is raised more unanswered questions. He did not believe that his father tried to kill Saito. That was a lie. He reasoned that Kawabata's friendship with Saito blinded him to his old friend's deception. It was Saito who stabbed Kato's father in the back. It was not the result of a struggle. It was cold betrayal.

He also found it hard to believe that his father and his family would be involved in a vendetta dating back to the dying days of the occupation by the Americans. He had never heard of any such plot. Surely, if it were true, there would be some information about it in the news. Those kinds of things have a way of becoming known at some point. He could not countenance the idea that his father of all people, would be interested in plotting against the emperor of Japan. He loved Japan, and he was a man of peace, a gentle and kind man, if not a little strict with Kato and his wayward ways. He was committed to the kimono shop and to his family and that was it, he held no other allegiances. Kato followed him in this regard. All that mattered was family and business, in that order.

Then Kato thought of his old friend Kenji. How did he get involved in all of this? He kept his friendship with Saito a secret. When he came to him for help, Kato stepped up and without hesitation volunteered. He did it for friendship, and a sense of shame because he stole Akiko from him all those years ago. Kenji was not the right man for her, he knew that when he saw them together, but he still felt rotten for what he did, literally taking her away from Kenji and marrying her.

But who poisoned his old friend and who wanted him dead? Kenji had said that he was close to finding out the location of a scroll. This had to be the scroll Kawabata was talking about. Kenji had to be working for Saito all along, because why would he give him the name of Kawabata? Saito would not have killed one of his own men, so it must have been Kawabata.

Kawabata said that his grandson and he met due to fate. This was the biggest lie of all. There was no such thing as coincidence. Ka-chan may have known Abe from his days at the Buddhist seminary and he certainly had relatives in the area, but that he should be on the same island, the same afternoon as Kato. That was a lie. Thinking back to that day, Abe and Ka-chan were smoking cigarettes on the island and walked back along the bridge, but who is to say that Abe did not meet Ka-chan on the island instead of walking with him to the island in the first place? Ka-chan might have been looking for Kenji because he found out somehow that Kenji knew of the location of the scroll. He followed him to Matsushima and was on the island the same time as Kato.

But Kato shot Kenji before Ka-chan could talk to him and force the location of the scroll out of him. He then assumed that Kato was involved with Kenji and Saito. Why else would he turn up at Matsushima? Kato then shuddered. Ka-chan was indeed an assassin. He was ordered by his grandfather to kill them both. He was planning to do that somewhere in Matsushima that day. But when he met Kato, he looked into his eyes and recognised him as the man who rescued him from the fire all those years ago. At that moment, Ka-chan could not obey his grandfather. He left the restaurant to talk to his grandfather before the earthquake and was told to get close to Kato and find out what he knew about the scroll. That was it. His friendship was just a ruse to get the scroll. What of Lijuan? Obviously, she was just getting played by a man even more ruthless than Kato was. Sure, he was a killer, but he would not manipulate someone like that for anything, not someone innocent.

What were the facts? Saito, and Kawabata know that Kato wiped out the terror group in 1995. They know that he is the owner of the sword that was used to kill everyone. Saito now had the sword in his possession. Joshua Tree told him that the Police suspect him of killing Kenji due to several witness statements that place him at the scene of the crime. Kato sighed. It was over. There was no way out this time.

Kato stood up and walked to the bridge. He crossed it in silence, looking out to the darkness of the forest in the distance. The river ran beneath the bridge, and he could see the reflection of the moon in the water. He reached the end of the bridge and found a seat to sit on so he could look up the river towards the forest. He could hear the cries of monkeys in the trees nearby. If these were the facts, he thought, what choice did he have?

There was only one. Itoh or Saito was involved in the death of his father. He could identify him. Kawabata was indeed a liar, and he had a role to play in the death of Kenji. He was probably the one who poisoned him. But Kawabata and Saito were warriors, fighting in an imaginary war against a nation that no longer cared about their insane ideas. How many other lunatics did Saito and Kawabata have working for them? What if they had a small army and they were all located in various parts of the Japanese government? If Itoh and Kawabata could hide effectively, then who else was lurking in the shadows? Kawabata mentioned five families: Saito, Kato, and Kawabata. There were two left he did not mention. Who were they? Where were they? What was their role in all of this?

There was only one choice. He needed to turn himself in, confess his role in the death of Nomura and bring the current situation to the attention of the authorities. It was too big for him, too difficult, he was only one man. Okubo was his old school friend. He could reason with him. Joshua Tree was his friend. He could help him as well. His information might lead to the prosecution of Kawabata. He had to confess. He would confess to Goro Fujita. He would do it at Myoshinji. The police no doubt would have found by now the bodies of the men who tried to kill Ka-chan, Lijuan and Kato the night before. Goro Fujita was bound to be at the scene. He stood up and walked along the main street of Arashiyama up to the railway line and then towards Kyoto. He found an all-night café. He stopped went inside, ordering some food and coffee and he waited.

19

It was only a few hours before the sun rose and Kato left the restaurant. He had drunk more than five cups of black coffee. He hailed a taxi which took him to the southern entrance to the huge temple complex of Myoshinji. As he got out of the taxi, a line of monks walked past in their dark robes and wide brimmed hats, chanting for alms. They were each calling out loudly in their voices a monotonous but harmonious tune. The chaos of the previous night left their daily commitments unaltered. Kato ran up to their leader, bowed, and gave him some money. The monks stopped, their leader bowed and rang a small bell, and they continued to walk along the street.

Kato turned and walked up the stone path, past several temples, turning left and then saw the enormous blackened wooden hall that sat high on a stone wall. For some reason, some of the wooden panels were open and Kato decided to go inside. On the roof was the painting of a huge swirling dragon, who seemed to follow people around with its piercing eyes. He had been there with Akiko a few years ago with their daughter and they found the view mesmerizing. He had been here with his Father too. This place was important to his family. It brought them together.

'Seeing a dragon for the first time is always a revelation,' said a voice behind him.

It was Saito.

He was in a plain suit, an open-necked shirt and was holding Kato's sword in his left hand. Kato did say anything but turned to face him.

'I found the sword quite by accident. Tamura-san showed me. He found it one day while he was cleaning. I must admit I was surprised when I saw the engraved dragon on the end. I began to wonder to myself, maybe I accused Kawabata-san without cause.'

'Kawabata said that you killed my father in self-defence, and tried to rescue his son, but were overcome by the smoke,' replied Kato. 'He said that he and my Father broke away from the vendetta but that you opposed them.'

Saito laughed out aloud. 'Did everything he say to you have the ring of truth to it?' he asked.

Kato said nothing.

'Your silence tells me everything,' continued Saito.

'Kenji was a good kid who needed guidance in life. He was a member of my organization for about a year. He did odd jobs. He was good at numbers, that sort of thing. Our paths crossed a few years ago when I returned to Kyoto, out of hiding. He came to the bathhouse a few times. I hired him only to do the accounts for me, but Kawabata must have seen us together and assumed he was one of my people.

'He wasn't. He was kidnapped by Kawabata a week before the tsunami. He wanted the scroll. He tortured Kenji, but Kenji only knew that it was located at a temple. In Kyoto there are 1,600 temples and shrines. They poisoned him with the polonium. I do not know where Kawabata got it from. I suspect from a foreign power. If anyone knew the right people, it would be Kawabata. Kenji escaped and came to me. He told me where he was going and what he was up to. I tried to talk him out of it. I had Sugawara, one of my men, follow him, all the way to Sendai as it happened. It was when he saw Ka-chan, or so he calls himself today. He called me, and I knew that Kawabata was behind the whole thing.

'Why would I try to set you up? I was angry with you, yes, that is true. I wanted revenge for what you did on the night of March 21, 1995. You arrived at my home in Takao and wiped out my organization, including my brother, whom you assumed was me. He was my twin brother, though not identical.'

'I called out the name 'Saito' when I came in the door,' said Kato. 'A man appeared and said he was Saito. I did assume it was you. I had never met you so how was I to know?'

'You had every right to take revenge for the death of your father,' said Saito. 'I killed him that night. I stabbed him in the back. He went that evening to talk to Kawabata's son to convince him to break with the vendetta. He and his wife had grave doubts.'

Kato sighed. 'But who killed the son and his wife?' he asked. 'I went into the house. His son had been stabbed to death. If you did not kill them, then who?'

'Ah Kato, you have been lied to. Kawabata was there with me. He killed his own son, knocked the wife unconscious, and set the house on fire. I told him that the boy was still upstairs, but Kawabata said to me that he wanted the stain of shame removed from his family entirely. No one associated with his son would be allowed to survive.'

'He said he was in Kyushu,' protested Kato. 'Are you saying that he was in Kyoto? Why would he kill his own son?'

'You don't understand do you Kato,' said Saito. 'Your father was the only one to break ranks with the vendetta. Kawabata and I remained committed the cause. Kawabata was, and I believe still is the leader of the vendetta. He and I were the ones who returned to my house that night to find everyone dead. I went into hiding and then left Japan with my wife, my organisation in tatters.

'Kawabata continues with his insane plans to topple the government. It just gets even more absurd with every passing year. His grandson is committed to the cause. Ka-chan should have died in the fire. He is as mad as the grandfather, even more insane. The girl, I don't think she is involved, she just likes the tea ceremony. But know this Kato, Ka-chan is a complete fanatic. He is devoted to the vendetta, this crazy plan to overthrow the emperor.

'Kawabata has regular psychotic seizures. He has had them since his youth when he survived the firebombing of Tokyo which killed his mother. It is why he started doing the tea ceremony, to counterbalance his insanity. This madness he passed onto his grandson. It skipped his son for some reason, a weak but nice man who just wanted a normal life.

'That is why your father had to die back in 1995. Shinya had made an alliance with an important family in Kyoto with ties to the emperor, someone called Watanabe. He talked about helping the people in Japan who had been ignored and marginalized, the so-called non-humans and the minorities. Shinya got all sentimental about building a better Japan, a fairer Japan. We wanted an old Japan, a return to the past, a return to the old ways. As soon as Shinya told us, I knew Kawabata would ask me to kill him.'

Kato felt his need to sit down and so he sat down on the wooden floor of the temple hall. He looked up at the ceiling. The dragon looked down at him.

'Where did you go?' he asked.

'I went to Indonesia and built houses for the poor. I was a carpenter in Japan. I felt the shame of your father's death very keenly and I thought that by way of penance I could do in Indonesia what your father tried to do here. In the mountains among the poor, I made my peace with the past and with your father's ghost who never seemed to find rest. In carpentry and nails, monsoon, and sweltering heat, I felt, for the first time in my life that I was doing some good in the world. Eventually Kawabata found out where I was and sent his people after me. I did not want the local people to suffer on account of me and so it was time to move again. I returned to Kyoto and rebuilt my organisation.

'I feared for you. I heard that you were back in Kyoto. I knew your father. You are just like him. He had a way of finding trouble. You do too. I thought I might be able to protect you in a way I could not protect him. I must admit I was angry when I found the sword and went to see Kawabata. I sent one of my men to rattle you in Kyoto. You gave him a real beating. You are just like your father. When I went to see Kawabata, I pretended to be committed to the cause, the vendetta, but I could see that Kawabata was completely insane. He wanted me to continue in our quest to rid Japan of the emperor as the puppet of America. He kept talking about the scroll. I refused to tell him where it was, but he was very insistent. I have until today to get it for him, or he has threatened to declare war on my family as an enemy of the vendetta. He murdered his own son Kato. There is nothing this man would not do for his insane cause.'

'I was attacked in Myoshinji last night by men I assumed were working for you and in Kyoto, near my office, some men tried to attack us,' said Kato.

'I only have three men left in my organization: the man who said he was in Matsushima, the man who roughed you up and another one. They are the only ones loyal to me and they would die for me. Sugawara is from the old days. He is the one who gave the police that stirring testimony about you. He is a brute but loyal and loyalty is important these days especially in a world that doesn't believe in anything. Beyond that, I have no one. I do not have the power to organise such an elaborate scheme.'

'You are saying that Kawabata staged it for our benefit?' asked Kato.

'Kawabata is a master assassin Kato,' said Saito. 'He holds all the strings. He probably hired them from someone, but they were not my people. I have seen them. They are being identified by the Police just up the path here. None of them are my men. I am tired Kato. I want to go to the temple, get the scroll and burn it, so that this insanity will come to an end. That is the least I can do for your father.'

'You have done much more than that,' said Kato.

At this moment Kato noticed that someone else had entered the hall. He could not make out his identity, but Saito sensed him as well.

'More people to see the dragon,' said Saito to the man who had entered. It was Noguchi, detective Fujita's assistant. He was wearing a brown suit and had his gun drawn.

'There is no need for guns in this place,' said Saito firmly.

'I will put down the gun when you put down the sword and move away from Kato-san,' ordered Noguchi.

Saito looked at Kato.

'As I said Kato-san, Kawabata's allies are everywhere, like this man. I wonder what price he paid for his complicity.'

'Put down the sword,' insisted Noguchi.

'I don't think he works for Kawabata,' said Kato finally. 'I think he is eager to prove himself to Fujita, his boss. Where is Fujita?'

'He is at the pile of bodies we found up the road and now I have found their killer,' boasted Noguchi.

'Just because he has a sword, it doesn't mean that he was responsible for anything,' replied Kato.

Noguchi began to waver with his pistol. He was unsure of what to do. Kato knew he had to resolve the situation quickly.

'Noguchi,' he urged. 'Listen to me, I must speak to your boss Fujita about what happened in Matsushima. Let this man go. He is just an old man who doesn't know what he is doing.'

'What are you doing Kato?' asked Saito, his face amazed. 'If you confess to anything, you will spend the rest of your life in prison.'

'I don't want anyone else to die because of me,' said Kato.

Saito looked seriously at Kato. 'I am not the only one Kato-san, Kawabata must be stopped, and you are the only one who can do that. In Indonesia I realised that the past is more complicated than we tended to believe when we were young. There are however others in the shadows, even crazier than Kawabata, who will proceed with the vendetta if he dies. You will cross paths with them soon. Trust no one Kato.'

Saito smiled.

Kato realized what Saito was about to do and standing up, he tried to take the sword from him, but Saito knocked him back with the sword handle and then turned to face Noguchi. He drew the sword, raised it above his head and yelled at the detective. He had not gone one step when a single shot rang out and struck Saito in the chest. He dropped to his knees, the sword fell out of his hand, and he collapsed. Kato went over and lifted him up on his knees. He knew immediately that it was a fatal wound. Saito had only moments to live. He looked up at Kato, with blood in his mouth.

'Kato,' he said. 'I'm sorry, I should have told you who I really was.'

Kato looked up at Noguchi. 'Get an ambulance and a doctor immediately.'

The detective stood there, frozen, unable to move. 'Get an ambulance!' ordered Kato. Noguchi turned and ran out.

'Kato,' said Saito, grabbing his coat, now covered in blood. 'You must get the scroll and keep it. It is the only thing that will keep you alive. Do not give it to Kawabata. Find the others. Destroy them. Stop the vendetta and save the emperor's family. Save Japan!'

'Where is it?'

'Under the persimmon tree near the temple at Kozanji. You will know it when you see it.'

He started to cough up blood violently.

At that moment, detective Fujita appeared with several other officers. He looked at Kato who shook his head. Saito was not going to make it.

'Is that you Fujita?' asked Saito.

Fujita came over to him and crouched down. 'There,' he said, pointing to the sword. 'It is mine. Kato's father gave it to me long ago. I killed all the people in that house in Takao.'

He lent forward and grabbed Kato's coat. 'Kato-san is innocent, do you hear me you lousy detective, you couldn't find me for years and I was hiding right under your nose.'

As he breathed these last words, he died.

Kato stayed with the body for a while as Fujita gave Noguchi a dressing down for using his gun. He would be suspended immediately following an investigation. Soon, Ueno-san, the head of the Kyoto Police department was on the scene and Noguchi was dismissed, pending a formal inquiry but the police chief made it clear that the young detective's career was over. Kato made his excuses to leave and wash off the blood. Fujita reluctantly agreed when Ueno stepped in and told him off, especially when he began talking about his quest to have Kato arrested for the murders in the house in Takao in 1995. Ueno was furious telling the detective that he had a dying man confess to the murders and he still wanted to prosecute an innocent man for the crimes. Kato left but he didn't go home to change. Instead, he caught a taxi to the temple grounds of Kozanji.

Kato left the car and walked across the road to a small path which led up the hill. At the top, Kato found a graveyard. It was small, surrounded by bamboo and overgrown with weeds. There was a gravelled entrance and a small, rusty gate. He pushed past the gate and found a bucket and a ladle and filled the bucket with water. He felt strange going to this place for he had no relatives here and he felt as if he was intruding into the homes of people he did not know.

He walked past the graves at the entrance, each of them stone pillars with the name written in vertical script, with small pots in front, some carefully preserved while others neglected. It was then that he saw it. Far at the end of the cemetery, well past the stones, there was a tall tree, its branches hanging over the graves, its old trunk winding up into the sky. It was a persimmon tree, but no fruit hung there. It was bare. The tree stood watch over the tombs, and probably had been planted at the time of the cemetery's consecration. At that moment, Kato could hear the ringing of a bell in the forest. That must be the temple he thought to himself, but what a secluded and solitary spot to rest the ancestors. It must have been very lonely for them.

Kato walked up to the tree and put down the bucket. The branches stretched back over the tombs. At the base of the tree was grass. He crouched down and looked more closely. He crawled around the base of the tree until he noticed that some of the ground had been recently disturbed. He looked around to see if anyone was there. There was no one at all. He reached over for the ladle and using the stick end of it began to dig into the dirt.

He managed to stab the ground with the stick and tore into the soil, but he was not satisfied with the progress, so he used his hands. Soon they were black with dirt under his fingernails, staining his shirt and jacket. It was then that he found it hidden just below the grass. His hands felt a wooden box, only recently placed there. It was long, and his fingers found the bottom and ripped it out of the ground.

He held it in his hands with amazement. It was a light wood, brown, but delicate, not meant for the ground at all, but usually preserved in a special place within a museum or temple. If it was what he thought, it was then he was holding in his hand one of the most precious documents in Japanese post war history. But it was a document for which people would kill and die and almost certainly needed to be protected and kept safe.

It was curiosity which made Kato open it as he sat under the tree. He wiped the box on his suit and then wiped his hands and opened the box. It was indeed a scroll, an old one at that. He took it out gently and untied a cord that wrapped around it tightly. Kato pulled it up and out to see it more clearly and as he did, his mouth opened in amazement. It was indeed what he suspected. It was a scroll of names with thumb prints in blood.

Kato was thinking this when he heard the ground stirring near the tree and he turned around. To his relief it was just a cat, a black cat with a bell around its neck. It came over to him and began to purr rubbing up against him.

'Where do you come from?' asked Kato. The cat moved around him and to his feet, looking back.

'You must be from the temple,' he said. 'You look well fed. I hope they are looking after you.'

The cat yawned and rested its head on its two front paws. Kato looked at the cat. It had a simple life a lot less complicated than his.

'We should swap places you and I,' he said. 'You can have this scroll and I can have your mat at the temple.'

The cat yawned but then her eyes saw something in the tree. Kato looked up. It was a little green bird, darting through the branches. It looked at Kato with his scroll, then at the cat and then as quickly as it appeared it was gone.

'Keep this a secret little friend,' said Kato. He turned to the cat. 'When I was young, I came to this temple with my parents. They wanted to tell me about a famous scroll associated with this place. It has little animals like you on it, it has frogs, rabbits, foxes and monkeys and they are all doing ordinary things, like humans do every day. Nobody is asking the rabbit, or the fox why they are behaving in that way, or why they are wearing funny hats or chasing each other over the fields, they just accept that this is the way of things. I like that. I have been one of those characters and my life has been lived out on that scroll.

'If I did not go to Matsushima, then I would still be in that procession marching along through life, playing, and living as if life would continue forever, the way it did my whole life. But it is time to get off now, to march to a different tune and play a different game and if I could, I would swap with you little cat, you could have my choices and I could have your morsels.

'I do not know the future. I went to Matsushima with everything I needed in life, and I did not really understand that until it was gone. As for the future, I must walk there alone and maybe this scroll can help me find the right steps forward. I do not think I am making any sense to you little cat. How can I put this in words you can understand? There are in this country some people, only a few who do not like the way the world is.

'They want to come and take away your mat and your meals and your temple and they want to turn everything upside down. Most of us like the world as it is, it isn't perfect and we are not perfect, but I will tell you this little cat, I will not stand by and see them tear this nation apart. I killed their kind before, and I will do so again. I will stand against them, and I will stop them, and your temple will be safe, and your mat and your freedom to walk in the grass. It is my promise to you.

'The old man Yamaguchi talked about three tsunamis, the three challenges of Japan. I do not think Japan had anything to do with it. I think he was referring to me. The first time I acted, I did so out of revenge, and I killed a dozen men responsible for my father's murder. The second time I acted, I did so out of desperation. I do not know how many I killed that day. The third time is coming, and I think it is coming soon and it will probably be the death of me, quite literally, but this third tsunami will simply ask me to make a choice. I am prepared to do what needs to be done. If I am still here, when this is all over, I shall visit this place and we can continue our conversation. I will bring some nice food.'

Kato returned the scroll to the box and put it under his arm. He stood up and looked down at the cat. She was looking up at him, her head tilted. She seemed to have sat in attention in front of him having listened to every word that was spoken. She seemed captivated and engaged, her eyes looking directly at him.

Kato smiled. 'You understood me, didn't you?' said Kato to the cat.

The cat looked at Kato and then ran between his legs, encircling him. Kato laughed. The cat turned back, purred softly, and ran off into the forest. Kato sat for a while under the tree and then returned to Kyoto. He thought about what Saito had said and so he wondered where he might be able to put the scroll for safe keeping. He went through the various options in his head when it occurred to him that there was only one place, but he had not been there for a few years.

It was an old storehouse owned by the Kato family on the outskirts of Kyoto. It was a kura, with a stone base, a wooden framed interior, and a thick mud bricked wall. In the old days, the kura was used to store important documents, money, and other heirlooms as it was more fire resistant than the wooden structures of the Japanese home. Upstairs, Kato's brother had renovated and placed a small bedroom and living room and library and downstairs was the kitchen and dining room. There was a small annex which contained a comfortable bathhouse and a small garden. The kura itself was next to a much larger country mansion owned by the Kato family which was now a museum that occasionally was used by local community organizations.

Kato chose to go there because his brother had installed a secret panel in the wall, known only to the two of them where he placed some important documents. It was he who designed the secret compartment under the tatami mat in the shop. Kato was always on the lookout for other secret compartments but to date had not found any.

Kato took a taxi to the outskirts of the town of Ohara and then walked half an hour to the farmhouse, and into the kura. He knew where the spare key was and put it safely in his pocket. He easily found the compartment, put the scroll and the box in the cavity, took out another box, put it on the table, then closed the compartment.

He opened the box. It contained a gun. He examined it closely. It probably had not been used for some time, so he spent the next hour pulling it apart, and cleaning it. He put the gun together and loaded it. He went to the bathhouse, got undressed, lathered himself and had a shower. He cleaned his teeth, washed his hair, and shaved. The bath was empty. He went upstairs and found a new suit in the cupboard, and a shirt that fitted, and a new jacket. He put the gun in his pocket, but then he stopped. He took the gun out of his pocket and put it back in the cupboard with the bullets. He left the Kura and walked along the road for a while and saw a waiting taxi that had just dropped off someone from Kyoto. He caught the taxi which took him back to the centre of town. He was planning to go back to his shop but on the way, he received a phone call from Fujita who asked if he wanted to meet up for a drink in a small Japanese pub, he knew in the suburb of Hanazono. It did not take long to get there once the taxi reached the city of Kyoto.

20

Kato opened the door to the restaurant. He was immediately confronted with a brief image of the face of a fat woman with cheeks that bulged and two tiny eyes that sat in hollow sockets on an otherwise whitish grey skin. Tufts of black hair jutted out at the edges in most unlikely places and her teeth were shiny and black. Kato wondered if he had come to the right place, so he stood back and looked at the red lantern that hung by the door and the shop banner which hung over the door frame in bright blue colours. He had come to the right place.

'Welcome! Welcome!' said the bulging fat lady and she stepped back to reveal that it was in fact detective Fujita wearing a mask. Kato surveyed the room. The restaurant, if it could be called one, was tiny. To the left sat a Japanese man for whom no mask could hide his wide cheeks, smiling face and stubble on his chin. He was sweating for smoke rose constantly in front of his face and the smell of chicken covered in teriyaki sauce wafted through the restaurant, along with the smell of barbequed fat and skin. He was sitting behind a wooden bar that functioned on his side as a barbeque and on the other side a bar with some stools. At the end of the shop, the bar trailed off to the corner and there was a door to a kitchen and there were some amenities for guests on the other side. There were two small tables towards the back of the room, with bamboo holders for wooden chopsticks and at the front of the room was a small, raised level which housed a small knee-high table with no chairs.

Noguchi was sitting at the bar slouching with a drink in his hand. Fujita moved the mask up to his forehead and drank from his half-empty glass of beer.

'Welcome Kato-san!' he said warmly. 'A beer for Kato-san,' he said, calling out to the chef and bartender. Kato took a seat on the bar next to Fujita.

'What are we celebrating?' asked Kato.

'Noguchi's short career in the police force,' replied Fujita.

'So, he has been suspended,' said Kato.

'He was suspended, and he has just quit,' said Fujita. Kato looked over to Noguchi. He was not talking but sullenly drinking his beer. Kato joined the two men for a beer, then another and another. They feasted on every part of the barbequed sparrow, the skin, the liver, the heart, the wing, and finally the sparrow itself. They munched on cabbage leaves and a few salads and bowls of white rice. The smell of barbequed chicken and meat was overpowering, and the smoke wafted to every corner of the room. Kato realised that he had not had such good food since he left Matsushima.

Fujita suddenly grabbed something and threw it to Kato and to Noguchi. Kato caught it, but Noguchi missed it and so he had to pick it up. They were masks. Fujita wore the mask of a lady with plump cheeks the so-called 'okame' mask, the one he wore when Kato walked in. The officer put it on and then wrapped a bandana around his head, so that most of his hair was concealed. He then tilted his head as if pretending his was an old woman and then reached into his pocket and pulled out another bandana. He carefully folded it and then placed it gently in both hands, bringing it up to wipe his forehead. He sighed and turned his head to the man who had been barbequing the chicken and pouring their beers for well on two hours.

His name was Kubota and he slaved fastidiously over the charcoal burner while his wife slaved in the kitchen cutting up the meat and putting the salads together. Fujita nodded and Kubota pulled out a flute. It was a traditional Japanese festival flute. He then reached down and pulled up a small Japanese hand-held drum and gave it to Fujita who sat down on a stool next to the bar and put the drum on his lap. He tilted his head to Kubota. With a thud and the shrill of the flute, the music began. Kato began tilting his face around and doing silly movements. He was wearing the mask of the village idiot, the so-called 'Hyottoko' mask.

The two men danced around the bar. The only one who was not doing anything was Noguchi who was struggling to put on his mask. It was the mask of a demon, its face red and two foreboding horns stretching out of its forehead. It looked like it had come straight from Hell. There was not much room for the three men to dance but dance they did. The music seemed to lift their feet and their gait changed and they found the right rhythm. The drum seemed to thud melodiously, and the tune was so delightful that Kato began to feel that he was somewhere else entirely. For some reason he imagined that he was in a forest, a deep forest and that these men were all in the forest dancing together, with the drum beating and the flute playing.

Eventually, when all three men were exhausted, the dancing stopped. They drank more beer and ate a little more and the dancing began again until it petered out a few minutes later when Noguchi realised that his fiancé wanted to meet up with him. They argued on the phone, but he apologised to her and said that he was drunk. Fujita seemed untouched by alcohol even though he had drunk as much as Kato, though Kato and Noguchi had very red faces.

Kato's mask was hanging over his forehead. He then thought of Noguchi. He was probably still quite distressed at killing the old man accidentally and his heart was probably a mass of unresolved emotions.

'You have a new kitchen,' Fujita blurted out to Kubota.

'Ah,' he replied nervously. 'Yes, it is about six months old. The house down the street burned down because of an electrical fault and we decided to make a few changes. The government recommended it.'

'Do you mind if I have a look at it?' he asked abruptly.

'You mean you want to have a look at Kubota's wife,' said Noguchi, speaking for the first time.

'Of course not,' said Fujita embarrassed. 'I already know she is the most beautiful in all Kyoto.'

'You must be blind,' replied Kubota. 'She is as wizened as a piece of piece of chicken skin after it has been marinated.'

At that moment, the door swung open, and Kubota's wife appeared for the second time with a plate of sashimi.

'And you have the face of a pig,' she said to her husband.

She turned to Fujita, 'That's why we don't serve much pork here. My husband is worried about eating someone in his family.'

Everyone burst out laughing.

Fujita took the pause in conversation to follow Kubota's wife into the kitchen. Fujita pulled out a cigar.

'If you want to smoke, go out the back, onto the street,' she said.

Fujita bowed deeply.

'I'm very sorry,' he said and went to the back of the kitchen and found the door which led to a narrow alley, shrouded in darkness. He turned left and walked slowly to the end of the laneway and found himself at the road. He thought he might for a short walk, find a vending machine, get some coffee, finish his cigar, and go back to the party. A bus passed by, rumbling as it went, on its way to Kyoto station. It stopped briefly at the bus stop. An old lady and two students got on. The bus edged away from the curb and continued its journey.

Fujita turned left again and began to walk slowly up towards the intersection. He was about to walk across it when he stopped himself. In front of him further up the road on the other side was a black car, its windows darkened and its lights off. Smoke could be seen wafting out of one of its windows. Even though the windows were darkened, Fujita could discern at least three people. Suddenly the phone rang. It was Ueno, the police chief.

'Fujita,' he said. 'Itoh's wife has just been killed. I am at the bathhouse now. Witnesses say they saw men there dressed as police officers, and heard the names 'Fujita' and 'Noguchi' at the scene. Where are you?'

'I am at a pub in Hanazono with Noguchi, where you went for your birthday last year. We have been here since about 5 pm. We have alibis.'

'Someone is trying to set you up for the killing of Itoh's wife,' exclaimed Ueno. 'Stay put. We are sending as many people as we can spare.'

Fujita hung up the phone. Help was going to arrive too late. He had to deal with this situation on his own. Fujita went to the edge of the building and to his surprise, two of the car doors were open and three men were walking across the road towards the restaurant. Fujita threw down his cigar and ran back into the restaurant through the kitchen. Kato was standing beside the cash register, but Noguchi was gone. The door was open, and he had stepped outside.

'Noguchi!' yelled Fujita and leapt towards the front of the restaurant. Kato and Kubota heard him and turned to face him surprised at his loud voice. Just as Fujita reached the register where

Kato and Kubota were standing there was a series of loud cracks and the wooden sliding door, which was half open splintered into a hundred pieces. The force of the blast knocked Kato and Kubota off their feet as pieces of glass and splinters of wood cut into both men, who shielded their faces as they fell. Mrs Kubota, in the kitchen at the time fell to the ground screaming.

There was another series of loud cracks as Kato and Kubota hit the ground and Noguchi was thrown backwards into the entrance of the restaurant. He had been mortally wounded by the first salvo and died in the second. Kato had been struck in the head and chest with glass and wood and Kubota was nursing a few more severe wounds caused by the glass.

'Get down and stay down!' screamed Fujita to everyone.

Kato looked over at him. He was not going to do anything of the sort. He crawled around the cash register to the charcoal-burner and saw Kubota's large sushi knife sitting there on the bench. He grabbed it. He thought he could smell smoke deep in his nostrils. He dismissed it out of his mind. Kato stood up, knife in hand. Fujita saw him and knew what he was going to do.

'Put down the knife Kato,' he ordered.

Kato looked down at him, ignored him and stepped out onto the road. He could see Noguchi lying dead on the ground, his eyes staring into space. The killer was walking slowly and confidently back to the car, with his weapon slung over his shoulder. Kato had recognized the sound. It was a battle rifle he was familiar with, the Type 64, a Howa gun, issued to the Self-Defence Force.

Poor Noguchi didn't have a chance.

He was murdered in cold blood.

His fiancé would have lost her husband and his parents would have lost a son. Kato was sick of this stupid vendetta. Saito, Kawabata, they were all the same, they all had to die.

Enough was enough.

Kato lifted the sushi knife and threw it at the killer, striking him in the middle of the back. He cried out in pain, staggering forward, dropping the gun, and falling to the ground.

The other two men were horrified. Kato immediately knew one as the guy who tried to rough him up in Kyoto a few nights before. He did not know the other man.

'We are not here for you!' said the man Kato didn't know.

'We came for the policeman only. He murdered our boss. Stay out of it. We do not want to hurt you.'

By this stage, Kato had reached the man he stabbed. He reached down and picked up the gun. He checked it. It was still loaded. Both men stood by their car, next to each other, not knowing what to do. Kato had deliberately given them a few seconds to run. He would give them no more mercy. The one closest to Kato opened the door and was about to get in when Kato called out to them.

'My name is Kato Masayoshi,' he shouted. 'My father was murdered by Saito your boss, in 1995. You work for him. You may not be here for me, but I am here for you.'

The man who was a stranger to Kato opened fire at Kato at the same time he fired the Howa. Kato was struck in the left shoulder and the man by the car was thrown back against the car, dead. Kato felt the bullet go straight through his shoulder and out the other side. He fell to his knees in agony and dropped the rifle. The third assassin, the one who had tried to kill Kato the night before, had been hit in the leg with one of the bullets, and tried to stagger down the street, limping in agony as he went.

Kato sat up again with great difficulty, as he was bleeding profusely, and grabbed the gun with his right arm. He took aim and fired it in the direction of the limping man. The shock of the discharge of bullets dislocated Kato's shoulder but brought the third man down to the pavement. He was still alive, but unable to run. Kato fell on his back in agony, as he could feel blood all around him. The pain was quite unlike anything he had felt before. He saw Fujita above him, grabbing him, lifting him up, trying to staunch the bleeding, calling out to Kubota to get bandages and call an ambulance. He felt Fujita telling him to hold on and not die. He felt his head fall to the ground and the last thing he saw were figures running towards him.

21

When Kato woke up, he realised he was in a hospital bed. It was about 1 pm, March 20, 2011. Joshua Tree was sitting by the window. He winced in pain as he realised that his shoulder was all bandaged up. He heard Kato stirring and put down the book he was reading. Kato could see it was Solomon's book.

'Any good?' asked Kato, feeling the pain when he spoke.

'Complete rubbish,' said Tree.

'How so?' asked Kato.

'There is that saying, *'the end doesn't justify the means.'* Or I can think of the other one, *'the road to hell is paved with good intentions.'* It is still the road to hell, and they would have known what they were doing.'

'You mean joining the Japanese was a mistake?' asked Kato.

'Look where the war got you,' said Tree. 'We dropped two atomic bombs, thousands of civilians died in the bombings, and there was enmity across the Pacific. I think the whole thing was a mistake.'

Kato laughed. 'You Americans say the strangest things. You think you can summarise everything in a sentence!' he coughed. It was painful. Tree got up and poured him a glass of water.

'What has been happening since I got shot?' asked Kato.

'Well, Honda called me late last night. I think Fujita called Seiji Oda, Oda called Watanabe, Watanabe called Honda and Honda called me. I know Seiji and Watanabe Sensei from the Jazz Bar, Monkey Blues, Oda owns it. Fujita, I don't know, but he wants you arrested.

'You lost a lot of blood. The men you shot died last night, and the man you stabbed in the back with the sushi knife died this morning after making a full confession to the police. They were in Saito's gang, and they thought that Fujita and Noguchi had killed Saito's wife. They were taking revenge for that, but also for the murder of Saito himself. The police suspect a third party. I heard the name 'Kawabata' mentioned by Oda to Fujita. You probably know who was behind it.

'The man you stabbed with the sushi knife was one Sugawara, who agreed to make a false confession that he saw you kill your friend in Matsushima. I passed on the good news to your friend Okubo. He was furious. Kenji Nomura's death is going to be ruled a suicide. Ueno is ecstatic because you turned up the Howa rifle. They have been looking for it for ages. It went missing a while back, along with some other weapons from some warehouse. The man who died also told them where he got it. The police made a few arrests this morning.

'Tokyo doesn't know what to do with you, Masa. Ueno and the rank and file want to give you a medal. You shot dead Noguchi's murderers in what can only be described as a 'shoot-out.' It hasn't been reported, but you know how things work here. But Tokyo and Fujita want you prosecuted. Who knows what will happen? Whatever happens, I think that your life will now be under the microscope.'

Kato sighed. 'It is probably for the best.' He smiled to himself. He looked at Joshua holding the book. He then saw that there were flowers on the table next to his bed.

'Where did you get the book?' asked Kato. 'Who gave me the flowers? I assume it wasn't you.'

Tree laughed. 'You have your signature sense of humour back again.'

He put down the book next to the flowers and smelt them with a smile.

'You have become a lot more popular than I remember you. The flowers are from someone called Ms Sasaki, who works at your shop. I have to say Kato, she is just a breath of fresh air, what a nice person she is. I remember meeting Tamura last year and I am glad he is gone. Just put that lady in charge and she will turn things around.'

'How do you know about the bankruptcy?' asked Kato.

'Oda told me, and Fujita and Watanabe actually, everyone seems to know,' replied Joshua.

'As for the book, your friend Ka-chan was here with his fiancé and his sister. They wanted to wish you a speedy recovery and hoped that you got better soon.'

Kato smiled and looked at his old friend. He seemed happier than usual.

'What is wrong with you?' asked Kato. 'You actually look happy, there is a smile on your face, is this a new look for you?'

Tree laughed. 'I have a date,' he said with a smile.

'A date?' asked Kato. 'You mean a real one, like I had with Akiko when we first met, you mean you might actually take someone to that temple you are always talking about?'

Joshua nodded.

'Well,' said Kato, 'I am happy for you. It is the first time I have seen you really smile in a long time.'

Joshua nodded.

'By the way, David Honda, who is he?' asked Kato with a sly smile.

'I think he is just someone interested in the future relationship of our two countries,' said Joshua cryptically.

'Well, whoever he is, next time you meet him, tell him this: Kenji was poisoned with polonium by the grandfather of the man who gave you that book on India.'

'And the grandfather of the woman I am going on a date with,' added Joshua.

'You just met her today and you asked her out?' asked Kato.

'I have met her before Masa,' said Joshua. 'But today I made a better impression.'

'Well,' said Kato. 'When you are not busy wooing the granddaughter of the man who has stolen nuclear material from the government, find time to tell your friend Honda to look into it. I will too when I recover from these injuries.'

'Well, you might be leaving sooner than you think. Watanabe called just a while ago, to make sure that you are still going to the Kitano Tenmangu shrine today,' said Joshua.

'You are joking, right? I have been shot,' said Kato.

'No reason why you cannot keep an appointment. You were just shot in the shoulder. It was not a serious wound. They popped your other shoulder back again. You were in worse shape in Iraq if I remember correctly.'

Kato laughed again. 'Ask the nurse to bring some more bandages,' he said. 'I need the use of both my hands if I am going to pray at the shrine.'

'I will speak to the doctor and explain it to him,' said Joshua. 'It will take some convincing though. I heard they said they don't want you to leave for some time.'

Joshua was able to convince the doctor and nurses to bandage Kato on the proviso that he returned to hospital as soon as possible. Kato was given some strong painkillers that worked but made him feel drowsy. Joshua helped him get dressed and out to the car. Seiji Oda was waiting for them. They soon arrived at the shrine. Oda parked the car, and they walked up the main steps flanked by two large fierce-looking stone beasts. They walked through the gate and over to the stone well to wash their hands. Kato lifted the ladle, dipped it in the water and let the water run over his hands. Even this simple act seemed to give him a sense of peace. He gently laid the ladle back on top of the bamboo mat which was covering the pond of cold water and shook the water off his hands.

Kato turned his face towards the shrine. They walked past the large wooden structure which housed the old wooden pictures and frames from years of long ago. Kato had always been amazed that the shrine officials decided to place such important pictures to rot in the elements, their delicately painted portraits and images ravaged by the sun, the wind, and the rain. 'Who would remember these portraits?' he thought to himself. Perhaps one or two of the older generation for whom these images ushered in memories of time long ago, times long gone.

'In time all is forgotten,' thought Kato to himself as they walked past the portraits to the entrance of the main shrine with the two statues on either side.

This place brought back so many memories for him. On his left, he remembered when he and his wife lined up on February 25 to enjoy the annual tea ceremony with the maiko and geiko from the oldest school in Kyoto, older even than the famed Gion. He also had come here on the second day of the New Year, the year of the Rabbit to pray at the shrine with his daughter. The crowds were overwhelming. It was a cold day and even though it was the second day of the New Year many hundreds of people crowded the shrine. His wife, being a Japanese Christian did not pray at the shrine, nor did she visit temples, but Kato never minded. Kato went through the motions usually and did not hold to any deep beliefs of any kind. As a businessman he was conscious of the importance of being seen to observe the rituals mainly for business reasons. Many of his clients were involved in both shrine and temple life and so it was important for Kato to be seen at least visibly at both the temple and the shrine even for the sake of appearances.

In his heart, Kato had not the slightest interest in anything beyond the grave, nor did he really in his heart of hearts believe that any of these religions conferred much power beyond the grave. His daughter seemed happy to attend with him, so he did not pry into her beliefs. Even though he had little regard for religion, he still enjoyed the whole experience of the shrine because it reminded him of important reference points as a Japanese man, in a rapidly changing world.

He walked into the courtyard. He expected to see Professor Watanabe, but he was nowhere to be seen. Perhaps he was running late. On his left, a priest was sorting through a straw bucket of plums freshly plucked from the trees, ready to be pickled for the coming year. To his right, a group of school children in their uniforms gathered around to collect some amulets and good luck charms for the year ahead. Their laughter, giggles and scampering around the courtyard reminded him of his daughter Ai. How he wished for her to be with him today. His home reminded him of Akiko, but everywhere he went in Kyoto reminded him of Ai. He remembered the day when she walked as a small child across the expensive fabrics in the kimono shop. He remembered the day she first wore a kimono for the summer festival. Kato laughed as he remembered all the faces of the boys turning as she walked past, next to her mother with her cheerful face and broad smile.

While he thought this, he realized that it was the first time since the day of the tsunami he was able to think clearly about his family without the fears of despair flooding back. Perhaps it was the laughter of the school children thought Kato, or maybe it was simply the passage of time. It was significant in any event he thought that this feeling would occur in the shrine. Perhaps he had drifted too far away from this place in recent years.

Kato's turn to pray had arrived. Joshua Tree was talking with Oda who had joined him near the stand for amulets and charms. Joshua refused to pray at the shrine because he didn't know enough about Shinto to make it meaningful. Kato respected that. He reached into his pocket and took out his small, knitted change-purse, removing a few coins which he tossed into the shrine.

Kato brought his hands together to clap but almost as he did, his ears began to ring. He could hear rushing waters and the smell of the ocean. He brushed off the sensation, but it had already made him dizzy and his mouth dry. He clapped again and the sound of the ocean became a roar. He stepped back to regain his balance, bowing slightly, and as he did, he looked up to the mirror which sat at the top of the shrine. He looked in horror as he saw his own reflection, but behind him there stood the figure of an old man. It was Yamaguchi and his hands were on his shoulders.

He regained his posture and tried to bring his hands together once more, but he found that he could not. The sound of the waves seemed to come closer. He was no longer in Kyoto. He was in Matsushima. He could smell the pine trees. He could see the body of Kenji Nomura in front of him and in the corner of his eye, he could see a red bridge. He saw Yamaguchi standing on that bridge.

'Do you want to see yourself as you really are?' asked the Nue.

Kato shook his head. He did not want to see that, not that. He saw himself shoot Nomura and the body falling to the ground. He saw himself enter the house with his sword drawn killing everyone in that building showering the walls with blood. He saw himself in that dank and dark room in Iraq, being tortured by the terrorists. He saw how he cut himself free with the piece of metal, grabbed the knife of his captor, killing him silently, taking his gun, freeing Joshua Tree and the other marines and stepping outside. He looked down at his hands. They were covered in blood. He tried to bring his hands together, but he could not.

'They are both gone Kato,' said Yamaguchi. 'But I am here and if you want, I will not leave you because I know you do not want to be alone. Imagine what we can do together, what havoc we can cause, but we can only do that if you let me stay.'

'Help me!' he called out loudly. He looked to his left and saw his daughter standing there. She looked so alive. He looked to his right and saw his wife. Akiko stood with her face still and calm.

'I cannot clap my hands!' he said to them. Ai grabbed his left hand and Aikiko his right. They were warm to the touch. He looked at them standing there and he could feel power surging through his veins and fingers. He brought his hands together with a loud clap, the sound which seemed to break his eardrums. Kato felt the lifting of a heavy weight from his shoulders as if he were forcibly unclothed by heat and every muscle and organ in his body was renewed. He was thrown backwards and all he could see was the sky above.

When Kato regained consciousness, he was lying on a tatami mat in the shrine office, his head propped up over some pillows. He looked up and saw Professor Watanabe, Joshua Tree and Oda sitting near him drinking some tea with the a few officials from the shrine. The priest pointed towards Kato. They thanked him, took off their shoes and went to join him on the tatami.

'How do you feel Kato-san?' asked Watanabe.

'I feel lighter,' he said. He touched his cheek with his right hand. 'I feel like I have been given a new skin, like I have been reborn anew.'

'What do you remember?' asked Joshua.

Kato thought for a moment. He remembered seeing his wife and child with him at the shrine, or rather he felt their presence. He also remembered that the influence of Yamaguchi and whatever he was being expelled from his body. He recalled at the bridge in Matsushima that he was physically ill. That must have been an ancient memory in his subconscious of an encounter with that evil creature. His ancestors must have crossed paths with that thing before. Whatever that parasite was, he was gone. He looked up at Joshua.

'I think I will spend the rest of my life thinking of an answer to your question Joshua,' he said.

He turned to Professor Watanabe.

'Up to a few hours ago, I was an avowed atheist. But now, I just do not know. I know this world is a big place and there might be room for some things I do not understand. There is more to this world than what we can see with our eyes. I am not the center of the universe, only one part of a greater whole.'

'That is a profound statement to make,' said a stranger standing behind all of them in the lobby. He bowed to Professor Watanabe, Joshua Tree, and Seiji Oda, took off his shoes and joined them on the tatami. He sat and bowed to Kato.

Professor Watanabe introduced him. 'This is Father Tanabe. He is a friend of mine. We play chess together and drink a little sake. He is the catholic priest at one of the churches in the city. He wanted to talk to you, so I have brought him here today.'

Kato sat up and looked at the man. He must have been in his eighties, with an extra-large pair of glasses sitting precariously on a small nose. His thin body looked as though it was being held up by the suit, he was wearing but that it might slip off at any moment. The priest looked at him and bowed politely.

'I was your wife's priest Kato-san,' he began. 'At New Year's Eve last year, Akiko-san told me that she had met her mother and father in a dream. They came to her and said that she would soon be joining them.'

'They are both dead,' said Kato. 'They died some ten years or so.'

The priest nodded. 'I told her it was a dream and that she should not let it worry her. She accepted my opinion, but I felt she did not change the feeling of her heart. She wrote a letter to you which she gave me two weeks ago after our last confession. She brought me flowers and thanked me for all that I had done for her. I did not think it at the time, but I think she had a premonition that something was going to happen to her. Anyway, she wrote you a letter. I have it here.'

'What a remarkable woman,' commented Oda. Joshua and Watanabe agreed.

The priest reached into his jacket and pulled out a long envelope. He presented it to Kato with two hands, his head bowed. Kato accepted it with two hands and bowed in return. He held onto it and said that he would read it when he got home. The priest thanked him, bowed to Watanabe and everyone else and left.

'I will see you at chess next week Tanabe-san,' said Watanabe. The old priest nodded and waved as he walked away.

Joshua Tree helped Kato to his feet and asked whether he wanted to return to his hospital bed. Kato looked at him astonished. He said that he wanted to be driven to his home first. Oda offered to drive him and let him stay a while and then later pick him up, take him to a restaurant for dinner and then back to hospital. This sounded like a good plan for everyone concerned.

As they walked back to the car, Watanabe asked if he could have a private word with Kato. The others agreed and walked on ahead. Watanabe looked at Kato.

'Has your problem been resolved?' he asked.

'Yes,' replied Kato. Watanabe did not ask for more information. He pointed to Seiji.

'He is a good bodyguard. Reliable. Trustworthy. You need one in your position Kato-san.'

'How will I find one?' asked Kato.

'You will know the right one when they come along,' said the Professor.

'It is important that you stay in business. Employ a new business manager. How much are you in debt?'

'Quite a lot,' replied Kato.

'Tell Seiji the amount. As I said before, I wanted to ask you to consider a business proposition. It is quite simple really. I need to rent your empty warehouses and properties around Japan. You simply need to provide the space.'

'What do you need warehouses for?' asked Kato.

'My role in life is to help minorities have a better life. Do you remember I told you a story of a family who moved people across Japan to give them a better chance of survival in a land of prejudice? Do you remember that?'

'Yes, I remember,' said Kato.

'Well, it was my family,' said the Professor.

'Professor Watanabe,' said Kato. 'What you are proposing is quite illegal and outrageous. Why do you think you could get away with it?'

'For two reasons,' replied the Professor. 'First, because the Watanabe family have got away with it since the 1870s, but also it was and is only possible if we use the right people. I need someone who exists in all three worlds, their world, the world of others and the world in between. You have close friends who are not Japanese, you have a deep commitment to our nation. You seem to understand the old ways but also the new ways. You exist in between the two worlds Kato, the old world and the new and you are comfortable in all three.

'I asked your father in 1995, he agreed but then he was killed. I have always felt responsible for it. I have kept out of your way, but our paths crossed again, and it is not coincidence. I have not always believed in the freedom to choose, but I do now, and I just let events take their natural course.'

Kato looked at Watanabe. This confirmed what Saito had said. His father had agreed to help Watanabe and his quest for a better Japan.

He felt closer to his Father than he had ever felt before and was glad he knew this about him.

Professor Watanabe stopped. They had reached Seiji and Joshua Tree waiting at the car.

'So, what you are talking about is a hidden road?' asked Kato. Watanabe smiled and nodded.

'Yes, that is exactly what it is. A hidden road,' replied the Professor.

Kato held out his hand. Watanabe looked at it.

'The American way,' Kato said with a smile. The Professor nodded and they shook hands.

Kato said goodbye to Professor Watanabe and climbed into the car. He realized it was now ten days since the tsunami struck. It seemed longer. Kato was in the clear. He was not going to be arrested for the death of Kenji. Saito's confession was enough to convince the police that Kato was not involved in the Takao incident. No one alive knew the truth. He had a clean slate. Akiko and Ai went to their deaths comfortable in the notion that he was a good and honest man. It was better that way.

When Oda stopped the car, Kato got out. Joshua and Oda were going to get a coffee and come back in an hour. Kato thanked them and walked up the steps to the house. Kato found the spare key under a pot plant. He turned the key in the door and pushed it inwards, stepping into the darkened entrance. As he opened the door, the words 'I'm home!' escaped his lips, but as soon as he said it, he held the door open and stood there.

The room was silent. He closed the door quietly and locked it, placing his keys on the cabinet next to the entrance. He turned on the light and the hallway lit up.

He slipped off his shoes and stepped up onto the floor, walking down the narrow hallway. He walked into the kitchen. He turned on the light and was immediately bombarded with memories, but they seemed so far away. He looked at a portrait of his wife and daughter which was stuck on the fridge with a magnet his wife bought at Tokyo Disneyland.

He decided to sit down at the small table which snuggled next to the wall. His eyes surveyed the table: a small branch of withered plum blossoms drooped over a small blue vase, a half-drunk cup of coffee, a mouldy crust of toast and his wife's open Bible. A bookmark lay on the left page, hastily placed. Kato looked at the worn pages. He looked and saw that Akiko had highlighted a verse with a red pen and it was marked March 10, 2011. Kato read it.

'I have no idea what that means,' he said to himself. He flicked through the Bible and realised she only marked that one verse. It was perhaps one of the last things she did at home. Kato picked up the bookmark and slid it between the pages. Respectfully, but firmly, he closed the Bible shut.

He remembered the letter given to him by the priest. He pulled out the envelope and opened it. It was handwritten by Akiko dated March 3, 2011. It read:

'Dear Masa, I will get to the point. I know what you did.

'The night you came back home, after your father was killed, you were so angry. I followed you to Takao in another taxi and got out discreetly and followed you to the building. You were good at what you did. I hardly heard a thing, except for a few muffled sounds. I went in and saw what you did. I lingered at the door to the house for the longest time and wondered what to do. I prayed to God for strength and wisdom.

'When I came home, I cried all night. I did not cry for the men you killed, but I cried for you. I prayed to God that he would change you. I trusted that he would. I married you believing that you would eventually change and put the anger behind you. When you left the army, I knew the same thing had happened in Iraq. You had the same look in your eyes for weeks when you were back, the same eyes you had when you came back from Takao. I cannot imagine what you and the others suffered overseas, but I know you succumbed to your anger and people died.

'You respected me, and my faith and you raised Ai properly. I forgive you. I forgave you a long time ago, but I knew, and I always prayed that you would change. I pray that you will replace that reservoir of anger with one of compassion for others, and if you do that, I think you could change the world.

'Akiko.'

Kato held the letter in his hand, frozen. It was as if time had stopped. His hand started to shake, and the letter fell out of his fingers to the floor.

Akiko knew.

She had always known.

From the beginning.

Kato immediately felt ashamed.

His eyes moved to an old picture on the wall of Akiko when they married. He could hardly see it for the tears. He stepped back along the hallway until he reached the entrance and felt a deep, abiding sense of shame rise in his heart, rushing through his veins and going up into his throat. He felt like he needed to breathe but could not and felt the walls closing in on him. He was not worthy to set foot in his house. He put his shoes back on. He bowed deeply, getting down on his knees and bowing with his face to the floor.

Kato wept loudly until he could weep no more. He did not know how long he stayed there crying. He cried for Akiko, for Ai, and for himself.

'Akiko, please forgive me,' he said, lifting his face up, his eyes red with tears.

He opened the door, and stepped outside, alone, into the darkness.

ABOUT THE AUTHOR

Michael J. Sutton lived and worked in Japan for ten years. While not lecturing in International Relations, and Political Economy, he developed an interest in playing the shakuhachi, the Japanese bamboo flute, visiting festivals and hot springs, and discovering the fascinating world of Japan's myths and legends, including the elusive yokai. These days, he is the CEO and Founder of Freedom Matters Today, looking at freedom from a Christian perspective. He has published four books on life, faith, and freedom. This is his first novel.

HISTORICAL NOTES

I wrote the original manuscript *of The Third Tsunami* in 2011 after the tsunami wreaked havoc along the northeast coast of Japan. I was astonished and horrified by the events of that day, and the subsequent nuclear disaster in Fukushima. I was also saddened when I heard and read about the discrimination suffered by the people unfortunate enough to live near the reactor. The way they were treated by many people was unforgivable.

As Mr. Solomon says in the book, there have always been minorities in Japan as there are in other countries. One of the aims of the Last Days of Old Japan series is talk about one of these forgotten people, the so-called 'yokai,' or non-humans. Another aim is to speak of friendship that transcends cultural barriers. We see this in the friendship between Joshua Tree and Kato and between Kato, Lijuan and Peter Wu. These friendships enable us to come to terms with the past and recognize a future where what unites us is more important than what divides.

I lived for a decade in the land of the rising sun. It is beautiful, it is tragic, it lives in the shadow of the past, and wrestles with the currents and tsunamis of the present. Most nations around the world struggle with the same issues, and the same questions around identity. I believe this search for self-understanding is a common one and a life-long project. The more we grow, the more we understand ourselves and the world around us. Most of the characters in my book are searching for their own identity and wearing various masks to cover up their uncertainty.

I wish to speak for the yokai as few speak for them. Behind these folk myths about local geography or imperial identity were people who sincerely believed in their existence. This means we ought to show respect and tread carefully. For centuries, local people believed in the Tengu, the Nue, the Kappa, the Kitsune, and the Tanuki. Every society has a Tengu, and he has many different names. These stories function as markers for cultural identity and morality plays. Sadly, the yokai in recent years have been cheapened and corrupted.

I sought to locate their stories in real places such as Matsushima and the red bridge, Zuiganji, Myoshinji, Takao, Arashiyama, and Hanazono. Mt. Kurama is a deeply spiritual place. The Tengu is said to reside there, but his origins are in China and possibly India. The Nue, Mr. Yamaguchi, is more complex. He may be a lingering fragment of an ancient myth or an amalgam of various stories. The tanuki or raccoon dog, and the fox are great Japanese shape-shifting animals. The tanuki is a trickster and the fox is almost always seen to be female. Their origins are also in China.

Mr. Yamaguchi tells us that the real monsters are people and that if monsters exist, then they would be trying to stay out of the way of humanity.

I wondered what monsters would do in their spare time, when they are not scaring us or waiting to attack us. The reader will quickly discover the identity of at least three yokai, and perhaps a fourth, if you are reading carefully. There are a few others lurking in the shadows but I will not reveal them at this time.

The Tengu stories are Japanese, but the Tengu is from China, and so are most Japanese mythical beings and characters. This means that these Japanese stories are versions of a broader cultural and historical context that spans parts of the world that is now home to billions of people. These are not Japanese legends but global legends with a Japanese flavor. Japan just like everywhere else, it is a melting pot for cultures, ideas, and myths. Japan is one of the destinations for the cultural Silk Road that began in India with Hinduism and Buddhism and then traveled to China, and Korea, and then to Japan. Accepting this cultural highway is not only the path to peace but it is the way to embrace a deeper and more inclusive sense of humanity.

Kato Masayoshi, Joshua Tree, Koichiro Kawabata, Ka-chan, Lijuan, Goro Fujita, Professor Watanabe, and Peter Wu will return…

In **THE LAST RONIN**, March 11, 2024.